Louise Bagshawe

A KEPT WOMAN

ORION

An Orion paperback
First published in Great Britain by Orion in 2000
This paperback edition published in 2001 by Orion Books Ltd
Orion House, 5 Upper St Martin's Lane, London WC2H 9EA

A CIP catalogue record for this book is available
from the British Library

ISBN: 0 75284 337 0

Typeset by Deltatype Ltd, Birkenhead, Merseyside

Printed in Great Britain by
Clays Ltd, St Ives Plc

This book is dedicated to
my darling husband Anthony.

Acknowledgements

My thanks are, as usual, due to all the people without whom there would have been no book. First amongst them is my editor Rosie de Courcy, who has a lucid, practically infallible grasp of what should stay and what should go. I must thank her for her patience and her perception as well as her good ideas. Michael Sissons, my agent, quietly and supremely confidently, steered me through a rough career patch during the writing of this book. All writers should be lucky enough to have him as their agent, but I'm glad they're not, as then he would have no time for me. I also want to thank Peter Matson, Tim Corrie, Brian Siberell, the team at ILA, and Alan Greenspan for their invaluable help steering my career during the time I wrote this book. I'm hoping to get a few more agents so I can have my own cricket team. Seriously though, I would be lost without them. My mother and father were beacons of sanity when I was throwing away previous manuscripts, and Alice and Seffi (hi darlings!) kept me focused on the important stuff. Thanks to Nigel and Melissa Huddleston for taking me under their wing when I first got to LA; and thanks to Susan Cartsonis for giving me my shot. Anthony had to put up with most of my whining, so I dedicated the book to him and named the hero for him. Michael is inspired by Anthony, so you'll be able to read for yourselves just how cool my husband is. All my friends deserve thanks, but I want to give a special mention to Fred Metcalf, Barbara Kennedy Brown, and Jacob Rees-Mogg. Finally, my thanks are due with this and every book to the whole team at Orion, especially Susan Lamb.

Chapter 1

Diana Verity looked at her reflection and smiled.

The mirror in her mother's bedroom was spotted slightly with age round its antique frame, but nothing could detract from the dazzling vision she saw there. Diana was a lovely girl who had never looked lovelier. It was marvellous to be a bride, but infinitely better to be a young, beautiful one, wearing a dress which cost more than some people made in a year, bedecked with minute silk roses and hand-sewn crystals, carrying a bouquet personally put together by the top florist in London. Her hair gleamed like spun glass; John Frieda had opened just for her, at an ungodly hour, and Joel himself had attended to the choppy fringe that swung so delightfully under the glittering tiara of Swarovski crystal, jet and cultured pearls which kept her small veil in place. Diana had been tempted by an all-over cathedral-length veil, but nothing should be allowed to obscure the view of her dress for her guests, not to mention the photographers from *Tatler* and *Hello!* who were massing outside the church.

You might as well not be married at all if nobody could see how exquisite you looked. Perhaps the pictures would even console Daddy for the colossal dent Diana had put in his wallet. Basia Zarzycka gowns did not come cheap.

'You look stunning, darling.'

Victoria Verity pursed thin, immaculately painted lips and regarded her eldest daughter with a critical eye. Diana was a gorgeous, selfish, spoiled butterfly, but today all you noticed was the butterfly part. It cost Ernie, her fiancé, a lot of money to keep Diana in the wonderfully groomed, plucked and polished state to which she had become accustomed, but Victoria had no doubt that when he saw his bride Ernie would think she had been worth every penny. A wedding day is trumpeted as the most important in a bride's life, Vicky thought, and maybe it is. But there is a certain type of groom for whom the wedding is almost equally important. She considered her future son-in-law with well-bred distaste.

Ernest Foxton was the bad boy of British publishing. After ruthlessly trimming down one of Britain's oldest imprints, firing staff *en masse* and pruning unprofitable authors relentlessly from its list, he was heading across the pond to America. Ernie had dual citizenship through his mother, and now it had come in useful. He'd been tapped to run Blakely's, the old-fashioned New York house whose shareholders thought it needed a major revamp. Ernest was a cut-throat businessman, Victoria reflected, and he knew the value of a beautiful, graceful English wife at his side as he networked through the charity balls and opening nights that constituted Manhattan's social scene. It was no surprise to her that a ring had been produced, and a fast wedding arranged.

Diana had risen to the challenge. She had never used her considerable brains – her mother felt sure they were considerable, if only Di would dig them out – for anything other than sneaking her way into the hottest Alexander McQueen show, or snatching up the last Prada limited-edition yellow calfskin handbag. She had dropped out of college, and taken a job at *Vogue* as a fashion assistant, accepting their minute wages and living on the generous allowance Ernie provided. Victoria knew Diana gave legendary dinner parties and was a bit of an 'It' girl. In snagging Ernie, her finest hour had come, and her life, presumably, would be one long American edition of *Jennifer's Diary* after another. With barely four months' notice, Diana had managed to put together a stellar guest list full of people she didn't care about, a delightful reception at Brown's, spectacular flowers, a string quartet and a handmade dress designed especially for her. Ernie would be proud.

'It's not too bad, is it?'

Diana turned round this way and that, admiring the tiny cap sleeves and almost indecently low bodice, the plunging back covered with a Greek-goddess silk drape and her white satin slippers stitched with delicate gold thread.

'It's almost too much.'

Susie Amberson, Diana's chief bridesmaid and younger cousin, gave Diana a jealous smile. It was *so* unfair that she should look like this, her brown hair all silky and gleaming, her slim silhouette sparkling with white and glittering like Cinderella. What on earth did Ernie see in her? There was a rumour going round the girls that last week Diana had flown into Manhattan *just to get her eyebrows plucked* at the John Barret salon in Bloomingdales. The wedding was already the talk of London. 'Sophie Rhys-Jones went for subtlety. I thought that was *so* tasteful.'

'Darling.' Diana turned those luminous blue eyes on her, which she had emphasised with blue mascara, and which still somehow managed to look natural. 'You couldn't be more wrong. Minimalism is so over. So nineties. It's all about modern classics today.'

'Modern classics,' Susie said, with a trace of sarcasm, all she dared. After all, you couldn't be rude to the bride, even if you were the maid of honour. Diana had chosen the bridesmaids' outfits and they were a picture of subtle beauty; moss-green velvet, Empire-waisted gowns, with tiny bouquets of pink rosebuds and small white clouds of baby's breath and a white rose in full blossom pinned

3

into everyone's hair. Susie scowled. Even the satisfaction of bitching that Diana had made her look like a heifer was denied to her.

'That's right.' Diana spritzed herself lightly with rose water – she would not use anything as unsubtle as a perfume today. 'A wedding where people are formally dressed. Full skirts and trains and veils and tiaras. Classical waltzes instead of cheesy eighties disco. Did you know I have an usher standing at the door who is passing out carnations to any man that turns up without a buttonhole?'

'How thoughtful,' Susie said nastily.

Diana gave her a blossoming smile, and Susie was left with the unpleasant feeling that Diana found her bitchiness amusing. She had meant to put a small fly in the ointment, and had wound up only helping Diana enjoy herself more. Which was just like Diana Verity: she never did a stroke of work; she just floated through life. It was obnoxious.

'I like to help people out when they are ignorant of the right way to behave,' Diana said.

Susie flushed and picked up her bouquet. Bitch. She hated Diana, from the tips of her satin slippers to the elegant, perfectly plucked and now almost legendary eyebrows.

'Hurry up, darling.' Victoria poked her head around from behind the screen where she was getting changed into her pink Chanel suit. 'We don't want to keep the carriage waiting.'

Ernie Foxton sat in his home office and tapped at the computer keys. It was a glorious, sunlit morning outside in Chelsea, and his best man, resplendent in his morning suit, was downstairs telling obscene jokes to the ushers. But Ernie was oblivious to all this. He had the blinds down, and the pristine creases in his trousers could only

4

be seen by the dull light of his computer screen. He was online, checking his stocks. It was a morning ritual which never changed. He saw no reason to change it now just because he was getting married.

AOL was up again. Terrific. He had made over 400 per cent on that baby and had no intention of cashing it in just yet. What else? His US trust had taken a small dive, in line with the Dow, but he wasn't particularly concerned. Ernie knew money and he knew the Dow only went one way, upwards. That's if you were prepared to wait a few months for the inevitable 'corrections' to right themselves. It was only the pikers, the fools who had blood instead of ice-water running through their veins, who sold when things got a little bearish. Buy and hold and you always make money.

He tapped a few letters on his keyboard. BLKY, the sign for his new publishing firm. Good, it was up one and an eighth, on the news that Grant Valentine had been fired and he'd been appointed to replace him. That was significant enough to impress his new bosses already, before he'd even stepped out of Concorde, or introduced his fragrant and deliciously decorative little wife. Ah yes. Wife. Better not keep her waiting. He quickly sold some cotton futures he wasn't sure about and bought a few more shares in Blakely's. A celebration.

Things were good, and they were going to stay that way.

Ernie switched off the computer and drew the curtains, allowing daylight to flood into the gloomy burgundy and mahogany tones of the room. A glass of Krug was fizzing pleasantly on the side of his desk, awaiting him. He picked it up and sipped reflectively. Just a little something to relax him before the ceremony. It was a bore, but you had to go through it. Besides, Diana had reassured him that the coverage was going to be fantastic. His parents, both dead now, had been a wide-boy city trader from the

East End of London and a cook at Chelsea FC. His father's hard work and financial flair had made enough money for Ernie to be sent to Eton, where he had learned little academically, but enough snobbery to make him violently ashamed of both of them. He'd worked like a demon with an eye only for money and as a result he'd made enough cash to wipe out the embarrassing stain of his parentage. The wedding today would be attended by a wonderful mixture of London society with enough titles for Ascot, and a bride who was undeniably top drawer, even if she had no money. Ernie didn't need money; he needed what Diana could bring him. In New York she'd be a marvellous asset. Just the right touch to complete his profile. He was sure he'd made the right decision.

Ernie shut off his computer and walked down his solid glass spiral staircase to where Gerald, his best man, a colleague he didn't dislike too much, was waiting with the ushers.

'Ready, old man?' Gerald asked him. 'Still enough time to bolt.'

The lads chuckled.

'That'd be a bit messy.' Ernie grinned. 'And we'd miss the booze-up afterwards.'

'True. Better get the car round.' Gerald adjusted his buttonhole and went off to summon the chauffeur.

'You know, Susie's awfully cut up,' said Gerald's cousin Harry. 'She always thought you were going to be hers.'

'Plenty of fillies champing at the bit, not just Susie, thanks. Anyway, I'll be married, I won't be dead,' Ernie said, winking. 'I'll need some time off for bad behaviour.'

They laughed, and went out to where the car was waiting.

Diana leaned back in her carriage and waved, just like the Queen. People stopped in the streets to cheer, watching a bride in full rig drive past in a horse-drawn carriage, and she basked in the attention. Some of the men stared at the creamy bosom spilling out over the tight bodice of her gown and whistled and catcalled. She thought she liked that most of all. Japanese tourists and the occasional American stopped to take photographs of her, and she tossed her veil back and gave them a dazzling smile – extra-specially whitened with cosmetic dentistry just last week, so she looked like one of those American models.

So what if it was ridiculously extravagant? It was her day to be extravagant. Daddy shouldn't complain about the cost. Since she'd started dating Ernie he'd stopped going on about settling down and getting a proper job, thank God. She had a job. All right, not one that paid the bills, but Ernie was doing that for her now. Diana glanced to her right and saw a young woman striding down towards Piccadilly, carrying a briefcase. She was wearing a nice suit – tightly fitted and lemon yellow, which always goes well with chestnut hair. Diana tried to peg the designer. It looked like a Richard Tyler, almost, but you didn't see too much of his stuff in London. LA was his territory. Maybe it was, though. Anyway, what a fool. Look at her, working all the hours God sends for some feeble little salary. She's a good-looking girl, Diana thought. Perhaps not quite as good-looking as me, but then again, who is? She bit on her plump lower lip to stop herself breaking out into an unattractive and unladylike grin. She should hook herself a nice, rich husband, and do things the old-fashioned way. They might be at the start of a new millennium, but the old ways never went out of style.

Her mother had squeezed her hand as she had helped her up into the carriage, lifting the lower folds of her dress, which Diana knew Susie was hoping would trail in the gutter or something.

'You're sure you're doing the right thing, aren't you, darling? I mean, you do love him, don't you?'

'Hush, Ma.' Diana gave her mother a peck on the cheek, very lightly so her lipstick didn't smudge. 'Of course I do. I love him madly, always will.'

She was pleased with that little diplomatic triumph. It was what her mother wanted to hear, and it wasn't *that* much of a lie. Of course she loved Ernie. He was dashing and he dressed beautifully, and he treated her so well. He'd never denied her anything she wanted, and they had a good time together. What more could you ask for? What was that old saying? It was as easy to fall in love with a rich man as a poor man. Diana had just seen to it that she'd fallen in love with the first sort.

Her mother and father did pretty well. Dad was a lawyer and had a nice practice in Lincoln's Inn. He had put three daughters through public school and had a pretty house in Kent. But it wasn't the sort of life Diana wanted; she needed more than the odd skiing holiday and riding lessons, she wanted to shop haute couture and buy herself diamond earrings, and fly first class, and holiday in the Seychelles, or better still, Mustique, on a private island somewhere. And she didn't see why she had to work like a slave to get those things. The good Lord had blessed her with beauty and style, and beauty and style were valuable.

I backed the right horse, Diana told herself, waving and smiling. Traffic slowed to a halt to let her carriage turn into St James's and there was the church up ahead, a beautiful old Anglican pile of eighteenth-century honey-coloured elegance, with a gratifyingly large posse of paparazzi parked right in front. Diana pulled her slim shoulders back and rearranged a few folds of chiffon and antique silk to give the best possible angle for the first shots. The light was going to be perfect, too. Everything was going to be perfect.

She started to sing.

'Going to the cha-pel, and I'm gonna get married . . .'

8

Chapter 2

Michael Cicero moved very slightly under his bedding. It was hard to move a body like his lightly. He was built for the boxing ring, not subtle ballerina-like shifts. But this morning he was motivated to try to shuffle lightly out of bed. For one thing, he had a hangover which was threatening to blow up his skull, and he figured that if he moved carefully enough, he might appease it. For another, there was a naked girl in his bed. On the face of it, that was not too bad a way to wake up. The trouble was, he couldn't remember her name.

He put his foot down gingerly on the bare hardwood floors of the tiny apartment. Glancing to his right, he saw two discarded rubbers about a foot from the bed. He grinned. One less thing to worry about, he thought, as he picked them up and threw them away. His place was minute, and not in the smartest area of town, but he kept it immaculately tidy. It was a matter of respecting yourself. Michael was big on respect; it was part of being Italian. He guessed it would be respectful to remember this chick's name.

He scratched his dark head, but he still had no clue. What was the last thing he remembered? The Five Leafed Clover on Hudson, about 8 p.m., St Patrick's Day and already a little buzzed. He must have picked her up there. Maybe she was Irish. The whole of Manhattan got a little bit Irish on March the seventeenth.

Michael padded to his bathroom, which was sectioned off from the rest of his studio flat by a dark wooden

screen, and retrieved his robe. It was thick navy towelling. He did not like to be seen nude in the mornings by
women he didn't know in any sense other than biblically.
Cicero wasn't vain, and he had no idea how good he
looked in the robe. The dark colour picked out his hazel
eyes, a legacy from his French mother, rimmed with thick
black lashes that were pure Italian. He would never be a
pretty boy; his nose was crooked from where a Second
Dan black belt had smashed up the bridge one Friday
night, and he was big, too, with weightlifter's arms and
thick kickboxer thighs. The type of teenage girl who
doted on Leonardo DiCaprio never looked twice at him.

But that was OK, because he didn't like them, either.
Michael liked women. Juicy, curvy girls like the one in
the bed. Her face was buried in the pillow, but she had a
nice handful of breasts and a gorgeous tight ass curving
out of a flat belly. He felt his groin stir slightly. Even
drunk, his radar for women was pretty good. She had
dyed hair, which he normally didn't like, but with a body
like that, he could excuse the lapse.

The dehydration started to kick in. Michael took a
seltzer from the fridge and drank it straight down, barely
pausing for breath. He felt slightly more human, and set
the coffee pot to brew while he took a quick, quiet
shower. The girl was snoring softly; she had probably
been as out of it as he was. He shaved and looked at
himself in the small mirror, then dressed in a white shirt
and black suit. It wasn't perfect, but it fit. He had six
suits, all the same make and cut, three navy and three
black. That way you didn't have to worry about what
you wore in the mornings.

Michael liked efficiency, especially when he had to get
into work. It was his own firm, so nobody was going to
fire him; but that was no excuse for slacking. He reported
to the mirror, and Michael Cicero looked a tough boss.
He was thirty and was going to make his business work,

or drop dead trying. It might be small, but it was still his. He dressed and acted for what he wanted his publishing firm to be.

The coffee finished perking as he fixed his cuff links. He got the shirts sent over from a woman in England, an old girlfriend, married to another man now but still a little in love with him. Michael preferred the European style of shirts, with holes in the cuffs for links to pull them together. He had to walk up six flights to his studio apartment, but his shoes were shined once a week, his hair was short, and his dress was as smart as it could be without any real money.

You didn't mess with Michael Cicero, in his office or out of it. He poured two mugs of hazelnut coffee, black and steaming, and took one over to the woman, shaking her awake gently, holding the liquid under her nose.

'Wake up, sugar.' He grinned at his own foolishness. You really didn't need a name at all. All girls had the same name. Sugar, aka Baby. It worked with everyone from old ladies to high-school cheerleaders.

'Ohh.' She groaned, and sat up, which made her small tits sway in a manner that almost made him decide to be late for work. 'Where am I?'

Michael wrapped her fingernails round the mug. They were too long. He couldn't stand the vogue for girls to have these take-your-eye-out monstrosities at the end of their hands. He was scratched all along his back, the soap had stung this morning. Guess she had enjoyed herself.

'You're on Leonard Street, downtown between West Broadway and Hudson.'

'Sure,' she said, uncertainly.

Her eyes focused and she gave a little start, like it was coming back to her. Her nipples hardened into tiny pink buds, and she drew back her shoulders and tossed her long hair.

'Oh Mikey, you were so great. I don't think it's ever been like that.'

He passed his rough hands over her skin, cupping her breasts, and kissed each nipple. Hell, it was only polite. She gave a delicious little shiver and threw back the cotton sheets invitingly. There was a nice curve to her leg, but her toenails were painted, which was a bad sign. She was the kind of girl who was great to fuck, but not to talk to.

'You flung me over your shoulder and carried me right out of Mick Rooney's!' She giggled. 'You're very strong.'

Memory flooded back. Her name was Denise. Great. He hadn't been wearing beer goggles last night, but looked like he'd had beer earmuffs on. She was giggling and pouting and she used a breathy, little-girl voice that was very annoying.

'Thanks, Denise. You were great too.'

Her face fell. 'It's Elise.'

'I said Elise. But drink your coffee now, baby. I'd love to stay and play but I have to get to work.'

'Can't you take the day off?'

'No,' Michael said, bluntly.

He was remembering the sex now. It had been OK; he'd moved her around the room pretty good. She had clutched and moaned at him. At the time he had hardly noticed her scratching him.

Elise stood up and bent over, picking up her scattered miniskirt and ankle boots and tight vest and jean jacket. Michael moved closer to her and rubbed his hands over her ass. She had a great ass, definitely. She was eager and thrust back against him while he played with her.

'Can I see you again?'

'Sure. Get dressed, and I'll go get a pen.'

She obediently tugged on her clothes, not bothering to take a shower. Michael winked at her as he made a big show of writing the number down, then walked her to the door, opening it firmly as she clutched at him.

Another ship in the night he never wanted to see again. He drank a second straight mug of black coffee, letting it slightly scorch his throat to wake him up. He was late, and he fought back the queasiness from the toxins swimming around his system.

The early rush-hour traffic beeped and honked faintly six floors below him. Welcome to another morning in Manhattan.

Green Eggs Books was Michael's dream. His father had a restaurant out on City Island, a popular place serving real southern Italian food, no Caesar salads, just herby bread and olive oil. He always left the bottle of Sambuca on the table with the espresso when his customers were done. It was a real good business, and his *gelati* were famous enough that he was thinking of adding an ice-cream parlour to the trattoria. He could have used the help, but Michael had doggedly gone his own path, so doggedly that the old man had given up. He complained, but he was proud. He liked the kid's bull-headedness.

The fact was that Michael Cicero, unexpectedly, unusually, liked books. He had never read any as a kid; his dad was big on softball but not so big on the local library. When Michael's mother died of breast cancer, he was only four, and his father had struggled to bring up the boy and his two sisters and keep food on the table. They shopped cheap for the last cuts of chicken and meat that the stores discounted towards the end of the day, and Francesco cooked everything up in a few pots and the four of them dined like princes even though they lived like paupers. One day an aunt dropped by the apartment, and left a smoked ham and an old encyclopedia she didn't want. Michael was bored, and he started to read.

Within a few months he had soaked up most of it. He

13

was like a sponge, and outpaced most of the kids at Junior High School 124, a mundane name for a mundane school in the Bronx. After that it was a scholarship to St Jacob's and a mile walk with another on the bus, there and back, every day. Michael loved it. He was out of the apartment, and he really got a chance to read. He had a passion for stories. Ancient Roman histories, translations of Alexander the Great, fantasies, novels. He read *Les Miserables* in ten days straight, doing nothing but reading, staying up sometimes till 2 a.m. using a candle by his bedside instead of the flashlight which might have alerted his dad.

College would have been nice but Michael was white and male and free of obvious disabilities, unless you counted a disastrous haircut and a passion for Kung-Fu movies. He lost scholarship places to women with worse grades than his, and his natural sexism deepened. There were always enough girls hanging around for him to be cocky and arrogant; though he was bookish he was also tough. He didn't enjoy team sports because he was too much of a loner, but he started curling his first weights at nine years old and never really stopped.

When he was thirteen Michael took up karate. There was no point wasting time with hockey and ball when the school gang beat him up for his lunch money every second day. Two months into his training, Michael kicked the hell out of the ringleader, and never got bothered again. He even beat up a few kids himself. If he ever looked back he might have been ashamed, but Michael didn't waste too much time examining his conscience. That was then; that was life on the street. Kick or be kicked.

The girls spoiled him. They did his homework, and tidied up his room. He had a way of blunt speaking some chicks seemed to enjoy. He paid on dates, even if a 'date' consisted of a soda and a candy bar at the local Five and

Dime, but he didn't compromise. If a girl complained about his karate schedule, they broke up. It never bothered Michael, because there was always another honey right there to take her place.

He thought of women as weak and pretty, future wives and mothers. He didn't mind if a girl was smart. In fact, he couldn't stand stupidity. He wasn't great at the bar pick-up game, because if a girl was stupid, Michael had an irresistible urge to tell her so.

Last week he'd hit some place on the West Side with his friend Big Steve who lived out in Westchester. Big Steve was still teasing him about the way the chick of the night had sat next to him, put her hand on his forearm and, gazing into his eyes, spilled out the story of her screwed-up life. Michael turned to her and said, 'You know, I really don't want to hear your sob stories. I just met you.' She was offended. Too bad. He was no good at pretending to be interested in bullshit.

The fact that women took the scholarship places when they had lower grades made him angry, but he took it on the chin. Columbia offered him a place to read political science, but he hated the attitude of the professors, so he left. In the end he attended a local college, and worked four jobs to pay for his tuition. His father hung Michael's diploma on the kitchen wall in his restaurant. It meant even more to Francesco than to Michael; his father had been a peasant from Naples right off the boat, and now his son was a Master of Arts. He backed off from the restaurant idea. His daughters, Maria and Sophia, had both made good marriages. Francesco was sure that Michael would do well, too.

Michael had taken out a bank loan and founded a tiny publishing company, for children's books, operating out of the East Village. He had faith that there was a huge market for children that just wasn't being reached. Kids like himself, kids who would love to read if only they got the opportunity, if they could be taught about letters by something other than *Sesame Street*. The market was out there for sure. He just had to find it.

He hired one assistant and talked to a friend from college, Joe. Joe's father owned a printing press and agreed to put out a small print run if Michael could come up with something to print. That was the trouble. He advertised for writers in the *Village Voice*, and got flooded with rubbish, full of spelling mistakes and grammatical errors. It was a huge mistake. Michael got his phone number changed so he didn't waste all day telling so-called children's novelists why their stuff wasn't going to make it.

After two months he had impatient creditors, a bored secretary, and not much time. The truth was, he knew nothing about publishing.

Francesco gave him the idea that saved him.

'Sure, there's good stuff out there,' he said, considering it pretty hard for a man who mostly read menus. 'It's just most of the good writers are dead. They died hundreds of years ago. Nobody writes like that any more.'

It was the answer. Michael bolted from his seat and drove back to his office. He could re-issue children's classics, and never have to pay the writers a cent. Edward Lear was as dead as a dodo, and after a while his stuff went into what was called 'public domain' – you didn't have to pay for it. It took him a week to find Seth Green: a smart, gay kid at NYU with a mad talent for drawing. He knocked out a version of *The Owl and the Pussycat* in three days. Joe's father gave them a break on the printing run, and Green Eggs had its first book.

Then all he had to do was sell it.

He didn't have a dollar for advertising, but he had passion. Michael loaded up copies of *Owl* into a knapsack and cycled round every kindergarten and library in Manhattan. For every nine 'no's, he got one 'yes'. After a month he had sold every copy.

About now, Michael was earning just enough to pay his assistant, his overheads and his rent, and even afford small luxuries like decent coffee. His big break could not be far away. He knew it. He walked down the rickety stairs of his pre-war apartment building to the street to spend one more day looking for it.

Chapter 3

Diana settled back against the black leather of the chauffeur-driven Mercedes, squeezed her husband's hand, and thought about New York.

Her things, what little there were of them, had already been shipped: real lavender bags and other small reminders of England, some new things from Chloe and Hussein Chalwar, and her wedding dress, dry-cleaned, boxed and pressed, to be presented perhaps to a daughter should she and Ernie ever get a minute to themselves to start working on one. Apart from that, she took very little. Only the Prada and Chanel had survived the move. What more perfect excuse could you have to start your wardrobe from scratch than emigrating to a new country? Ernie was still buried in his new reports and balance sheets for Blakely's and just signed off whatever Diana wanted. And to conquer New York, nothing but the latest stuff would do.

Her engagement ring, a not so subtle diamond rock, now glittered next to a thin band of platinum. Diana glanced down at it smugly. Her status had taken rather a leap. She was now Diana Foxton, Mrs Ernest Foxton. In fact, there was a large box of creamy Smythson's writing paper in the boot, zipped away in her Gucci luggage (Louis Vuitton was so yesterday) with her new name emblazoned all over it. Diana crossed her legs under her sage-green Joseph suit, her string of pearls at her neck, and tried to get used to it. To be honest, she preferred her maiden name. A part of her missed being Diana Verity.

But that was silly; married women didn't keep their own names, particularly when they weren't going to work.

'Do you think they'll have got our place ready, darling?' she asked. 'I need a really good bath when I get off a plane. I always feel so sticky and bloated.'

'Course they will.' Ernie had his nose in a report and answered her absently. 'I told you, the supervisor's hired us a temporary maid. She'll have done everything, even stocked the fridge.'

'I bet there won't be any bubble bath.' Diana pouted. 'I should have stocked up before I left.'

'I can't be expected to sort out your toiletries,' Ernie said, rather shortly.

'I know that, sweetie.'

Diana glanced out of the window as London swept past and wondered how much she would miss it. Susie had given her a big hug at the end of the reception at Brown's, and told her the scene would never be the same. She might miss Catherine Connor and Emma Norman, her girlfriends who used to drink with her at the Groucho and Soho House. But there were only so many times you could go to the Met Bar, and that old Liam and Patsy, Jude and Sadie, Tara and Tamara thing was just . . . played out. I want *fun*, Diana thought impetuously, pushing her dark hair back from her blue eyes, sweeping a soft hand finished with a plain French manicure across delicate cheekbones dusted over with a sheer tinted moisturiser and just a hint of bronzing powder. Her reflection in the rear-view mirror showed that the Stila lip gloss she had chosen for today was a definite improvement on her old matt look. She resolved to wear nothing but lip glosses from now on in. Or at least until she got bored with them.

So the clubs were done. What about London's culture? There *was* an awful lot of it, but what Londoner ever bothered to go? The British Museum, the National

Gallery . . . just pretty piles of stone you drove past on your way down to the King's Road. She might miss her family, but Daddy had been pretty sour once the wedding bills had finally come in, and Ma was still bugging her about Ernie not being the right chap, and her sisters Iseult and Camilla both thought she should get a job, which was insanity, of course. Why should one get a job when you could, instead, spend your days shopping and lunching and having fun?

Diana batted away all the criticism. It was mostly down to jealousy, anyway. Ernie was *so* dashing and *so* successful, the sad fact of the matter was they just couldn't handle it.

Camilla was a lawyer and made about a hundred grand a year, and had twins. She had absolutely no fashion sense and lived south of the river, in a big Victorian pile with a garden. Yet Ma was always holding Milla up to her as some sort of shining example.

Diana remembered the farewell tea Milla had given her yesterday afternoon in her garden. She had cried and given Diana a big hug and offered her a slice of home-made flapjack.

'But you'll be so bored in New York. You don't even know anybody.'

'I'll make friends, Milla. I made lots of friends when I moved to London. I'll just do it all over again.'

'Friends? That crowd you hang out with?'

'They are my friends, so don't be horrible.'

'I wonder how many of them you'll keep up with once you reach Manhattan,' Milla said, rather shrewdly for her.

'There are such things as phone lines. And think how enjoyable it'll be in New York in spring. We'll throw lots of dinner parties. You love throwing dinner parties.'

Milla looked out at her two terrors trying to dismantle the oak tree in the garden. 'What about your job?'

'Not everybody *wants* to work. I've rather had enough of *Vogue* and, anyway, Ernie's going to pull some strings in case I decide I do want to go back to it.'

Diana pushed a lock of chestnut hair back behind her ears, in which new sapphire and ruby studs, a wedding present from Ernie, glittered merrily. They were rather flashy, but jewels were jewels. Her beloved husband was actually making noises about getting her a part-time job, which was tiresome. She was hoping for a couple of years off from fashion writing and ringing up designers telling them what non-size Stella and Shalom were this week. It was good in that one got the perks – free samples, big discounts . . . but she thought that, given a little time with the ladies of New York, she would be getting the perks without doing the work, which was just about the story of her life.

'Well, that's good, angel. In the end you'd get bored with nothing to do.'

'Nothing to do? Oh Milla!'

Diana laughed, and for the millionth time her sister marvelled at how bewitching she looked when she smiled, lit up like Oxford Street before Christmas, the beautiful white teeth and slightly imperfect nose and sparkling eyes all crunched up together and simply adorable. It was easy to see how London had fallen under the spell of her incorrigible, layabout sister. If Milla had any reservations, they were about Ernie. It was true that he seemed devoted, and gave Di whatever she wanted. Some men loved a high-maintenance girl. It was just that Ernie didn't seem to appreciate Diana's ravishing smile the way Milla would have wanted him to. He always seemed a bit distracted. Oh well; perhaps that was just his way.

She poured tea for her sister, stirring in milk and sugar for herself and a slice of lemon for Diana. No doubts about the wedding, though. What a triumph. All the nasty little London scenesters who professed to love Di had been absolutely seething with envy. And Diana had been so gracious, kissing everybody, laughing so the whole room lit up, making a point to forget no one, not even the crusty old great-uncles Dad brought down from Shropshire. She had danced the first dance – a lovely stately waltz – and then later, had led the whole party in a mad disco-dancing frenzy to 'Venus' by Bananarama. Ernie had moved around the room, smiling and getting his picture taken, seemingly oblivious to all the boy-friends and husbands casting longing looks at Diana. She was so radiant, so charming, so discreetly flirtatious! Milla sighed and bit into her flapjack. She'd miss her sister. Diana was impossible, but impossible not to adore, too. She started to tell Diana about the people she knew in New York, watching her blue eyes glaze over. Milla's girlfriends were lawyers and bankers; not the trophy wife sort she supposed Diana would gravitate to.

Recalling the conversation, Diana smiled gently. Dear Milla. If only she could get her to loosen up just a little bit, how wonderful it would be! All that money, and no time to enjoy spending it. She glanced across at Ernie, buried as he was in his report. What had her sister said about him?

'The city's buzzing about Ernie.' Milla had been admir-ing Diana's amazing trousseau before the wedding and helping her select candidates for her going-away wardrobe. There would be no honeymoon, as Ernie wanted to get to his new job as quickly as possible, but Diana had said lightly, 'Our whole lives will be a honeymoon,' so maybe there was no cause to be concerned.

'Buzzing how?'

Diana picked up a cream silk shirt, wondering if it would survive the trip. It contrasted so well with everything from burgundy to eggshell blue. You really couldn't do without cream silk and cotton. It gave you neutrality without washing out your complexion the way white tended to do. 'Nothing good, I hope.' She gave Milla a quick glance and started to listen. Gossip about Ernie! That was interesting. It was good to be marrying a man who other people talked about.

'Blakely's picked him because he was ruthless at Hatfield Books.'

'Businessmen should be ruthless, shouldn't they? Anyway, under Ernie, profits went up. You can't deny that.'

'I don't, but people say he was still pretty cut-throat, even by modern publishing standards. He fired over a thousand people. He closed a printing operation—'

Diana shivered. She didn't like to think of people losing their jobs. 'He never told me that.'

'Why would he? I expect you didn't ask.'

'I don't know too much about his business. He probably hated having to do it.'

Milla recalled the nasty jokes that had circulated in *Private Eye* and decided not to share them with the bride to be. Ernie Foxton had legendarily issued the P45s two weeks before the Christmas party at Hatfield's London offices so that the company's champagne bill would be lower.

'A lot of authors who had been with Hatfield for years were dropped, and they stopped publishing poetry and other prestigious books.'

'Prestigious doesn't pay the bills.'

'I suppose that was Ernie's thinking. But it caused waves,' Milla said, tentatively.

Diana frowned slightly with her beautifully shaped brows. 'Well, I don't know about that. I imagine they will find other work. Ernie's job was to make the company profitable. I think he did all right, don't you?'

'He certainly did,' Milla said dryly.

Ernest Foxton ran such a tight ship they had given him the nickname 'Captain Bligh'. The head of the sales force, who had been with Hatfield man and boy for twenty years, had been called up to Ernie's office and given twenty minutes to clear out of the building. The logo which had been the company's signature for half a century was instantly wiped out and replaced with bright neon colours that stood out on the shelves. New writers were dropped from the list, old staples were cleared out wholesale and mid-level authors lost the editors they had relied on as Ernie fired some staff and rearranged others. With the closure of the printworks, and the farming out of printing to contractors, Ernie had personally eliminated about a third of the workforce. Maybe it was necessary, Milla thought, but did he have to be quite so brutal? The horror stories were legion. Pack up your books and go, and if you contact any of our writers we'll sue. Pregnant women fired in their ninth month, lifelong company men sacked and told not even to expect a bonus. The atmosphere over at Hatfield had been just a little bit short of France during the Reign of Terror. It was Ernie's revolution, and it had been a corporate bloodbath.

Of course a few people had come out of it pretty well. The shareholders loved Ernie: their moribund stock had risen five and three-eighths. Then there were the superstar blockbuster writers, the best-selling authors who now got an even larger piece of the pie. And finally, there was Ernie himself, who had shot up from middle-manager to big cheese. He had been rewarded with stock options, cash bonuses, a bigger office, a Lamborghini and, finally, a new job from half a world away, offering him double his salary. Ernie was a two-million-dollar-a-year executive and he was only thirty-eight. The world was his oyster now, and he could afford the delightful Diana, and any other toys he might want.

'Well, there you go then. I expect most of the talk is about how much money he made for the company.

People are too tied to tradition. All Ernie did was try to give the place a facelift.'

'The company he's taking over in New York is going to be a tougher proposition. They have a very prestigious fiction list and publish a lot of well-loved popular authors. I don't think they'll react the same way if Ernie decides to go for slash and burn again.'

Diana selected a pair of Manolos that set off her outfit perfectly and congratulated herself inwardly for her luck in not having taken them down to the charity shop yet.

'Nobody loves businessmen, Milla, but they do love results. Sometimes tough decisions have to be taken. Ernie's a very kind soul, you know. He's already discussed all the charities he thinks we should get involved in in America.'

All the most visible ones, Milla didn't say.

'I'm sure you're right. I just thought you'd want to know what's being said.'

'And I do.' Diana gave her sister a kiss on the cheek. 'Of course I do. You're a darling to warn me. I need to have ammunition when the New York literary establishment starts being horrible to my husband and making snide jokes at parties. You need to look out for that sort of thing. I'll watch his back, so he doesn't get insulted for twenty minutes straight without knowing what's going on.'

'Sounds good. Now tell me about your place, again.'

'Central Park West,' Diana rhapsodised, 'mid-seventies, twelfth floor, *extremely* good building, the committee turned down Barbra Streisand two years ago because they didn't want photographers hanging round . . .'

As she launched into her description of the glories awaiting her just a stone's throw from Saks, Diana seemed so perfectly happy that Milla allowed her worrying inner voice to be quieted.

She can handle Ernie, Milla told herself. Diana can handle *anything*.

Chapter 4

I could like it here, Diana thought to herself. She lifted the crystal flute of freshly pressed raspberry juice her maid had brought her, and took another exploratory stroll round their apartment. Huge windows almost as high as the ceilings looked out over Central Park, and the blue lake sparkled in the sun. Beyond that, even Harlem looked peaceful from this distance. On the horizon, when the sky was clear, like it was today, you could even make out the blaze of colour that was Westchester County. Ernie wanted her to go out to Westchester and find them a little holiday cottage. All the Wall Street boys and Park Avenue surgeons had places outside the city, and Martha's Vineyard, Diana thought, was just too much of a cliché. Ditto the Hamptons. Plus, there was the small matter of Ernie's finances. He was rich – such a hit at Blakely's already – but he didn't have real American dollars, the kind that Calvin and Kelly Klein, Steven Spielberg and Kate Capshaw possessed. Diana didn't want something in the Hamptons if hers would be the smallest place for miles around. She preferred to head out to Scarsdale or Bronxville, and find some rustic little gem for the weekends. Westchester was full of city refugees – her new best friend, Felicity Metson, had told her it was the second-richest county in America, after Beverly Hills.

It hadn't been too hard, settling in. Paul Gammon, the chairman of the board at Blakely's, a crusty old social register stalwart who idolised the Brits, had thrown a party for their second night in town. All very select, no celebrities, just the money crowd. Diana had worn a classically simple gown of pewter silk and the drop diamond and citrine earrings Ernie had bought her the day she closed on their apartment; her make-up nothing more than a slick of foundation and a whisper of bronzer. She knew how to invoke the look of the old money she had never really had, and it worked like a charm. As Ernie boasted to the stock-market whizz-kids about his overhead cuts back home, Diana worked the wives. Business was so boring. It was much more fun knowing how to spend money. And it was the wives – sometimes the mistresses, too – who held the key to social acceptance here.

London had been a cakewalk, Diana thought, sipping her juice. A few photo shoots here, some blue-blooded relatives there, beauty and a rich husband. You could shop divinely for three weeks around Bond Street and never hit the same store twice. But grown-up exclusivity was about more than velvet ropes and your name on a guest list guarded by a gorilla in a tux. Americans had their own way of doing things, and Diana intended to fit in. The new girl in town needed all the perks of the Manhattan elite: the secret phone numbers the top restaurants gave out so that important customers always got a table; the names of the best manicurists, masseuses, dog-walkers and private shoppers; invitations to the right galleries and parties. Diana had a determined look in her eye as she moved from group to group, in Mrs Gammon's mahogany-panelled drawing room high above Park Avenue. She offered little cards, collected names, and promised a lunch here, a tea there. Ernie was a publisher, and publishing still carried prestige in New York. And, after all, women are curious creatures. Diana knew they would want to check her out.

She planned her first two weeks like a general. Helen Gammon had provided her guest list – of course Diana would do nothing so crass as to scrawl down phone numbers at the party – and she worked her way through it. A flurry of lunches, trips to the beauty parlour and expeditions to Prada and DKNY followed. Some of the ladies were fun, most were bitchy, all were rich, skinny and bored.

'I'd like to throw a party,' she announced that night when Ernie returned.

Her husband looked at her absently. Diana had hardly been around the house since they'd arrived, and that was just fine by him. At work there was so much waste, so many bodies not making the sales, not pulling their weight. He was busy trying to work out who to fire first. His revolution was blasting away the corporate cobwebs, and that was exhilarating. Let Diana do her thing, as long as she didn't bother him too much. She never had when they were dating. Why should things change now they were married?

'Party. Is it necessary?' Ernie sighed. 'I've got things to do.'

'I know you do, darling. You're being so clever. But things like that help with the business. You needn't plan it, just keep the twenty-first free. And I'll need some money, of course.'

'Surprise.' Ernie grunted.

Diana pouted. 'But darling, it'll be so *impressive*.'

It was the way to his heart, or at least to his wallet. Ernie liked spending money where it showed. Fast cars, flashy jewels. Maybe her engagement ring *was* just a little vulgar, it was so large, but Diana had never complained about it. Could a diamond really be too big?

'All right.' Ernie nodded. 'Just one, then.' He ignored his young wife's knowing smile. She thought one would turn into two or three. But if he didn't like what she produced, it wouldn't.

At least Diana had come and asked for a budget. Some American wives just spent first and asked questions later. His girl knew better.

It's my way or the highway, Ernie thought, and returned her smile with one of his own.

'Let's go into dinner.'

The dining room was a triumph. Diana had worked with Richard Hesson himself, the hottest, campest interior designer in the city. He was known for his uncompromisingly masculine rooms, maybe to make up for his uncompromisingly feminine looks, but who was she to judge? The room was all dark woods, a heavy walnut table from some eighteenth-century French farmhouse, rich red *toile de joie*, and a scarlet carpet. The maid had the table laid for two, one at each end, with crisp Irish linen napkins, small silver vases filled with creamy yellow roses, and beeswax candles in antique silver candelabra flickering invitingly. Diana almost sighed out loud with contentment as she moved to the lower end of the table, across from her husband. This was so . . . *civilised*. A lot better than her grotty London flat. She was only missing a little intimacy, and Ernie would probably get round to it once he had settled in more at the job.

'Tell me about your day,' she suggested, as Consuela laid the appetiser before her; tiny baked potatoes served with butter and flakes of truffle.

'Not much to tell.' Ernie forked the food into his mouth, barely taking the time to taste it. 'Showing the lads how to run a modern business. Lots of bullshit talked in books.'

His wife nodded and waited for Consuela to uncork the Merlot. They would eat quietly and then she could probably get away with a long drawn-out bath and *Friends* while Ernie retired to his study, to trade stocks on the Net or some such. Mentally Diana started to plan her first party. She fully intended to make a splash here.

Ernie talked away at his wife, offering up anodyne stories about his new offices, the incompetence of his assistants. Nothing of real importance, but why should he tell Diana about business? She wasn't the kind of girl to give a damn. Sure, once in a while, a female came along who understood money. Usually ugly ones, frustrated types. Janet Jensen, a new underling of his, was a prime example. Ernie tried to imagine Janet spending days picking out the perfect duck-egg-blue trim for the guest bathroom – impossible, the hatchet-faced old boot. Janet types had brains; Diana types were arm ornaments and then there were sluts, Ernie's favourite kind of girl.

After dinner, he gave his wife a brief peck on the cheek before heading to his study. It wouldn't hurt for her to butter up the Yanks. It was part of the reason he'd slipped that three-carat Tiffany rock on her finger.

Ernie shut the thick mahogany door behind him. Diana's touch in the office was more old-world subtlety; dark greens, leather, a Persian rug, bookshelves crammed with Victorian tomes that might have been in his family for generations. It was a room his friends' fathers from Eton might have had; a gentleman's library, complete with a muted oil of some ancient dame in a riding habit on the far wall. Ernie half loved and half loathed it. If he had dug a little deeper, he might have recognised the screaming sense of insecurity he always had around Di's good breeding. But Ernie wasn't into digging deep. He was into instant gratification.

His bride would be an hour or longer at her *toilette*. Ernie didn't want to disturb her. Who needed to see women do their private, slightly revolting, stuff? Shaving legs and armpits and plucking and waxing and filing . . . it made him nauseous, thinking of women like that. Ernie didn't think much of the traditional idolatry of the female body. Most of them ran to fat, let themselves go, had moles, hair and dimpled skin. Whatever his reputation as a raider, he didn't have a matching one as a playboy like so many of the wide-boys kicking corporate ass in the big city. He could get it up and he certainly got around. Furthermore he realised that having the right woman was important, like having the right car. That was why Ernie had chosen Diana. She was the best, which was what he had to have. But she didn't do much for him.

Ernie slid his thin frame into the ancient leather armchair and flicked on his computer, the only modern touch in the room. His stocks came up, and he cast an eye over his portfolio. How long could the Dow go on this crazy run? Almost indefinitely, maybe. He couldn't concentrate on trades tonight. His mind was running on Blakely's: not the sad, overpaid, underworked old war-horses, company men since their early twenties, who he'd fired today, but the PR girl from Hastings Inc., their new contractors.

Mira Chen. She was probably twenty-five, but she looked younger, apart from that icy, bitchy curve to her lip. Thin as a rail with small, curved breasts which jutted out at an unnatural angle, definitely fake. Their fakeness aroused him. She was a girl who liked to show it off. Her dresses were tight, dark, low-cut, worn with a jacket so snug it made him wonder if she was wearing a corset. Yeah . . . a corset cutting off her blood-flow, pinching, pushing the little apple boobs upwards, trying to make something of them. Her long nails were painted bright red. How the hell she typed with them, he didn't know. Mira's thin lips too were always scarlet. Ernie thought about her pale, creamy skin, the eyebrows that she had plucked so thin she had pencil up there in place of them. It was a fake, painted look. He loved it.

What's more, as Mira shuffled her papers, and pre-tended to listen to her boss giving the presentation, she had looked over at Ernie. He was good at reading the faces of his lackeys. Ms Chen was showing neither fear nor agitation. Rather, the look she sent him was slow, assessing and cruel. Ernie had found his throat drying up. He had snuck a look at the skinny, muscular legs protruding from the tight little tube of a skirt, encased in see-through black hose, they tapered down to a pair of high, arched heels, black, with little spiked metal stilettos. It must hurt her feet to be crammed into those, he had thought vaguely through the cloud of lust that enveloped him. When the presentation finished, Ernie told Dick Hastings, her boss, that they should meet again.

'I have more questions.'

'Let's rearrange,' Dick said, smoothly. 'Unfortunately I have a three o'clock uptown.'

'No problem. One of your co-workers could probably help me out. You.' Ernie turned to Mira. 'You're free now, right?'

'Absolutely, Mr Foxton.' She had a nasal Brooklyn tint to her voice, and she was eager. He imagined Mira was a thrusting, grasping little bitch. The way her colleagues glanced at her suggested to Ernie she wasn't well liked. But she had a tiny, compact little ass, as flat as a boy's. Who cared about popularity contests?

His gushing secretary showed out the other suits, bowing and scraping, and Ernie shut the door behind them, turning to Mira.

'Interesting presentation.'

'I noticed you were gripped,' Mira said.

Ernie scowled. He wasn't used to being sassed by people at work, especially women. He opened his mouth to rebuke her, but she held up one hand with those sharp talons. 'I think public relations is very complex. I'd feel more comfortable discussing this in a social setting. That is, of course, if you found that acceptable, Mr Foxton.'

There it was again, that tightening in his groin. As he

looked at her, Mira ran the tip of a pink tongue across her glossy red lips. A coffee, Ernie thought. What could that hurt? And he was the boss. Nobody would dare to complain.

'I could probably give you half an hour,' he said, briskly.

Mira's mouth curled up at the corners in a slow, deliberate smile. She knew a mark when she saw one. With some men it was written right across them, all she ever needed to do was lay the bait. If a man didn't respond, no harm done.

Ernest Foxton had a fearsome reputation for ruthlessness, but he also had that thin, petty look about him that usually meant only one thing.

He liked to be treated badly and dominated by women. The gossip was that his wife was a stuck-up, spoiled, ladylike little princess. She would be no threat. The seedy clubs Mira went to were full of high-powered businessmen with a weak streak somewhere deep inside that got off on pain. Only last week she had been forced to finish with her ex-boyfriend, the CEO of a Fortune 500 company, something to do with industrial machinery, or some such. His wife had found out, which was too bad. Mira had definitely been discreet, as long as the gifts kept coming. Most likely the moron had shouted out her name in his sleep. At any rate, the sugar daddy – sugar slave – position was vacant. And if she knew men, Ernie Foxton was a prime candidate to fill it.

'That would be great.' Mira stared at him coldly. 'There's a coffee place not far from here that I like.'

Without a word, Ernie gathered up his notes and followed Mira out of his office. Through the opulently decorated lobby, she kept up a loud stream of chatter about brand management and focus groups and Internet presence. Ernie told his assistant they were stepping out for a meeting. He wasn't listening to what the woman was saying. His gaze kept trickling down her hard legs to the spiked metal stilettos. He found his throat was dry.

She kept up the talking until they were a block away from the coffee house. Ernie sprang to open the door for her. She didn't thank him. She indicated a banquette away from the window and he sat there, quietly. The place was gloomy, although it was noon outside. Looking up, Ernie saw that there were erotic prints set against the black walls, 1930s maybe, ink etchings of women – semi-nude – with whips, restraining men. Homoerotic pictures, too. The ambience was dark and, as he looked around, he saw the patrons were well dressed, but furtive. It felt secret and forbidden and terribly exciting.

A waiter materialised into view from nowhere and turned to Mira.

'I'll have herbal tea. He'll take black coffee,' she said, shortly.

As the man sidled off, Ernie looked at Mira. The expression in her eyes was such that he didn't say a word. He swallowed, dryly.

'I don't take my coffee black,' he muttered, after a while.

She looked him over with contempt and reached under the table. Ernie felt her talons dig into his hand as she grabbed it, waiting just a second to feel if there was any resistance. Then his hand hit something cool and smooth and firm. Her skinny thighs, as tight as a man's. He gasped with excitement. His cock hardened, he was suddenly afraid to move, afraid that anybody could pass by and see the state of him. Damn, she was a bitch. And a slut. His fingertips, squeezed so tight in her grip that the blood was cut off, were feeling her pussy now. No panties, and she was shaved totally smooth.

Ernie groaned.

'You'll take your coffee exactly how I tell you to take it,' Mira hissed.

Chapter 5

The days rolled on, and Diana was satisfied. At least, she kept telling herself that. Her little dinner parties, given with élan and verve, were the talk of the town, not least because Diana made sure to invite all the gossip columnists, flattering them shamelessly. Ernie's business was going well, too, from the looks of things. The stock price of the company had risen after his first month in charge, and that was all she wanted or needed to know. Diana was more concerned with digging out the *right* – it was her new favourite phrase. There were many stylists dotted around the soaring skyscrapers, but Diana wanted to find the *right* one – the man with the best razor cuts to trim her long hair, to keep it glossy and perfect. The *right* dinner guests, the delicious mix of celebrities, socialites, big businessmen, and one or two scandal-hit divorcees, with perhaps a poverty-stricken but talented poet thrown in somewhere. She had already picked the *right* decorator, and with the help of her friends, she was aiming to find the *right* everything. From pedicurists to psychics, New York had its favourites – but, Diana thought, sighing, it was so *boring* to follow the crowd. As if she would be seen dead in a pashmina shawl, for example. There was a very fine line between stylish and fashion victim. Perhaps it was the incessant sameness of New York moneyed life that had her ... well ... restless.

She was meeting Natasha, Jodie and Felicity at L'Urbane, the newest hot spot, run by two Frenchwomen who promised to steal all the crowds away from Bliss.

There was a three-month wait for an appointment, if you were one of the peasants. My girlfriends don't fall into that category, Diana thought smugly. And apparently the hour-long oxygen facials would give you a complexion to die for. She studied her own smooth skin in the mirror of the solid-gold Cartier compact Ernie gave her after her last dinner party got him a great write-up in the papers. He was revelling in being a social lion, getting the kind of acceptance in the States he could never get at home. Back there, Diana thought, her husband would always be second to her. It was the quietly inflexible class system that Ernie would never be able to buck. In America, with the right kind of press, he could make it.

And America was all about status. Ernie drew a lot of satisfaction from it, Diana mused, why couldn't she? She was doing everything right. So what was missing? Love? That was a fairy story girls should grow out of when they grew out of Cinderella. The best thing you could hope for was to find a guy who you got on with, who didn't bother you overmuch, and who didn't paw you in bed. She had no complaints about Ernie in that regard. Since the job had kicked in, he hardly ever wanted sex, and when he did, it was dutiful, fast and distasteful. Diana gritted her teeth and just prayed he would keep away from her. She'd read in *Glamour* that 80 per cent of women never had an orgasm. Was that true? She looked at her rich girlfriends' husbands and thought it might be.

Sex was for men. Sex for women was a huge myth. It was better to seek real pleasure from life, Diana told herself. She had a rich husband, a life of luxury, she was young, and beautiful, and envied, and never had to do a stroke of work. It was . . . she grinned to herself softly . . . the American dream. The ennui would pass, she must just be tired. A life of leisure could be exhausting. Maybe this spa would be the thing to refresh her.

The limo pulled in smoothly to the kerb, her driver

easily negotiating the Fifth Avenue traffic. L'Urbane's frontage, a quietly opulent canopy of bronze silk, was spread out to welcome her. Diana slid out of the car while Richard held the door open for her. She tugged her tailored jacket closer around her breasts, snugly encased in La Perla mocha lace this morning, and gave a tiny smile to the hot-dog vendor who whistled as she strutted into the lobby.

The girls were waiting for her. Diana gave them a little wave.

'Darlings, it's so good to see you.'

'Diana! At last.' Natasha stood, all skinny blonde elegance, and moved to kiss the air at the side of her face. Jodie and Felicity waggled manicured fingers and gave her the small grimaces that passed for smiles among many New York wives since the press broke the story that smiling gave you wrinkles.

Natty Zuckerman was married to a press mogul, Jodie Goodfriend to an investment banker, and Felicity Metson was recently divorced from a real-estate magnate. Felicity was the youngest of the three, just a little older than Diana, and was her closest friend over here. She was currently dating a US Marine major stationed at Fort Hamilton, and liked to give Diana all the juicy gossip. And wasn't gossip the best thing in the world – after a nice designer sale at Bloomingdales?

'Shall we go in? It's the seaweed wrap to start with,' Felicity said, eagerly.

'Sounds good.' Diana smiled at her friend, vaguely aware that Jodie and Natasha sometimes gave Felicity a hard time, just because she was divorced, which was unfair, of course. Some people were just tolerated. Diana tossed her newly platinum bob, her roots eliminated as of nine this morning, her head covered in a glossy cloud of corn-gold, shining hair.

'Ladies. Please to come this way.' A beautiful Indian

lady in a sari of rich crimson and gold appeared before them, bowing low. The changing rooms were individual, of course, and inlaid with mosaics on the floor. The taps were gold-plated, and the countertop solid marble in pale pink. L'Occitane shea butter and honeysuckle soap was laid out for her, next to a crystal vase crammed with roses and the delicate buds of actual honeysuckle blooms. Wow, Diana thought. The Americans certainly know how to pamper a woman.

She knew she ought to be thrilled at the thought of a half-day of massage in the company of her girlfriends. Impatient with herself, Diana struggled into her swimsuit and shook her head. She *would* enjoy this. New things, she found, always alleviated the boredom.

Michael Cicero stretched in the half light of dawn. His arms felt like they were on fire. Three sets of curls with thirty-pound weights had made his biceps scream, but he gritted his teeth and forced himself through it. Exercise was the physical stress that helped him cope with the mental stress of running his company. Besides, he didn't intend to allow his muscles to slide. Guys today, many of them, looked like they could hardly lift a gallon of milk without panting. Just because he wore a suit didn't mean that he was going to go soft.

He pushed himself up lightly on the balls of his feet and stepped into the shower. Getting up at 4 a.m. to sneak out of a girl's apartment was tiring, but it had some definite advantages. He didn't have to worry about hustling her out while not appearing rude. The chick had been attractive, too, Jessica, an old flame he called up periodically, a grad student at NYU, one of those cool chicks with an out-there CD collection and a nice line in little leather backpacks. She wore her hair too short for his taste, but she was very well endowed, and with those tits bouncing towards him, he could forget other aesthetic considerations. Jessie was ravenous in bed. She didn't want a relationship and neither did he. He enjoyed her simply, clutching her back as he thrust into her, making her buck and wriggle, his hand gently trailing over her pussy, teasing her while he thrust. Michael liked his women responsive and took the time to make sure they were. In his opinion there were no frigid women, just lousy lovers. He grinned at his steamy reflection in the bathroom mirror. Most guys were weak and couldn't hit it. That helped him. When women found a guy who could make them pant, they'd do anything for him.

He loved women. The trouble was, he reflected, that he loved too many of them. Settling down with just one? Impossible. Maybe, someday in the future. But if Michael was honest, he sometimes doubted that day would ever arrive. He shrugged and towelled himself off. Romance wasn't his style. He had work to do.

Outside his apartment it was very cold. New York's snap into winter couldn't be far away. A bitter gust whipped down from West Broadway and into his jacket. Shivering, Michael ducked into the subway. Whatever people said about the New York subway, it was warm.

He arrived at the office to find Susan already there. Today she wore a smart, short red shirtdress that buttoned up along the front, with a fitted jacket over it. Jessica had concentrated his mind against her temptations, though. Michael nodded a brisk good morning to his assistant and asked for his schedule.

'You have a ten thirty uptown, at the Blakely's headquarters, with a lunch to follow. And that's all today, Mr Cicero.'

Michael had made it quite clear: in the office, it was Mr Cicero from the staff – which was Susan, at this point. Susan said to herself this was totally arrogant.

'You've got my files?'

'Right here, sir.'

She felt a little tingle in her skin as she said that. Her nipples tightened sweetly. No wonder Leslie thought she was on fire in bed lately, she spent her whole day at work dreamily frustrated.

'Wish me luck,' Michael said, grinning at her.

Oh, my. Susan steadied herself with one manicured hand. 'Oh, I do, Mr Cicero, really, I wish you the very best of luck, there's no way you're not going to wow them—'

'Thanks.' He cut her off, absently. She could see his mind was already on the meeting. 'I'll get a cab on the street. Make sure Seth has the artwork he needs, OK?'

'OK, Mr Cicero.' Susan sighed.

He walked out.

Damn, Michael thought. The chick this morning had made him forget he had this meeting. He was getting old. He walked hastily away from Zabanda's, so the moussaka reek didn't cling to his suit, and jumped in a cab on the corner of Madison. It was a pretty big morning this morning. He had pitched their latest list to a new group of buyers last week and got some good orders . . . major bookstores, even an order placed by Amazon.com. It seemed that the clean, crisp, old-fashioned editions with his own special typeface and sweet illustrations were making waves.

He'd expected some interest from the big houses, and he hadn't been disappointed. Everybody was singing the same tune. Michael settled back into the black leather seat, and got ready to wince at the fare. If he took any one of these job offers, he wouldn't have to watch cab fares ever again. They had different voices: the young, hip, book mogul, the old lady known as a killer editor, the crisp accounting type with the seductive figures. But the trip was the same. Give up Green Eggs and work for us. Commissioning editor, right off the bat. He could pay off the student loan and stop dressing off the peg. Hell, he could buy his own apartment on the West Side someplace.

Michael turned them all down flat, even the lady who came to his office. Not interested. He didn't branch out on his own so he could report to some other asshole. He liked being called sir. He hated calling other men the same thing. In fact, he refused to do it. Taking a salary? That was for guys without balls. He was going to make his own path.

The sixth call had been from Blakely's. Michael had read about the changes there in a trade magazine, but he hadn't paid any attention. What the big firms did couldn't impact on Green Eggs, so why would he care?

Ernie Foxton, the new president, apparently had his own ideas as to why Michael should care. In the call his assistant had made last week, she hadn't mentioned a job for Michael, no salaried post at all. Mr Foxton, she informed him, wanted to talk about a 'joint venture'.

Michael was instantly suspicious. He had a tiny, two-person Mom and Pop outfit; he was just on the verge of hiring a salesman to make it three people, and the biggest publishing house in New York wanted to set up a joint venture? Why?

But there was no denying it. Blakely's were the big time. If he could work something out . . . Michael saw financing. He saw distribution, not himself and his staff of one in a beat-up old van but fleets of shiny new trucks. He saw a national, not a local catchment area. He saw printing costs plummeting. He saw . . . he didn't know what, it was cloaked in a vague, golden cloud . . . a vision of opportunity.

But he knew Ernie Foxton's reputation.

All he had to do was wow the toughest cookie in the business.

*

Ernie relaxed in his burgundy leather Eames chair and assessed the decor of his office. He liked the floor-to-ceiling sheer glass walls that gave him such a wonderful, vertigo-inducing view of midtown. The traffic crawled seventeen storeys below him, peaceful from his perspective, dotted all over with the tiny yellow bugs that were the New York taxis. He was an East End boy, and he was still trying to get used to the size of everything over here. The buildings, the billboards, the tits on the women . . . everything was *bigger*. The feng shui expert had been round yesterday . . . was that trickling Zen fountain in the left-hand corner there to help wealth go in or bad vibes go out? Ernie didn't care. He had a rockery in his bloody office, designed by Zaban's, the most expensive firm on the West Side. The rumour was they had a commission for the renovation of the Kravis wing at the Metropolitan Museum. He would drop the name at his next dinner party, for sure.

Diana told him that, as usual, everybody had accepted. He, Ernie Foxton, would host a gathering including two financiers, one famous *Vanity Fair* writer, the Yankees' third base coach – he hated baseball, but anything Yankees was golden in New York – a supermodel and . . . who else? A novelist or two? Whatever. Diana was doing a wonderful job as hostess. Hopefully, she wouldn't bat an eyelid when he turned up with Mira Chen.

Ernie's groin stirred a little. Mira. He loved the way she dressed, in those mean power suits and the three-inch spike heels. He knew there was nothing above the hold-up stockings, either. It was so easy to imagine her in a little Domino mask with a whip in her hand. Mmm-hmm. She'd be really cruel. She wore those heels to advertise it. Even on a warm spring day, it was always spikes for Mira, never slides or sandals. And waist-wrenching, tiny corsets under her tight jackets.

It was indescribably thrilling. She gave him orders. Ernie's cock was as hard as her smile. She took him out to a dark, damp little club on East Thirty-Sixth Street, where a succession of strict girls in black leather humiliated, leashed and aroused him. He wore a mask. He was no longer the terror of his industry, the feared hatchet man. He was just a slave grovelling around their cruel, contemptuous, anonymous spikes. It was dirty and sordid, and it aroused him in a way Diana had never managed to do.

Sure, she was the perfect arm ornament. He wasn't complaining. And as long as he could still see Mira . . .

He'd had a headhunter poach her from her firm and given her a commissioning editor's job over in popular fiction. If there was any talk, he hadn't heard about it. A smile curled round Ernie's lips. Frankly, he didn't think anybody would dare.

His phone blinked. He let it flicker for a few seconds before he picked it up.

'Yes, Marcia?'

'You asked for a reminder at ten fifteen, Mr Foxton.'

Ernie scratched his head. 'What is it this time?'

'Mr Michael Cicero. He's already waiting in the outer lobby.'

'Let him wait.' Ernie loved to keep the little people hanging. It reminded him of his power and impressed on them how lucky they were to see him at all. He flipped through his monogrammed leather day-planner. Oh, right, of course – the Green Eggs guy, the possible comer. Well, Blakely's – and himself – had courted the kid assiduously. Now it was time to remind him just who the big boys were in this scenario. He wanted Cicero on board – but only on his terms.

'When it turns quarter to, you can send him in,' he told Marcia.

Let him cool his heels for thirty minutes. Time for the

poor man to appreciate the Degas in the lobby, and the Jamaican Blue Mountain coffee and imported French petits-fours that they would be serving him. That was what Blakely's could offer. He liked dangling the carrot, to soften up his prey a little. And making him wait. It was important to show the little people who was boss.

Chapter 6

'Show them in,' Ernie said, finally. He liked saying that. It made him feel like a king granting an audience and that was really what he was, in a way.

Marcia ushered in the courtiers. First came Peter Davits, known as the Russian, an excellent number-cruncher, head of the business affairs department. Ernie gave him his job so he could slash the jobs of others. No point in carrying lots of fat. Close behind him, Janet Jensen, an all-American girl and his closest ally in restructuring the Blakely's list. Who needed to carry poetry titles that never sold, to invest in young authors and take silly risks with literary fiction? Nobody could say that he, Ernie, carried no literary fiction. He did. He carried authors that sold, just the same as he invested in pulp romances that sold. He didn't believe in catering to long and loyal readerships. To Ernie, a loyal readership was one that bought about three-quarters of a million copies per title – and anything upwards of that.

The screams of pain and anguish that had rattled about his ears in London were being unleashed in New York, but, ensconced in his glass palace up in the rarefied air of the steel and concrete Manhattan canyons, Ernie did not hear them. The PR department of Blakely's had their orders. They issued nice blanket statements about modernising the firm and not being fettered by the last millennium's traditions. Ernie thought that last millennium bit was a nice touch. He'd written it himself.

He cultivated the opinion makers with the chic parties,

lunches and dinners that Diana threw, and he was getting pretty popular. Everybody wanted to come to his dinners. Gradually the printed articles were tapering off. The *New York Times* and the *Village Voice* still shouted inky columns of protest, but really, who cared? – old readers he was no longer selling to, authors that he'd dropped, and a few stick-in-the-mud journalists.

Ernie smiled at Peter and Janet and the flunkies they'd brought along with them. He was retrieving the data about Michael Cicero he'd stored away from the inner filing drawer of his brain. A natural salesman with a nice little list. Sometimes illustrations were all it took to make a difference. Look at Dorling Kindersley. Zero to 90 million pounds in about five years, and still resistant to imitators.

His kids' department had being trying to copy Cicero's style, without marked success. They kept coming up with bright, friendly, Disneyfied illustrations whereas Cicero's style was real old-fashioned . . . it had a touch of darkness, what his (now fired) children's commissioning head had called 'the tangled forest'. Personally, Ernie thought Blakely's own were just fine, and told them to 'make it a bit more evil'. But the villains still looked like they walked out of Sesame Street. Ernie liked them, but the buyers didn't.

Whatever Michael Cicero had, he wanted to get. And he thought the other guys, offering him a salary, were missing the big picture. Who wanted a salaried employee who could walk out? What you wanted was the company. That was where the big money was. Owning.

Of course, he wasn't about to tell Cicero that, nor spend any serious money. As yet, the guy just had potential. But if he fulfilled that potential, Ernie Foxton wanted to own him, to get him in so deep he could never break the golden handcuffs.

'Everybody settled? Great.' He gave his little group a

warm, conspiratorial grin. 'Let's bring him in. Softly softly catchee monkey, remember.'

Michael flipped through his brief statistics – he only had a year's worth – his blown-up illustrations, and his customer lists. He told himself that getting angry would serve no purpose. Maybe something urgent had come up. Maybe this was how it always was in the big firms. Possibly, even, Susan had gotten the time of the appointment wrong. He told himself he knew he had a temper and now was a good time to practise that control he'd been meaning to get to.

His watch tick-ticked. He studied the painting. He went over his presentation in his mind.

By the time he'd been kept waiting for ten minutes he was very aggravated. By the time he'd been kept waiting for twenty minutes he was angry.

At twenty-eight minutes, the president's secretary emerged from the outer office. Her office was bigger than his entire firm. What Ernie Foxton's office was like he could only imagine.

Cicero's gaze flickered lightly over the woman. She was slender with a tiny waist and a very flat butt, which he found unattractive. Her pantsuit was tan, with a matching, tiny cashmere cardigan, neutral make-up, glossy hair and a classic strand of pearls. She was a pretty trophy, the kind he could only dream about right now.

'Mr Cicero? Mr Foxton is ready for you now,' she said, condescendingly.

She smiled down at him with a fake smile, and her eyes swept over his suit. Cicero realised she was judging him by it. He dressed off the peg; this wasn't designer, just a plain suit. And the shoes, ditto.

He stood.

'It's eleven. Our appointment was for ten thirty.'

'Yes, I know. Mr Foxton had some other business he

had to take care of first. I'm sorry you had to wait.' She snapped him another frosty smile.

'Thanks for the explanation. Good morning,' Michael said. He gathered his materials together and turned around, towards the elevators.

The fancy secretary was confused.

'Mr Foxton's office is that way.'

Michael glanced at her. 'I'm not going to Mr Foxton's office.'

The girl panicked. Nobody had ever walked out of a meeting with Ernie Foxton. Was he really going to leave? 'But – your meeting – *sir*,' she blurted, 'they're all waiting for you.'

'Sorry. I have some other business to take care of,' Michael said.

The elevator doors hissed open, and he stepped inside and pressed the button, ignoring her flustered cries of protest.

He rode down and out into the street. Seventh Avenue was a beeping, swarming madhouse, with glass and concrete towers jabbing their long fingers into the sky. Michael was immune to the delights of the scenery, however. He clenched and unclenched his fingers as he strode along. What had Blakely's been going to suggest? Maybe he would never know. But one thing was for sure. You didn't get respect by lying down and tattooing a big 'Welcome' on your back.

If they want me that bad, they'll call back, Michael thought. He wasn't sure if that was true or not. Maybe he was insane. Maybe he'd just blown the biggest opportunity of his young life.

He hit the nearest bar he could find and ordered an early lunch. It was fifteen bucks for a burger and fries, but they would serve him up a Jack Daniels on the rocks, cold, fiery and nerve-settling.

*

48

Marcia had a fierce, whispered conference with her assistant. It was not a pleasant conversation. Then she had to push open the door to Ernie's office. He was lounging around with Mr Davits and Ms Jensen and several other big-shots she recognised. She dreaded having to give him this news in front of them. Ernie Foxton did not take kindly to public humiliation.

'Here he is,' Ernie said.

Marcia stammered, 'No sir. He just left.'

Ernie stared at her. 'What?'

'He said the appointment was at ten thirty,' Marcia quavered.

Out of the corner of her eye she saw a couple of the lower-level execs bite their lips and look downwards. They seemed highly amused, but they were hiding it real carefully. Good idea. Mocking Ernie Foxton wasn't the shortest route to career advancement.

'Yes, it was. So what?'

'Jennifer explained to him that you had been detained by business, sir, and he said he had business too, and he got on the elevator, and—'

'OK. Right. That's enough.' Ernie held up one hand, red-faced with annoyance. Everybody took his waiting-game treatment lying down. Who was this little prick, exactly? Some broke chancer from downtown? And he was showing Ernie up in front of half the staff? He swallowed hard. An unpleasant thought came into his head – Michael Cicero making a deal with one of the other big houses, and producing serious numbers, and the story of how he, Foxton, had let him get away, spreading right around the New York scene. Whispered little jokes at his dinner parties. A snide remark from the Blakely's chairman. An unfavourable line in one of the Wall Street company analysts' reports. 'Has he got a cell phone? Go look it up.'

'Yes, sir.'

'Hurry up.'

'Yes, sir,' Marcia blurted, and fled to her desk. Nobody in the office dared look at him; for a moment, the only sound was Marcia tapping frantically on her keyboard. She ran back in. 'It's 917 555 1455.'

'Get him for me. No, wait. I'll do it myself.'

Foxton punched in the number and forced himself to smile, like this was just par for the course.

The waiter had just brought Michael's burger and drink when the phone buzzed. He dipped a thick, chunky French fry in mustard, bit down on it, and then picked the phone up.

'Cicero,' he said.

'Hey, Mikey,' said a man's voice.

'It's Michael.'

The guy laughed warmly. 'Of course it is. Stupid of me. Michael, this is Ernie Foxton. I'm really sorry I was delayed earlier.'

'That's OK,' Michael said. He felt the adrenaline crackle through him. He took a sip of JD.

'I was wondering if we could get you back in and see if we can still swing this meeting. I think Blakely's has some very exciting things to offer you. I have a good number of our people here waiting to have a little chat with you.'

Michael glanced down at his burger. It was rare and nicely bloody. The fries were home-cut, too, with sharp mustard. And besides, he'd paid for it.

'That would be good,' he said.

'So we'll see you in ten minutes,' Foxton told him.

'No can do, Ernie. I'm having lunch. How about a half hour?' Michael said easily.

There was a momentary silence on the other end.

'Right. Half an hour it is,' Ernie Foxton said, as warmly as he could manage.

The phone clicked dead. Michael gazed down at his

50

burger. It sure looked good. He was really going to enjoy it.

'So what do you think?' Diana asked Claire Bryant.

Claire nodded. The newly laid terrace garden was beautiful. 'I adore it,' she said simply. 'Another triumph for you.'

Claire was the latest in the long lines of New York wives and fiancées to come calling, and Diana was playing the polite hostess to perfection. Claire was an heiress herself and had recently become engaged to Josh Salzburg, the young Internet-stock king. She was unfailingly good natured, well dressed, and interesting, but, Diana reflected, there was something about Claire that made her just a bit uneasy. Claire was interested in local politics; Hillary Clinton and Rudy Giuliani duking it out in New York, that sort of thing. The race for the White House just made Diana yawn. Plus, Claire actually read the *Wall Street Journal* and dabbled in stocks. True, she wasn't a workaholic; Diana loathed those hard-edged New York women, the type of go-getting American girl who just made her feel bad, and she only had them over to her apartment on extreme sufferance. Sometimes the wives of Ernie's top executives fell into that career-girl category, and then, to her annoyance, Diana just couldn't cut them. But Claire Bryant still seemed full of excess energy. Diana had invited her out to the shopping excursions, spas and Broadway matinees she attended regularly with Jodie, Natasha and Felicity, but Claire was busy half the time. Busy! What did that mean? Diana wondered. Sure, Claire had a little interior design business, but Diana just thought of that as another toy, something to occupy her while Josh went out and made the real money. Why couldn't Claire just relax with the rest of the girls?

'You know, you really do have a flair for design. You

could work in that area. Why don't you consider it?' Claire pressed, setting down her Limoges cup.

'I simply don't have the time, darling,' Diana said, a little defensively. Claire always made her feel that way. 'Let me show you out. Give my love to Josh.'

'I will.' Claire kissed her warmly. 'Say hi to Ernie.'

When Claire had gone, Diana gazed out at the terrace of her apartment and congratulated herself. Really, Central Park West was the place to be. The view over the leafy greens and blue splash of water was very soothing, such a necessary contrast to the hustle and bustle of the Big Apple. Actually, though, she thought she was fitting in rather well.

It was easy for an Englishwoman to make a splash in New York society. First, there was the accent, of course, that had never hurt anybody. Diana found it conferred cachet as soon as she opened her mouth. And she thought she was very popular among all the young New York wives . . . she was something of a rarity, in that her husband was not in his late forties or early fifties and on the third model already. She liked to dress a little unusually, too. Most of these ladies had abandoned the big hair and shoulder pads of the eighties, but they were still stuck on that social X-ray thing . . . if the scale showed a hundred and fifteen pounds they screamed and went on a diet. And they were slaves to fashion.

Diana dressed differently. She had her own personal style which didn't pay attention to what the designers had in the stores. She loved to show off her firm curves and wear court heels. Diana eschewed the itsy-bitsy skirt and the designer sport-styled anoraks and went for a 1940s look. Pure classic. Tight skirts which hugged the firm curve of her bottom, neat jackets that sliced down to her small waist over her larger bust, a softly waving, sheeny-shiny Veronica Lake haircut. Of course, there were some concessions to the Natty Zuckerman set;

Diana went blonde at Oribe's, and had her brows done weekly at John Barrett. Crisp white shirts were her trademark, along with a dinner-party menu that had nothing fat-free on it – unless you counted vintage champagne. At first she had raised some brows, sure. But when the husbands started to flirt, the wives started to take notes.

Soon her proper little twin sets and neat, tweedy skirts were the talk of the gossip columns. She was a regular in Liz Smith's column and Heidi Kirsche's page, always photographed in make-up by Chanel, with a little tote, or a subtle clutch evening bag in the sweetest designer gowns – long, always long.

She dressed like a princess and acted like one too. In a matter of months, she had become one of the most courted wives on the luncheon circuit. And as she fondly thought, the most popular.

Her latest triumph was to redo the terrace. Surely Ernie would be thrilled. It would be a perfect surprise. Jodie Goodfriend had put her wise to that delightful Westchester gardening specialist, who, for a price, would make house calls. And a few measly thousand later, she was looking at an instant garden – a leafy oasis of potted orange trees, entire beds of moss dotted with large balls of stone, terracotta urns stuffed with exotic grasses and shrubs, and delicate silver bells strung between the branches. Instant topiary hedges carved into balls and arches covered the entrance, and the clever little gardening man had promised her he would install some climbing ivy and wisteria next week.

Idly Diana flipped through her diary and looked for a space. She wanted two or three girlfriends over to enjoy this masterpiece. If it was a sunny day, they could have a wonderful girly, gossipy lunch, under her orange tree in full blossom.

Her phone buzzed and she reached for it. Ernie had

had extensions installed in every room in the place so that she wouldn't have to dive for the receiver.

'Darling. It's me.'

Diana beamed. How nice, he was calling to check in on her. His gestures of affection had waned a little of late.

'I have such a marvellous surprise for you, sweetheart. I—'

'I'm sure it'll be fantastic, Di.' Ernie's common East End accent was showing through. It grated on her. She also knew it was a sure sign that something was seriously bothering him; Ernie downplayed his origins to the best of his ability. 'Look, I need you here. Got to put a little dog-and-pony show together for someone.'

'But I've got a manicure at three. It takes for ever to get an appointment with Marcus,' Diana said, disappointed.

He was snappy. 'I really couldn't care less. Get over here, would you?'

'Who is this horrible man?'

Diana wanted to stamp her foot. It had taken her two weeks to get a slot with Marcus and this was her first time. Most likely he would take umbrage and not see her for a month now. And *all* the girls were going to him. Except her.

'Horrible is right. He's a little idiot. But we want to land him. So be a good girl, and get yourself in a cab, all right?' her husband said, and hung up.

Diana stamped her foot. Blast it. She dialled Marcus's number and prepared to grovel. Meanwhile, she decided that Ernie could be a royal pain in the arse. And who was the odious guy cutting into her alone time?

I hate him already, Diana thought.

Chapter 7

Michael relaxed into his chair. It was hard, but extremely comfortable, obviously custom made for Ernie's office. Not the kind of furniture he'd have picked himself. He didn't like showy, curvy chairs. For Michael Cicero a chair was just there to be sat on, not to be noticed. This little ergonomic number was just too accommodating, he might get drowsy on the job and that would not be acceptable.

Today, however, he permitted himself to enjoy it. Today he was being worked on, not the other way round.

Ernie Foxton was standing in front of him, concluding his presentation. The enthusiasm the Blakely's people had shown for Green Eggs Books was amazing. It made him feel like John Grisham, or something. He was taken aback by how badly they wanted to get into bed with him. Janet Jensen, the dark, intense little woman, and Peter Davits, who seemed smart, had given him the hard sell for thirty minutes apiece. Janet's department was enthusiastic about children's literature and talked movingly about the lack of intelligent stuff for little kids to sink their teeth into. Peter Davits calculated that they could bring the company up millions of dollars in net worth in almost record time. His pitch was tough to resist, too. There was streamlined distribution, with a new fleet and a hungry sales force, apparently the best in the business. Ernie told him about booksellers and the global reach and mission of Blakely's.

In summary, they were telling him he could be the next

Beatrix Potter. Amazing for children, and a multi-million-dollar industry at the same time.

'You *have* to go with us, Michael,' Ernie Foxton said. His voice dripped sincerity. It was rough, and Michael recognised him as the limey equivalent of blue-collar made good. 'It'll be something new for New York. For America. Kids deserve this kind of book, and not just the lucky few who live round here. It's time to go professional and stop fucking about. Don't you think so? Excuse me, ladies.'

'Yeah, I guess I do. I'm really flattered you show so much interest in the company,' Michael said, carefully.

Ernie gave him a warm grin.

'Not interest, mate, passion. Passion for books. Passion for quality.'

'I need to think it over a little and discuss it with my advisers.'

Ernie fought back a snort of laughter. His advisers? Right, like this little prick had advisers. Instead, he tossed him an oily smile.

'Don't take too long, all right? We truly believe Green Eggs is the firm for us, but the chairman is keen to buy something – if it isn't you it'll be somebody else. I don't have the leeway I would like.'

'But the company?' Cicero asked, bluntly. Ernie noted the square, stubborn set of the man's jaw, and swallowed. The thickly muscled body made him nervous and ill at ease, and Michael was some schlep, some years younger than Ernie and over a million bucks poorer. He detested the way Cicero looked at him as though they were equals. Didn't he know who Ernie Foxton was?

'Not buy the company' – that was a slip of the tongue, and Foxton chided himself – 'buy ourselves a partnership. Think about this. All the other houses offered you a salary. We are offering you partnership, because we believe in you.'

Michael hesitated. He loved passion. The figures sounded good. Was it a smart move to turn down a winning lottery ticket? That's what this sounded like.

Ernie shook his head. 'No pressure right away. I'll send the suits back to the grind' – he flashed his troops a charming smile – 'and you can come out with me and my wife. We're a personal firm, here. Blakely's cares who it deals with.'

'Sounds good.' Cicero extended a ridiculously firm handshake to Ernie.

'Great. Great.' Damn it, Ernie thought, I got him. And in about three months I'll have the firm, too. Once this arrogant little bastard's taught us all we need to know. 'Diana's actually got a table for me over at the Russian Tea Room. Come along and have a drink.'

'Sounds very good.' Michael relaxed.

The waiter deferentially ushered them to one of the choicest banquettes in the house, and Michael tried to ignore all the rubbernecking businessmen who were leaning out from their tables and staring at Ernie and himself. He understood that they were trying to figure out who he was.

You haven't seen me before, he thought, thrilled, but soon each and every one of you will know who I am.

'You can't let business encroach on your pleasure time,' Ernie said genially. Michael couldn't have disagreed more, but kept silent. The guy was making a lot of money. He must know what he was doing.

'There she is.'

Ernie waved at a female walking towards them. 'My wife, Diana Foxton.'

'Excuse me, darling, I was just freshening up,' she said. She leaned forwards and kissed the air at the side of her husband's cheeks. 'And who's this?'

'Michael Cicero. A new business associate of ours. At

least, I hope so,' Ernie said. 'You'll thank me for introducing you, Diana, it's somebody your own age to talk to.'

Michael stared at her. He knew he was staring, but he found it hard to stop. There was something so wonderfully, vibrantly beautiful about the girl . . . was it the arch of her slightly thick brows, the daring comfort of the tiny, perfect little sweater that draped over those stunningly sexy breasts, that tilted upwards at him, almost aggressively . . . or could it be the sweet blue eyes and lusciously shining platinum hair, that he longed to dive into, just breathing in the clean scent of her shampoo? She smelled of baby powder layered over the sweet breath of perfume from her skin.

'Delighted, Mr Cicero. Or can I call you Michael?'

Diana smiled charmingly at the rude boy who was staring at her. Honestly, did Americans have no manners at all? She extended one hand in a delicate, well-bred gesture.

Cicero shook it. His handshake was firm and dry. There was a lot of power in his grip. He was a big, coarse sort of man, Diana decided. Look at those muscles; he must lift an awful lot of weights. She rarely met men of this sort; they made her edgy. Cicero's dark eyes and fighter's nose were too much, altogether. He was bristling with testosterone. It was strange to see a man with a body like that in a suit. Surely his natural job would be as an extra in some Hollywood action flick, possibly starring Sylvester Stallone or Arnold Schwarzenegger? He was shorter than Ernie, but so much stockier. And why were his eyes raking over her tights and shoes? Was there a run in them, or something?

Diana resisted the urge to look down and check. Why give him the satisfaction? Anyway, who cared what he thought? A man like this would not appreciate the finer points of fashion.

'Michael, please, Mrs Foxton,' he said.

The voice was deep, too, Diana thought, and coarse. He was probably another working-class boy made good, much like her husband. Oh, well, it didn't do to be snobby. But he was so young for Ernie to be applying a full court press.

'Then you must call me Diana, and that's settled,' she said, bestowing a radiant smile on him.

They sat down to drinks for Diana and Michael, and a light lunch for Ernie. He ordered beluga, and wolfed it down like it was a hummus dip. Meanwhile, Michael nursed an espresso and watched Diana while he talked business to Foxton. He tried not to drool all over his saucer, but keeping his control got a little easier as the minutes passed. Michael didn't think he had ever met a more beautiful and stylish girl, but, on the other hand, he'd never met a more vapid, stupid, spoiled little princess, either. Listen to her. She was discussing landscape gardeners and bitching about her so-called friends' masseuses. The prices she was flinging around would have paid the rent on his shitty little apartment for a month.

'Excuse me.' Ernie stood up. 'My beeper has just gone. I have to get back to the office. Here, Michael.' He fished in his well-cut pocket and handed over a business card; it was stiff vellum, embossed with tiny gold letters. 'This is Jack Fineman, my lawyer. He'll be able to help you out, go through the figures and such like. I'll get a copy of the contract messengered to you.'

'Thanks,' Michael said. He pocketed it, stood and shook Ernie's hand. 'I'll be in touch.'

'Like I said, don't be too long. The chairman is breaking my back to get a deal with somebody. We really want it to be you.'

'I hear you.' Michael grinned at him, and then Foxton was gone.

He looked across at Diana Foxton. She didn't seem particularly thrilled to be stuck with him.

'I'll drink up and you can get going,' Michael said.

Diana arched a brow. She could, could she? Who did this man think he was? Ernie had asked for the dog-and-pony show, and he'd got it – and surely she wasn't required to lay it on any thicker. She felt a small wave of resentment wash over her.

'Thank you. Very kind,' she said.

'Not that I mind spending the time with you,' Michael added. Her tone was extremely cold. Stuck-up little madam. He guessed it wouldn't do to tell her to grow up and get a life.

'What a relief.' Diana arched her back a little, like a cat. 'But I'm in no hurry. I missed several appointments to be here and rushing out of the door won't change anything.'

'That's bad. Really.' He was apologetic. 'It must have been something important.'

'It was *vital*, actually. It takes for ever to get an appointment with Marcus Walker,' Diana informed him, frowning lightly.

'He's your doctor?'

'My manicurist,' Diana said, pouting.

Michael laughed. He couldn't help it. He squared his shoulders and looked at her. 'For pity's sake, girl, listen to yourself.'

'What do you mean?' Diana demanded, stung.

'Your manicurist is hardly vital. Air's vital. Water's vital. You need to get your priorities sorted out, lady.'

'My priority is to look good.'

'I'd say you've already achieved that.' Michael gave her a lazy grin. 'Why don't you do something with your brain?'

'I used my brain to make Marcus squeeze me into his

client list,' Diana snapped, 'and thank you for the career advice, but I think I've done just fine on my own.'

Cicero tried to make himself shut up, but he couldn't. 'Well, you've married a rich man. So I guess that's mission accomplished.'

'You are an extremely rude person,' she said, drawing herself up. Partly to frighten him with her superiority, and partly because when he leaned forwards, she caught the masculine scent of him, and those dark eyes were fixed on her. He was disturbingly unreconstructed. Over the top button of his shirt she could see the thick wiry hairs of his chest, curling up. Ernie was smooth as a baby down there.

'I get that a lot.' Michael stood, his dark eyes still boring down at her. He was angry at himself for losing his temper, and angrier at her for being such a goddamn bimbo. No woman was perfect; when you found one with a decent body and a little elegance, she turned out to be grasping and as dumb as a rock.

Maybe he'd even blown the deal. Cicero suddenly wanted to get it signed before Ernie Foxton talked to his wife. 'Here, allow me.' He pulled out his wallet and slapped down a hundred.

Diana looked at the bill like it was something nasty she'd found stuck to the sole of her shoe. She lifted it in her long fingers and handed it back to him.

'I don't think so. I'm sure this place is a little rich for your blood. Ernie would want me to settle up.'

Flushing, Michael took his money back and left her without another word.

What a stuck-up little bitch, he thought.

He hailed a cab on the street. Fifteen minutes later, he was back in his office, and Susan greeted him with an expectant look.

'Mr Cicero, welcome back. How did it . . .'

He turned to face her and her voice trailed off. He had the slightly reddened face he got when he was truly angry – and that was a real bad time to be around him.

'Not well.'

Susan didn't press the point. Timidly, she handed him over the thick package that had been sitting on her desk for an hour.

'Blakely's had this messengered over. They said it was your contract.'

Michael ripped open the envelope and took out about eighty pages of densely printed legalese. He fished the embossed vellum card out of his pocket and tossed it to his assistant.

'Get me Jack Fineman on the phone,' he said. 'Quick as you can. We may not have much time.'

Once Diana Foxton went bitching to her husband, she would blow this deal for him. Blakely's was offering a partnership. Michael wanted to kick himself. Why couldn't he just have kept his mouth shut around the selfish, spoiled little princess?

Fineman was brisk and businesslike. 'I would love to represent you in the matter, but I can't. Conflict of interest.'

'Fair enough. Tell me who I should be talking to?'

'Let me see . . . somebody skilled, not connected with Ernie . . .'

And not too expensive, Michael felt like saying, but his pride wouldn't let him.

'. . . Jane Grenouille, she's your woman. Grenouille and Bifte, they have an office on Fifty-fourth. I recommend her,' Fineman said warmly. He gave Cicero the phone number. 'I can fax the contract over to her right now, if you like. It's standard, shouldn't take too much of her time. Oh, and Michael – Ernie Foxton already signed it from his end, so if you countersign within twenty-four hours it's nice and binding.'

'What if I delay beyond that time?'

'Then you need to get him to sign another copy. I guess they put a time limit on it in case another deal gets worked out in the meantime and you force them into bed with you.'

'Thank you,' Michael said quietly.

It never occurred to him to ask how Fineman knew Ernie had signed the contract.

He rang Jane, who sounded young and vivacious and a little ditsy, but seemed to have an excellent grasp on the legalities. She suggested a few changes and told him he should jump on it.

'We'll get a few things policed up, though.'

'Are they vital?'

Michael suddenly had an image of Diana Foxton going home and sobbing on her husband's shoulders. If he signed today, the deal was valid, and Ernie couldn't rip it up.

'No. You'd lose the twenty-four-hour window by the time we got the renegotiation back.'

'I'll get back to you in a little while,' Michael said.

He hung up and looked around his tiny office, breathing in the wafts of moussaka and lamb with minted yoghurt from the taverna. His print shook slightly on the walls as the booming bass of the record store leaked up through his basement.

He was hesitating. And why? Because he didn't like Ernie and Diana.

But Ernie Foxton had promised him a partnership, not a salary. They had offered up financials, editorial rights, distribution, new offices and a sign-on bonus of a hundred thousand dollars.

If he signed he would have a real company. If he signed, he would have a real office. If he signed, he could afford to take Diana Foxton out to a fancy restaurant, and get a suit that people would not sneer at.

Michael visualised Diana's look of arrogant pity. He took the contract and put it in his briefcase.

There was a timid knock on his door. Michael looked up to see Susan Katz smiling at him breathlessly.

'So what do you think?' she asked.

Michael grinned.

'I think we're in business,' he said.

Chapter 8

In the half light of the early morning, Ernie Foxton woke and looked at his wife. The first rays of dawn had slunk across Manhattan, creeping up from the hustle of the fishing nets and the fresh-produce markets, covering Wall Street's bustling bankers all striving to be at their desks before the other guy, until they were washing the sleek high-rises of the skyscrapers and the elegant brownstones round the Park. From his bedroom window, all he could see was sky and greenery. Central Park was attractive, if you liked nature, which Ernie didn't. And he had the terrace garden his talented bride had thrown together.

Diana lay there, sprawled over his bed – he still didn't think of it as their bed. Her long, dyed-blond hair was gorgeously dishevelled on the satin pillowcases she'd ordered so as not to tangle it. One hand was flung sleepily over the cream silk sheets, manicured to perfection with a simple French polish. Of course, Diana would never go for anything tarty like scarlet red talons, the type that Mira liked to wear, that she wanted to rake across his back. He longed to let her do it, but it would leave a mark. Mira said he deserved it, that Ernie was a naughty little boy who ought to be punished. He felt a twitch in his cock just thinking about her.

Ernie looked over Diana's body: slender, but still curvy. He wasn't sure he quite liked the round, womanly fullness of her hips and breasts, and her thighs weren't pure muscle, like Mira's when she gripped the sides of his back with them as she rode him like a pony.

What a turn on it was when Mira had sat next to him at dinner and ground her spiked heel into his foot. There was his young wife, such a good girl, in the flowing, dusty-pink chiffon gown, sweeping round her ankles, hair and make-up to a simple minimum, and then, when he looked around, there was petite, boyish, cruel, brazen Mira, in her outrageous little black number, no bra so her hard nipples peeked through the fabric. Mira had lowered her lashes and stared at him last night, all through dinner. It was hard when he was trying to play King of the Castle with all the movers and shakers, but those black little pools had been merciless. It was like she was daring him to look away from her. With Diana right there. And when he'd had to, her cruel smile seemed to promise the most delicious punishment.

They were going to meet up tonight, after work. Mira didn't allow disobedience, hell no. The things she did to him with that riding crop. But somehow she knew not to let her commands interfere with his work. She liked the little baubles and presents he gave her and she liked his status. So when she ordered him, sharply, to be nude and on his knees, blindfolded, in the club, she told him 7.30 p.m. – enough time to pleasure her, and still be back at the apartment in time for dinner.

His wife couldn't compete, how could she? Their sex was dutiful, never passionate. Diana endured him and he rarely made it with her, thinking about Mira when he did so to get him off.

But Ernie wasn't discontent. Nobody could match Diana as a housekeeper and hostess, when she wasn't shopping for England. Her latest party had been a wonderful success. He had a stack of gilt-edged envelopes on his mantelpiece so thick she was almost a social secretary. And other men looked at his wife with a kind of glitter in their eyes, which made him happy. Ernie loved having the toys that the other boys wanted. He 'worked' later at the office, to give him time with Mira, and he came home to a lovely catered dinner, or a well-dressed Diana waiting patiently with their tickets to the Met in one gloved hand. His friends' wives were all over her, too. It meant she was a hit in New York. So he was, all in all, quite satisfied, he told himself, regarding her narrow waist and the firm curve of her behind without wanting her. Diana was expensive, but she was great PR. She reflected on him all the class he couldn't quite manage himself. Yes, all in all, she was a great investment.

The phone at his bedside purred softly. Diana's choice, so that it wouldn't wake them too harshly in an emergency.

He lifted the receiver. 'It's five to six in the morning,' Ernie said, 'so I hope you've got a good reason for calling this early.'

'I don't need a reason for anything I do.'

Oh man. It was Mira. Ernie sat up, his skinny body excited, the silk sheets pooling around his groin. 'You can't call here. You might wake my wife.'

'I can do anything I want to, you little worm. And stop whispering.'

'I – I can't,' Ernie croaked, hoarsely. He glanced down at Diana, looking at her body, her even breathing.

'Never mind about that, you simpering Brit moron. Be at the corner of Sixth and Twelfth in thirty minutes. And expect to be punished like you deserve. You *do* deserve it, don't you?'

'Yes,' Ernie muttered, flushing. His dick was hard now.

'Louder.' Her sexy voice was a guttural hiss in his ear.

'Yes. Yes,' he breathed. 'Look. I'll be there.'

'You better be.' Mira smashed the receiver down, and Ernie hung up, thrilled to his bones. What would she do to him today? He guessed there was only one way to find out. Gingerly, swinging his thin body away from Diana's curves, he put his bare feet on the hardwood floor, and padded across the polished mahogany to where his wife had laid out his work outfit over a chair.

It took Ernie five minutes to shower, five minutes to dress, and another thirty seconds to leave, closing the apartment door softly behind him.

Only then did Diana Foxton open her beautiful, shocked blue eyes.

How dare he? she asked herself.

It was the fiftieth time she had asked herself that question that morning, and it was only 7 a.m. The maid was silently spooning fresh summer-fruit compote into Diana's crystal dish, and refilling her glass with pomegranate juice and champagne, so she smiled sweetly and pretended to be interested in Liz Post's column in the paper as she played with the ivory spoon in her hazelnut vanilla coffee. It didn't do to show emotion in front of the help, but inside she was fuming. Diana's gaze flickered from the newsprint she wasn't reading to the springtime beauty of the Park that she wasn't taking in.

It had to be that strumpet who had embarrassed her last night. Turning up in basic black was bad enough, but in a dress so tight and tarty it belonged on a high-school kid with a bad reputation? Diana had been so sweet to her, too, sitting her next to Ernie – humph – what a rich joke – and asking her questions about her boring work she seemed so obsessed with. Why, she'd even tried to give Mira some invaluable beauty advice, recommending Clarins, Aveda and Bobbi Brown, to steer her off those fire-engine reds and overly plucked brows. So flashy. So eighties. And it would seem her husband – her newly wed husband – the husband of Diana Foxton, the toast of Manhattan – *preferred* that two-buck tramp!

What a humiliation! Could there be anything worse than this? Diana wondered, absent-mindedly sipping the mimosa she'd felt she needed for strength this morning. Lying there, listening to him make a secret date with some slut?

Diana scrutinised her reflection in the glass top of her terrace breakfast table. It was puzzling. Was there anything wrong with the face that stared back at her, the smooth skin, the almond-shaped blue eyes, the pretty little nose . . . maybe the nose . . . maybe it could be a little more chiselled, a bit more modelly, but she'd always assumed men *liked* the slight imperfections in the face that made her, well, her. Were her eyebrows not arched properly, were her teeth not bleached as bright as they could be? She wouldn't second-guess her perfect sense of style, but what, for goodness' sake, could make Ernie prefer the tramp from last night to herself?

They'd been married for six blissful months now. Yes, Diana insisted to herself, they *had* been six blissful months. The wonderful parties, the celebratory dinners over Ernie's latest business triumphs, her *sensational* redecoration of the apartment, the terrace garden, really, everything. Except possibly the sex. Sex was a frightful bore, when it came right down to it, but Diana didn't let that faze her. Basically, she knew she was simply more worldly wise than most of her fellow females, or maybe more honest.

Women hated sex.

They had hated it since time immemorial. The clever woman simply made allowances for the needs of men, let them do whatever they wanted, and tried not to protest too much. After all, who really enjoyed sex? Men. Men had orgasms at the drop of a hat. All a man needed to arouse him was friction.

Diana sipped her drink, watching the morning light play on the fluted stem of the glass, allowing the bubbles to fizzle against her tongue. They were using Cristal, which was the current in *vogue* choice of the Yank set, but which she thought was inferior, all things considered, to Dom Perignon or Taittinger.

Yes, it was a pity that women were built so differently. She had never met a woman who reached climax with her man in bed, although the magazines were full of articles about it, which were pie-in-the-sky lies as far as Diana was concerned. What women did in bed was sigh, cry and lie, and watch the minutes – or seconds, in Ernie's case – go by. Sex, after all, was what men liked, and it was a price a girl knew she had to pay.

Diana detested sex. It was like a bad boyfriend – all promises and then all let downs. Sometimes, not often, but sometimes, you would get a bit excited, get that nervous, squirmy, edgy feeling in your belly, get slightly damp in that secret place between the legs. And then you went to bed with him, and you wound up frustrated and angry, lying there trying to get his big heap of a sweating, smelling body off your body and your aching nipples.

It had been that way with Jack, the naval second lieutenant who had been her first boyfriend. At least Ernie didn't frustrate her, because he never even aroused her in the first place.

The best part of married sex, Diana thought viciously, was when Ernie rolled over and went to sleep. Of course, it only lasted a few seconds. Then he started snoring.

But could Ernie get better from somebody else? He was nothing himself in the sexual stakes. Huffing and puffing and grunting and making death's-head rictus faces. Maybe the other girl was a better faker than she was. Frankly, Diana found it just silly to lie there moaning like Meg Ryan in *When Harry Met Sally*. If she started all that, she'd just burst into giggles, which would make Ernie's unimpressive penis do a nice impression of a soft, floppy worm.

Diana tried to imagine Ernie with another woman. Was she jealous? Not exactly, she decided. She was angry though, very, very angry. She had never complained about his aggravating sexual antics. She had been an ideal hostess. And this, this was how he repaid her – his new bride!

'Consuela,' she said.

'Yes, Senora Foxton.'

'Could you bring me my cellular phone and my diary?'

'Right away, Senora Foxton,' her maid said, hurrying off.

Diana clenched her fist and angrily dive bombed her spoon into her compote in childish resentment. Ernie might think he could get away with treating her like a silly little fool, but he was sorely mistaken. She had friends here, too. And she was going to hold a council of war. No way was she losing her man to some two-bit little American whore.

'Darling, it's *so good* to see you.'

Natasha Zuckerman kissed the air on both sides of Diana's cheeks. 'Not a moment too soon, either. Felicity and Jodie were wondering what happened.'

'Gridlock,' Diana murmured, 'so sorry to have kept you.'

She had summoned the three ladies best suited to give her advice, Diana congratulated herself. Natasha and Jodie were happily married to big businessmen, and Felicity was divorced – something she could help Diana prevent. She'd thought about asking Claire Bryant, too, but had decided against it. Claire had a bit of a feminist streak, the side of her that made Diana uncomfortable. She tossed her head arrogantly. Claire Bryant would just tell her to confront him, get a divorce. Diana didn't want to hear that.

These girls would tell her what she did want to hear.

'Not at all,' Natasha purred. 'It's murder trying to get

71

down to the Village at lunchtimes. But my spirits are restored because you chose Mono.'

'The food's terrific and it's all herbs, hardly any fat.'

Privately Diana thought her friend could use a little meat on her skinny hips, but she didn't want to belabour the point. It was much easier to get the girls out at the last minute if you could find somewhere that had decent low-fat cooking, even though as they only ever had salads and breadsticks it really didn't matter where she chose.

'Wonderful to see you all.' Kisses were exchanged, and Diana saw everybody was sipping Perrier water. To hell with it, she thought, ordering up a nice glass of Chardonnay big enough to bathe in.

'Sweetie.' Jodie looked very concerned. 'All the urgency, and the last minute – what on earth has happened?'

'Something awful.' The wine came, and Diana took a big gulp. 'I need your advice.'

'Your personal organiser crashed.'

'Your maid has been taping your cellular calls.'

'The IRS want to investigate Ernie,' Jodie suggested excitedly.

'No. It's much worse than that.'

'What could be worse than the IRS?' Felicity said, horrified.

'I think Ernie's having an affair,' Diana muttered.

There was a shocked silence. And then, to her amazement, all three of her girlfriends started to laugh.

'What's so funny? I don't get it,' Diana said, rather offended.

'Oh, don't look like that, darling,' Jodie said, patting her hand reassuringly. 'It's nothing, really, except we assumed you knew. Of course Ernie's having an affair. Everybody knows that.'

'Well, I'm shocked. I think it's just awful of Ernie to be sneaking around behind your back,' Jodie sniffed. 'I rather assumed you knew as well. People thought the two of you had an open marriage.'

'An open marriage!' Diana said, flushing bright pink with shame. 'Of *course* not!'

'Well.' Felicity put her water glass down with a determined thud. 'Seeing as you don't know, Di, somebody's got to tell you. It's not just an affair. It's affairs. Ernie's a womaniser. Everybody knew about it.'

'Everybody except me,' Diana said.

Chapter 9

Diana smiled, chewed her food precisely, pushed her salad around her plate, and tried hard not to display too much emotion in front of her friends.

'But, angel, it's Mira Chen at his office. They are always working late. My maid's husband knows one of the cleaners over at Blakely's,' Natasha told her.

Felicity made an angry stabbing motion in the air with her fork. 'And before Mira wasn't it Henrietta Johnson?'

'Maurice Johnson's wife?' Diana asked, amazed. The Johnsons were bankers and had moved to Miami last month. Luckily for them, she thought. To think she'd played tennis with Henrietta in that tournament on Long Island. And all the time she really wanted a set of mixed doubles with Ernie!

'But of course. She had nothing to lose. Very discreet, but I knew the signs,' Natty added.

'We thought you did, of course, or we'd have said something.'

Diana pushed her hair out of her eyes. 'If I'd known, wouldn't I have done something?'

'I don't see why,' Jodie said judiciously. 'So many hubbies do it. It leaves us girls free to make our own arrangements.'

They seemed so calm and collected. Diana didn't want to seem overly naive. Maybe this was just the way of it in America.

'Isn't that awfully cynical?' she said.

'I prefer to say practical,' Natasha pronounced.

Diana took another sip of her wine. 'Do your husbands stray like that?'

Shocked heads shook. 'Of course not, darling,' Jodie said, with a touch of smugness. 'He's got no reason to.'

Diana blushed; she suddenly felt her inexperience, and her foreignness, and, strangely for her, an unpleasant little wash of failure. She was furious at Ernie for exposing her to pity. Thank goodness I've got my girlfriends, she told herself. People I can rely on.

'Maybe you spend too much time at home, sweetie.' Natasha signalled for the check. 'No, no, let me, I insist, you're having an awful day. Too bad to find this out. And so long after it started, too.'

'We're always here for you,' Felicity said softly, giving Diana a warm hug.

'Call if you need anything,' Jodie pressed. 'Anything at all.'

And with a lot of air kisses and warm pressings on her arm, they suddenly melted into the sunshine.

Diana stood for a moment watching her friends leave. She felt such a fool. Grateful to them, of course, but what a silly girl she'd been. Maybe she had been wilfully blind to it. Ignored all the girls that liked to drape themselves over Ernie's arm at her parties. He'd been very receptive, but she'd thought it was just flirting. After all, in England, what mistress would be so crass as to hit on a husband at a dinner party in his own home, in the presence of his wife?

She absently retrieved her coat and overtipped the coat-check girl.

'Shall I get you a cab, ma'am?' the maître d' was asking.

She glanced at him, not noticing the glitter in his eyes as they swept her form in the silk shantung dress that was tight in all the right places.

'No thanks. I'll walk.' She smiled. No need to advertise

to the whole world how she was feeling. Diana went through the door another man held open for her, hardly even looking where she was going. She needed to walk round and gather her thoughts.

Tears prickled in her eyes. Obviously she was not the prize she had imagined. How it hurt to hear Jodie saying of course *her* man would not stray, *he* had no need to. But Ernie had felt that need.

What on earth could Mira Chen and Henrietta Johnson and all those other *tarts*, Diana thought viciously, do for her husband that she couldn't? A sullen fury took hold of her as she marched along the street. Maybe it was the fact that she was too easy to please, always there. Surely Ernie had lied to her when he said that he liked the idea of a traditional wife. Talking to Jodie and the others, a traditional wife seemed to be one who let her husband screw around without making a fuss, while she did the same – except that their husbands were somehow exempt from this rule.

In the future she thought she would confide more in Felicity. Felicity had been through a divorce and was single now, she couldn't triumph over Diana. Oh stop, she chided herself, they were being supportive, trying to help you. She wanted to believe that, so she told herself it was true.

Well, I've done my wifely duty, Diana thought, getting angrier by the second. I've thrown his parties and entertained his contacts, I've dressed perfectly, I decorated his house, hired his servants and fucked him whenever he asked for it. And I refuse to lose him to some trampy little slut. I don't see why I should sit at home while he fakes his meetings like I fake my orgasms. I can work too, if that's what he likes. I can get a job. I could—

Here her imagination failed her, and she stamped her foot in the street. A few Japanese tourists giggled and

76

stared like she was a mad bag lady. Diana pouted and hailed a cab.

'No, of course I don't think you're crazy,' Milla soothed her.

The long-distance line was crackly, and there was the sound of screaming children in the background, and a hissing noise like something was cooking on the stove. What *right*, Diana thought, did Milla have to sound so happy and contented all the time? She weighed a good ten pounds too much, she wasn't even married to somebody rich and she worked like a slave.

'I've always said you should get a job. It helps concentrate the mind. There has to be more to life than shopping.'

'I don't see why,' Diana said mutinously.

'And Ernie may not be cheating on you after all. These women don't sound like such good friends to me. They sound jealous.'

'They're not jealous. I trust them.'

'Well, that's very nice, sweetheart. Mary, stop that, please. Put it down, it's supper in just a second. But consider how quick they were to give you all those names. Pretending to be sorry for you when actually they were just gloating.'

'Milla—'

'All right,' her big sister said gently, 'just remember, you can do anything you put your mind to. You worked at *Vogue*. Maybe you could do something along those lines over there.'

'That's a great idea. It would put me right back on the cutting edge,' Diana mused.

'Of course it is. Anyway, I have to go, because the potatoes are boiling over. And just don't trust those women. God bless, darling.'

'God bless.' Diana blew Milla a kiss and hung up.

Somehow she always felt better after talking to her sister. Ernie would see her differently once she was working again. And the great thing was, she could take a job at a very low salary indeed.

She looked round her husband's den, with the extensive his and hers Rolodexes. Somewhere among those exclusive hairdressers and flavour-of-the-month manicurists were her old numbers from London; if she made a few calls she could get an excellent list of contacts and just go from there. Within a week, Diana exulted, I'll have a wonderful job and he won't be so certain of me any more.

She pressed the kitchen buzzer and told the cook to make duck à l'orange, Ernie's favourite, for dinner tonight. No need for a big scene. She hadn't got her job lined up yet. Besides, Milla was probably 100 per cent right. Ernie was faithful. Diana decided that maybe she'd misunderstood the call this morning. Maybe it *was* a business acquaintance. Ernie loved to make money, and she loved him to make money. I can't blame him for working hard, Diana said sedately to herself. She looked around the opulent, barely used little den, and past the mahogany walking-cane case out to her flagstone-floored hallway, with its gilt-framed paintings and subtle sconce lights on the walls. She was living in paradise here. Why rock the boat?

'But I don't understand,' Diana protested. The managing editor's office was immaculately decorated in tasteful white, with framed covers and black and white photographs of models. 'You've seen my portfolio of work for *Vogue*. Why isn't there anything for me?'

'I keep trying to tell you, Mrs Foxton.' Kathy Lybrand leaned forwards, her long-nailed bony fingers folded one over the other. 'We prefer single girls here at *City*

Woman, and besides, you're about five years too old for our magazine.'

Diana swallowed both her anger and her pride. She was getting the run-around, and it had been the same way at American *Vogue, Glamour, Marie Claire, Elle* and all the other major fashion mags that she had targeted over the last fruitless week. She, Diana Foxton, was 'too old'. At twenty-nine! She wasn't about to go crawling to some old mumsy *Redbook* or *Family Circle* type thing. Besides which, Diana had a sinking feeling that, even if she changed her mind, the answer there would still be no.

'Can I be frank?'

'Certainly,' Diana snapped. 'Why stop now?'

Kathy gave her the smile of a feeding cobra and ploughed right on. 'You're a society wife, Mrs Foxton, and that's just great for you. At *City Woman* we like our assistants to be hungry, ambitious and driven.'

'I'm driven,' Diana said, annoyed.

'Yes – by your chauffeur.' Kathy chuckled at her own joke. 'It's hard to find a girl who's excited about sweating her way up to a contributing editor position on thirty to forty thousand a year when that's about your yearly budget for clothes.'

My yearly budget for clothes is a lot more than that, Diana thought, rather spitefully.

'In conclusion, if you want to find something to fill your time, might I suggest that you do whatever the other Fifth Avenue wives do – volunteer to organise charity balls and luncheons and write letters to *Town and Country*,' the businesswoman added with a sneer. 'Although I never saw why they didn't just give away the money to charity and add on the cost of hosting the thing. Perhaps that's because of the lack of paparazzi involved in just writing a cheque.'

'Thank you for your speculations,' Diana said crisply, 'I'd rather you kept them to yourself.'

'I dare say you would.' Kathy tapped her long nails on the desk. 'I'd rather you didn't waste my time in the office just because you once had my boss to dinner. Lots of people need the job you're asking for to put bread on their tables – *and* they have a passion to work. That's the kind of people we're looking for.'

Completely discomfited, Diana sprang to her feet.

'I'll show myself out,' she said in her coldest, crispest tone, the one she used when personal shoppers were late for an appointment or some hapless maître d'couldn't fit her and Ernie in at the last minute.

'You do that,' Kathy said, ignoring her rage completely. Diana paused at the door to her office, hoping that some snappy quip would spring to her lips; something really cutting and harsh. But nothing suggested itself, and the managing editor was already busy with the papers on her desk.

Diana marched out of her office, barely able to stop herself from slamming the door, which would have been childish, and given the bitch more satisfaction. The only difference between this interview and the others was that in this one the insults had been open. In the other ones, they had been veiled. But Diana knew when she was being mocked.

The elevator ride down seemed eternal and depressing. The sinking feeling in the pit of her stomach matched the sinking feeling in her life. Diana gazed at the well-put-together, slim, curvy figure that gazed back at her from the shiny elevator inner doors. It was a beautiful reflection, no two ways about it. But how long would it stay that way? She was trembling on the threshold of thirty; and she hadn't felt this depressed since she turned twenty and could no longer call herself a teenager. Too old to be a fashion assistant? But that was – unfair.

Ridiculous. Ageist. Diana wanted to hit somebody. She felt a few tears prickling at the back of her eyes, and that was unforgivable, because they would make her mascara bleed and her foundation would go all grey.

I'm supposed to be the hottest new bride in town, Diana thought. So why do I suddenly feel so abandoned and useless?

By the time she got home it was 4 p.m. The sun was still high in the sky, and yet she felt exhausted. Right now all she wanted to do was to get into a hot bath and then go to bed.

'*Buenos dias, senora*,' Consuela said, giving her a bright, fake smile. 'Senora Felicity and Senora Natasha call for you. They say to ring them. Also, Senor Cicero waits in the guest room.'

Diana steadied herself against her dark oak balustrade, trying to process this information. She certainly didn't want to deal with Natty and Felicity in her present mood. And who in the name of goodness was Senor Cicero?

'Mr Cicero?'

'*Si, si*. Ees friend of Senor Foxton.'

'Oh. Let me go and say hello,' Diana said faintly. She searched her memory, trying to figure out exactly which of Ernie's myriad business contacts this man was. And why had he come over to the house?

She hurriedly smoothed down her skirt, and slapped on a smile she didn't feel, and pushed open the door.

'Oh hell,' Diana said, 'it's you.'

Chapter 10

A month earlier, Michael walked purposefully down Seventh Avenue and people got out of his way, as they always did in New York. He was young, true, but he carried himself like a much older man. Most thirty-year-olds didn't wear heavy-cut, dark suits and sober Paisley ties. And most thirty-year-olds weren't built like a Giants linebacker. But then again, most thirty-year-old males in this city weren't running their own companies out of a midtown skyscraper.

In bars, at night, Michael had sometimes been mistaken for a stupid guy. Some men – weaker men – took one look at the hard, thick chest, and the muscular arms and strong thighs, and assumed he was a jock, an idiot. Michael didn't mind. It was human nature to be jealous. Like a beautiful blond woman, he was thought to have no brain. It was more enjoyable to cut down sarcastic remarks with words than with fists, of course. Besides, when Michael asked another guy to step outside, he usually took one look at him and then backed down.

Since he started wearing suits, he got a little more respect. But he didn't care about the thoughts of lesser people, he would force them to respect him. Actions spoke louder than looks.

Green Eggs was his ticket out. As he strode along the sidewalk, looking up at the towering buildings on either side of him, Michael felt the headiness of it. A week ago he was driving around trying to hawk tiny print runs of his books to libraries. Now, suddenly, it was the big time.

I could have had it before now, though, Michael thought. If I had sold out. He congratulated himself. What a fucking awesome buzz this was. He had held on to his baby company, had refused to take a salary. Now he was actually in partnership with Ernie Foxton. Independent control and mainstream money. It was a dream, and it was his.

The Blakely's building loomed up ahead of him. Michael stopped dead, leaving the businesswomen in their tight suits and the workmen clutching their Styrofoam cups of coffee to push forward round him, waving down the yellow cabs that crawled along the semi-gridlocked roads or diving into the subway stations. He looked upwards. The tower was magnificent, covered in opulent black polished granite. It glinted in the morning sunlight, sparkling like marble in some Venetian palazzo. The name of the firm was etched on a large brass plate in royal-blue lettering. Michael noticed that Green Eggs had not yet been added to the list of companies housed there. He'd have to remedy that.

The thought gave him an electrifying thrill.

Revolving doors made of solid dark glass provided an entrance to the lobby. He could see his reflection in them. The young man facing him was heavyset, in a smart suit, with an intense look of concentration on his face. Michael resisted an impulse to wink at himself. He grinned, and pushed into the lobby. Time to get to work.

Ernie was looking out of his window as Michael Cicero arrived, but he didn't see him walk in off the street. He was staring out at the billboards for the movies and DKNY jeans balancing amid the concrete forest of midtown, but he did not see them either. Small red lights blinked in and out of focus on his telephone bank as Marcia dealt with them. Right now he was distracted. He was talking to Mira Chen.

'You like the job then. . .?' he asked nervously, fiddling with the tie on his thousand-dollar Armani jacket. The costly clothes never seemed to hang quite right on Ernie, not that he gave a fuck. He dressed in the most expensive suits and shirts of the season. Top of the range, whatever it happened to look like. Ernie thought this gave him a sophisticated air.

'You like the job then, *what*?' Mira demanded, in a low hiss.

'I mean . . . you like the job then . . . Miss Chen,' Ernie half whispered. He didn't dare to call her Mistress on an open phone line, even though Mira was now his employee. He imagined her tiny, boyish body, her long legs tapering down to pointed, cruel stilettos. Mira was the first time he had cheated on Diana. Ooh, she knew how to treat a naughty boy like he deserved, Ernie thought. He had the first stirrings of an impressive hard-on.

'It's barely adequate. I need more money and a bigger office.'

'It's the best I can do for now . . . Miss Chen,' Ernie whimpered.

'It's not good enough. You need to be punished for even thinking I would accept this,' Mira snapped, hanging up on him.

Ernie gave himself a second to contemplate what tonight's punishment might be. It was a delicious picture.

His buzzer sounded, snapping him out of it. Ernie felt his hard-on wither and die.

'Yeah, what is it?' he barked at Marcia.

'Excuse me, sir,' his assistant said, nervously. 'I saw you were done with Miss Chen . . . you asked me to let you know when Michael Cicero got into the office.'

Ernie switched his focus. He felt a surge of adrenaline. The fly had finally crawled into the web.

'Reception said he just signed in, Mr Foxton.'

84

'Excellent. I'm going to take a little orientation meeting,' Ernie said. 'You can route my calls to Peter or Janet.'

'Yes sir,' Marcia said.

Ernie rode down to Michael's floor in the regular elevator, the peasants' elevator, as he thought of it. Normally, he rode in the brass and velvet, air-conditioned president's car, which only he and his guests could use. It was non-stop from the lobby to the sixteenth floor. But Michael Cicero didn't get offices up near the executive suites of Blakely's. He had a basic set of rooms on the fourth floor. At this stage, there was no point in putting any more cash into Green Eggs than they had to.

If the children's book sector wound up profitable for Blakely's, Green Eggs would get all the cash it needed, but by then, Michael Cicero would not be a part of it.

Ernie smiled as he thought of Jack Fineman's cleverness. The backdoor deal with Grenouille and Bifte had made sure that the contract was badly presented to Cicero. There were plenty of outs for Blakely's and few outs for Cicero. He would learn that nobody walked out on Ernie Foxton.

Of course, Michael didn't have to learn that just yet. A happy employee was a productive employee. Ernie wanted to get the best out of him, to pick his brains before he kicked him out.

Michael Cicero was thirty and self-made and he thought he knew everything. It would be a pleasure, Ernie decided, to show him how wrong he was.

'So what do you think of it?' Ernie asked loudly.

He pushed through the plain wooden door without knocking, and was pleased to see a young woman, presumably Cicero's assistant, jump out of her skin. The space was boringly decorated, clean and functional.

There was nothing of the black leather and gilt-clock elegance of the other Blakely's offices, not to mention any trace of the opulence on Ernie's floor. Cicero had no Eames chairs, no hand-woven Persian rugs. He had secretary cubicles and swivel-back chairs from an 'economic' office supply place.

But Cicero was walking around his small space as rapt as if Ernie had assigned him a wing at Versailles.

'It's amazing.' He glanced into the corner office, slightly larger than the two beside it, where he would sit. 'You even got us our own kitchen.' Michael laughed. 'Susan is thrilled she won't have to go on a bagel run twice a day any more.'

'And you've hired your new people?' Ernie asked. He really didn't care what Susan thought. She was pretty enough, but girls like her were two a nickel in New York. He didn't promote women up from assistant positions and he didn't want to fuck her, so she didn't feature on his radar.

'Yeah. I spoke to Felix last week. Everybody will be coming in today, making changes to the run we have ready to go. Of course, they will have to get used to all this.' He waved a brawny arm around his offices, and Ernie realised the bitching about luxury wasn't going to come. To Michael Cicero, this *was* luxury.

'You have to bring your illustrators up to meet Janet and me.' Ernie smiled warmly at the younger man. His lawyers had told him he had to make sure of each piece of talent, individually, to really fuck Michael over. Last thing he wanted was Cicero walking out before he had got hold of his talent. 'We take pride in really getting to know a team we work with.'

'I'll do that.' Michael repressed his distaste. He hated corporate therapy-speak that called workplaces 'teams' and 'families' and then didn't hesitate to fire a guy who was underperforming. Plus, the limey was thin and had manicured hands and what looked like a fake tan. He was a million miles away from Michael's idea of a guy. But he was the one coming up with the money. So far, there had been no memos, no corporate interference. Just production dollars, meetings with finance guys and lots of cheques.

Michael reminded himself it was no more cheap paper and flimsy covers. No more riding around Brooklyn and the Long Island Expressway with a van full of products. For that, he could deal with Ernie and his corporate babble.

Ernie stuck out a bony hand, and Michael shook it, careful not to crush it in his.

'Great to have you on board,' Ernie said. 'We love nurturing talent. We think you're really going to create a very special endeavour here.'

What the hell does that mean? Michael thought, but he just smiled. 'Thanks. The guys will be arriving shortly. I'll send them upstairs when they get here.'

'Good. Remember, you're part of the Blakely's family now,' Ernie told him. Then he flashed an insincere smile at Susan Katz and was gone.

Susan closed the door behind Ernie and looked at her handsome boss. He was leaning over the windowsill outside his office, surveying the street. Nobody was here; the creative gang didn't show up to work until ten o'clock at the earliest. She indulged in a brief, glorious fantasy that Michael would turn around to her, thrust up her neat little burgundy skirt, grab her thighs around the cream-coloured lace hold-up stockings she was wearing today, and throw her over her cubicle desk and just fuck her brains out.

'So what do we do now?' Susan ventured.

Michael turned around and handed her a neat sheet of folded paper from his jacket pocket. 'This is the call sheet for today. I made it up last night.'

'Yes, Mr Cicero,' Susan said, sighing.

Of course. Work. She was insane to think there could be anything else in Michael's life.

Michael Cicero could never clearly recall his first few weeks in business. It merged into one long, confused, exhilarating, exhausting blur. While Seth and his other illustrators worked with Blakely's production team, he was hiring salesmen, visiting booksellers and making presentations. At night he was wiped out, but still didn't want to leave. Susan Katz, reluctantly, would leave the office, in a breath of perfume, wishing him goodnight with her pencil-lined mouth, tossing her gleaming hair back across her shoulders, and Michael, oblivious, would head out to a bar when he could no longer squeeze in even one more call.

The line was coming together. The response was superb. He felt he was living on a cloud of adrenaline and energy. He snatched a sandwich or burger when he could, and fit in his workouts by rising an hour earlier. Every night, Michael wanted to celebrate.

What he really wanted was a woman.

There was no shortage of girls, of course. There never had been. Poor Susan, if Michael had met her in a bar he would have jumped her bones without thinking twice. But the office was sacred to him. Three times a week, on average, he picked up a girl, usually one he had banged before; girls he knew, clean, dumb, gorgeous girls, women he could take in small doses. They had big breasts, small waists and round, firm butts. Unfortunately, most girls were stupid and Michael couldn't take stupid. He was polite and kind and didn't lie to anybody. Nine times out of ten, they wanted a return encounter. He liked Janet, who wore a bra two sizes too small, so creamy, jiggling flesh poured out over the top of the black lace, and Elsa, the fitness instructor, who had that delectable ass, curvy, jutting and muscular. He laughed at her when she complained about it. When would girls learn that most guys didn't want a tomboy? Every time Elsa leant over to pick up something from the floor, he got a twitch in his groin.

But all the girls who banged Michael so eagerly, all the condom packets he went through, didn't satisfy him. He wanted a girl he could talk to when she was done giving him head, preferably expertly. And if her technique wasn't perfect, he'd be happy to give her practical lessons.

He thought he'd found her when he met Iris. She was in a bar on Twenty-fourth and Eighth, but then again, so was he. She was a paralegal, with hopes of becoming a lawyer some day. She had an excellent body, a curvy ass, good tits, and she knew several words of more than one syllable. Michael asked her out and, to his surprise, found she wouldn't give it up on the first date. Nor the second. She made it to three before sharing his bed, and when she did so, he found she could suck him well. Better than well. She wasn't the classiest girl, but he figured you had to make allowances. And he was full of adrenaline, and she was there.

One evening, three weeks into their relationship, after a more expensive dinner than he could really afford, Michael had taken her home, banged her, and was now wondering how long he had to wait before he could ask her to leave, without being rude. A girlfriend was great, but he had to get up in the morning.

Iris lay sprawled across his bed, reading his tabloids: the *News* and *Post* which Michael only bought for the sports sections. Iris liked to ring all the jewellery shops advertising discount diamonds she couldn't afford, and then move on to the gossip pages. She propped herself up on her slim elbows, which let her breasts sway nicely, her nipples still hardened from his tongue on them earlier.

'Anything interesting?' Cicero asked. Play nice, he thought with an inward sigh.

'Yeah. Something about your boss.'

'Where? Let me see.'

'Oh, so *now* you're interested,' Iris teased, but she handed over the inky sheet. 'It's a bit about the wife, actually.'

'Diana? She's a snotty little bitch,' Michael said, unthinkingly, and then cursed himself. He shouldn't say things like that. Not even to Iris. Discretion was important in a business like his.

'You met her?' Iris demanded. She sat up with a sigh, butt-naked, and he admired the firm lines of her stomach. She sighed, wistfully. 'They're always taking her photo. She looks so great. She throws, like, the hippest parties, and everybody goes.'

'Do they now,' Michael said, absently. He scanned the article to see if it said anything about Ernie. It didn't; he was about to throw it out.

'Sure. All the celebrities, the politicians, basketball players, everyone ... and her clothes, such incredible clothes!'

Iris babbled on, but Cicero paid her no attention. He was looking at the shot of Diana, in a soft cashmere sky-blue sweater worn over a silk taffeta skirt, emerging from a dinner at City Hall. She looked ... out of his league. Classy, like a princess or something. The thought of Ernie Foxton banging that was literally incredible. He tried to picture it: he failed.

Diana Foxton. There was something about her he should remember, wasn't there? Something he had meant to do that had slipped by him?

Oh, shit, Michael thought. Of course. They had fought – stuck-up madam that she was. Class, sure, but didn't she know it – and he had signed his deal before she could go running to Ernie and blow it for him.

But in fact, she hadn't said a thing. Ernie had never mentioned it. Nobody had said boo to him. Mrs Foxton had actually kept that plump, sexy little mouth shut.

He should thank her. He had meant to go and thank her. She could have made things hard for him, and she had chosen not to.

Credit where it's due, Michael thought. He resolved he would see her tomorrow.

He looked across at Iris, her legs up in the air, lying on her stomach now. Her ass stuck straight up in the air. He was sure she lay around naked deliberately. Whatever, she was a great piece of ass.

'Get over here,' he said.

Chapter 11

Michael Cicero looked at Diana.

He was lounging on Ernie's antique Chesterfield sofa which she had found at huge cost with the help of two decorators. Diana couldn't accuse him of being rude, at least not directly. His feet weren't propped up on her Indian ottoman, he wasn't smoking and dropping ash on to the Persian carpet.

But something about his manner set her on edge. Diana's skin prickled when she noticed his body, lean and hugely muscled, looking even bigger in that new suit he was wearing, arranging itself comfortably on the leather, relaxed, confident. Cicero didn't seem in the slightest bit put off by the fact that he was lolling on a fifteen-thousand-dollar piece of furniture; nor nervous that he might knock over one of the eighteenth-century vases. He wasn't even staring reverentially at the pictures and mentally calculating how much they cost. He didn't seem, Diana realised with another shock of annoyance, to care.

His suit was charcoal, hand tailored. It was no designer she could pick out. The shoes – John Lobb, maybe? Diana was hazy on men's fashions, but she knew instantly that Michael Cicero had come into money and that he had aggravatingly good taste.

'That's not the most pleasant way to greet a guest, ma'am,' Michael said with a lazy smile. His eyes flickered over her, and for the first time, Diana noticed it. She blushed slightly and drew herself up, angry at having been caught in blatant rudeness. You couldn't allow yourself to slip like that. This arrogant man was some kind of business acquaintance of Ernie's.

I won't endear myself to Ernie by putting off his colleagues, Diana thought.

She glided into the drawing room and offered him the warmest smile she could muster.

'I'm sorry, I didn't mean it how it sounded.'

'Oh hell, it's you?' Michael quoted, with a broad grin.

Diana was slightly flustered. 'Well, I – I guess – it came out—'

Cicero held up one hand. 'Hey, that's fine. I understand. Don't worry about it.'

Diana bit down on her lip. 'You were waiting to see Ernie here? I'm afraid he'll be at the office for quite some time.'

'No. I came to see you.'

She paused, not quite sure she'd heard him properly. 'You came to see *me*?'

'You're going to ask to what do you owe the pleasure, aren't you?'

'Something like that.'

'Please, have a seat.' It was amazing, the way he could so generously invite her to sit down in her own apartment. He did it with such force of will that Diana found herself settling on the armchair opposite him.

Michael watched the way she tucked her slender legs in behind her automatically as she sat down. Her back was rigid, her bearing ladylike. She was one class act, he thought, and judging from the way she was dressed, she cost exactly what you always imagined these dames fetched. He thought about Ernie Foxton. Maybe she liked Ernie's take-no-prisoners business style, who knew? The guy had nothing else to recommend him. Prancing around in his flashy clothes, with his designer offices, and weak limbs – probably never seen a set of weights in his life. He hadn't had the right body language with his girl either, when they were at lunch. Hadn't even held her hand. Hell, if she were my woman, Michael told himself, I'd be all over her.

He decided that the unyielding rigidity of her back was due to the fact that she never came. A little mouse of a man like Ernie couldn't melt the ice over that exterior. No way.

He pulled himself sharply back from his reverie. She was a spoiled little minx, and she looked exhausted – from her long day of shopping, probably. Best that he said his piece and got out.

'Well, actually, I figured I should come around and thank you,' Michael said.

'Thank me for what? I'm sure you don't owe me anything.' Diana pressed a little button on the table, and Consuela glided into view. 'Could you fetch us a pot of coffee and some cookies, please, Consuela?'

'It's not necessary. I won't be staying. My company, Green Eggs, signed a deal with Ernie's company last month.'

'Really? I don't pay much attention to his work,' Diana said vaguely.

Then it's not his business nous, Michael thought, just good old-fashioned gold-digging. He refused to believe that the gorgeous creature in front of him could love anybody at all apart from herself, and certainly not Ernie Foxton.

'Well, yeah, we did. It meant I got new offices, some cash to play around with, great distribution, more staff, a printing facility . . .'

'Congratulations,' Diana said, slightly coolly. Why on earth was he telling her all this? It pained her to see this – this thug from the wrong side of the tracks sitting in front of her and congratulating himself on his shiny new offices and fleets of staff, or whatever it was, when she herself could not even get a lousy editorial assistant's job.

'And in a way I have you to thank for it.'

'I don't see how.'

Michael swallowed. This was the bit he hadn't been looking forward to. 'When we had lunch that time, I guess I let rip some. And since you were Ernie's wife, I expected you to go running home to him and tell him. It could have blown the deal. Not the main deal, because I signed real fast, but some bonuses and stuff.'

'If you're coming here to apologise for what you said that day at lunch, I forgive you.'

'Not at all. I'm not apologising,' Michael said quickly, struggling not to snap when he was supposed to be thanking her. 'I just want to thank you for having kept it to yourself.'

Diana bristled. She'd wanted him to eat humble pie, and apparently that was not on today's menu. But what could she do when he was here thanking her?

Her blue eyes settled on his face. It was handsome and square jawed. She had visions of him with maybe dozens of women. That was usually what made men so cocky. This one had been the same way even when he'd showed up to lunch in that cheap suit and bad shoes.

'That's no problem at all.' I'm going to be gracious if it kills me, Diana thought. 'I don't go telling tales on people. Whomever Ernie wants to deal with, that's his business. I hope the takeover works out well for you.'

'It's not a takeover, it's a partnership.'

'Whatever. I hope it makes you very rich.'

'I certainly hope it's good for the company,' Michael said neutrally. 'For both companies.'

Diana felt a great wash of exhaustion rock her. She didn't feel up to an in-depth discussion of this guy's successes right now. She pressed one slender hand to her forehead. 'Look, Mr Cicero – I wonder if you would be kind enough to excuse me. I've had a really bad day, and I was looking forward to a bath and bed.'

'Of course.' He stood up, and she couldn't help but notice he was short, and very stocky. He was about five ten, and his lack of height just made his body look bigger. 'I'm sorry to hear that. Why was your day so bad?'

'I couldn't get a job.' Diana half clapped her hand over her mouth. Had she just said that? She must be tired.

'You were trying to get a *job*?'

'Do you all *have* to look so surprised? Yes, I worked before my marriage. I was a fashion assistant at *Vogue* in England. Ernie's an American citizen, so as his wife I have a right to look for work.'

'Hey, hey, slow down.' He sat down again. 'I'm sure you do. Now, who's "you all"? How many interviews did you go on?'

Diana wondered how she had gotten into this, but there was no point in lying now. 'Seven. And the last woman was just rude to me.'

'I'm sorry.' Michael tried, and failed, to imagine the woman in front of him going to seven job interviews. Seven in one day would mean that she was almost serious about getting a job. 'She was rude, huh? What did she say?'

'She said I should sit at home and throw charity balls for the paparazzi.'

Michael burst out laughing, and Diana couldn't take it any more. She stamped her foot.

'You're worse than she was! How dare you laugh at me! You're in *my home*!'

'Look.' Michael smothered his laugh and walked closer to her, putting his hands on her arms. His touch was very strong, but subtle. 'I'm truly sorry I laughed just now. It was just such a rude thing of her to have said.'

That was a lie, but a little white lie couldn't hurt. It wouldn't comfort her to know that he'd laughed because

96

that was exactly what he'd thought Diana should do himself. Cicero felt an unexpected small pang of guilt. The girl was trying, right? He had to give her credit for that.

'It was, wasn't it?'

'Very. Look, if you're serious about working, you could maybe come and do something in my office.'

'Like decorating it?' Diana brightened. 'I'd be excellent at that and very reasonable.'

That would be a coup. She'd love to tell her friends that she had her first decorating commission. That might actually be fun.

Michael Cicero was giving her a surprised look with his dark eyes. 'No. I have the wall colour I want and a print and some furniture.'

'I *think* I could manage something rather more exciting than that. I could start with some Eames chairs, and—'

'My budget for decorating isn't really large,' he said, dryly. She was a fox, no doubt about that, but she was definitely starting to irritate him again. 'I mean, say, being my assistant, helping to file, and make phone calls—'

'Fetch tea and coffee?' Diana asked sarcastically.

The sarcasm washed off him like water off a duck's back. 'Exactly. Tea, coffee, frank the mail, whatever needs doing. It's like a Girl Friday job. It would be hard work and it wouldn't pay much.'

'Sounds great.'

'Look, if you don't want it, I understand. You're a rich lady. Thanks for taking the time to see me,' Michael said, courteously, offering her a stiff little bow.

'No – wait, please.' Diana ran and caught at the elbow of his jacket. Her pride was stung. He agreed with the nasty hag from *City Woman*, he thought she should stay at home and run charity balls. I'm more than that, she thought fiercely. I can handle a job! Why does everybody except Milla assume I would fail? The thought of Mira Chen, in the office, the little businesswoman, probably right now taking a 'meeting' with her husband, made her furious. 'I'd love the job. It doesn't matter about the pay. Just as long as I can start as soon as possible.'

'Pay would be fifteen thousand a year.'

'Sounds good to me,' Diana said, insistently.

Michael could have kicked himself. Who on earth would have thought that the woman would actually say yes? But that was fine. She'd quit in a week. A chick like that – society lady with the body of a forties sweetheart – had probably never worked an honest day in her life.

'We have new offices in the Blakely's building. Fourth floor. You won't be too near Ernie, I'm afraid.'

'That's fine,' Diana assured him. 'What time do you open the office? Publishing normally starts around ten, correct?'

'Correct. It normally does. But Green Eggs is a bit more ambitious than most. I like to be in the office at eight thirty. I'll see you there at that time tomorrow. If I'm a little late, the security guard will let you in.'

He chuckled inwardly, watching her pale. Any second now she'd fling the job back in his face.

'Oh, and by the way.' He thought he'd spice up the mix for her. 'I take my coffee black, and I like it fresh brewed twice a day.'

Diana swallowed hard. Insufferable man. He was playing with her. He wanted her to quit.

'See you tomorrow at eight thirty,' she snapped. 'Let me show you out.'

'You do that.' Cicero was strolling out to the door. That arrogant walk he had, it was like he owned the place. 'I'll look forward to working with you.'

Diana went upstairs and ran herself a hot tub, shaking Floris Lily of the Valley liberally into it, and revelling in the cloud of fragrant steam as she sank her long limbs into the water. Her feet had a very unaccustomed ache from tramping round the streets of New York all day long – it was amazing how hard it was to get cabs in midtown at lunchtime – and she wasn't used to the humiliations she'd been asked to suffer. Well, *Elle* and *Marie Claire* would regret bitterly that they hadn't snapped up the new Diana, the new businesswoman Diana, once she'd made her mark in publishing. She was determined to be upbeat about her new job. Fifteen thousand didn't sound very much, and, of course, it was dollars, not even pounds. But it was a start. It could be her handbag money, or maybe she'd put it in the stock market, and wind up really rich like the Rockefellers. There were consolations. Diana considered the delicious necessity of buying a completely new wardrobe full of business suits, maybe even kitsch pinstripes, who knew? There were endless possibilities, and then of course one needed work shoes and handbags to go with them. She could almost forgive Michael Cicero his coffee remark. Did he really expect her to fetch his drinks? Of course not. That had to have been a joke. At any rate, she would show him that she could not be bossed around the way he seemed to be planning.

She started daydreaming about life as a working woman. Ernie would be entranced and surprised, and he'd just have to work harder at catching her in. Then there would be so much less time for extracurricular activities. Yes, Diana thought, she had made it far too easy for him to enjoy the pleasure of her company. But all that would change.

Fuelled by enjoyable thoughts of revenge, Diana climbed out of her bath and swathed herself in her rich, navy Ralph Lauren gown. She lazily reached for her Crème de la Mer and slathered it all over her hands and body, rubbing it into her knees, her aching shins and feet.

Then she sauntered into her walk-in closet and stood in an agony of indecision for several minutes before plumping for her pink silk Richard Tyler number. She just managed to finish spritzing her perfume before she heard the front door open.

Ernie was home.

Chapter 12

Five miles away, in SoHo, Felicity Metson was considering her options.

Diana Foxton was such a little fool. Nobody liked her – who could like that combination of perfect dressing and inane naivety? It was too unfair to watch her swan into town with no reputation, nothing, only a rich husband in a city full of rich husbands and that blasted accent, and just take over the social scene. Her body didn't fit in – a good ten pounds she had on most of the girls – and her dressing didn't fit in – such perfectly tailored, wonderfully subtle clothes; even if she was wearing Prada and Gucci she managed to make them look English. You glanced at Diana and you got an instant sense of Merry Olde Englande, with – well – castles and Labrador puppies and oh, what was that game they had that was even more boring than baseball? Oh, cricket; yes, that was it. Of course, Ernie was just another rich flyboy made good, but that wasn't the point. A rich husband was pretty much wallpaper.

Felicity moved around her pale-cream apartment, idly dusting the Moda Italia furniture that was so stylish and uncomfortable, and the stacks of How to Get a Man books she kept like bibles at the side of her bed. Because, after all, even though a husband did nothing more than provide the requisite background for a wife to shine against, he was a necessity. How could you throw wonderful, aggravatingly perfect dinners like Diana Foxton without the moolah necessary to hire just the right chef, get the perfect table bouquets of twigs and wild berries, and buy the French crystal that everyone drank out of and the Royal Doulton everybody ate off?

It was too bad, Felicity thought, pouting, that Hector, her own husband – landed after a campaign planned with military precision – had decided that, after all, he preferred the company of slender, sexy young men. It was simply embarrassing to be this young and divorced. She glanced down at her man manuals – *The Rules, Getting To I Do, The Art of War for Lovers* – and thought about Ernie Foxton. What on earth had Diana got to complain about? Ernie was a good worker and seemed to give her carte blanche when it came to running her home and her life. Felicity went to her wonderful 1970s bar and mixed herself a vodka Martini, even putting in a jumbo olive, because style was all about the details. Diana was mad, the silly little chit, running around town telling all and sundry. And the faces of Jodie and Natasha saying their husbands didn't cheat! The whole world knew that Zuckerman liked to pork the nanny whenever possible, and Natasha went along with it because if it was kept in the house it was under her control. All she did was change the model regularly, as if there were any danger her hubby would divorce her – far too much money down the drain for that. Felicity lifted her glass to Natasha, who was a wife who knew how to play the game. It suited her to be married and it suited her husband to be married. With this open admission, this senseless bleating, Diana was laying Ernie and herself open to ridicule.

In Felicity's experience, if there was one thing men couldn't stand, it was ridicule.

The Zuckermans and the Goodfriends would have blabbed it all over town by now. Felicity had kept quiet and congratulated herself on her subtlety. When Ernie first started hearing the rumours, he would investigate the source and find out that she, Felicity, had been the only discreet person in the whole silly business. What a fool Diana was to worry about the little oriental tart Ernie had brought into the office! That was not the type of woman an obvious social climber like Ernie would ever marry. She would never be able to mingle properly at the Met, the way the classiest Chinese and Japanese ladies did with such effortless ease. She was a cheap little slut who had no social graces, and besides which, she thought small. She was, Felicity decided, most likely just sticking Ernie up for the odd platinum watch and diamond bracelet, instead of the small gold ring which really counted. Ernie was no fool. He wouldn't swap a Diana for a Mira. But if Diana wasn't careful, she would most likely find herself swapped for someone else.

The phone at her bedside buzzed. It was Tom. She let the machine pick up.

'Hey babe, it's me. Got a forty-eight-hour pass at the last minute. Wondered if you wanted to do dinner or something. I'll try you later.'

Dinner or something? Well, that was very romantic, Felicity thought disdainfully, wiping his message with one flick of her Chanel Rouge Argent sparkling finger-nail. Tom just didn't get it, did he? He looked good in dress whites, and he was a novelty in her circle, certainly better than nothing. A recently divorced girl could not afford to be seen anywhere unaccompanied. But the salary of a Marine major was never going to keep her in the style to which she'd become so very accustomed. Why, if she married Tom she'd be the richer partner and need a pre-nup. And besides, who could see her, Felicity Metson, dragging herself from base to base and deferring to the wife of a lieutnant-colonel?

She squirmed with shame on the sofa as she thought of her divorce. God, what a stigma! A girl her age actually cast aside! It was no comfort to think that Hector had been a faggot. If she had somehow been smarter and let him know, subtly, that both her eyes were blind, he could have had the gardener, the pool-man and the chef and she would never have batted an eyelid. It wasn't so different to what Natasha was doing. Felicity swung her skinny legs and mentally chastised herself. What a rookie error, to try to persuade Hector that his position demanded he be straight, that he could shut his eyes and just do her instead. She'd made him uncomfortable. As Diana was most likely making Ernie uncomfortable right now.

Of course, *I* was married for a good five years. And silly little Miss Perfect has only been wed six months, Felicity triumphed, taking a spiteful sip of her Martini. What a terribly amusing thing it was to see the beautifully put together Miss Limey with that aggravatingly classy accent take such a swift tumble from grace, and then be stupid enough to broadcast it to the two biggest gossips in town! They would be repeating this story at Bliss facial spa and Oribe's salon on Fifth and, in fact, all over New York. She made a mental bet with herself on how long it would take to get back to Ernie that his wife had been blabbing? Not long, not long at all. And then, how he would prize discretion, and want to silence the gossips.

Felicity made a mental note to find out all she could about Ernie Foxton. Judging from his apartment, he was doing wonderfully well. And if she played her cards right, he could soon be back on the market. Just as she was herself.

Diana settled into the high-backed, carved oak chair opposite Ernie's. She'd had a little love table installed at one end of the bedroom for their most intimate dinners. His favourite food, champagne, flowers, candles. It would be special for a lot of men, but she did this for

Ernie on a regular basis. A pleasant home was her end of the bargain. Why couldn't he keep his?

'How was your day today, darling?'

Now that the moment was here, she was nervous. She had no idea how to handle it.

'Not too bad. Lots of meetings. Always the same.' Ernie's accent was starting to grate on her. 'Nothing you'd be interested in. Have a good time here?'

'I might be interested in your work if you'd tell me about it,' Diana said sweetly.

He looked surprised. 'I doubt it. You've never shown any interest in anything without a label on the back, have you?'

'I could be. I spent some time at *Vogue* before we got married.'

Ernie speared his lamb and shook the piece at her, smirking. 'Yeah, but that was hardly a real job. You were just mucking about waiting for me to pop the question. And I didn't mind. What were you going to say, that we now had two million *and* twelve thousand a year?'

He giggled in his high-pitched way.

'It's true; I have been a bit of a butterfly,' Diana admitted, stifling her annoyance. She tossed back her silky hair to show it off to its best advantage in the candlelight, but Ernie only seemed interested in the cranberry relish. 'But I think the working life has a lot to offer a woman.'

'Like a salary. Lucky for you, you don't need one.'

'I think it's important to be independent,' Diana said firmly. 'I've actually gone out looking for a job. And I've found one. In publishing.'

That got him. Ernie lowered his knife and fork theatrically and stared at her. 'In publishing? But you've got no experience. What are you doing? Who for?'

'I'm going to be assisting one of your colleagues. Michael Cicero at Green Eggs.'

Ernie half choked. 'You what?'

'I'm going to be working for Mr Cicero,' Diana said, sliding one long, curvy leg over the other and shaking her shoulders slightly so that her dress moved around the full ripeness of her breasts.

Ernie looked at the sensual movement of his wife, but she did nothing for him. If Diana could get a little kinky, get a riding crop and paddle his buttocks mercilessly the way Mira had done this morning, maybe he'd have some desire for her again. But Mira had squeezed out the last drop of juice from him, and he didn't think he could get it up for Diana with a crane. Now she wanted to work for that little asshole Cicero, huh? Well, he, Ernie, wanted a spy in that office. Besides, it would mean she had less time to wonder where he was at night.

'If you want to, babe, I think that'd be a great idea.'

Diana preened. 'I'm sure I'd be able to understand your business more once I get the hang of it.'

'Get the hang of it? You'll quit in a week.'

'Why would you say that? Of course I won't quit. I'll be good at it. I'm sure I'll be indispensable.'

'Rumour has it Mike Cicero's a slave driver.'

Don't talk to me about rumours, Diana thought. She lifted her glass. 'I can handle it. Let's have a toast. To business.'

'To business,' Ernie repeated dutifully, wondering what had got into his meek little wife.

He took some paperwork into his den as soon as Consuela started to clear away the dishes. If he could stay up late enough Diana would fall asleep and he wouldn't be expected to perform like a trained monkey. I'm *stressed*, Ernie whined to himself. He shut the heavy oak door behind him and gleefully booted up his computer so he could log on to the Internet. He loved the Net, it was an isolating little cyber-world that kept him well away from his flesh and blood woman. So far Diana had never disturbed him in here. Ernie told himself smugly that she knew better.

He had just clicked his mouse on to his favourite online trading site when there was the unmistakable squeak of the door. Without glancing round, Ernie told Consuela he wouldn't be needing anything else and she could retire.

'It's not Consuela. It's me.'

Ernie twisted around in his revolving chair. Diana stood in the doorway, the light from their soft sconces filtering through her dress, outlining the silhouette of her. She was built a lot like that film star, Catherine Zeta Jones. He so much preferred Mira's hard, tarty, boyish little body.

'I got some work to do, OK, babes?'

'Not really.' Diana took a deep breath and glanced out of their huge, six-foot windows looking downtown through the canyons of glass and concrete. Manhattan was Ernie's gift to her, and it was glittering in the night like a web of jewels. 'I think we need to talk, darling.'

'We just did talk,' Ernie said, a nasty squirming feeling in the pit of his stomach. Fuck. Was she on to him? It felt just like when his Ma used to scold him, back at school, in front of the other kids. He began to feel the first stirrings of resentment.

'Who were you talking to so early the other morning? I heard you on the phone. You told the girl on the other end not to speak so loudly in case you woke your wife.'

'How do you know it was a girl? It wasn't a girl. It was Peter Davits, he's my head of business affairs. He needed an early morning meeting and I wanted to make sure I didn't disturb you.'

Diana relaxed and Ernie breathed out. Well. It was easier than he'd expected to wriggle out. 'Look at you, you're all jealous. Don't you know I got the best wife in

New York? You know I need to work all the hours God sends, sweetheart. To get nice things for you. Same as it always was. All right?'

'All right,' Diana said, smiling at him uncertainly.

'I really need to finish up in here. Why don't you go get some rest and I'll be in as soon as I can. You've got a big day tomorrow. New job.' Ernie tried to finish that last sentence with a straight face.

'You're right.' Diana padded across the study in her delicate Moroccan slippers, embroidered in golden thread, that sparkled as she moved. She kissed him, and there was the scent of baby powder on her skin. Very clean, very wholesome, very spoiled. Ernie decided he'd have to find some way of letting her know what the score was. He hardly asked much of her. Looking the other way, it was as old as time, wasn't it? What wife could do less?

Ernie clasped her to him and dramatically breathed in, sniffing the air. 'Wow, you smell great, honey. Why don't you go to Tiffany's tomorrow and get yourself a little something to celebrate your new job?'

'Thanks. I will. Don't be too long,' Diana said, pressing his shoulders and gliding off.

Ernie waited until he heard the bedroom door shut, then picked up his cell phone and dialled Mira's number from memory. If he was lucky, his Mistress would be home, and maybe order him to another early morning rendezvous tomorrow.

Chapter 13

The alarm buzzed in the darkness, and for a few seconds Diana didn't recognise the sound. She lay sprawled in her silk sheets, trying to work out, half conscious, why that horrible noise wouldn't stop.

Ernie's bare foot pushed at her, and with a start, Diana sat up. Groggily she hit the button to turn the wretched thing off. In the darkness of early morning, the luminous dials on the clock silently told her it was 5.50 a.m. The bedroom was chilly, and her sheets and pillows seemed blissfully, temptingly soft and warm. For a second she hesitated, but only for a second. Diana glanced back at her husband, snoring in the sheets, and thought of Mira Chen's nasty little smile. She, Diana Foxton, was not the type to give up so easily. She jumped out of bed and staggered into the shower.

They had separate bathrooms, because Diana couldn't stand to have Ernie watching her toilette. A woman must cultivate an air of mystery. When she needed to floss, or pluck her eyebrows, he didn't need to watch, did he? She loved to appear perfectly groomed and pulled-together at all times. She turned the heavy brass shower knobs to her pre-programmed temperature setting and clicked the water pressure to power. Time to wake up. The jets, steaming and brutal, hissed into action, and Diana slid aside the frosted glass doors and stepped in.

Ah! Normally she adored her black marble, roomy shower, with its inlaid gold and silver stars that made you feel as though you were washing yourself in the night sky, but today the water was invigorating and harsh. Her shoulders and back were pummelled into wakefulness, and little rivulets gushed down over her forehead and across her nose and mouth. Her sleepiness evaporated, and Diana congratulated herself on her willpower as she reached for the shampoo. True, they were really not far from the office here, and she had a chauffeur on twenty-four-hour call, so she wouldn't have to wait for a taxi. But I left enough time to dress and make up, Diana thought. Pleasant visions of herself gliding beautifully into Michael Cicero's office, immaculately presented, drove her on. That bastard had more or less offered her the job as a joke. He didn't expect to see her on time, let alone put together. But I'll show him, Diana thought, excitedly.

She took her time in her gilt and marble sanctuary. Hair was easy – she always went for a glossy, well-conditioned, natural look. Make-up was somewhat more difficult. At *Vogue*, of course, there was the option to be fashionable. In a regular office, it probably wouldn't do to be daring. Languidly, Diana settled on a pretty, neutral look, a sheer mousse foundation, soft berry lips, nothing but mascara on the eyes with a touch of concealer to mask the terrible sleep deprivation. The bathroom window looked out past her terrace to Central Park, and as dawn hit the New York skyline, revealing a few ant-like figures making their morning circular rounds past the lake, Diana rubbed La Prairie moisturiser into her shapely calves and told herself being a working woman wasn't at all bad.

She buzzed the kitchen and told Paula, the cook, to have some vanilla coffee perking and warm her up a croissant. All this fashion was giving her an appetite. She finished blow-drying her hair, smoothed it with a touch of shiner, and selected the belted navy shirtdress that was the most appropriate thing for work that she had in her wardrobe. Clothes shopping would need to be after hours or at the weekend. Maybe she'd pick up a nice burgundy leather briefcase from Coach while she was at it.

Finally, she was ready. She spritzed herself with Clinique's Aromatics Elixir, clip-clipped as quietly as she could on her high blue strappy Manolos out of the bedroom, and went downstairs to bid Paula good morning and pick at her breakfast. Freshly squeezed juice, fragrant coffee and a small croissant, just to settle her stomach. After Paula had left the room, Diana, delicately sipping from her cup, regarded her reflection with the utmost approval. Everything worked magnificently together. In fact, she looked very like Grace Kelly.

Yes, Diana told herself. Being a working woman would be fun, fun, fun!

Michael awoke at quarter past seven in the way he liked best, which was to say Iris's lips were wrapped around his cock, and her tongue was flickering over the head of it. To be honest it was a little late for him to be awake; a hangover from busting this chick up for hours the night before, he guessed. But Iris's tongue was flickering over his penis in that soft, feather-light, sexy way she had, darting over the tiny ridge of skin that he loved a girl's lips on so much, then sliding her mouth down the whole length of him. Yeah, now he was awake. His fingers tightened in her hair. Oh, man, was she ever good at this. A faint question as to how exactly she had gotten so good at it danced in the back of his mind, but it was a distracting thought, and he tried to squash it. She was a smartly dressed, clever enough chick, with a pretty face and a body he'd have liked to add twenty pounds to, but it wasn't all that bad. She was a bit earnest, but she was a nice girl. He thought so. Well, sure, she qualified. Very few girls resisted Michael's full court press for any length of time; normally he measured it in hours, not dates. So

Michael felt hopeful about this one. Though he never articulated the thought to himself, he respected the situation of the family, and one day, maybe, just maybe, he'd like to be married. There were a hundred girls around in New York he could fuck – married girls, engaged girls, girls who propositioned you right to your face – a huge turn-off – girls dating other guys, and just the common or garden variety of girl who would agree to every nasty little thing you suggested right away, before she even knew your surname. He'd fucked some of these girls. It used to be all of these girls. When he was a bit younger, Michael had carried a full condom pack in his hip pocket at all times. But now, the girls just looked more tired, less appealing. When he woke up with one, it felt cheap, maybe a little dirty. Like when you ate a full box of Crackerjack out at a ball game and then felt sick later. Plus, there was the ever more annoying problem of how to get them out of the bed, the apartment, and his life. He'd even stopped giving out his number, so he didn't have to deal with the pleading, whimpering phone calls. Iris had put a stop to all that. She qualified as a nice girl so he didn't like to speculate how she'd become as good as she was at what she was doing right now.

Iris smirked and angled her head backwards and took him deeper into her throat, and Michael groaned. Somehow it was no longer quite so important to keep one eye on the clock. Damn. Feel that sucking. His cock was always more awake than he was in the mornings anyway.

'I gotta go,' he breathed.

'Not right yet, baby.' She broke off and lifted those puppy-dog eyes to his.

'Stop talking,' Michael growled. He pulled her lips back on to him and spread his thick, hard thighs on the bed. Her bleached-blond hair was bobbing up and down in an amazingly distracting way.

Wasn't he doing something new at work this morning?

He didn't remember. He didn't remember anything. He didn't even know where he was. There was nothing on his mind but his hard thickness, and Iris's clever, eager mouth surrounding and sucking him.

Michael gasped and abandoned himself to the moment. This was better than an alarm clock any day.

He got out of the subway on Seventh and Fiftieth an hour later, washed, shaved, newly suited, and with his mind cleared and body relaxed. Iris and he had a date that night, but he wasn't thinking about her any more. She was filed away in the back of his brain. The commuters around him marched past up the grimy steps and poured out into midtown, everybody intent on the day's hustle ahead, getting those dollars, making that sky-high rent roll. How was it that he'd signed a deal that upped his compensation to sixty grand a year, Michael asked himself, and yet his financial problems were worse than ever?

He pushed open the door to the Blakely's building and exchanged morning greetings with the security guard. Michael made a point of asking how people were doing. When he'd been a doorman as one of his four jobs working through college, people had treated him like a piece of furniture, even people he saw day in, day out, for months. Cicero never let people push him around, but he reckoned politeness didn't cost a dime. And in Manhattan, politeness made you stand out, too.

The elevator came and he looked over his half-decent suit. The first thing he'd done when the money came in was to get a bank loan and invest in some clothes. Shoes and suits did not come cheap. Then there was the new apartment; for two thousand a month he got a tiny, first-floor, one bedroom TriBeCa walkup with a minute alcove that served as a den, but it was in a good location. From now on he was going places, and he should start with a good address, personal comfort was secondary. The apartment had space for one double bed, and that was about all he needed. His bills were already starting to mount, so he had very little stuff. Hell, minimalism was supposed to be fashionable anyway. Not that Michael really cared. It suited him to live where he did, so everybody else could whistle. Iris had expressed surprise the first time he took her home, but when she saw his expression, she'd wisely concluded that maybe she should shut up.

The fourth floor was deserted, as usual. Michael racked his brain. Something was meant to be different today. What was it? He asked Joey to ride up with the keys, and remembered as he unlocked and switched the lights on: Diana Foxton was meant to be here. Michael grinned privately to himself. What was more likely, he wondered, that she'd be late, or that she wouldn't come at all?

The sooner she realised that it was a foolish idea, the better. He really didn't need a time waster in the office.

Diana swung her heels delicately out of the back door of the Bentley which Richard was holding open for her. She smiled and tipped him her usual ten dollars, and looked up at the Blakely's building. This was a first, wasn't it? To come here and not be picking Ernie up? She pushed through the heavy glass doors, speed-dialling Felicity on her cell phone as she did so.

'Darling, are you awake? No?'

Diana punched the elevator button as Joey Petano, on the front desk, drank in the itsy-bitsy heels and clinging silk dress.

Felicity sat up in her bed, cell phone pressed to her ear. When Diana called, she had to be awake. Even at this ungodly hour.

'For you, of course I am, Di, sweetie. What's new? More bad behaviour from Ernie?'

'No, no. He's being a lamb. He said it was a man he met the other morning. Anyway, I have got myself a job, working for an affiliate company in the Blakely's building.'

'Really.' Felicity's heart sank. If Ernie had got her a job so that she could be close to him, actually in his office, maybe the marriage wasn't shaky – maybe their intelligence was all wrong.

'Yes. Not on his floor, about twelve storeys below . . . and he had nothing to do with it, I got it myself.'

'That's wonderful,' Felicity said, her face creasing in a genuine smile. She twitched open her curtains to let the morning light in. 'A new start for you, dear. What does Ernie think of all this?'

'He thinks I'll quit, but I won't. Anyway, must dash, the elevator's here and it'll cut me off.'

'Do call me later, sweetie,' Felicity suggested kindly, as her friend hung up.

She relaxed against her pillows. That meant Ernie would be at home on his own right now. Languidly, Felicity punched the speed-dial for the Foxtons' private number.

Diana stepped off the elevator at the fourth floor. The office lights were on; maybe some inefficient cleaner had left them on the night before. The door had a small, unostentatious plaque next to it. *Green Eggs Books. A Blakely's Affiliate Company.* Not very impressive, frankly. Nothing like the bronze etched plate and statuary that greeted the visitor to the main Blakely's office, with her husband's name emblazoned all over it. She would have to see what she could do about that.

She pushed open the door and looked around, disappointed. Judging from the way Cicero was dressed she assumed he would at least have come into a little cash. These offices were clean, spare, functional and little else. Architectural plans were mounted on the walls, which were cream and, as she peeked into the individually locked offices, she noted that the furniture was some kind of plain, rather old-fashioned brown wood. Sure, it was light and airy, but couldn't they have been a little more extravagant, a bit more imaginative? She'd soon persuade Cicero that her touch was needed to brighten the place up and—

'Nice to see you, at last.'

Diana jumped out of her skin and spun around. There he was, lounging against the only open door in the whole place. He looked relaxed, confident and cocky. One dark eyebrow was raised as he examined her outfit.

'What are you doing here?' she gasped. 'You scared me.'

'I scare a lot of people. I don't see why I should scare you, though. It's eight twenty-five.'

'I'm not late,' Diana said defensively, wondering how long he'd been standing there. Had he watched her raising herself on tiptoe peeking in through all the windows? She blushed. 'You said eight thirty.'

'I said *I* would be here at eight thirty, and therefore you should be in at quarter past. You're ten minutes late.'

Normally she'd have about an hour an a half left to lie in bed right now. Diana swallowed. 'I'm sorry. It won't happen again.'

Michael registered somewhere deep down that she hadn't offered him an excuse, but he wasn't all that mollified. The girl was outrageously, scandalously beautiful. What did she think she was doing, turning up to his office looking like that? It was a good thing Iris had been busy this morning, he told himself, or he'd very definitely have his concentration shot all day.

'Can we talk about your clothes, Mrs Foxton?'

'You can call me Diana. And yes, you can.' She waited proudly for the compliments she knew were about to flow almost against his will. It must kill Cicero to give her compliments. 'Go ahead.'

'They aren't suitable for the office.'

Diana started. Had she heard him right? But yes, he was standing across from her with folded arms and a direct, frank black stare.

'What's wrong with how I'm dressed, Michael?'

He paused. Actually, he hadn't taken the time to stop and analyse it. Her neckline wasn't low-cut, and her skirt reached to below the knee. The silk fabric clung sensuously to every inch of her, but you couldn't see anything. Maybe she was actually old-fashioned enough to wear a slip, or maybe she just wasn't wearing panties. Oh hell. Now his groin was starting to miraculously recover. Stop thinking like that, Cicero, he lectured himself sternly. *Cut that out.*

'Your shoes,' he said, grasping at a straw. 'Strappy sandals aren't good for office attire. And I prefer Mr Cicero, Diana.'

Chapter 14

Diana struggled to keep her cool. 'You prefer to be called *what*?'

'Mr Cicero. This is my company, and I'm the president. I like a formal attitude; it promotes respect.'

The big brute was staring her down. He was deadly serious. Diana wondered angrily if she should go back to Mrs Foxton, but she didn't want to look childish. Blast him!

'If you have a formal office dress code, *Mr Cicero*, you should have told me that before I got into work. Then I could have conformed to it,' she shot back.

Michael suppressed a smile of admiration. She was quick on her feet for a spoiled brat. But he wasn't going to give her her head – Michael was the boss here, and he had guys ten years older than he was reporting to him now. It was vital to maintain control, otherwise things would start slipping. And he didn't like it when things started doing that.

'We do have a formal dress code,' he replied, 'but you're right, we don't have it written up. You can bring a dictation pad into my office after you've made my coffee. And that'll be your first task as my assistant. You'll meet the other people you'll be reporting to later.'

'Other people? I thought I was your assistant,' Diana said, bleakly.

She had the most awful feeling that this job wasn't going to be nearly as much fun as she'd anticipated.

'You're one of them – the most junior, as I said, a Girl

Friday. Susan is my senior assistant, so you'll answer her phones when she's busy, make her coffee, and do whatever filing and photocopying she needs. She'll show you where all of that stuff is.'

'Great,' said Diana, with heavy sarcasm that Michael totally ignored.

'Follow me. I'll show you the kitchen.'

Diana made a face at Cicero's broad back as she teetered behind him towards the kitchen. It was functional like the rest of the space and absolutely tiny. She hadn't seen a kitchen this small since she was sharing a flat with her girlfriends back in London.

'Here's the kettle, the coffee machine, tea, coffee, and cookies. I keep milk and half and half in the fridge, employees can put their personal foods in there too, if they have bagels, or whatever. One of your duties is to keep the kitchen clean and nicely stocked. Our budget is forty dollars a week for everything, so keep within that. Mugs are up here.'

'Where's the dishwasher?' Diana asked, horrified. He was telling her she had to clean up a kitchen?

'There isn't one. You'll do all that yourself. Mostly you won't spend much time in the kitchen, though.'

'Good,' Diana said faintly.

'You'll be too busy filing and typing.'

Diana steadied herself. Was it her imagination, or were her shoes already starting to hurt? She couldn't take much more of this, and the day hadn't even started yet. But Cicero was looking at her – in these heels, he was maybe an inch shorter than she was, but it still felt like he was looking down at her – like he was trying to hide a smile at her dismay, like he expected her to quit any second.

Diana was spoiled and lazy, but she was also extremely stubborn. Her pride made her lift her head as she smoothed down her dress.

'Sounds good.'

'So we'll get to it. Fix me a coffee, and one for yourself, if you want, and then come down to my office at the end of the hall, and we'll make a start.'

'Right,' Diana agreed.

She watched him as he turned sharply on one heel and marched off down the corridor. I hate him, she thought. Resentfully, she switched on the percolator and started to fish around for the filter cups. Thank God Felicity could not see her now. It was all *too* humiliating.

Ernie had invited her over out of curiosity. He dealt with prying industry reporters every day, and he knew veiled insinuations when he heard them. This Felicity woman, a good-looking bird, one of Diana's crowd, he vaguely remembered her. It was weird for a woman to call a man out of the blue, wasn't it? Anyway, Ernie enjoyed gossip. He had closed some good deals from indiscreet tidbits from wives. Who was this Felicity hitched to? He couldn't recall. But Mira had not called this morning – probably disciplining some other guy, the hot little slut – so Ernie had time to muck about.

He had Consuela prepare a lavish breakfast and serve it out on Diana's recently landscaped terrace. He dismissed her, and settled down to wait. You didn't need the servants listening in when business was being discussed. Little bastards might go out and place orders with some online broker and make money off your insider info. Ernie didn't know if Consuela's English was up to that, but he didn't propose to take any chances. He had got rich by following a number of principles, one of which was to never take anything for granted, and another of which was never to trust a soul.

Felicity was ushered onto the roof terrace about forty minutes later, and Ernie was not disappointed. She was a lean little madam, much more in the standard New York style than his Diana, whippet-thin with glossy platinum hair, and a sharp, short dress in cranberry silk matched up with – nice – steep stilettos. They could do some serious damage walking up and down his back. Ernie could almost feel the sharp heels in his skin. His groin stirred mildly. He was intrigued.

'Felicity, nice to see you again. Take a seat.'

Dreadful accent, Felicity thought, sitting down and making sure to leave him a high view of her thighs, grasped at the top by viciously strong hold-ups. She *was* wearing panties, if you could call a see-through Calvin Klein thong panties. What a delicious pad they had here. Quite wasted on an English country lass like little Diana.

'What a stunning garden. Diana really excelled herself,' she cooed as she settled opposite him.

'Yeah, I s'pose she did. Want a juice?'

Ernie lifted the pitcher of squeezed blood oranges and made to pour them for her. He felt slightly adrift; he didn't know quite the right thing to say, the way Di always did. This girl's sharp spikes were in his face, though. He couldn't concentrate. Ernie glanced admiringly at her long talons, blood-red, just like Mira Chen's. Mmmh. Not bad.

'Thank you. I suppose you're wondering why I've come?'

'The thought had crossed my mind. Though it's a pleasure to see you,' Ernie added, as gallantly as he could.

'I hope – I hope you won't think I'm being forward if I asked you to keep what I tell you in the strictest confidence,' Felicity purred.

Ernie perked up. Good, she *was* gonna spill the beans on something valuable.

'Not in the least. I'm very discreet, and I like my friends to be, too. As far as I'm concerned this nice breakfast never happened.'

'I hoped you'd see it like that,' Felicity murmured. 'To be honest, I didn't know who else I should turn to. But I'm rather worried about dear Diana, and I thought you should know what people are saying.'

Ernie's brows knitted together and he leant forward on his wrought-iron seat. 'And what, exactly, are people saying, Felicity?'

Ernie stormed into his office, flinging his coat at a quailing Marcia.

'What's the schedule for today?' he demanded.

'You have Goldman Sachs at ten thirty, lunch with Dom Floyd from—'

'Never mind. Just print it off and bring it in here. With coffee. And hurry up,' Ernie snapped.

'Yes, sir.'

'And get me last month's sales breakdown by region. What are you waiting for?'

Marcia sensed his mood and fled with a muttered apology. Ernie slammed his inner door and flung himself into his dark leather chair, spinning as it swivelled, murderously angry.

Thankfully Felicity had had the sense actually to come to him. What would he have done if she hadn't told him what was going on? Ernie loved gossip; but he absolutely hated gossip that was directed at him. What bloody right did Diana have to go around whining and mouthing off to a bunch of New York tarts like Jodie Goodfriend and Natasha Zuckerman? Their husbands would be laughing at him over lunch at their clubs today. Probably by now the story had gone all round New York. Ernie had no doubt at all that he'd be reading about it in the gossip columns at some stage this week. He looked out of his huge windows at the stone forest of midtown. Full of people who might be reading about him ... discussing him ... *laughing* at him.

Ernie had found it hard going at first, climbing the New York ladder. His social life had been the answer. Diana and Ernie, the new golden couple in town. I'm a good husband, Ernie thought. She spends for England and I never say a word but the first little problem, and she's washing our dirty laundry in some downtown café, making me look ridiculous.

He could just see the headlines. '"Princess" Diana in Marriage Mess!' His lovely façade shattered for no reason. It wasn't like Diana actually enjoyed sex, or that he'd showed her up in public – he'd never taken Mira to any of their habitual restaurants, or squired the bitch to some public function. If Diana felt she'd had a problem, she could have come to him, couldn't she? But noooooo, Ernie thought, angrily, to himself. Not to me, to some clique of witches which is as good as taking out a front-page ad in the *New York Times*.

He swivelled round on his ergonomic chair and sipped his fragrant coffee, served up by Marcia in a Limoges cup. It did nothing to soothe him. What were riches and power if you looked ridiculous?

In five minutes of brooding, Ernie had convinced himself that he was the victim. He was the one who had been played falsely. That silly little cow. Diana was a fucking embarrassment.

He pulled a report on distribution out of his desk drawer and went through it with a yellow magic marker, slashing whole sections and finding extra places where they could lay off workers and boost profits. How this frigging company had survived so long without going under was a mystery to him. It carried so much fat, and for what? For a so-called gilt-edged reputation? The only things he wanted round him gilt-edged were his stocks, Ernie mused. Anyway. Back to the current problem, one more damn thing he had to worry about. He had a PR department here that took care of press problems for him, and it was highly paid and effective. Diana was his at-home PR department, except that she'd now be getting him exactly the kind of attention he spent a fortune avoiding.

Why couldn't she be more understanding? That was the question. Ernie brooded angrily. Marcia came back in with the sales report and he snatched it from her without a word. Who was Diana kidding, exactly? There had been an unspoken agreement between them from day one as to what this marriage was going to be. It wasn't that many girls who were kept in the lap of luxury without ever having to lift a finger, was it? Sex with Diana had been OK at first, but it was boring as hell now. She wasn't a fit match for him.

I work *hard* to keep that little cow in the style of a fucking movie star, Ernie thought. Least I should be entitled to is a little fun. All on the down note, no scandal, nothing.

He thought of Felicity. She was a good mate, that girl. Felt he should be warned, but didn't say a word against Diana. She'd made lots of jokes, like she didn't believe the story Diana dreamed up, but if it was true, who really cared? What had she said? 'A wife does one job, a mistress another. That may seem very European to you, I suppose—' and laughed. Ernie wasn't sure exactly where the Yanks got the idea that in Europe every married man had a mistress and it was socially acceptable – from what he could tell it was exactly the opposite – it was the New York way of doing things. But he liked Felicity's joke, and he agreed with her. Got her head screwed on, that broad. Who was she married to? Couldn't recall. Come to think of it, he didn't recall a wedding ring either. He'd have to look her up. Marcia kept a Rolodex out there with a few choice facts about everybody he knew. That way, if Joe Bloggs called, he could ask about baby Janie Bloggs or his recent fly-fishing vacation in Canada and give a good impression of somebody who actually gave a fuck.

He thought he might give Felicity a little Rolex. Just a thank you. At least he had a chance of containing the damage now. Yesterday night he'd felt bad when Diana asked him about it. Now, wounded, angry, victimised, Ernie burned with indignation. He'd have to have a little heart to heart with her and lay down the law.

'Marcia,' he said, pressing his buzzer to the outer office, 'get me Mira Chen on the phone. See if you can fit in a PR meeting with her about five p.m.'

'Yes, Mr Foxton,' Marcia said, carefully neutral.

Ernie breathed out. It was the best he'd felt all day. And anyway, if Diana didn't like it, it was his way or the highway.

Diana stumbled as she pushed open the door that divided her tiny cubicle from Susan Katz's small, neat office. Oh bugger, bugger! There went another strap. That was a five-hundred-dollar pair of shoes ruined, just ruined! She looked down at the nail of her right forefinger and saw that it was damaged. Chipped! What was the point of finding the best manicurist in town and waiting for weeks on an appointment and then walking around with a chipped nail? She felt like crying. Her mascara had smudged so badly from her perspiration she'd had to wipe it off, her ankles were swollen from all this ridiculous running around, and she was up and down fetching everybody's coffee like some sixteen-year-old waitress.

The phone on her desk trilled annoyingly.

'Just a minute,' Diana called out towards Susan Katz, who had just buzzed her – again. She snatched up the phone. 'Green Eggs, Mr Cicero's office.'

Damn. It was so humiliating, having to say that. Michael Cicero acted like he was Julius Caesar. Of course assistants did do that but not her, not Diana Foxton. Being a working woman was more work than she was used to.

'Diana! Darling, it's me, Claire.'

Diana bit her plump lip as a new blush rocked over her. Oh, man. Claire at least ran her little design business. Now she would know just how lowly a position Diana had taken.

'How are you? I heard you got a new job.'

'If you can call it that.'

'Don't be silly.' Claire chuckled warmly, in a way that reminded Diana of Milla. 'Practically everybody starts out as a secretary. It can lead on to great things, you know. And the top assistants make a lot of money. Josh would be lost without his.'

'Well, it's only temporary.' Just until Ernie starts to miss me. 'I was getting a bit bored,' Diana lied furiously.

'Good for you. I knew you had too many brains to be out there as a professional shopper, like those wretched Miller-girls.'

Diana's fist clenched. She had done just fine as a 'professional shopper'.

'That's so sweet of you, Claire, but I've got to dash. My boss is buzzing me.'

'Take care. And congratulations,' Claire said warmly.

Diana hung up and hurried into Susan's room.

'You buzzed me, Susan?' Diana asked, annoyed. She was in the middle of filing endless vacation rosters. Susan had buzzed her five minutes ago, too. What could be so important?

'Yes,' Susan said, coolly, and with evident enjoyment. Bitch. Bitch! Diana thought, but not out loud, as that loathsome Michael had told her Susan Katz was her immediate boss. More like Catty than Katz. Susan Catty. Kit-Catty, Diana thought. 'I wanted another herbal tea when you're ready.'

'I'm just doing this filing, right now. Why don't you get your own tea?' Diana snapped.

'Do you have a problem you'd like to discuss with Mr Cicero?' Susan asked sweetly.

'No. That's fine.'

'Whenever you're ready then. That'll be all,' Susan said, waving her away dismissively.

Diana glanced at her watch. Could it really only be 2 p.m.? Was it worth it? There had to be some better way to get Ernie's attention.

Chapter 15

Susan watched Diana go and scowled at her departing back. Unbelievable. She had worked for Michael day in, day out, before they got these flash new offices and the sales reps and the commissioning editors, and she had been indispensable. She'd done more than filing and typing: she'd organised his entire life. She'd dressed so carefully, too, and never once protested at the long hours and the total lack of flirtation from him, the handsome bastard. And now this.

Who the hell was Diana Foxton that she should just swan in here? Who ever heard of a twenty-nine-year-old Girl Friday? Susan hated her already. That marvellously sensual shirtdress with the lining – pure silk, of course – beautifully belted, a sort of Forces look, like a feisty World War Two heroine. Did anybody have the right to be so lovely?

Susan didn't kid herself about Diana's beauty. She knew exactly the kind of girl Diana was – not model perfect, because despite the evident amounts of hard cash that had gone into making her skin, teeth and hair as shiny as a prize racehorse's, she would never fit the rail-thin Gwyneth Paltrow ideal of boyish beauty. But the old-fashioned kind of man, the type, in fact, that despite her boyfriend Susan was becoming more and more afraid she really liked – that kind of man would be attracted to Diana like a nail to a magnet.

As a woman considering a rival, Susan watched Diana move down the corridor, stumbling on her silly heels, and assessed her. Great ass. Susan went jogging in the Park for hours and lifted weights with her heels and she would never get a high, tight rounded butt like that. Did Diana have to walk with that wiggle? At least that was probably the heels. And her cheeks and lips! Susan wore neutral make-up, too, but she never managed to make it look like Diana's, like there was just a whisper of colour on her cheeks, like her skin was just naturally, softly glowing . . .

I'd have assumed Michael was fucking her, Susan thought angrily, except that he doesn't screw around in the office, and that now there's that Iris chick – oh yeah, and Lady Diana here is married to the big boss of Blakely's.

Of course, that had to be it. It wasn't that Diana was Michael's latest toy, it was that her husband had given them all this extra cash and clout. Michael was doing some kind of favour for Ernie Foxton.

Susan resented Iris – but there were obvious reasons for that. She didn't really know why she loathed *this* stuck-up little madam so much. At least Diana no longer looked quite as polished, quite as perfect, as she had prior to all the filing Susan had her do. She lifted the neatly printed-off dress code that Diana had written up, pointing out her own violations. Flat shoes. Minimal make-up for female employees. No jewellery other than a watch, signet and marital rings, plus any religious items. Skirt length was to be on or below the knee. Judging from that shirtdress, Mrs Foxton was a fashion plate. There was no question but that she'd quit. Flat shoes? Fat chance.

Susan worked hard and shared an apartment with four other girls, and Diana was doing this job solely to pose and—

The buzzer on her desk sounded.

'Susan, could you bring me in the bookseller reports, please?'

'Coming, Mr Cicero,' she said, her spirits rising.

Diana sat in the file room and brushed angry tears off the end of her nose. No way was she going to let the vile Susan see her like this. Or any of the other people in the office. Jake Harold was the new commissioning editor, and there was Rachel Lilly, the distribution chief, and Felix Custer in business affairs, and Michael. Diana cordially detested all of them; barking orders at her, telling her to do this and do that, no matter what else she was trying to finish. Rachel, Felix and Jake all had assistants and all the assistants were absolutely hateful too. Well. Diana dabbed the end of her sleeve to her eyes and put down her load of filing. Filing was really beastly, nasty stuff; but it would have to wait, because Susan Katz wanted her herbal tea.

The kitchen wasn't empty; Kara and Helen, Jake and Felix's assistants, were in there eating yoghurts and lounging against a wall. They stopped talking as soon as Diana appeared. She pasted a smile on her face.

'How's it going?' Diana murmured.

'Oh, not bad.' She had the definite impression that redheaded Helen had just been talking about her. She did not enjoy that nasty smile that was hovering on the girl's lips. 'We're just discussing . . .'

'. . . the traffic,' Kara said, hastily.

'Oh, it's dreadful. Insane.' Diana tried to be friendly. 'Excuse me, I have to get Susan a herbal tea.'

They drew aside.

'Where do you guys live?'

'East Village.'

'Alphabet City,' they said, exchanging looks. Who did the limey broad think she was? Everybody knew she lived on Central Park West in a place that was bigger than their entire apartment buildings.

'I have to go downtown tonight,' Diana lied manfully. 'We could give you a lift.'

'Your *husband*'s coming to pick you up?' Helen asked. Helen tugged down on the navy Sears suit she'd bought on sale last week. She was thirty-eight, and the chances of finding a suitable man seemed to plummet with every month that went by. She was a new hire to this company, but she didn't like Diana either. Young women who married older men meant older women couldn't find a decent man to save their lives.

'Oh no. Ernie works late usually. No, I'll send for my driver when I'm ready to go.'

Send for my driver? Kara thought. She was still paying off her student loan.

'I think we'll manage,' Helen said dryly.

'Excuse me,' Kara snapped.

Both women turned on their heels and marched out, shooting Diana nasty looks.

Hell, she thought, *what's got into them?*

Tired, exhausted and horribly messy, Diana struggled through her first day. Her cubicle was tiny and window-less, Susan was on her back all day, she had paper cuts on her fingertips and snags in her nails, and the work they did ask her to do was boring in the extreme. Her shoes were broken, her sheer make-up had not survived and she felt wiped out. On top of which, everybody in the office was sneering at her. Sneering! At her!

Diana tried to console herself with the thought that her beauty budget would have eaten up about half Susan's salary, but she felt ugly and heavy and klutzy, and that didn't much help, either. Outside Kara's window, across the hall, light, miserable rain was starting to fall and grey clouds obscured the tops of the skyscrapers. Diana sighed and looked at the clock for the millionth time that afternoon. Only four fifteen. Time must run on a special slow schedule in offices.

Her phone buzzed and she wearily depressed the button.

'Hi, Susan. Herbal tea or coffee?'

'It's not Susan, it's me.'

Just what she needed. Diana bit down on her lip.

'Yes, Mr Cicero.' Ooh, that hurt. Mr Cicero. She wanted to slap him, but that probably wasn't wise. Damn him for offering her this lousy job, and damn him for smirking at her so that she was too proud to quit! 'What can I get you?'

'Nothing. You can get in here. Bring a notepad.'

'OK.' Diana grunted. There was a low chuckle from the phone.

'Careful, you're sounding a little too enthusiastic,' Michael's disembodied voice said.

Diana hung up on him and marched into his office. She shut the door behind her, and the whirring sounds of the Xerox and their constantly ringing fax machine were silenced. Almost involuntarily, she drew in a long, shuddering sigh of breath.

Michael was standing looking out of his window at the wet, crawling traffic marching slowly up Seventh Avenue. Diana regarded the stocky, firm set of his back, the muscles visible even through the newly tailored cloth. He turned round and gave her a broad smile, tilting his head and showing her his busted-up nose.

'I read your dress-code report,' he said. 'Take a seat.'

Diana flopped into the chair in front of him and scowled. 'There's something wrong with the report? I do think, Mr Cicero, you might have said something before now.'

'I only just got around to reading it,' Cicero said flatly. 'I had more important things to get to.'

Of course you did, you patronising jerk, Diana said to herself. 'I see.'

Cicero lifted her two pieces of paper in one large paw and waved it at her. 'I read this. I was quite surprised.'

'It can't have been *that* bad,' Diana protested, angrily.

Hell, Michael thought, look at that girl. He told himself not to start thinking about how a female employee looked. She'd annoyed him when she swanned in this morning looking so gorgeous and polished and disturbing, and now that she seemed to have gone ten rounds with Mike Tyson, she was . . . stunning. Undeniably. And still, so arrogant. The aristocratic, upward tilt of her head, the soft, defiant slight pout of her lips . . . Cicero had an intense desire to crush her to him and kiss all that rebelliousness away.

'It wasn't,' he said, as coldly as he could manage. 'Why don't you let me finish before you interrupt me?'

'I'm sorry, Mr Cicero.'

'It was actually quite well done. I gave you very spare notes and you produced something clear and business-like. You've got a crisp turn of phrase.'

Thanks for the English lesson, Diana thought. 'I'm glad you were pleased. Does this mean I get a promotion?'

She crossed her legs, the wrong way, to hide her busted strap as best she could, and tossed her blond hair behind her shoulders.

'No, it doesn't. You need more than one job done well to get promoted. It might mean that I increase your workload, though. Give you some other basic duties and rosters to type up. Such as guidelines for ordering in office supplies. We don't have an office manager here, so all my executives take care of that stuff themselves.'

'Sounds thrilling,' Diana grunted.

'Don't be sarcastic, please, Diana. Everybody starts at the bottom.'

'I suppose you started at the bottom, did you?' Diana demanded. She knew she should drop it, but somehow her mouth was no longer listening to her brain.

'That depends.' Her boss lolled back in his chair in that confident way of his. His dark eyes on her made her shift in the chair. 'If you call working eighteen-hour days and cycling for miles with two boxes of books, going door to door trying to shift them, starting at the bottom, then yes, I qualify.'

Diana shrugged. She didn't particularly care to hear about Michael Cicero's struggles. Nobody here gives a damn about me, she thought. Why should I care about them?

'Now, take this down. These are our rules about calling in sick, vacation planning and reordering supplies. I'd like you to type them out like you did with the dress code. Maybe you could put together a small folder for everybody with all our separate policies in. It can be your project.'

My, how thrilling, Diana thought. 'What about all my filing and typing?'

'You'll still be doing that. This will be additional.'

Diana pushed herself to her feet, furious, and took a step towards Michael Cicero. To her extreme annoyance, he did nothing but grin.

'You want to quit?' Cicero asked. There was a gently amused note in his voice. 'It's OK, really. This is very basic, very easy work that lots of kids would like to do. I can see why you wouldn't want to persevere. You hardly need the salary.'

'It's got nothing to do with the salary,' Diana said, fuming. 'It's to do with the work.'

'What work? All you have to do is file and answer the phones and make some coffee. You should see the hours Susan Katz put in when she first came to work for me. You maybe think writing up a few reports is too tough?'

'Of course it isn't.' Diana sat down again. 'I wasn't going to quit – Mr Cicero.'

'Then why were you standing up, glaring at me?'

Diana shook her head. 'I was – just stretching. I'm perfectly happy here,' she said, bristling with hostility, 'and I'll be happy to organise all your reports.'

'Good.' Michael looked down at his notepad, which offered some refuge for his eyes, away from the serious double threat of her breasts. 'Then let's get started.'

It was only half four when Diana left the office.

'Do you mind if I leave early, Susan?' she asked. 'My head is splitting. I think I have a migraine coming on.'

Susan Katz smirked. 'Of course not. I'll be here for at least another two hours. If the refrigerator is clean, you can go home now.'

The look on her face said she just couldn't wait to tell Michael about this.

Well, thanks, ma'am. 'See you tomorrow, then,' Diana said, as cheerfully as she could fake. She switched her computer off at the wall and tidied up the papers on her desk, rather than give the bitch any more ammunition. She was so enervated, she could hardly think straight. All she wanted to do was to sink into the limo, go home and get into a spa bath. What madness had possessed her to tell Michael Cicero she didn't want to quit? Oh well. Time enough for that tomorrow. All Diana cared about was getting out of that door.

As the elevator doors hissed shut behind her, Diana felt her spirits lift. Tomorrow she'd quit, and that bunch of catty secretaries could go to hell with their herbal teas and their filing. She would have to find another way to be interesting to Ernie. A vacation, for example. Yes. Right now that sounded really good. Diana poked her head out of the door and saw the familiar, comforting sight of Richard, her driver, with the limo purring sedately at the curbside, waiting for her. As he opened the door for her, muttering something about a pleasant day, Diana felt as though she were shrugging a backpack full of heavy weights from her shoulders. A bath was what she needed. Americans didn't bathe, they showered, but she needed a soak, an hour with a cloud of scented water courtesy of Floris and then a long rub-down with some Shea butter from L'Occitane. Once I've changed for dinner and taken off these shoes which pinch like hell, Diana told herself, firmly, I'll feel more human. She might call Felicity and see if she wanted to do something, maybe catch a last-minute show, like *Rent*, or *Chicago* again. Possibly the answer was just to make an emergency call to Anne-Marie, her French reflexologist, and have her rub her feet for an hour.

Ernie liked to keep a full bar stocked in the back of the car, although he rarely drank during the day. It was just there to impress other CEOs. Right now Diana was grateful for it. She poured herself a Bourbon and Coke and sipped it through the heavy crystal, watching midtown slip noiselessly past her sound-proofed, dark-ened windows.

Eventually she started to relax. The tight coils of pressure in her back began to unwind. It was dark and cold outside, but their building loomed up in front of her, well lit, friendly and welcoming. Her stupid little job suddenly seemed a total joke. She would quit tomorrow, definitely. Let that bitch Susan make her own goddamn coffee.

The doorman blinked at her as she swept into the lobby, giving him an automatic smile. Diana didn't talk to the help much, but she made a point of smiling and being friendly. Ernie tended to ignore them. The heavy, gold-decorated elevator hissed open, and Diana stepped inside and pressed the button for the penthouse, turning her key in the lock.

The apartment was well lit even though Consuela had a half day off. Maybe she had forgotten to switch off the lights. Diana kicked off her shoes, groaning pleasurably in anticipation of her long soak.

Then she froze. There was a voice coming from the bedroom. A woman's voice. Diana knew her staff and her friends, and this wasn't one of them. A prickling burst of adrenaline crackled through her skin. Could it be a burglar? But that was impossible. Security here was outstanding. Even the elevator shaft was wired with alarms. Maybe Consuela had invited one of her friends over while the lady of the house was at work. If so, she would have to deal with it herself. Ernie would fly into a rage. Sighing, Diana slipped her shoes back on and walked quietly over to her bedroom.

It *was* a woman. Tall and much thinner than Diana, almost bony from the back. She was standing bent over in front of Diana's exclusively designed walk-in closet, the small inner sanctum that was just hers, where even her husband and her best friends never came. A tight fist of anger closed around Diana's heart as she noticed what the woman was wearing: one of *her* dresses, a silky, red velvet evening gown by Richard Tyler, cut to drape over her voluptuous curves like a a toga over a Roman goddess. It hung loosely off the bony shoulders of the intruder. With a simmering wash of rage bubbling up inside her, Diana glanced down to the woman's feet. They were poking out of *her* brand new Manolos, the strappy sandals she had so delighted in when she picked them up in his boutique last week. Diana was disgusted now. She would never wear them again, she knew that. Were jobs so easy to come by in America these days that Consuela would do this to a good employer?

Diana found the voice that seemed to have frozen in her throat.

'Excuse me,' she said, loudly and coldly. 'Exactly what do you think you're doing?'

The intruder spun around, mouth open, starting with a little jump.

It was Mira Chen.

Chapter 16

Diana stared down at her. Her brain seemed to be as frozen as her body.

How repulsive. How disgusting. How – how *silly*. Mira Chen. The name had been haunting her suspicious thoughts for days, and now she was here in the flesh. A small part of Diana, a small corner of her brain – the part that said 'you're drunk' when she was – couldn't help but run over the face and figure of her rival. She had hardly noticed her at the last dinner party, there was nothing there but a vague memory of hating the tight, tarty dress the woman had worn.

Diana's red dress hung off Mira like a nasty smell hanging in the air. It was so much too big for her. She felt a sudden pang of insecurity about her body. The extra folds of fabric, peeling back off Mira, seemed like a fresh insult. I should lose a few pounds, Diana admonished herself. No more sour cream and chopped egg yolk with her caviar. She tried to shake herself out of her random thoughts. The fact was that there were only three keys to the elevator. Consuela would not pal around with a woman like Mira Chen, and the second key was sitting tight in Diana's purse.

Ernie had let Mira in. Ernie had let her try on Diana's clothes. Maybe Ernie had given her her own key.

Mira was red-faced, sputtering like a landed fish.

'We didn't think you'd be home,' she muttered, eventually.

Diana steadied herself against the solid oak of her

doorway. There was a rush of blood to her head and her heart. Desperately she tried to pull herself together. We?

'Is Ernie here?' she managed to say.

The door from Ernie's private bathroom swung open and he entered their room. His skinny frame was wet from the shower, and he was wrapped in his navy-blue cashmere bathrobe. *I gave him that for Christmas*, Diana thought.

'You're early,' he said, looking at her stupidly. 'Why are you home?'

'I had a headache.'

She didn't ask him what they were doing. It was painfully, embarrassingly obvious. The girls' voices came back to her. Everybody knew. It was all over town.

She dug deep for a reserve of dignity. How little he must really care about her, to do this to her. Fucking that tramp in her apartment. Letting her try on her clothes. *What other things of mine has she worn?* Diana wondered. *Paraded around in?*

She turned to Mira.

'Get out of my things, and then get out of my apartment.'

The small, compact little body was already struggling out of the dress.

'Hurry up,' Diana said coldly, 'or I'll have to call security.'

She looked at Ernie. He had gone red-faced with embarrassment and now, as he faced her, with spite.

'You can't call security,' he said nastily, 'I asked her here.'

'I realise that.' Diana's voice seemed to be coming from someone else, some other girl located at the far end of a tunnel. 'But I didn't, so if you don't want this all over the front page of the papers I suggest you let me handle it.'

Ernie fell sullenly silent. Tears had started to prickle at the back of Diana's eyes and she fought for better control. She turned on her rival. 'Hurry up, Mira, would you? Hadn't you better get going? I think some of your regulars down on Forty-second Street will be getting impatient.'

She was rather proud of that sally. Maybe not the wittiest, but not bad at the last minute. Diana regarded Mira Chen. She was super-skinny and her hair was broken and tattered at the ends. And this was who her husband had been with all the nights she'd waited up alone?

'Ernie is my only regular,' Mira said smugly.

'Somehow I doubt that. Now get out,' Diana snapped. 'I want to talk to my husband.'

Mira looked over at Ernie as she struggled back into her pants, but he avoided her eyes. 'I'll see you later, honey,' she purred, and swept out past Diana, deliberately joshing past her shoulder.

'Oof.' Diana pinched her nose. 'Next time try to use a little less of that lavatory air freshener you're wearing. You're going to stink up my clothes.'

Mira opened her mouth for a catty comeback, but Diana wasn't having it. 'Get out. Your lap-dancing job is waiting. Plenty of dirty old men in booths want value for their Viagra.'

She shoved Ernie's mistress into the elevator and punched the lobby button, then turned back to her husband. Ernie was busily tightening the robe's soft belt around his skinny little frame. His hair was plastered with sweat. Hell, she thought. She knew she'd never get that image out of her mind. Sexuality was something best avoided, in Diana's opinion, but although she didn't know what turned her on she knew what turned her off. Mira in her clothes? Her stomach was churning. She wanted to vomit.

Weakly, Diana steadied herself on one of the wide sofas. Now that bitch was gone she felt she had nothing holding her up. Central Park swam outside their huge windows, and Diana's knees buckled and she sank onto the leather.

'What the hell do you think you're doing?'

Ernie had righted himself and now he was shouting at her. His plucked brows knitted together and his face was purple. He wiped the sweat off his forehead. 'You came back early. It's your own fault.'

'Oh, right,' Diana said, faintly. 'I see. It's my fault you were unfaithful, fucking some slut in our bedroom?'

'She might be a slut,' Ernie said nastily, 'but at least she *can* fuck.'

Diana breathed in. Time had stopped for her.

'Then that makes one of you, I suppose,' she snapped. She was completely adrift. What was the smart, groomed, pulled-together woman's response to catching her husband in flagrante? Her style was failing her. She had no idea how to act. Those betraying tears were thickening her voice in the back of her throat and squeezing out of the corners of her eyes, no matter how she tried to blink them back.

'I'm a fantastic lover,' Ernie insisted. His voice had gone high-pitched and wavery. '*You're* the one with the problem. Mira says I'm the best she ever had.'

'And how much are you paying her to tell you that?'

'You can talk. You don't exactly come cheap, darlin'.'

'I am your *wife*. I deserve more than this.' Diana sobbed.

'Oh you do?' Ernie's tone was nasty. 'You deserve what, exactly? After going and talking about our personal business to a bunch of slappers that have blabbed it all round town? You couldn't come to me, love, could you? No – you have to make me look like a fucking idiot and have girls ring me up—'

'What girls? Who rang you up?' Diana wept. 'I did come to you, Ernie! And you lied to me!'

'But not until you'd already gone to a bunch of harridans. Let me give it to you straight, girl.' Ernie folded his thin arms and stared at her. 'You aren't made for sex and a man needs that. I thought you'd be discreet. Understanding. If you hadn't shoved your nose in my business you would never have been hurt.'

'You have to give up that whore. I want her fired,' Diana said, trying to ignore the large tear that had splashed off her lashes onto the end of her nose. Thank goodness she'd had to wipe off her mascara earlier. Waterproof never was.

'Well now, that wouldn't be fair. She could bring a sex-harassment suit, too. And she'd win. I don't want to take the chance.'

'At least have her transferred. To another country.'

'No,' Ernie said reflectively, 'I don't think I will. It's not her fault. Maybe I like having her here. Maybe if you were better in bed I wouldn't need her. Anyway, I work fucking hard and you need to deal with me 'ow I am.'

Diana drew herself up to her full height and wiped the tears from her eyes. 'You're going to have to make a decision, Ernie. If you really need a little slut like that, go ahead. But you'll have to choose. Her or me.'

'Don't you try to threaten me,' Ernie screeched at her departing back. 'And don't think I'm moving into a hotel either. I paid for the bloody pad and I'll come home when I feel like it.'

'And when will that be?' Diana demanded, one hand on the door. It was so hard to see with water in your eyes.

'Whenever I fucking feel like it,' Ernie snarled, 'maybe after I'm done with Mira. Tell you what, Di. Don't wait up.'

Diana burst into tears and ran from the room.

She rushed out onto the street and tried to get a cab, but it was rush hour and nothing was free. Diana fought to stop herself dissolving into a messy puddle. No cabs, and now she had to walk down to the Park in her broken, achy high heels. She caught sight of herself in a shop window. Her hair was blown into messy strands, her ankles looked swollen, her eyes were reddened and her make-up had run. Oh please, Diana thought, don't let anybody I know see me now.

A horn was blaring loudly in the traffic. Diana tried to ignore it and moved forwards, tightly gripping her handbag.

The horn blared louder.

'Diana!'

She spun on her heel, and saw Felicity Metson, leaning out of the window of her BMW, looking trim and polished in a new pink hat and shades that reflected the early evening sun. 'Whatever is the matter?'

'Oh, Fee, thank God you're here,' Diana sobbed. She ran forwards into the traffic and Felicity leaned over to unlock the back door.

'Darling, hop in. Whatever can have happened? Were you mugged?'

'Nothing like that. Oh, Felicity, I can't go home,' Diana said weepily. 'Can you take me to your place? Could I stay with you tonight?'

'Of course you can, sweetie. Although I can't think why you would want to.' In the front seat, Felicity's fist curled into a cruel little ball.

Something had obviously happened. Something bad. The perfectly pulled-together Diana was crying in the street. Felicity had been on her way to pay her a visit, ask her out to lunch tomorow, try to dig up some more dirt on their shaking marriage.

Felicity had looked like this the day she found out her husband was gay. It was the face of a woman in the pit. A girl who felt utterly, completely betrayed. And she was going to want Felicity to pick up the pieces.

Terrific, she thought. *I got her*.

The rain had started up again by the time they got downtown. Diana lay curled up on Felicity's uncomfortable leather couch, swathed in an enveloping white towelling robe. She had taken a long, hot bubble bath at her friend's insistence – 'absolutely nothing feels quite so bad after a hot bath, sweetie' – and felt a tiny fraction better. She was still crying, but at least her face was washed, her wretched shoes had been kicked off, and Felicity had provided her with a mug of hot chocolate and a large box of Kleenex. The hot chocolate was fat-free and taste-free, but at least it was warm. Right now, Diana thought, she would take what she could get.

Darling Felicity. What a trouper she was. Diana smiled gratefully at her friend and listened to the rain drumming on the roof.

'I don't want to rush you, darling,' Felicity said, kindly. If you took off all the make-up and the smart dress and towering heels, Diana Foxton looked – well, beautiful. Unfortunately. But she also looked very soft and vulnerable. What had happened? Felicity tucked a straying platinum strand behind her diamond-drop earring and leant forward, trying not to look too much like the vulture she was. 'Tell me whenever you're ready. Or don't tell me at all! Whatever makes you comfortable.'

'It's Ernie.' Diana looked down and reached for another wad of Kleenex. She was bitterly ashamed, but there was no getting past this, and anyway, Felicity was an angel. She'd swooped down and rescued Diana, she'd run a blessed warm bath, she'd fetched slippers and made up her tiny guest room. Diana could trust her. She was divorced herself, she'd understand the pain of a cheating bastard. 'I – I walked in on him.'

'Walked in on him?' Felicity pretended that she didn't

understand, but her whole skin was prickling with thrilling anticipation.

'Yes. He – he was – having sex.'

'With someone else?' Felicity did a good impression of somebody shocked. 'Oh, Diana! I thought you must be wrong about him, at lunch. Who on earth could he prefer to you?'

'Do you know who?' Diana said painfully. 'You won't believe it. Mira Chen. It *was* her. To think, she's been to dinner with us. And there she was, the little hooker—'

'Oh, no. What a tragedy. What on earth did you say?'

Diana sobbed and blew her nose loudly. 'I'll tell you, I'll tell you. Fee, could I possibly stay here? Just for a couple of days? He won't leave the apartment and I can't face going back there.'

'Of course you can.' Felicity reached forward and stroked Diana's damp hair. 'Stay with me, dear, and don't worry about a thing.'

Chapter 17

Diana woke up before her alarm. She glanced at the glowing numerals of Felicity's bedside clock and saw that it was only six fifteen, but she still got up. There was no way she would be able to sleep now.

Felicity had lit a comforting, crackling little fire in her wood-burning stove last night, and now, in the dawn light, it was ashen and cold. The empty bottle of Chardonnay they had shared lay on her eat-in counter-top. Nobody had cleared it away. Diana looked round Felicity's apartment. Decent, above average for Manhat-tan, certainly. But it could not compare to the exquisite life of servants, interior decor and fine furniture Diana had carved out for herself with Ernie. Her husband.

Diana groaned. She felt groggy from the alcohol, and there were small blisters on her feet. Plus, she had no clothes. Unless she wanted the guys at Green Eggs to see her in last night's clothes, there was nothing for it. She'd have to go back home.

She regarded her reflection in Felicity's mirrored kitchen cabinets. There were dark circles under her pretty eyes, and stress and alcohol seemed to have aged her ten years. Panicked, Diana dived for her handbag and retrieved her Gucci sunglasses. They were tinted pink, so that you looked at the world through rose-coloured lenses. Very funny. What was rosy about her life?

Outside, in SoHo, New York was already awake and bustling. Diana watched a Chinese vendor bicycling through the streets, intent on buying the freshest stock at the market stores before his rivals. Manhattan was one big Darwinian experiment, and up until yesterday, she'd welcomed the competition. In her particular pond she'd been one of the biggest fish. Survival of the most stylish. Which nobody could say she wasn't.

The hired-help mafia would, of course, have her now. The doormen had seen Mira enter; Ernie hadn't even had enough respect for her to keep Mira out of their home. It would take about a day for the news to leak up through the ranks of Manhattan society, maybe three before veiled items appeared in the gossip columns. The triumph of her enemies would be bad; the pity of her friends even worse. And, of course, word would reach England. Oh hell.

Diana pressed her neat nails to her throbbing head. There was no help for that. The question was, what would be her most dignified response? Live with Ernie and pretend it never happened? Out of the question, he hadn't even fired Mira Chen yet. Stay here? She glanced back across the neat little oyster-white apartment to Felicity's bedroom. Thank heavens for one good friend, but she couldn't impose and, besides, how humiliating to have to share the details every night of her lousy job and cracking marriage. No, the best thing was to rent a luxurious, fully furnished place with Ernie's money until he came to his senses. Diana allowed her anger to start to build up in her stomach. She would not let him get away with this. Think of the gorgeous fairy-tale wedding that darling Daddy had paid for!

The bustle of the early morning was increasing. I don't want to be seen out like this, Diana thought. She tiptoed back into her room and dialled her chauffeur's number. Luckily, Richard was right there and promised he'd be down to get her in twenty minutes.

She dressed and fixed herself a cup of coffee and tried to concentrate on more important things. What was she going to wear today? Diana was suddenly very grateful to have her shitty little job. It meant that she could hide from Ernie, Consuela and even Felicity. She could make her calls from the office, and maybe Felicity or Natasha would know of a suitable place where she could stay. Then Diana would have Consuela deliver her things, and hey presto, she could glide elegantly, temporarily, out of Ernie's life. Until he came to his senses.

She clenched her fists as she stared out into SoHo. Where was her driver? Quietly, Diana picked up her bag and tiptoed out of Felicity's place, gently shutting the heavy door behind her. The corridor in her friend's building was grey and actually cold, not even heated. Diana shivered. The sooner she resolved this with Ernie, the better. She punched the elevator button; better to wait in the lobby for Richard, avoid any more questions Felicity might want to fire at her. It was too much to have to sit around in dirty clothes. She sighed; Felicity was kind, but she wanted to know *everything*. Of course, that was her way of being supportive, Diana guessed. But she didn't want to dissect every tiny thing in her marriage. She wanted to fix it, and go on as they had before.

She sat down on the functional black leather bench in the lobby and watched the street outside. What would it take to win her back? Mira's exile, a promise never to stray again, and a really substantial present. There was an emerald and diamond necklace with matching earrings at Cartier's, a beautiful set that glittered like drops of the sea set round with stars, African emeralds that were pale green like the shallows of the ocean washing on to a Greek beach.

Diana jumped into the car when it pulled up, giving Richard the kind of frozen nod that told him not to ask any questions. She hadn't worn last night's clothes since she was a teenager. Richard moved the car smoothly through the morning traffic and acted as though he didn't even notice her.

She suddenly had the nasty feeling that he'd done this before. Probably lots of times. Dropping Ernie off, or picking Mira up? Or maybe even another girl?

He held the car door open for her as he pulled into the underground car park. Luckily, all the husbands in the building had already left for Wall Street and none of the wives were up yet. Diana summoned the elevator and managed to tilt up her head and ignore the attendant. How I'm dressed is my business, she thought resolutely.

She stepped off at her floor and went into the apartment. Consuela bustled her plump ass over to open the door and cooed at Diana's exhausted look.

'Meees Foxton, where you been? I was worried . . .'

'Staying with a girlfriend downtown. Nothing to worry about. Is Mr Foxton here?'

The maid shook her head. 'Oh no, he is gone one hour.'

Diana breathed out with relief. At least there would be no more embarrassing scenes this morning. 'Consuela, I am going to visit with a friend of mine for a little while. I want you to pack up my summer clothes and my make-up and shoes and call Mrs Felicity Metson.' She grabbed one of the Mont Blanc pens that Ernie kept piled by the phone and scribbled the number down for her. 'My jewels, too.'

'Yes, senora. You will be here to supervise?'

'No.' Diana checked her watch. 'I'm jumping in the shower, then I have to go to work. If you could bring me some breakfast up to the bedroom?'

'*Si, senora.*' Consuela looked as though Diana was in imminent danger of losing her mind, but she thought the Anglos were mad anyway, and did not argue.

Diana ran upstairs, flung her dress into the dry-cleaning basket, and gratefully jumped in her shower. As she scrubbed and rinsed, she ran her fingers across the embossed gold stars embedded in the metal. She'd miss this place. Hopefully, she wouldn't be away for long. Just enough time to crack the whip on her errant husband.

The hanging clock on the wall outside told her it was seven thirty already. Diana towelled off roughly and blasted the hair dryer at maximum as she searched through her wardrobe. OK, there was a neat green Prada jacket she matched with an on-the-knee Joseph skirt of the same colour and Ralph Lauren black pumps, plus the lightest, sheerest Woolford hose. There was really no time to make up, so she buzzed Richard again and used nothing but coloured moisturiser and neutral gloss.

Diana wanted to be at her job early today. Ernie wouldn't expect her to show up, nor would Cicero. She'd be on time, and she'd show them both.

Consuela opened the door and nearly dropped her tray.

'Meees Foxton! Are you all right?'

Diana had never got ready so fast in the entire time Consuela had known her. Was she visiting a baby? Was someone sick?

Diana nodded and swooped down on the mahogany tray. 'I'm fine, Consuela.' She lifted the crystal flute of orange juice, downed it, and then took the croissant, still in its napkin, and marched out to the lift.

Consuela waited for her to come back, crazy lady. When she did not, the older woman sighed, plopped down on the bed, and started to eat Diana's *pain au chocolat*. Packing was hungry work. There was no point in wasting it. And that coffee smelled too good for a mad Englishwoman to pour away.

Michael looked down at Iris's sleeping form. Her skin was still mottled from the way he had left her earlier, gasping and bucking underneath him. She was responsive, sure, but then Michael thought all women were responsive – once they found the right man.

Thank God she had rolled away out of his arms in her sleep. He couldn't stand to be crowded, but he hadn't wanted to wake her up and tell her that. Sometimes he liked the warmth of her body, when she rubbed that curvy butt up against him and got him hard, and he would nudge up her leg and take her just there like that. Iris had nice breasts, too, surgically enhanced, maybe, but firm and nice. She was skinny, but she refused to eat, although she sure did love to fuck. He remembered the night before, when she'd booked the restaurant and turned up in that short little purple number, the fringed dress, and underneath it, nothing but skin, nothing but her neatly trimmed little bush, already all slick and fired up for him . . .

He glanced over her sleeping form. Her tits stood up like hard melons when she lay on her back, but he didn't knock her for that. The girl took care of herself. A good sign. That dress was slightly cheap, though it had turned him on . . . maybe he could get her some more suitable stuff to wear for eating out.

He swung his thick legs out of bed and walked over to his dressing area. Definitely the worst part about having a girlfriend was that he couldn't bundle her out of the apartment in the mornings. Iris slept the sleep of the dead unless his cock was nudging at her. Maybe she was the perfect woman: she never got in the way.

He bent down and picked up a couple of forty-pound free weights and did a few sets of curls. The blood and lactic acid sang through his biceps and rushed around his skin. He felt the cobwebs lift from his head. Outside, TriBeCa was barely stirring yet. He thought he could shower, shave and get into the office for seven thirty today. It was an important week for the company. He wanted to be able to think.

Ernie Foxton was an obnoxious little limey fuck, Michael thought, then grunted and hefted his iron weights and told himself not to be biased. As long as the business was good, who cared? Let the Blakely's guy muck about in his dandified suits and fake tan. He had provided Michael with an amazing distribution chain, and professional, cheap printing works. Their sales force was eager to go with new products, too. Cicero thought maybe they had the sleekest sales force in the business, possibly because Ernie had upped the quota and was firing the men who didn't produce.

Jean Fellows was the Blakely's head of children's fiction. She was a fat, hairy woman who didn't seem bothered by the sprouting mole on her chin or the dark moustache nestling above her upper lip. Gossip in the publishing world about Jean wasn't too good. Six secretaries had resigned in eight months. But again, she's not my problem, Michael thought.

He had a mission for Green Eggs, and Blakely's was going to help him get to it. Yeah, it was truly aggravating having to go up to the sixteenth floor every Monday morning and give an account of his plan, but what the hell, there was no getting anything for free. Michael was about to execute his first serious line of books. Seth had been working overtime on them and had drafted in a couple of friends, as well. Michael had a line on a guy with a new font that looked like easy-to-read handwriting, and an old woman from Queens, who specialised in intricate initial letters that reminded Michael of the ones he'd seen in medieval manuscripts. He'd investigated paperweights, covers, photographic processes and he'd investigated every aspect of producing a series of stories that would look like nothing kids had seen before – not unless they'd been born around the turn of the century.

He laid down the weights, stretched for a second and jumped in the shower. Five minutes later he was washed and shaved. His suit and notes for the bookseller presentation were lying on the chair. Michael dressed, and debated whether he should stop for a pot of coffee. He thought not, on the whole. The warm scent of it might wake Iris, and he couldn't wait this morning, not even for the wet sensation of her lips sliding up and down his cock. *Stop that, Michael.* He grinned at his reflection and ran a hand across the newly smooth surface of his chin. It would be stubbly again by mid-afternoon, but now he was dapper and ready to go.

He felt the adrenaline in the pit of his stomach. He left the apartment quietly and walked across the street to the subway, hardly seeing all the other commuters as he shoved his way onto the crowded train.

He could no longer think of these books in the way that he'd dreamed them up with Seth, crammed in Seth's tiny walkup studio in Alphabet City, eating pizza and attempting to ignore the roaches, deciding if *Cinderella* was the way to go or whether to choose more out of the way stories, like the *Billy Goats Gruff*, getting blasted on German beer and trying to remember what it was like being a kid.

'People think kids are stupid, is what it is.' Seth was cramming pizza into his mouth and gazing lovingly at a picture of his recently departed boyfriend, which used to freak Cicero out, but he'd got used to it. Seth was unapologetic, and you had to respect that. As long as he didn't kiss any guys in front of Michael. He didn't take tolerance that far. Fuck that.

'Yeah. They do. Kids will pretty much perform as well as you set their expectations.'

'*The Lion King.*' Seth made a face. 'Can't we do any better than that? Barney? Is that what it is?'

'Did you hear,' Michael said seriously, taking the time

to pronounce his letters because the beer wasn't going to affect him, dammit, 'about that school down in Alabama? This new teacher got her classes mixed up, and she thought the remedial string was the advanced string. She ditched all her stuff and started hitting them with Shakespeare.'

'What happened?'

'They all started making As.'

'See? We give kids the early texts. Smart stories. Actual adjectives. Multisyllabic words.'

'What are you, the writer? You just draw the pictures.'

'Scary pictures. Dark forests.'

'Looming mountains. Give me some pizza, you greedy jerk. Monsters. With teeth. Height. Tall castles that look like castles.'

'Not Mickey's Magic Kingdom.'

'We're going to make a fortune.' Michael had grinned.

Now he wasn't thinking about the kids any more. Maybe it made him a bad person, just another greedy suit, but today it was all about the sales. Getting the line out to the booksellers was just the first step. Covers had to be presented, reviewers courted, press obtained, and then there was space. What good did it do him if Barnes & Noble stocked the line if they didn't rack it out front? Getting the thing in the front of the stores where the casually shopping mom would buy it – that was vital.

A new line had a shot, it always had a shot. But if the books didn't make it in the first month, they'd be shoved aside, replaced with the latest cheap horror story for teenagers or *Sweet Valley High* kids soap opera. And his little company would never get another chance; at least, not for years.

He had an opportunity here, Michael thought, and it made his blood pound as he stepped off the train. Midtown was still mostly empty. He could get into his office and practise his presentation. First the Blakely's people needed convincing, then the booksellers and then the public. Life for him was nothing but meetings. His presentation today would really determine Green Eggs' future.

Harry was on reception today. Michael wished him good morning and asked for his keys, but he told him the lady already had them. That was a surprise; Susan was enthusiastic, but he didn't expect her in at this hour.

Michael stepped off the elevator and shoved open the doors to his offices, and stopped dead in his tracks. The shapeliest ass he'd ever seen, swathed in tight, demure, amazingly sexy dark-green cotton, was pointing at him, bent over from a waspish waist. He breathed in sharply and felt an unwelcome tightness in his groin. He knew he should say something, but he was rooted to the spot.

She lifted herself and turned around.

'You're staring at me,' Diana Foxton said.

Chapter 18

Felicity flipped open the note from Diana and read the few brief, gracious lines. Yes, she had definitely gone. She was going to check in at the Paramount tonight, and would find a furnished apartment from there.

Felicity tapped the crisp paper against her bronzed skin. Excitement zipped through her veins. Humming a little tune to herself, she sauntered into her master bathroom and started to prepare herself for the day ahead.

As Felicity washed her golden hair with the rich jasmine-scented conditioner they made up for her specially at Frederick Fekkai, she found it easy to convince herself that she was doing Diana a favour. Ernie Foxton would never change and if Diana was that bothered about a little fucking, a little standard extracurricular activity, well – he wasn't the right man for her. You needed to be open about new things. Diana could stand to lose a few pounds, and fit in with the New York crowd. Felicity stepped out of the shower and blasted her hair with her sleek professional dryer, mentally rehearsing her wardrobe and make-up choices for the important day ahead.

First she'd have to run this entire situation by Natty and Jodie. It was important to spread the word, to put the Foxtons' rocky union out there into the realm of gossip, speculation and nasty items in the press. Ruminatively, Felicity selected a buttercup-yellow pair of slim jersey pants with a knitted, off-the-shoulder silken top.

The sensual fabric poured over her like melted butter, clinging to her thin frame and emphasising her tan. No, Diana wasn't suited to New York society, Felicity decided with a wonderful glow of self-righteousness. Perhaps they did things differently across the pond. Such a fuss about nothing! It was kinder to help both her and Ernie see the light.

There was no denying, she thought as she brushed out her blond hair and finished it with a gleaming spritz, that Diana had made a success of her first months here. But how quickly she'd fallen from grace; being foolish about little, inconsequential Mira Chen, and going to the wives with the news; as well as busting in on Ernie, and then – unbelievably – moving out. Felicity stared approvingly at her fine cheekbones in the mirror as she dusted blusher across them. Why hadn't Diana simply backed out of the room, pretended not to have seen it? No harm done ... She was practically *asking* for somebody to interfere. Perhaps that's what she wanted, subconsciously, Felicity thought. Yes, Dr Modal, Felicity's therapist, would definitely say so.

Felicity wandered into her eat-in kitchen and set her Krups machine to grinding her mocha walnut decaff. She had a small fruit salad, all she would eat, prepared in the fridge. So important to keep the weight under control.

Married barely six months! Why, even in America, how much money would a first wife walk away with? Surely not that much. Of course, there were outrageously good divorce lawyers in New York. But both Foxtons were Brits, even if Ernie did have dual citizenship. Felicity applied her fire-engine-red lipstick with grim purpose, lining and blotting like a pro. Hadn't she read someplace that the English had crazy divorce laws that gave the wife little more than support? She'd need to investigate.

She poured out her coffee and gazed at her reflection in

the long mirrors of her closet. Delightful. She looked fresh, American, a rich Manhattan lady. The kind for whom it was just a sacrilege to be divorced. Felicity had done her time in the horrible outer reaches of society, frozen out of every important party unless a spare woman was needed, sat at the lowest tables at the charity balls, completely left off certain ladies' dinner lists and, finally, placed in Siberia at all the important restaurants.

Felicity shuddered. Never again. She had done penance and learned her lesson, and it seemed as though, miraculously, the universe was offering her a second chance. This time, she would do it right.

Once word got out about Diana Foxton's hysterical behaviour, every unattached twenty-something in town would know that Ernie Foxton was fair game. It was moving fast that would secure her the prize.

She felt a thrill of gratitude towards Diana. By coming to her, the silly little English girl had given Felicity a head start on everybody else, and if her prey got away, it would not be for any lack of trying.

She dialled up Natasha and Jodie and arranged a small, intimate lunch at the Four Seasons. They both accepted right away, which meant they must realise she had some important gossip to share. Next, she dialled Ernie's number, but the machine picked up, so she replaced the receiver. She tried his office, and Marcia told her that Ernie was in a meeting, but would call her back. She left her number, and then paced about the room, eagerly awaiting his call.

Felicity Foxton. It had *such* a ring about it.

'I'm not staring at you.' Cicero recovered his composure. 'I was rather surprised to see you in so early.'

'No need to be.' Diana straightened, and looked at him with icy hauteur. Michael took in how she was dressed, with the schoolgirl black flat penny loafers, and some tight, neat little green suit. Her face had half the cosmetics that were on it yesterday, her hair was swept back, and he couldn't help thinking she was the most stunning creature he had ever laid eyes on. 'You said yesterday I was late. I didn't want that to happen again.'

'I see.' Michael repressed the impulse to scratch his head. 'That's good. Maybe you can brew me a pot of coffee.'

'Already done,' Diana said. The words were polite, but the tone was clipped, sarcastic, almost insulting. Her blue eyes were ice as she looked at him. He guessed she was saying in no uncertain terms that a girl like her was out of his league.

Well, he didn't have time for battles. If she wanted to try to put him down today she was going to need to do better than a cold look. Michael had his own problems, and he didn't have time for Diana's.

'Good. Bring it into my office,' he said, shortly. 'And find me the files on the new line.'

He walked away from her. Outside Green Eggs, sure, she was a big shot and a princess. But in this office she was the recipient of a charity job. Michael felt his good mood evaporating already. If Diana were single, he thought, he would take her out, and crush her to him and kiss her until she was squirming and ready to beg for his phone number, and then he wouldn't give it to her. Well, maybe he'd bang her once or twice. Probably twice. But that would be it. Girls like Diana were high maintenance, and that meant trouble. He didn't need to work at a relationship, Michael thought. He worked hard enough in business hours.

And anyway, Diana was married to that prick, his boss.

He reminded himself he wasn't meant to be thinking about Diana. He was going out with Iris.

Michael flipped on the lights and reached into his desk

for his notes. They were all here, thick sheaves of them, his handwritten scrawl extending over eighteen pages of yellow foolscap. Maybe little miss rich girl out there could type them for him. It gave him something of a kick, to think of those perfect, glossy nails tapping menially on a computer with his work. Yeah. If she wanted a job, let her work for the money.

He lifted the receiver and dialled Seth, who cursed him out with a string of blue epithets that would have done credit to a particularly angry sailor.

'You need to wake up. Get your butt out here,' Michael said firmly. 'I may need back-up, and besides, what if they need to talk to a creative?'

'Is that what I am? A creative?' There was a pitiful groan on the other end of the line. 'It's the middle of the night, and you talk as though I were an advertising executive. I'm not a suit, Mike. You're a suit.'

'It's just one day. Get out here, you lazy bastard.' Michael cupped one hand over the receiver. Diana Foxton had glided into his office with notes and a steaming mug of coffee. His stomach growled slightly. 'Put it down on the table, Diana. So what were you saying?'

Seth continued to protest. Michael didn't know why other people were just not as committed as he was. Diana was still hovering on the edge of his vision, and her waist and legs were intensely distracting. Just because she'd covered them up, didn't mean they weren't distracting.

'Get here by quarter to ten at the latest,' he said, hanging up on his partner. He eyed Diana.

'You brought my notes?'

She nodded and made a brief, clipped gesture to the folder she'd laid on his desk in front of him. The huge sparkler on her left hand caught the light as she waved it. It had probably cost more than his entire apartment.

Michael bristled. 'Then what are you waiting for? Don't you have work to do?'

'Oh, I have plenty of work to do.' Her cool English accent was so confident, so refined. 'But I'm afraid I have to object to your language.'

Michael blinked. 'Excuse me?'

'Certainly, I will excuse you. This time,' Diana said.

'I don't think I follow you,' Michael said coldly. The chick had some set of balls. Rebuking him in his own office, when he ran the damn place. Maybe she thought being Ernie's wife meant she could throw her weight around? If so, he would be happy to disillusion her. He frowned.

'I did not use any language to you.'

She stood her ground, eyeing him, he thought, like he was some drunk bum who was crashing one of her rich-chick dinners. 'Not to me, no. But in front of me. You asked me to dress appropriately for the office, Mr Cicero, and I did. But I would ask you to speak appropriately for the office in front of a lady.'

Michael coloured with annoyance. 'I suppose you are going to sue me for sexual harassment,' he snapped.

She gave a delicate little laugh. A million-dollar laugh. Maybe more.

'I doubt it. I – we – hardly need the money. And that's an American thing. I don't sue, I just handle it.'

Oh you do? Fighting talk, for somebody who did one day's work in her whole life, Michael thought. He inclined his head. 'Very well, Diana. I stand corrected. You can go now.'

'Thank you, Mr Cicero,' Diana said quietly, and left his office, shutting the door gently behind her.

Michael slumped in his chair and drank his coffee and tried to concentrate on his notes. It was very hard. Damn that spoilt society brat. Damn her. He looked at his watch. Hurry up, Susan, he thought, I really need you here.

'She didn't,' Natty Zuckerman breathed.

'Oh, but she did,' Felicity half whispered, with just the right note of affection and concern in her voice. Jodie Goodfriend said nothing, but shook her perfect little blond bob.

They were seated at one of the best tables in the Four Seasons. Felicity's hawk-like gaze had already spotted Barry Diller and David Geffen, the entertainment moguls, and Cindy Crawford with Randy Gerber. The 'Mrs Zuckerman' and 'Mrs Goodfriend' had proved to be key. She could never have been sat at the last minute without them, and, of course, not in a decent section like this, where ladies could see and be seen. The discreet golden rings on the fingers of the older women flashed at Felicity like laurel wreaths of victory. Mrs Ernie Foxton might not have quite the same punching power, but it would be a close thing. Give me six months, Felicity thought, and they'll bump Cindy herself to seat me.

The waiter approached with a little more champagne. Cristal at this place cost the same as a seat on a plane to Europe – if you went coach, of course. Felicity nodded with an imperious air. Her guests were extremely socially secure, and therefore they could drink at lunch if they chose to. Anyway, wasn't champagne supposed to be virtually calorie free? All the supermodels drank it. Felicity couldn't afford business class much these days and, of course, she would never fly coach, but she had splashed out for the champagne and the meal. She had known these women for years, and when she was really Mrs Metson, they had been close. Felicity was desperate to regain her footing.

The soft music and flattering lighting, the small

portions and overdressed plates, soothed Felicity's jangling nerves like nothing else. This was the life she was born for. Would Natty and Jodie support a palace coup? Gently, so gently, she tested the waters.

'I worry about Diana. She took her clothes, and I think she's actually moving out.'

'Tell me more,' Jodie murmured, pushing her curly endive lettuce round the fine china plate.

'Well. This must be in complete confidence, of course. We have Ernie to think of too,' Felicity said, dropping her voice responsibly. 'But Diana barged into the room without knocking, and it seems he was found in a . . . *compromising position*.'

Natty Zuckerman put one hand over her mouth and arched her elegantly plucked brows. 'No! She actually forced her way in?'

'She saw everything too,' Felicity said, affecting sorrow. 'She thinks the staff heard them. Very embarrassing.'

'Very,' Natty agreed, a smidgen too enthusiastically. 'It'll be all round the city by now.'

'You know how people talk,' Jodie agreed. Now she could blab to all her girlfriends and blame the maids and Diana's doorman. It was a terrific story. What a fool Diana Foxton must be. 'And she was so popular, too. The *Post* write-up on her last two parties . . .'

'Yes. "The Queen of New York",' Natty Zuckerman quoted.

Felicity fought to hide her triumphant grin. She couldn't stand these two, and they couldn't stand her, but they were all on the same team. Natasha and Jodie had been giving elegant little parties for years, but neither of them had ever captured the columns in the way 'Princess' Diana had done. They were jealous, and she recognised at once that they shared her desire to see the English girl take a tumble.

'That's what I'm afraid of. For Diana's sake, and, of course, for dear Ernie's. I don't think I can forget that Ernie is a friend too.'

'A good friend,' Jodie nodded.

Natasha speared a piece of her healthy steamed broccoli and looked Felicity square in the eye.

'If you want my confidential advice, my dear,' she said, 'you have a definite duty to talk this all through with Ernie. We can't allow him to be so severely compromised.'

'Where will Diana be staying? Will she be going home?' Jodie Goodfriend enquired.

'I think at a hotel,' Felicity pretended not to know, 'and then a short-term furnished apartment.'

'That's an excellent idea. Space to cool down. Perhaps you could go and have a private talk with Ernie,' Jodie said.

Felicity lifted her champagne flute and sipped reflectively, like the idea had never occurred to her. Natasha gave her a tiny nod. It was the green light. The wives would be on her side, not Diana's, and the English girl would get no warning of what was coming. She almost felt sorry for Diana. Her party was definitely over.

'I'll do that,' she agreed.

Chapter 19

Ernie looked around the packed room and grinned quietly to himself.

Michael Cicero had the booksellers in the palm of his hand. Each successive Green Eggs cover was greeted with warm smiles and nods of approval. They were leaning forward in their seats, like they could hear the cash registers ringing already. You could tell when a buyer was faking it; this was the real thing. That faggot, Seth Green, had a good line when he talked about the creative team of illustrators. The large letters with the complicated patterns – so much crap, in Ernie's honest opinion, but he didn't care about his personal taste. The kids overruled him. Ernie hated kids anyway: they were whiny little brats without anything interesting about them. Except, of course, their ability to nag their parents for books.

The kids' book sector in America was dying fast. Who read any more, when there was Disney and Buffy? Did parents take the time to read stories to kids? No. They stuck them in front of a VCR. If Cicero's Green Eggs could breathe life into the sector, so much the better. They needed a Harry Potter.

Besides, the sellers and distributors weren't looking at Cicero. Ernie's careful PR department had done their highly paid job, and, to them, Michael Cicero was just a kid himself, the 'product manager' on the line. Product managers were very replaceable. To the trade, Ernie Foxton, Wall Street magician, the bottom-line king, had come up with this idea. If it flew, he'd get all the credit. If it tanked, Cicero was there to take the fall.

The presentation finally concluded with huge applause and a rush towards the sales department. Yes! Ernie's skinny fist balled under his desk as he accepted congratulations. Now they had the hard product, the really enjoyable part of his Green Eggs takeover could begin. Ernie hadn't forgotten the way Michael Cicero had made him grovel. He'd been longing for payback. Now his production people had seen the little wop's goods, which he'd been so secretive about in that broom cupboard on the fourth floor, they could duplicate them.

Sell or stiff, either way, Michael Cicero was *out*.

Ernie glanced out of his windows at the crawling traffic on Seventh Avenue and the huge billboards of Broadway. Mira had ridden him well this morning, and Diana was out of his hair, too. Who gave a fuck about her little temper tantrum? It was *good*, he decided, that she'd caught him. That would lay it on the line for her without him having to bother. Cicero, Diana, anybody who annoyed him, from now on was going to be swept out of the way. Glittering Manhattan loved him. What did anybody else matter?

He shook hands with the suits and nodded, friendly like, at Cicero as he bulldozed past him on his way downstairs. He was polite to Ernie, nothing more. Didn't Cicero know he held his future in the palm of his hands? Ernie bristled. He'd teach the cowboy some respect. He glanced across the room and saw Marcia giving him that wary look of hers. It was about time he had her replaced. Transferred, to avoid any kind of a suit. And her replacement could be a younger woman with less of an ass, a thin, hard-looking girl like Mira Chen. Not Mira, though. You had to be wary of the law over here. Besides, Ernie thought, smirking, it was about time somebody other than Mira got a crack of the whip – so to speak. There were a lot of cruel women with stilettos and a taste for thong panties and money on the island of Manhattan.

'Give me the call list, Marcia,' he said, smiling warmly at her, to let her know she wasn't being sacked.

She handed it over deferentially. 'Here, sir. And there was another call for you just now. A Mrs Felicity Metson.'

'Felicity.' Ernie smiled. 'Interesting. Get her back for me, and hold my calls until I've finished talking with her.'

Gossip about Diana? Another warning? Classy tart, Felicity. Just the kind of girl he needed on his side right now.

Maybe she'd know what the hell his wife was doing with herself.

Ernie looked round his outer office. Everybody was doing their jobs, not looking him in the eye. That was fine, though. As long as he made money for this firm, they would be quiet as mice on tranquillisers.

It's good to be king, he thought.

Diana was sitting at her desk, typing, when the phone rang. She'd thrown herself into this shabby little job today. There was nothing else to do, except check on Consuela and leave messages for her girlfriends. Jodie and Natty were not at home, nor were Melissa or Robin, so she'd done the mindless work Susan Katz had given her. Diana was in a bad mood, and not even attempting to make conversation with the other bitches in the office. She got them herbal tea and coffee when they asked for it, then marched back to the file room or her desk. As she moved about the office, typing, filing, working, never wasting a second, they seemed to draw back from her, like they were scared. Diana reflected they probably hadn't heard about her and Ernie yet. They probably thought she was cooking up some elaborate scheme to get them all laid off.

Good. Let them worry. She was busy.

That rude oaf, Michael, had stormed off upstairs with his troops to do his silly presentation. Diana typed out daily meeting schedules and conference notes, spell-checked and printed, faxed, photocopied and carried, until her hands were covered in paper cuts and she had swollen ankles. Now she was taking his messy handwritten office rules and vacation schedules, and turning them into policy documents. It was better than filing, after all. Diana found that she was taking care with this, amazingly enough. It was too bad the way that lout Michael ordered her about, without giving him any ammunition. She didn't want to let Susan Katz triumph over her more than she was already doing.

Her phone buzzed and she picked it up.

'Michael Cicero's office.'

'Darling, is that you?' Felicity gave a little laugh, and Diana twisted in agony on her seat. Oh great. Now Felicity knew she, Diana Foxton, was nothing more than a secretary. In fact she was *reporting* to a secretary. Diana blushed scarlet to the roots of her hair. 'How nice to hear you sounding so businesslike.'

'Oh, it's so much *fun* to work,' Diana managed to say, 'a completely new experience.'

'Yes. Maybe that's what'll turn Ernest around,' Felicity suggested.

'I really don't care whether it does or not,' Diana lied, 'it's very enjoyable. Something I can do for myself.'

'Indeed. It's terrific you've got a hobby,' Felicity purred. 'Anyway, the point is, sweetie, I've been doing some digging, and I have a marvellous little list of furnished places I thought you could use.'

Diana was touched. It was good to have people she could rely on.

'Thanks, Fee,' she said. 'Fax it over.'

For the first week Diana did nothing but check in at the Pierre and enjoy herself. The suite had a phone, a fax, a silver bowl full of freshly cut blazing red roses replaced each morning, and a view of the Park that reminded her of home. She took sauna baths and massages, manicures and pedicures, and managed to feel just a touch more human. All her friends came to visit and offered advice on the reconciliation, which Diana chose to ignore. To be quite honest, she thought, it's bliss being away from Ernie. I'll let him miss me.

The trouble was that the Pierre rang her up at work, and that turned her so-called colleagues into utter tyrants. They so hated the idea of anybody else having any fun. They seemed to violently object to the fact that her chauffeur dropped her at the office and that she went home to her gilded oasis each night. Besides which, Diana told herself, guiltily, as she sipped her fresh almond coffee and gazed out from her balcony over the warm colours in the Park, swathed in her thick white robe, the bill was getting – possibly – perhaps – just a smidgen too rich.

She handed in her work, bought herself a complete new wardrobe for the office on Ernie's card, and reluctantly went apartment hunting.

'But it's all so shabby,' she complained to Felicity. 'No views, no decor . . .'

'It's not that bad, sweetie,' Felicity reminded her, 'you need to show Ernie how well you can make do on your own. And it's only temporary.'

They were in a top-floor apartment near the Flatiron, a one-bedroom snip at three thousand dollars a month. It had red-brick walls, and a plain white bathroom and oak closets.

'It reminds me of a Holiday Inn.' Diana sniffed.

Felicity looked across at Diana and allowed her growing dislike to have a free rein. Nobody had forced the spoilt little prima donna into this wretched, serviceable hovel, suitable for, say, a middle-management wife. Nobody had forced her to leave Ernie's opulent apartment and move here, where there wasn't even a walk-in closet. Diana had made her plain, unimpressive queen-size bed and now she would have to lie in it.

'Well, I'm sure that by now dear Ernie has been calling and begging for a reconciliation. Maybe you should just go home,' Felicity purred.

She sat down delicately on the bed and felt the mattress. It was lumpy. No more interior designers for Diana Foxton. From now on it was Bed, Bath and Beyond, and lucky to be able to afford that. Felicity knew for a fact that their usual crowd had been cutting Diana off. Dinners had turned into lunches, and lunches into quick drinks after work. Well, as she knew, nobody liked to be associated with the stigma of impending divorce. It really was very ugly. And somehow the wives always felt it would be catching, like a nasty bout of Spanish flu.

Men had the power, in the end. Men could always get rid of you and replace you. A woman of a certain age had no friends but her divorce lawyer and her pre-nup. Who else was going to marry her, once she was past thirty-five? There were twenty-eight-year-olds around every unwary corner. So, the wives really couldn't stand a girl who dragged divorce back on to their husband's radar screens. A nice settled life was to be cultivated.

Diana was infected and she was being put into quarantine.

Felicity took careful note as a frown creased Diana's perfect white brow. Of course Ernie hadn't been calling. He'd spent the week closeted with the divorce lawyers she had put him on to.

'He just needs a little more time.' Diana sighed. 'Well, it's ugly and squat, but at least it's clean. I suppose I can put up with it for now. Until he comes to his senses.'

'Absolutely.' Felicity soothed her. She patted her blond hair and told herself that this would make dining-out fodder for years. 'I'll call the Pierre and tell them to send your cases over.'

'But we have to sign the lease, and all that stuff,' Diana said, a bit perplexed.

Felicity waved her bony hand lightly in the air. 'Darling! I already spoke to the leasing agents and you're pre-approved. All you do is write them a cheque for six grand, and you can move in tonight. They even have the phone and electricity already turned on.'

Diana opened her mouth, then shut it again. She didn't know what to say. Felicity had been such a bedrock, but wasn't she moving just a little fast? Surely I can't complain that this is too convenient, Diana thought. I guess she's just a very efficient girl.

'Thanks, Fee. What would I do without you?' She gave her a hug. 'Let me call you tomorrow and we'll have that long brunch on Sunday.'

'Sweetie, I can't wait.' Felicity pressed her sleeve in a very light, detached manner. 'What a bore that I have to run now. We could have organised a little apartment christening with the girls.'

Diana threw up her hands. 'Oh, heavens, no. I think I'd die if any of them saw me like this. Thank the Lord that it's not permanent.'

'Of course it isn't,' said Felicity, gliding out of her door with a smile and a little wave.

Diana sat on her standard-issue armchair, covered in boring beige cotton, and tried to suppress the waves of misgiving washing over her. She felt a pang of loneliness when Fee disappeared, and it seemed she had nobody else to call. Why hadn't Jodie Goodfriend rung her back more than twice? It was too bad having to leave a lot of messages. Really, people weren't very prompt. Mentally she crossed several people off her next dinner-party list. Even Natty had only come to drink with her twice, and then for a mere two glasses of white wine at the Rainbow Room. Hardly worth coming out for. Gosh, Diana thought miserably, I'm at the point where I'm ready to ask Susan Katz if she'd like to go out for tea after work. Not that I even feel like it after eight hours of wretched grunt work. What a failure her job had been. If it was intended to bring Ernie crawling back to her, it hadn't exactly produced results. She'd already have quit if it hadn't been for the sneers of Cicero and her husband.

The phone rang, and Diana jumped half out of her skin. Who could it be? She hadn't given the number out to a soul. She didn't even know the number yet.

'Mrs Foxton? Madam, it's Carlos at the Pierre. I wanted to check the bellhop had the correct address for your cases.'

He read it off in a perfunctory way.

'Yes.' Diana managed to lift her tone, to show how unembarrassed she was by this address. 'It's temporary.'

'I'm sure, ma'am,' Carlos agreed, with the blandness of the terminally uninterested.

Diana's head swam. Hell. Now she was reduced to trying to justify herself to a concierge.

'Just bring them right over,' she told him, and hung up.

To distract herself, Diana went downstairs and wrote the front office a cheque. They gave her her keys, her phone number, and her gym pass. Maybe she'd go for a swim in the building's tiny pool once her clothes arrived.

It was important not to be conquered by this. And I *won't* call Ernie, Diana insisted to herself. I don't care how long it takes him. Let him do the crawling back.

Ernie was showing Sir Angus Carter out just as Felicity

arrived at his apartment. He made the introduction, and watched her venal little eyes light up at the title. Cool as a cucumber she was, though. Nothing like Diana. At dinner last night she'd said she thought most marriages benefited from a little piece on the side. Discretion was what counted. Damn, how he agreed with her.

All this week, Ernie had had to endure the thinly veiled references in the *Post* and *News*, the snaps of his wife leaving the Pierre in those dark glasses, wrapped up like Jackie F***ing O. They'd even run a shot of Mira Chen, a half-nude still from some porno she'd apparently done back in college. Nice, really. He'd had a stab of regret, staring down at those aggressive little tits peeking out of the bondage halter, that he'd had to get the personnel department to terminate her for lying about her criminal record. She'd tried to order him to stop, but Ernie had just laughed at her.

'I don't think so, darlin'. Not this time.' Mira had begged and blubbed, and he knew he'd never be able to crawl to her boots again. 'Now be a good girl, and don't make it hard on yourself. I promise you, one word about me to the press and I'll have the cops up your ass like a twelve-inch dildo.'

'How can you,' Mira whimpered.

'Very easily.' His power gave him a little thrill. Not sex, but better. *There are a hundred replacements for the Miras of this world, but only one of me.* 'Maybe I'll send you a little something, but that's it. Don't even fucking *think* of trying blackmail, because I'll go right to the police. Remember, my whole office already saw what you got.'

'Ernie, I thought we had something good,' she wailed.

'So did I,' he said, and hung up.

He'd waited three days. When she didn't call, he sent her a pair of diamond earrings, anonymously. She could flog them before she got herself a new boyfriend. He felt no guilt. Love was a romantic illusion for suckers. Had that little whore thought she could actually be his wife? His wife wouldn't be the type who sucked cock in another woman's bedroom. Undemanding, presentable and savvy, that was what he wanted in a wife. He glanced across at Felicity. Maybe she could fill Diana's vacancy. She seemed to know the score.

Chapter 20

Felix Custer entered his boss's office with the warm grin of a man who is about to impart some excellent news. He was fifty, and at first he'd baulked at the idea of working for someone nearly half his age. But he'd been laid off by HarperCollins, and most employers in America were so addicted to youth that his age and experience had actually handicapped him. He'd taken what he could get. Cicero was bullheaded, blinkered and sharp as a tack. Now the figures were in, Felix was going to look like a genius. The profits, the reorders, the low overhead from these unbelievably basic offices – the company had the best bottom line he'd seen in years.

This was his first report, and it was going to be a show-stopper.

Custer smiled at his colleagues. It was strange to be on a winning team of people who actually liked each other. The street below them seemed busy and vital, the huge spinning neon news tickers wrapped round the sky-scrapers impressive, futuristic. Before midtown had just stressed him out. He was starting to enjoy it again, like a kid.

Michael Cicero was so determined, it rubbed off on everybody. Even Helen, Felix's flighty assistant, had started to spend less time playing solitaire and more updating his Rolodex. Jake Harold, the commissioning editor, and Rachel Lilly, who coordinated their distribu-tion, also looked smug. No wonder. These numbers would make anybody look smug. Felix's wife had started boasting about his work again.

Everybody was so damn happy in this office, it was like you expected a blonde chick to bust in and start singing about the hills being alive with the sound of music.

There was a rap on the door.

'Come in,' Felix said genially.

It swung open and Diana Foxton marched in. Custer's good mood evaporated around the edges. She was an amazingly pretty girl, but nobody here noticed that. It was like looking at a lotus flower encased in a block of ice. Diana did her job well, if you could call it a job. Nobody spoke to her, because she was rich and cold. She had a 'Do Not Approach' sign emblazoned on her forehead in neon letters. Felix disliked her as much as anybody else in this place, and passed on financial filing to her. She always took it without complaint, briskly and efficiently, and said nothing. It spooked folks, how silent she was. Diana ate lunch at her desk and went home on the dot of 6 p.m.

He couldn't deny she was good, though, she had a way with words. But when Felix took the time to congratulate her, he'd had nothing but a 'Thank you, Mr Custer,' in a tone that would have made an Eskimo freeze up.

'Susan called in sick, so Mr Cicero asked me to take the notes on this meeting,' Diana said.

'Have a seat,' Felix said, coolly. 'Where is Michael?'

'Just taking a call from Ernest Foxton,' she replied, blue eyes looking up at him like she had nothing whatsoever to do with that person. It irritated Felix. She was probably spying on Green Eggs for her husband, and she made out like she'd never even heard of him. 'He'll be right out.'

Diana crossed her legs. They were beautiful pins, strong-calved, slim-ankled, encased in very expensive-looking hose . . . he could tell that by the way they shimmered . . . and they rode all the way up from her crocodile court shoes to her neat, eggshell-blue skirt. She had teamed this with a silky, milky shirt and a matching jacket, as well as a discreet string of pearls round the creamy hollow of her throat. She had a tiny dusting of freckles round her nose, and a full, slightly swollen mouth. Felix decided, clinically, that she was one of the most lovely women he'd ever seen. A trophy wife for Foxton. Surely the rumours of impending divorce could not be true. Where would Ernie get a better-looking arm ornament than that one?

The door swung open again and Michael Cicero strode in. Felix drew himself up. There was something about Michael that made you sit up straight and focus. He had the air of a battlefield commander about him. Whenever thoughts of his age crept back to Custer, Cicero's bulldozing manner made him forget about them again. There was simply no time to worry about his age. Michael kept the whole team too busy for that.

'I hear good things,' Michael said. No preamble, of course. He wasn't good on the niceties. 'I'll get to your reports individually. But give me a summary first. What's the picture?'

'I'll go first,' Rachel said, with a sidelong nasty glance at Diana. The women here had taken against her worse than the men. Rachel was a pretty girl, too, mid-thirties with neat blond hair, but she was nothing to look at. Maybe Diana didn't understand just how off-putting that whole ice-queen thing was to men. 'Our sellers are fighting them off in the Mom and Pop stores, and Barnes & Noble, B. Dalton and Waldenbooks have all racked us out by the sales register. We're just trying to ensure even distribution round the country – to be fair. I've been taking a lot of international calls, but we'll need a much bigger print run to cope with that demand.'

'The press loves us,' Jacob Harold said, jumping in, not to be outdone. 'I even got a slot on *Good Morning America* for Ernie Foxton.'

Michael nodded. 'Excellent, but why wasn't that given to me? It's our line.'

A shadow of confusion passed over Jake's face. 'You know I work the PR side with the Blakely's people, Michael. They told me you had turned it down.'

Cicero paused. 'Maybe I did.' His large frame shifted on the chair, like he was thinking hard about something. He shook himself slightly and turned to Felix. 'How are we looking, chief?'

'Pretty good.' Custer heard his voice light up with pleasure. 'You and I decided to keep the executive staff compact and multifunctional, and to cut down drastically on our projected overhead budget—'

'You mean we only hired a handful of people and we chose simple offices,' Michael said.

'Exactly. Combine that with the success of the first printing of the series, and what Jacob tells me about lack of returns, and I'd say the first quarterly profit margin is—'

Felix smiled warmly and gave out the figure.

'Wow,' Rachel said, rather endearingly.

Michael blinked. 'Are you sure?'

'I checked the figures several times. They depend on certain variables—'

'You're sure, right?'

'Yes,' Felix said, grinning. 'I'm sure.'

'Am I right in saying', Jake asked, loosening his collar, 'that that level of profitability means we will receive that bonus promised in the contract?'

'That's correct. Two hundred and fifty thousand apiece,' Felix said, almost licking his lips.

'Before you start drooling, let's go through the reports,' Michael said, dryly. 'We still have work to do.'

*

Sixteen floors above him, in his glass and chrome palatial offices, Ernie Foxton was also discussing their figures.

'Beautiful.' Jean Fellows was turning the Green Eggs *Cinderella* over in her hands, but she wasn't talking about the thick, glossy paper or the delicate watercolour pictures. Her eyes were on the sales figures projected onto the wall in front of them by Peter Davits. 'I never saw sales like it in children's fiction. It's because of the illustrators.'

'And you got the names and addresses?' Ernie Foxton demanded.

Fellows turned her fleshy neck towards the president of the company. 'Yes, just as you said, Mr Foxton. I took the names and addresses and signed them all to new individual contracts with Blakely's. Exclusive contracts, with a no-compete clause. For one year.'

Ernie rubbed his hands. 'Terrific. That'll shut the little fuckers up.'

He beamed at his own deviousness. No-compete clauses were normally put in the employment contracts of film presidents and engineers, but why not use them for scribblers and paint splashers, too? It meant that if they refused to work for Blakely's, they couldn't draw for anybody else – for example, a new firm that Cicero might be tempted to set up, once he figured out what was happening to him. The only job they would have would be to sling hash in some fast-food joint. Ernie was learning about the so-called artistic temperament. Seth Green didn't understand what he'd signed, but that was his problem. He would draw for Blakely's, or he wouldn't draw at all. To a guy like Seth, revolting little faggot, that'd be unbearable. Same for all the other kids Cicero had recruited.

'You spoke to the booksellers? Amazon and the other online people?'

'Of course,' Janet Jensen said, primly. 'They don't care

about our office politics. They just want to know that the line will continue. They all saw you on TV, Mr Foxton. They give you the credit.'

'And so they should,' Ernie said shamelessly. 'It's a Blakely's line, and I run Blakely's.'

'Very well, too,' Janet said, giving him an oily smile. Ernie didn't mind. What the fuck? It was true.

Tonight he would call Jane Grenouille at her firm and prep her on how to deliver the bad news. He had such a nice surprise planned. Of course, Diana would be getting it in the rear twice, which was more than she'd ever gotten from him. Frigid bitch. Felicity was right. He was well shot of her.

Ernie's thoughts drifted away from victory to the new maid Felicity had hired to tend to his personal stuff. She was neat, compact and Eurasian, with milky skin and slanted eyes. She wore stiletto heels four inches high around his apartment and tight little black dresses over her boyish body. He loved thinking about the insults which would pour out of her cruel little mouth, given half a chance. Felicity made herself scarce three nights out of five. She did what she was told, except in the bedroom where she was demanding and raked his skin with her nails. He could get it up for her, no problem. She ate next to nothing, and she sucked him with such enthusiasm and leapt to his touch which she directed. It was a pleasure to eat out her neatly trimmed little pussy. Sometimes she even braided the small strip of pussy hair she had left and affixed little bows to it. In public, of course, you'd never know. Last night he'd taken her out for the first time, and he'd enjoyed the stares of the crowd.

Felicity reminded him that the whole of New York would be watching to see how he handled Diana. The way they watch my business, Ernie thought. But that's OK. Let them watch, I'm going to show them how it's done.

'Great meeting, everybody.' His tone told them to get the fuck out. He buzzed Emma, Marcia's replacement. 'Emma, get me Sir Angus Carter on the phone. Right now.'

Michael did something he never did, and gave everybody the rest of the day off. Helen and Kara whooped, gathered up their bags, and were out of there in under two minutes. His executives were more restrained but, still, they didn't exactly protest. It was 78 degrees and sunny outside, and they could get back to their homes before the rush hour, and eat watermelon on their sundecks, and think about the sweet two hundred and fifty K they'd get for riding along with him.

He pretty much wanted out, too, today. He loved his job, but it wasn't every day you found out you were about to become an instant millionaire. His dad had been in tears when he rang him and told him. Right now, Michael reflected, he wanted head from Iris, a bottle of chilled Taittinger rosé champagne, and . . . he'd figure out the rest later.

He was just finishing up with Diana Foxton. He resisted telling her to thank Ernie for him. He'd *earned* this golden-handshake bonus, he thought. They were making money because Blakely's was making even more money. That was what he had to bear in mind.

Diana was handing him the last set of letters that needed his signature. She seemed remarkably unexcited about today's news, but then again, why should she care? It wasn't like one pre-tax million dollars would rock her world, exactly.

'Nearly done here.' He nodded at her. 'I expect Susan will be back tomorrow. You did a good job today, though. Now you can take the rest of the day off to go shopping.'

She looked at him coldly. 'How do you know what I'm going to do with my day?'

'I just assumed—'

Diana gave a clipped little laugh. 'Of course. Doesn't everybody? But I'd rather you didn't.'

Cicero ignored the snub. 'What will you use your time for, then?'

Diana blinked. Was somebody actually asking her a personal question? Everybody in this bloody place had been ignoring her for weeks, much like her supposed girlfriends who'd been blanking her *en masse*. Diana was too savvy a social operator to ignore the signs any more. Obviously, it had to do with the separation. Why, she couldn't imagine. Ernie was a liability socially. She had shown these New York witches how the game was played, and now the jealous bitches were taking this opportunity to snub her.

'Museums, actually.' She'd been planning on going shopping, sure, but why let Cicero think he had her all figured out? A wave of bitterness washed over her. She smoothed the pale-blue silk around her knees. Why the hell didn't Ernie call her? He must be going crazy without her. Some nights it took all she had to stop herself picking up the phone.

'Really? There's a nice exhibition at the Met, I heard.'

'There are several,' Diana snapped at him. Arrogant jerk. She so objected to being thought a moron. She wasn't a little bimbo like Helen or Kara. 'I'm planning on taking in the St Francis of Assisi exhibition. They have some very important medieval works on loan from Italy since the earthquakes destroyed the church there.'

Michael arched one of his thick brows. His chest was very broad as he leant over her, scribbling his signature on the letters. Despite herself, Diana felt a sudden, surprising shock of desire. It had been so long since a man had touched her. Ah, but remember, honey, she told herself, you get all worked up, then he takes you to bed, and it's nothing but frustration.

Of course, that had been with Ernie. Diana thought about the way all the businesswomen who visited this office flirted so shamelessly with Michael. It was probably just their perception of his power.

Susan Katz, that kitty cat, definitely wanted him. Definitely. Diana was savagely glad that he had a woman. She couldn't stand Susan and her bullying ways.

It was a mystery why all these girls would chase a man like Michael, a man without money or position.

Diana breathed in the scent of his body. No cologne, nothing but a very faint, mannish musk. She held herself in, to stop herself squirming. It would be insufferable for this macho pig to get any idea she thought twice about him.

He gave her a sidelong glance out of those dark, thick-lashed eyes.

'I didn't know you knew anything about art,' Cicero said.

'Oh, I don't. But I know what I like.'

Michael grinned. Diana Foxton, the art critic. On a whim, he pulled out two sketches from his desk drawer: mock covers for the second wave of Green Eggs books.

'What do you think of these two?'

Diana tilted her head, and plain gold stud earrings caught the light. Michael wondered idly what it would be like to take his thumb and stroke it along the soft ridge on the side of her neck.

'This is much better.' She pointed to the left-hand drawing, one of Seth's. 'It's realistic. The other elephant looks like a stuffed toy.'

'Interesting. What about this and this?'

He put down two more pictures. Diana leant forward and pointed to the right one. 'This one uses colour more subtly. I prefer the line detail.'

184

Cicero was surprised. That was just what he thought. He pulled out his book of thumbnail sketches. 'Which of these would you use to cover the *Seven Little Tailors*?'

Diana sat down, unconsciously pushing him out of the way. She had forgotten how much she disliked her boss and was lost in the pictures, blocking out everything else. Michael bent over her. He could see the tops of her breasts, just subtly revealed through the open neck of her silk blouse. Instantly, his cock stiffened.

It's the headiness of the day, he told himself. I need Iris. I need to get laid.

'This one.' She flipped the page, and showed him a small image, black-and-white pencil only. He'd never noticed that one before. Sometimes you could go crazy looking at hundreds of different cover ideas. 'If it was coloured, maybe a watercolour. Look at the lines, the detailing. It almost leaps out at you.'

Cicero examined the picture closer, and was shocked. It was perfect. Exactly right for his book. He'd missed it because it wasn't a finished image, it was black-and-white.

It was better than the one he'd chosen. Better than the ones Jacob and Seth had chosen, and she'd picked it out, right away.

'You know, I think you might be right,' he said, slowly.

'Of course I'm right.' God, how cold she was. 'It's the obvious choice.'

'Come in earlier tomorrow,' Michael said. 'I may have some more work for you.'

Diana's back tensed up. He grinned as he saw the aggravation writ large on her pretty face. He fantasised briefly about sliding that skirt up over the curves of her butt, bending her forwards over his desk, and gently palming her until she was begging him to stick it in her.

'I don't think I can be asked to handle anything more,' Diana said. 'I work hard enough as it is.'

Cicero handed her the letters and gave her an amazingly annoying wink. 'Yeah, well, I don't think so. Be in tomorrow at eight.'

Chapter 21

'As far as I can see, Mrs Metson is correct.'

Ernie smiled at Sir Angus Carter. He had that plummy aristocratic English voice that Ernie, the barrow-boy, always detested. Fucking snobs. Diana was from that same snob-ridden class. But he couldn't fault the words that were coming out of Sir Angus's mouth, even if the sound of them was grating.

Sir Angus shuffled his papers. 'Mrs Foxton has no case whatever in the United Kingdom. She has only been married for seven months, one of which was spent outside the marital home by her decision. She left without word and made no attempt to contact you, Mr Foxton. Irreconcilable differences . . . whatever you would like. No judge in the United Kingdom would, in my opinion, award her a penny.'

'She has recently taken a job, too,' Felicity chimed in. Her arm snaked through Ernie's; her blood-red nails rested on his sleeve. She wore a pair of thin, arching high heels and a tight pink dress.

'Indeed.' Sir Angus pushed thin wire-rimmed spectacles up the bridge of his aquiline nose. 'Which means she will find it hard to claim that Mr Foxton was intending to support her.'

'I've taken a few preliminary steps myself,' Ernie said. 'I've put all her stuff together in boxes, and I transferred all but ten thousand dollars from the joint account. Didn't want to close it. Thought we'd be subtle.'

Subtle, Sir Angus thought. Subtle? This moneyed oik in

front of him was about as subtle as a neon orange ball gown. If Diana Foxton could not be commended on her pre-marital fiscal arrangements, she could be roundly condemned on her taste in men. She would lose millions in this divorce. Personally, he thought it would be a small price to pay to rid oneself of Mr Ernest Foxton.

'Hmm. I think that is wise. Mrs Foxton has only one power in this situation. She can contest, and delay, the divorce.'

The American she-hawk with the talons paled. 'For how long?'

'For five years,' Sir Angus said gravely.

'Unacceptable.' Felicity jumped to her feet. 'There has to be *something* we can do.'

'There is. You can make her an offer. Any lawyer she consults will tell her of her financial position.'

'What about immigration? If she's not Ernie's wife, she doesn't have the right to stay here, does she?'

'Immigration is not my field, madam. I suppose it might be another thing you could threaten her with.'

Ernie rose, feeling magnanimous. 'Draw up an offer, Angus—'

The lawyer stiffened. He'd worked hard for that knighthood.

'– and tell her that I'll give her two fifty, American, if she signs the papers, and if she delays over a year, absolutely nothing.' Ernie ignored the pallor of Felicity, beside him. 'Tell her I can wait her out. We all can.'

As annoying as Michael Cicero was, Diana felt it was her duty to pop down to the Metropolitan and view the exhibition in case he gave her some snotty test tomorrow morning, and she actually enjoyed it. The colour and richness of the nine-hundred-year-old paintings still had the power to amaze and delight. She was moved to go down to St Patrick's and look at the Catholic cathedral. It was very soothing: the candles glowing, the people kneeling at their devotions, or standing head bowed in front of fine carved statues of the saints. She felt her soul calmed to the extent that she left, walked to Barnes & Noble on Fifth and bought a novel instead of diving into Saks for some retail therapy. It was ironic, really: the Temple of God next to the Temple of Mammon.

Diana had a sudden desire to be on her own, coupled with a ravenous hunger. She dived into a Friday's which was right next door. It was ideal; absolutely nobody she knew would be seen dead in here. She ordered a greasy cheeseburger and fries, and ate it with a large chocolate milkshake while she read her trashy novel. In fact, for a couple of hours she was able to forget Cicero's demands, Ernie's silence, and her friends' treachery. She pulled her hair out of its snug chignon, and sat reading and people-watching, savouring each crispy peppered fry and sip of creamy chocolate.

She took a cab home, and determined to wash her hair, dress, and go out. Maybe she'd call Felicity, the only one who was still talking to her. This was meant to be the city that never slept. There had to be a million fun things for a young woman with money to do.

Almost as soon as she walked through the door, the phone rang. Diana half jumped out of her skin; the phone never rang in her apartment these days. She had gone from the queen of the city to a Trappist monk in one fell swoop. She picked it up, her heart racing. Maybe, at last, Ernie had seen the light.

'Hello?' a soft voice said. 'Diana?'

She felt an intense stab of disappointment. It wasn't her husband, it wasn't even Natasha or Jodie. It was only Claire Bryant.

'Hi, Claire,' she replied.

'Diana, where have you been?' Her friend sounded cross, which was unlike her. 'When you go to ground, you really go to ground. I've spent weeks trying to find you. In the end I had to ring Felicity Metson, and pry it out of her.'

Diana felt slightly guilty. Why hadn't she called Claire? It was true that Claire had made her feel foolish for thinking of work as the ultimate four-letter word, but Claire had always been there for her, when they talked. Her other so-called friends had bailed out when her husband did, except Felicity, of course. But Claire had actually made the effort to find her.

'To be honest, I wanted to be on my own for a little while. Ernie and I are having some . . . slight troubles.'

'Slight troubles? I heard it was worse than that.' Claire paused. 'Look, can I give you some totally unwanted advice?'

Diana sat down on her bed. 'Go ahead.'

'You have to see a lawyer and you have to go home. If he's cheating, who knows what the girlfriend is trying to get out of him? Why should you be living in a cramped one-bedroom apartment when you are the wife? Go and see him, don't stand on your pride. And get a good lawyer, just in case.'

A lawyer!

'I'm sure it won't come to that,' Diana protested. 'Ernie just needs to see he can't treat me this way. When he asks me home, I'll come.'

'I hope it won't, but you can't leave it all up to him. Look, take this number down. These are my lawyers, and they're very good.'

'But I thought everything was great between you and Josh.'

'It is, but I was in the Girl Scouts. Be prepared, you know. And keep in touch. I'm here for you.'

Diana hung up and was brushing her hair, thoughtfully, up to its normal state of glossy suppleness when the bell rang.

She opened the door.

'Ms Diana Foxton?' Steve Santuro asked.

He blinked once or twice. Steve served papers all day long – divorce papers, court summonses, notices telling people they were being sued. America was the litigation capital of the world, and Manhattan was the litigation capital of America. Steve made a great living, so he put up with the oaths and curses, the drunken husbands getting nailed for child support, the fat wives getting the elbow. But he'd never served papers on a chick like this.

She was wearing a simple pink cotton dress with little puffy peasant sleeves, and a scoop-neck that revealed high, lovely collarbones and golden skin. She had a thick gold bangle round one wrist, high slides in her hair, long legs, and curves that would make a blind man see. Goddamn, Santuro thought. Her hair was blond and shiny and it looked like it came straight out of a shampoo ad. Any second he expected her to toss it from side to side for the cameras. Her breasts in that thing! Steve felt himself bead with a light sweat. They were soft and fighting to get out of that little blouse. They even looked natural. What woman these days actually stuck with her own tits?

'Mrs Ernest Foxton,' the vision corrected him.

Ernest Foxton was a damn fool, whoever he was, Steve thought. Perhaps he was gay. Letting go of a peach like this? What a sexy accent, too. He loved the way those Brit chicks spoke.

'Uh. Yeah. Mrs Foxton, right.' Steve blushed and wanted to get out of there. 'I, like, have a delivery for you. Could you sign?'

'Of course,' she said. She smiled with bright white teeth and carefully wrote her name on his board. 'What is it? Flowers?'

'No ma'am. I'm afraid not.' Steve went the colour of a ripe tomato. 'It's some legal stuff.'

He thrust the papers forwards awkwardly.

Diana didn't understand. She took the papers and flipped them over. She read the lettering on top. Carter & Carter, Solicitors, Grays' Inn, London. What the hell was this?

'What is this about?' she demanded imperiously.

The spotty little delivery boy cringed and mumbled something about it all being in there.

'Have a good evening, ma'am,' he said, and bolted.

The cab plunged and weaved through the New York traffic like a swallow, ducking in and out of lanes, running lights, blasting the horn. Diana sat in the back, oblivious to the noise and the crowd of people. She was furious to the point where she could see nothing but her white-hot anger. Who the hell did Ernie think he was, exactly? Divorce? Divorce *her*, after seven months? As if she had done something wrong, when he was the one fucking that little hooker in his office in front of everybody. She had been the *perfect* wife and this was how he repaid her. She was Diana Foxton, and she was not the kind of girl you could use up and throw away like a rag doll!

The joint account had nearly a million dollars in it. First thing tomorrow, she would go straight to Tiffany's and buy herself some *serious* jewellery. It was the least Ernie could do. All this time she had been waiting for his apology, to put this unpleasantness behind her, and instead, he'd been doing – this!

He had the gall to offer her a lousy quarter of a million dollars? He was worth ten times that much! He sat in the apartment Diana had selected, in the rooms Diana had designed, on the couch Diana had dug out at great expense and effort, and he offered her peanuts for a quickie divorce?

I'll show him, she thought, curling her small fist. I'll show him what he can expect from a woman like me.

The cab screeched to a halt outside her apartment building. What a blessed relief it was to be pulling up to home, to a decent address! Her so-called friends had never been afraid to visit her *here*. When she'd finished with Ernie, she'd start with them. Diana had visions of the wonderful parties she would throw for a *completely* new set, from which Natasha and Jodie and that bunch of hags would most definitely be excluded.

She threw a twenty down on the seat in front and told the psychotic cabby to keep the change. He didn't argue; Americans never thought there was such a thing as too much money. The cab disappeared in a screech of rubber, and Diana strode into the lobby, ignoring the deferential crawling of the doorman and receptionist, and rode the elevator all the way up to their penthouse. The attendant opened his mouth a couple of times, but closed it again after she shot him a look. Good. She really couldn't be bothered with the opinions of the little people right now.

The doors hissed open and Diana marched out into her stone-floored lobby. There was the sound of low, murmuring voices. Ernie obviously had guests. Well, too damn bad. If ever there was an excuse for a scene, this was it.

She brushed aside the greetings of Consuela and Paula and marched into the drawing room.

Ernie was sitting there, with his arm draped over Felicity Metson.

He looked up.

'What are you doing in my apartment?' he said.

Michael moved a large paw through the air, grabbing at Iris. Her breasts were bouncing in that way he loved. Wedged deep inside her, he thrust to the rhythm of his blood. He was muscular and covered with sweat, the way he always got when he fucked. Her ass was resting up against his knees, it was too bony for him, but she wasn't bad. She liked to reach behind him and cup his balls feather-light with those soft fingers as she rode him. Her blond hair moved over her face and trailed across her tits. She was grinding at him energetically, but she kept talking, which aggravated him. He found it hard to get off when she was distracting him like this.

'A – million – dollars,' Iris grunted. 'Oh! Oh! And I bet it's just the beginning, too.'

Michael plunged back and forth, angling his cock in the way she loved. 'Shut up, honey.'

'You're a genius,' Iris breathed. Her skin was mottling, and he saw her nipples all purple and full with blood. 'I always knew you wouldn't stay poor. I knew you weren't a loser.'

Some part of his brain registered her talking, but it was nothing to worry about now. His whole world was the sweet thickness of her wet pussy clamping around him, in and out, involuntarily gripping him. 'Just shut up, OK? Shut up.'

'But – it's – so *exciting*,' Iris babbled. 'A millionaire!'

Michael growled low in his throat. If she wouldn't shut up, he would shut her up. He lifted her up by her scrawny hipbones, and tilted her slim body backwards on his knees, thrusting his cock deep inside her. Yes, he could feel the nubby head of it against the wall of her, that yielding, melting spot which turned any woman crazy. She groaned and tried to buck away from him. Often at first, the sensation was so strong they couldn't take it. Mercilessly he held her in position, and shut his eyes, and thrust and thrust, and now she was gasping and sobbing and shuddering on top of him. He felt her pulse, her groin muscles in spasm around him, contracting in and out, in and out, violently, as he milked her. His orgasm started and he felt his balls shrink small and tighten with the pressure, and ruthlessly he kept at it even as she subsided. His world exploded and the release came, so that he wasn't even aware of her or her cries, or anything other than the tightness and pleasure of his cock pumping into her.

Michael breathed in, hard, and came out of his stupor. The white-hot pleasure of riding Iris dissipated like mist on a bathroom mirror now he was done. He lifted her gently and rolled across the bed.

She was gasping and whimpering. 'Oh, Michael, that was incredible. That was so incredible.'

He eyed her. She wasn't so groomed now, she was reddened and perspiring, and her hair was plastered to her angular face. He saw his thumbs had left small white marks around her waist. Her nipples were still up and full, pointing out at him like angry missiles.

'What did you mean that I wasn't a loser?' he asked, softly.

She shrugged, breathing heavily. 'What I said. I had faith in you. I knew you would make money, that you wouldn't stay a loser, living in this dump, you know, no car.'

Michael looked at her expressionlessly. 'And what if I hadn't gotten that bonus?'

Iris stood up and stretched her heated, slender body. Now he was denuded of his lust, Michael considered her more critically. She needed to eat more, for sure, and do some squats. She needed a bigger butt. It was annoying to have all those sharp angles digging into him when he was trying to fuck her.

Iris padded across the room and reached for a large towel, wrapping herself daintily up in it, like he hadn't seen everything she had to offer from every angle.

'Really.' She drew a hand through her hair, tugging it back. 'Why make problems where they don't exist? I make way more than you do, but I knew that wouldn't

195

last.' She moved towards the bathroom. She didn't like anybody to see her looking less than perfect. 'The point is, you did make this bonus, and you're going places, so we don't really have any problems.'

Smiling coyly, she blew him a kiss and tiptoed into the bathroom. Iris tiptoed all over the apartment when her shoes were off. Michael assumed that for her it represented nature's high heels. She was a high-maintenance girl, all the way down the line. They didn't really have any problems, huh? Think again, baby. He stood wearily and thought about the mechanics of dumping yet another girlfriend. Another gold-digger. Did a girl think it was attractive to be told you were now acceptable because you'd made a million bucks? Were all girls like this? He was drained from sex, too tired to think about it now. Iris would shower, then he would shower and fall straight into bed. Tomorrow night they would have their talk. He was going places, but it would be without her.

Michael lay on his futon and regarded the high towers of Wall Street right outside his window. The moon was rising in the sky, and so was he. Tomorrow he would go to Ernie Foxton and take delivery of the cheques for himself and his staff.

He was a millionaire. He had made it. It was one of the sweetest moments of his life.

Chapter 22

The alarm buzzed in her ear. Diana reached out and hit it with one weary hand. She'd been awake for hours. There was too much to think about for her to get any sleep, and she had to be into the office at eight this morning.

She lifted herself out of her lumpy bed and looked at the grey, muggy dawn that was breaking over Manhattan. Uptown, up high in her penthouse, where the air was clearer and the Park was green in the sunshine, that two-faced bitch Felicity Metson was sleeping in her bed, with her husband. Diana groaned. Oh, she must have looked ridiculous last night, standing there dumb as a rock, her mouth open like a dying flounder on the beach.

She beat herself up for her stupidity. When her other friends had melted away like the San Francisco morning mist, she had counted on Felicity. She should have known something was up. Diana looked around her clean, functional, soulless apartment with loathing. Fee had wanted her in here and out of Central Park West ASAP – to keep the coast clear for herself.

Claire had been right about the scheming mistress. Only the mistress in question wasn't Mira Chen. It was her best friend.

'Of *course* I was your friend, darling.' The image of Felicity, smiling smugly like a crocodile about to swallow a fish, swum back into her mind. 'I was your friend *and* Ernie's friend, too. You made such a ridiculous fuss and a spectacle of him. Clearly he wasn't the right man for you.

I'm just helping you get closure on the process *you* started.'

'I started it? I fucked Mira Chen?'

'It wasn't only Mira.' Oh, the satisfied look on Ernie's face as he'd come out with that one. 'You knew the score when you married me, you stuck-up cow. You're so frigid, you forced me into it.'

Diana had stood and gazed from one to the other. She imagined Felicity laughing, giving a blow by blow account to Natasha, Jodie and the others. Probably she had been doing that all along. She imagined the married women, sitting on the best banquettes at the Russian Tea Room, talking about Mira and Ernie, and the scene at the apartment, and her low-class living quarters, and laughing, their champagne flutes clinking. She couldn't move. It was like being in one of those nightmares where her feet were stuck to the ground with superglue.

'You bastard,' she whispered.

Ernie gave a braying laugh. 'You bastard,' he mimicked. 'Is that the best you can do, love? You've seen my offer, have you? Our lawyer says you haven't got a prayer. Check it out; we've been together barely seven months, and *you* walked out.'

'Because you were cheating,' Diana said. Her tongue seemed stuck in her throat. 'I'll sue, here in America. You won't have a dime left.'

Ernie laughed at her. It was amazing, Diana thought, how she'd managed to blind herself. She'd thought he loved her. 'I don't think so, babes. I've filed for divorce in England, and you took a job over here, you moved out, no phone call, nothing. By the way, don't bother trying to empty the joint account. I've already done it.'

'What?' she gasped. She steadied herself on the ottoman sofa that she'd scouted out after months of trying at the Amsterdam fine antiques fair last year.

Ernie waved one thin hand condescendingly at her.

'Don't worry. You got ten grand left in there. Can't see my ex-wife on the streets. People might talk. Should tide you over. Plus two fifty for being a good girl.'

'But I'm your *wife*,' Diana said. She blinked back the tears, she so badly wanted not to cry in front of Felicity, that smug, aggravating bitch, but she had no choice.

'Not for long,' Ernie said, smirking.

Diana had howled in misery and stumbled back into the lobby. As she stepped into the elevator, the sound of barely muted giggling from Felicity had reached her, rising up like the hideous bubbling of a cauldron. She had ridden down to the lobby with tears streaming down her face, and the elevator attendant had been reduced to studying his shoes very carefully, making her, Diana, as invisible as a lurching drunk on a bus.

Mercifully the cabby who had taken her home – she had no wish to be told by Richard he couldn't drive her any more – didn't ask any questions, either. This was New York, and misery was common. People minded their own business here.

Diana shook her head, to get rid of the memories. This was real. This utter nightmare, it was real. She had checked last night, and this morning she couldn't even afford her rent for more than a couple of months. Ernie was determined to cast her off, to make a beggar of her. She was suddenly, pathetically grateful for the grinding routine of her job.

Determined to make the best of it, Diana regarded her tired reflection in the mirror. She was a pro at beauty. She had time to take care of those dark shadows, to wash her hair, to put on her best stuff, to douse herself with her bottle of Joy – the most expensive scent in the world. No matter how bad things got, she still had her beauty.

I always relied on it, Diana told herself, and I still can now.

*

Diana turned up at the office at five to eight. She was wearing one of her sexiest business suits, a camel cotton, tailored suit with a sharply cut jacket that emphasised the flare of her breasts and bottom, and the dainty narrowness of her waist. Her face was a muted, glowing palette of berry and bronze colour, the concealers had erased the shadows, and she wore her hair up, neatly, in a French chignon. Defiantly, her engagement and wedding rings still glittered on her left hand. A fragrant cloud of scent hung about her, if you dared to get close enough. The sheerest Woolford hose and butterscotch Patrick Cox courts completed the look.

She'd relished every whistle and whoop even as she pretended to ignore them. Male validation, Diana told herself, its what I need right now.

Her mood had improved. At twelve thirty today, she had a meeting with Herb, the best, hardest divorce lawyer in Manhattan. Hearing the name Foxton, the assistant had instantly cleared a time slot for her. She'd show Ernie where he could stick his two hundred and fifty grand. If he was left without a cent, it wouldn't be her fault.

Meanwhile, she had to deal with Michael.

Her boss was already waiting for her. Diana took in the dark suit, the black shoes, the thickly muscled chest. Cicero looked the same as he always did. She felt a small, fresh surge of nervous adrenaline. What the hell kind of hoop was he going to have her jump through this morning? More work? Like she needed that right now.

'I'm here,' she said, bluntly.

Cicero looked her over. What a gorgeous creature she was. He mentally peeled off the light cotton from those stupendous breasts and that grade-A ass. She annoyed him, the way she was so effortlessly perfect every second of the day. How he'd love to slide that tight skirt up over the creamy rounds of her butt, push her over his desk, and trace his name with the tip of his tongue across the freckled valley of her breasts. He thought he could have those nipples hard and dark as sea-washed pebbles in twenty seconds. He imagined her losing her composure, that glossy hair sweaty and tangled as it fell across his chest, the flat stomach bucking against him, her elegant fingers clutching at him as she wriggled about under him . . .

Michael made himself look up. He was glad these pants had a roomy cut. He mustn't allow this girl to cause him any loss of control. Besides which, she was married. She was fully off-limits.

He'd bet she'd squirm like an eel, though.

'So I see.' His voice was remarkably businesslike and calm. 'I've got some more work I'd like to try you out on.'

'I think I have all the work I can handle.'

'That's for me to decide,' Michael told her, bluntly. 'I want you to look over some more pictures and designs.'

'What for?' Diana tossed back her gleaming dark hair. He thought about catching it, and wadding it in her mouth while he roped her hands and feet together and played with her until she was lifting her body up to him, helplessly. 'You don't file pictures. Don't tell me you want to start filing all the pictures as well.'

He grinned down at her. It was the most cocky, annoying grin imaginable.

'What are you going to do – stamp your foot?' he asked.

Diana's face darkened. 'I'm not in the mood.'

'Too bad, if I am,' Cicero said.

He twisted the key in the lock of the door. It was quaint, the way these offices opened with a key. Upstairs it was all codes and passwords. Diana noted how Cicero hated overheads. What a contrast to her husband's – was he still her husband? – yen for luxury. How much was the private jet, the two choppers, the monthly flights out to Atlantic City and the golf-club schmoozing for the super-agents and star writers costing his shareholders? Plenty, but Ernie didn't care about OPM, other people's money. Only his own, from which he'd almost completely cut her off.

There was a heavy tread on the stairs. She turned to see a besuited man coming towards them. She recognised him, it was Reggie Shropton, one of Ernie's in-house lawyers.

'Hello, Reggie,' Diana said politely.

A faint spot of red rose to the pallid centre of his cheeks and he didn't look up. He was clutching two sets of papers.

'Hello, Mrs Foxton.' She blinked; it used to be Diana. 'Mr Cicero. I am afraid I have some papers for you.'

Cicero reached out and grabbed them. 'Papers already? Starting early this morning, huh?'

'In a manner of speaking.' He lifted his head and stared at Michael with fishy eyes. 'I'll have to ask you to give me that key.'

'Excuse me?' Cicero snapped.

'These are termination papers for yourself and Mrs Foxton. Every other employee at Green Eggs has been served. The company is withdrawing its stake and closing down the operation at this time. As per your contract, a month's salary is enclosed in lieu of notice.'

For a second Michael said nothing. He was trying to process the information, and it didn't compute.

'I suppose it would be far too much to hope that you're joking.'

'I never joke,' Reggie said thinly.

'Apparently somebody at Blakely's does, though. I have a contract.'

'With a company consolidation clause, valid for the first eight months, that invalidates further obligations on the part of Blakely's, including office space, overheads, health plans – and bonuses,' Reggie said. There was a nasty glitter in his eye.

Diana recognised it. It was a favourite look of Ernie's. Her heart dropped. Her job had evaporated. As little as it had been, it was all she had.

'I'll have to ask you both to leave. I hope you can do so quietly and not force me to call security,' the lawyer said.

'That won't be necessary,' Diana said quietly. She nodded to Cicero. 'We're leaving. You can tell my husband he will be hearing from my lawyer later today.'

'And mine,' Michael Cicero added. His thick, bull-like neck was red with anger.

'Certainly,' Reggie Shropton said, in a tone that implied he really didn't care.

They walked out together. It was a nasty experience. Holding on to the severance forms, they passed several Blakely's staff as the elevator spat them out into the lobby. Janet Jensen was one; she gave a nasty little snigger as Diana brushed past her.

Michael Cicero said absolutely nothing to her, but she could feel the anger prickling out of his skin, like the static on a balloon. Wordlessly, he took her arm and shepherded her across Seventh Avenue. He was silent until they got to Broadway and Fifty-first. Then he yanked his hand from her elbow and glared down into her eyes.

'What the hell is going on here?'

'How would I know?' Diana asked, angrily brushing her hair back. 'Don't look at me as if I had something to do with this.'

Cicero gave a short bark of laughter. 'Man, that's a good one. You little English girls can sound so sweet and innocent when you feel like it. It's almost as if I didn't know you were married to that weak little jerk on the sixteenth floor.'

Diana bit back the retort. Doubtless her divorce would be all over the papers tomorrow, but until that happened, he didn't need to know everything. The sun sparkled on the glass of the skyscrapers and over the billboards advertising the Broadway shows. She was standing on the sidewalk, but she felt unbalanced, almost like she was dreaming. The whole situation was surreal.

'I didn't know a thing about this,' she said, ice cold. 'I'm not privy to everything Ernie does. I got fired, too.'

'Bullshit.'

'Do you mind not using that language?' she said, primly.

He stared at her, like she was from another planet. 'You know what, lady? I do mind. Funny, huh? A man works all his life to start a company. Nights. Days. Sleeps on the floor. Gets something good out there. Turns down other deals. Takes this one – and gets shut down, overnight, by – what? A blackguard? A bounder? I prefer to say asshole. I think it's more accurate.'

'I worked hard enough at that company. If you didn't cover yourself legally it's not my fault.'

'Right.' Michael's dark eyes drilled into her. He was so bestial, so ferocious. A million miles away from Ernie's thin, spiteful little body. 'You worked, sure – like Marie Antoinette playing at being a milkmaid. Now what? You whistle up your chauffeur and go back to your Central Park penthouse.'

'That's not fair,' Diana said, sullenly.

'The hell it's not. You want to know why you were so disliked by the girls in the office?'

'Not particularly.'

'Well, I'll tell you anyway. You talked to them about a drink after work and dropping them off where they live.

They barely make rent; you're boasting about your chauffeur-driven limo.'

Diana flushed. 'I wasn't boasting. I was offering them a ride.'

'How many office dogsbodies do you think get driven to work, Diana?'

'Dogsbody,' Diana snarled, 'right. That's what I was to you. A dog. Somebody you enjoyed kicking around just because she had a bit more money and a bit more class than the rest of you. Nothing but shabby jealousy. I made an effort for your wretched little company.'

'Wretched, huh? Is that what you told your husband when you ran upstairs with your spy's report?'

Diana was enraged. 'I didn't spy on you. Why don't you stop blaming other people for your problems and look in the mirror. Or better still, stop whining and do something about it.'

What a bitch she was, Michael thought. Beautiful, but such a bitch.

'That's a great idea. I'm going to see my lawyer.'

'Me too,' Diana said. 'Goodbye, Mr Cicero.'

She turned on her heel and walked away from him.

Chapter 23

'You did what?'

Herb Brillstein, the lawyer Claire recommended, stared at her in horror. The chair she was sitting in, expensive dark-green leather though it was, suddenly seemed very uncomfortable. Diana shifted in her seat. She glanced out over Fifth Avenue, looking serene and calm from the eighteenth-floor offices of Brillstein, Brooks, the most savage divorce lawyers in Manhattan. When she rang, they had fallen over themselves to get her into their offices. Ernest Foxton's wife. But during her introductory session with the head of the firm, Diana felt the temperature drop several degrees every minute.

'You departed from the marital home? Voluntarily? And you haven't contacted your husband in weeks? And you weren't working, but you took paid employment?'

'That's right.' Diana blushed. 'I just didn't want to be around him.'

'So you let *him* move into a hotel. You haven't been married long, Mrs Foxton, less than a year. Your position is very weak. You need to move back into your home immediately. How long were you dating before you married?'

'Two years,' Diana muttered.

'Maybe we can work with that. But you must go home, Mrs Foxton. At once.'

Diana left the office feeling rather dazed. The lawyer made it all sound so simple, but she hadn't thought that way. 'Take possession of the marital home.' She hadn't expected divorce; only for Ernie to see the error he had made and to come crawling back to her. Diana shivered in the thin winter sun. Was her mistake going to be fatal? Reconciliation was not a possibility. Not with Felicity's laugh still haunting her nights. She didn't want to go home, and the immigration lawyer had said that she could stay as her marriage to an American citizen was made in good faith. The dinner parties, written up in the New York tabloids, proved that. But now she had lost even the shitty little job she had. She wondered how much her lawyer would charge per hour, and winced. Offices like his carried a lot of overhead. Yes, it was imperative to get a decent wad of cash out of Ernie. If she had to bite the bullet and live with him for a few months, so be it.

Diana had no illusions. Ernie had fired Michael Cicero like he had fired many men before him. But he knew that she was working in that office too. The firing had been a deliberate insult.

She was going to have a fight on her hands.

She had no idea how big a fight.

Her cab pulled up outside their building on Central Park West, and Diana stepped out carefully, trying to avoid getting salt stains from the icy slush on her Ralph Lauren brogues. She had selected her outfit with care; a dark Donna Karan dress with a Hermes bag, simple and classic. She was carefully made up, and her blond hair was secured in a neat chignon. So far the press had not got wind of the separation, of her firing, but if a snapper was there, Diana wanted to be ready for them. She considered removing her sunglasses from her bag, but decided against it. It might look to Ernie as though she wanted to hide red-rimmed eyes, and Diana was not prepared to show weakness.

She stepped through the door and made for the elevator.

'Excuse me, madam.' It was the deep Texas twang of Brad, the security guard. He approached her, blushing slightly, and hung his head. 'Do you have an appointment?'

'Of course not. I live here.'

Brad's flush deepened. 'I'm afraid you'll need an appointment to see Mr Foxton, ma'am.'

Diana's brow arched delicately.

'You know me, Bradley. I'm Diana Foxton. Mrs Foxton.' She unsnapped her bag, letting her engagement ring sparkle in the light, and fished out her keys. 'See? I live in the penthouse. I can show myself up.'

'I'm sorry, ma'am. The apartment is only in your husband's name. He's informed the building management not to let you up.'

Diana breathed in sharply. A bolt of anger and fear surged through her.

'You might want to give me those keys,' Brad suggested, taking a step towards her.

Diana drew herself up and stopped him dead in his tracks with a single, icy glance.

'Don't even think about touching me unless you *and* your company want to be sued for assault. I'm keeping these keys.'

'Yes, ma'am.' The guard stepped back instantly. 'But you'll find they won't work any more. Mr Foxton asked us to let you know, if you turned up, that he had the locks changed.'

She shook her head. 'Very well; I'll be back with a warrant.'

'Yes, ma'am,' Brad said, politely and implacably.

She went back to her rental place and called Herb Brillstein.

'Damn. You never should have moved out.'

'Well, I did,' Diana snapped. 'How do we fix this?'

'I need to take him to court. We'll retain you on a no-win no-fee basis, so don't be concerned about that.'

'If you win, how much is your fee?' she asked.

'Fifty per cent,' he said. 'In the meantime, you'll need to live on whatever budget you can. Please keep records of everything.'

'I'll be sure to,' Diana said, faintly.

She hung up.

Diana looked around her with disbelief.

The rental apartment was small and cramped. Instead of antique furniture and delicate oriental rugs, the decor seemed to be right out of Ikea. Red-brick walls decorated with black-and-white posters of babies and tall house-plants in terracotta pots. There was a small television, and a kitchenette – she wouldn't call it a kitchen – with a microwave, a fridge and precious little else. When she said, 'Where's the dishwasher?' Rita, her potential room-mate, just laughed.

Her bedroom – the one the letting agent had boasted about – looked out over a gas station on Tenth Avenue. It was cramped and contained a single bed, in functional pine with a white cotton coverlet.

'I like the bedspread,' Diana lied. 'Where did you get it?'

Her prospective landlady examined her Lee Press-on nails and said, 'K-Mart. Half price, in the sale.'

'That's great,' Diana said weakly. 'A bargain.'

'*Si*, bargain. Like thees apartment.' Another quick once-over of her nails. 'Only thousand a month, one month deposit payable in advance.'

Diana almost crumpled with embarrassment, but she knew she had to do this. 'A thousand is too much. Nine hundred is all I can manage.'

Rita looked up from her nails and fixed her heavy-lidded eyes on Diana. 'I got three other people who want the place. For thousand.'

'Yes, but they're flaky. I'm quiet, and responsible.'

Rita considered. 'Eef you will clean up whole flat, each week, I say nine hundred. I like English people. Very clean. I like also clean.'

Diana swallowed. She glanced round the train wreck of the living room: empty Domino's pizza cartons, beer cans, make-up towelettes and two overflowing ashtrays. There were probably cockroaches. Then she thought of the bad news her lawyer had delivered: she had little or no case. Her best hope was to refuse to grant a divorce, and hope that Felicity was so desperate for a ring that she would get Ernie to up his settlement.

At any rate, she had no money, and this was at least a Manhattan apartment with her own bedroom and a working washing machine.

Diana was just too proud to go crawling back to England, or take charity from Claire. 'That's a deal,' she said.

Diana moved three cases of clothes into her bedroom. She had no room for the rest of them. She had to pay to put most of her stuff into storage, another expense she could barely afford. After she'd unpacked, taking everything meticulously out of its tissue-paper wrapping, she had four suits, five dresses, six shirts, four pairs of pants, and only four pairs of shoes. It was heartbreaking.

'So many clothes!' gasped Rita, eyeing her suspiciously. Nobody with such clothes should live in a place like this. They must be knockoffs, or else the English girl had stolen them. 'I never seen such nice things.'

'Thank you.' Diana forced down the retorts that came to mind. Her snobbery would have to take a back seat. She needed this place.

'Yes, well. I show you clean stuff. Come.'

Diana followed Rita's ample bottom into the kitchen where a filthy bucket containing a mop, a brush and a dirty washcloth was shoved under the exposed sink.

'I don' have Roach motel,' Rita commiserated. 'We need get new one. Anyway, I leave now. You clean.'

She picked up some ugly-looking candles with pictures of angels on them and squeezed out of the door in a waft of cheap perfume and cigarette smoke.

You can do this, Diana told herself, swallowing down the lump of tears that threatened to rise in her throat. Sure, it's shaming to be cleaning up filth on my own, but I live here. It's either that or live in a dump like this.

For five hours she scrubbed and swept and washed filthy dishes. She collected three bags full of garbage, and struggled down six flights of stairs to the groaning dumpster at the back of the building. The tiny Hoover sucked up so much dirt that the burgundy carpet turned out to be bright magenta. Diana tied a towel over her nose and mouth, and beat the rugs out of the window while clouds of dust billowed up, choking the pigeons.

It took her for ever, but when she was done, the tiny apartment was clean. Under the piles of rubbish she'd discovered a tatty leather couch and one armchair. The floors were hardwood, maybe she could persuade Rita to throw out the revolting rug. Even the air seemed cleaner and fresher now that she had sucked out so much filth. She threw out some of the ugliest plants, certain her new room-mate would never notice. Exhausted, Diana peeled off her dirty jeans and T-shirt and crept to the shower room to rinse herself off. There was no bath, of course. That was a luxury she was going to have to live without.

Shattered, exhausted, miserable, Diana slunk back into her tiny, hot little bedroom, stretched out on the coverlet, and shut her eyes. She was asleep when her head hit the pillow.

*

She rang nobody. What would she say? 'I'm living in Hell's Kitchen, I've been fired from my job and my marriage, and I clean to make part of my rent?' No, it was too humiliating. She'd get herself a new job, Diana decided. She had youth, class and a certain notoriety. Maybe she couldn't afford the best restaurants and the charity lunches any more, but she wasn't going to let that beat her. She was Diana Foxton – still – and she had a brain.

Saying little to Rita, Diana swallowed her pride and went back to every magazine that would see her. Every place she went she heard the same story.

'We need current experience.'

'We're looking for younger girls.'

'We have no vacancies at this time,' the sickly sweet *Vogue* personnel officer assured her, 'but we'll be sure to check back with you when something turns up.'

She tried other places. Even publishing houses. She got little for her trouble but blisters and stares. Wasn't that the ex-wife of Ernie Foxton? Diana sat there and sweated out the horrors of the interviews, the snide comments, the pointed questions. Working for a swiftly shut subsidiary of Ernie's didn't seem to count for anything.

'Yes, well. It wasn't *real* work, Ms Foxton.' The people at HarperCollins were polite enough, but the woman here was telling her the same story. 'The company receives hundreds of applications each month from college students and other qualified personnel who've formerly worked here.'

'I see.' Diana gazed despairingly into her lap. She had eaten humble pie for weeks now, and what good had it done her? Maybe she should give in and take Ernie's paltry cheque. Maybe she should crawl back to London with her tail between her legs. The curse of *Hello!* strikes again.

'Can I make a suggestion?'

The polished young woman across the desk was giving her the first kind smile she'd seen in days.

'Sure.' Diana shrugged. 'I'll listen to anything at this point.'

'You need contacts,' she said. 'Some friend that'll give you a job. Because nobody else is going to hire you.'

Diana managed to make it three blocks away before the tears started. The lump rose up in her throat, like a betrayal. Every morning she got up, washed her hair and made up with costly cosmetics that she wouldn't be able to replace when they ran out.

It got harder and harder to keep her head high.

None of her former friends would talk to her. Natasha seemed always to be out when she called. She'd left four unreturned messages for Jodie and five for Laura before the nasty truth sank in. She was a pariah, and none of them wanted anything to do with her. Except Claire, of course. Claire had always told her she could get a job on her own. Somehow going to Claire and begging for help would be worst of all.

She refused to call Ernie. Partly out of pride, partly because she wasn't sure he'd take her call. Diana imagined being put off by his secretary. 'I'm sorry, Mrs Foxton, he's not available. Can I take a message?'

She shook her head. It would never come to that. Nor was she going to run back to Daddy. What a laugh Felicity Metson would have over that.

There was a Starbuck's on the corner of Fortieth and Park. Diana ducked into it and ordered herself a large cup of black coffee with a sweet shot of Amaretto. She took it to a corner table in the shadows, and decided to consider her options. If there were any.

Papers for the customers hung on wooden racks. Absently, Diana lifted the *News*, and stared in horror at Rush and Molloy. Her own face, beautiful, sorrowful, was staring out at her from the grimy newsprint. She was looking exhausted and was entering a subway station.

Next to it was a snap of Felicity, wearing a long Calvin Klein evening gown – how conventional, Diana thought – dressed up with a diamond necklace and long drop earrings. Enough ice to sink the *Titanic*. Ernie, in a ridiculous tuxedo and cummerbund, was at her side. They were attending the super-prestigious New York Literary Lions bash – one of the charities, Diana remembered, feeling sick, that she'd been asked to chair. OUT WITH THE OLD, IN WITH THE NEW, read the headline.

> *Nobody can say Ernie Foxton doesn't practice what he preaches. The slash-and-burn downsizing in his company obviously extends to his marriage. Former society queen 'Lady' Diana is now taking out her subway tokens, while new Fox flame Felicity M. sparkles brighter than the fourth of July. Diana's reportedly scrabbling for a job, too. We say good luck to her. If you can make it here, you can make it anywhere!*

Oh my God, Diana thought.

'Are you OK, hon?'

The waitress was hovering with her refill. 'You look kinda pale.'

'I'm fine.' To prove it, Diana sipped at her sweet coffee. 'Thank you.'

'If you're sure,' the woman said, melting away.

Tears of shame and humiliation prickled in Diana's blue eyes, but she forced them back. No way was she about to break apart in public, and no way was she going home. There was a bubbling knot of anger in her stomach. Goddamn Felicity! She visualised Felicity laughing at her with the other girls. Her small fist curled into a defiant ball on the table.

I *will* get a job, Diana vowed, even if I have to wait tables.

What had all those women said?

No experience. No references.

Diana looked out across Park Avenue, at the rich society matrons and the dog walkers, the doormen standing outside co-op buildings, several of which she had reviewed and rejected. That was her world; not this! She flipped through the paper, barely seeing any of the headlines. It was something to keep her from breaking down in public. The English were all about the stiff upper lip.

Suddenly she stopped. In the business section, which she never read, there was a tiny headline, tucked away in the bottom left-hand corner of the page. AFTER THE EGGS . . . THE BACON.

> *Which young entrepreneur – for all of five minutes – is starting again? In the same East Village digs he busted out of barely a month ago? Ah well . . . easy come, easy go, Michael. We hope East Eleventh isn't too much of a drop from the multinational midtown tower . . .*

Her heart jumped. It was him. It had to be him.

Diana's fingers curled round her coffee cup. Michael Cicero had done nothing but be rude, crude and obnoxious to her. Was she desperate enough to go asking for his help?

A breeze ruffled the edges of the paper, flicking it back to the picture of her. Once again, Felicity's diamonds glittered mockingly up at her from the black-and-white ink.

She picked up her bag and stepped out onto the street to hail a cab. No more goddamn subways.

Chapter 24

'There's nothing we can do, Mr Cicero.' John Motta, the Italian lawyer who was assigned to him, at least gave him the courtesy of an explanation. 'Grenouille and Bifte aren't employed directly by Blakely's, so there's no obvious conflict of interest. You said you signed a disclosure and explanation policy form.'

'She lied to me. Straight up.'

'Right, and she's probably getting a backhander from their main lawyers. Difficult to prove. It would cost you plenty, and we wouldn't take a case like this on contingency. Too tough to win.' He smiled, showing one gold-capped tooth. 'Suing lawyers is always a mess.'

Michael sat there. 'You're telling me they can take my work, my company, my fonts, my illustrators and my contacts, and I can't do a thing about it?'

'Zip. They had you believing you were in partnership, correct?'

'Damn right.'

'You never were. You were an employee until the bonus phase kicked in. They terminated you just before that happened, without prejudice.'

Michael got to his feet and paced around the plush offices, looking out at the financial district spread before him to the south. In the soothing, air-conditioned atmosphere of Greenbaum and Fischer, he was hearing these calm words telling him his dream was dead.

'It seems prejudiced enough to me. I have to start over. With nothing.'

'A legal term.' Motta bit back a smile. He admired the man's anger and passion. A pity none of it was tempered with realism. Foxton had done a major number on this boy.

Motta, usually very detached, was sorry he had to drop a few more bombshells.

'You had a no-compete clause, good for one year.'

'And?' Michael asked, his voice dangerously soft.

'That means you *can't* start again. Not children's publishing. Not children's books in any form. Plus, Seth Green, and your other creatives – they can either work for Foxton, or not work at all. At least not in the book business. If they want to be illustrators, they have to wait a year to do it for you.'

Michael's heart did a slow flip in his chest. That was it then. He could not take a year off work. Game, set and match to Foxton.

'I'll call Seth,' he said after a few moments. 'He has to draw. Stopping him drawing would be like stopping Pedro Martinez from pitching.'

The lawyer nodded. 'I'm sorry we couldn't help.'

'Not your fault.' Michael turned to leave, then stopped. 'Just one last question. Am I barred from working in children's fiction, or from all kinds of books?'

'Let me check.'

Michael's pulse sped up as the smaller man ruffled through the papers. Already he had begun to formulate schemes for his revenge. What if he came out with a new poetry line, accessible stuff, or maybe travel guides, or even—

'Yes.' Motta's tone was final. 'I'm sorry. You cannot work in the book business for the next year.'

'Thank you,' Cicero said.

He paid his bill on the spot, at the receptionist's office. This was an episode in his life he wanted over and done with.

He pictured Ernie Foxton, waiting to get his revenge for having to beg him to re-enter his offices. Michael had to give him credit. It had been pretty complete.

You little fuck, he thought to himself. *I'll get you.*

The problem was, he had no idea how.

First Michael had sex with Iris. Then he told her.

'I've got no money, no bonus, no company and no job. From now on, it's cooking ourselves from the discount produce left over in the deli at the end of the day. You can cook while I look for work.'

Iris had looked at him and laughed. 'This is a joke, yes?'

'No.' Michael noted the look of shocked horror on her face and enjoyed himself for the first time that day. Iris's skin was still flushed and pinked from her long session of sex. Ever since she'd assumed he'd come home with two hundred and fifty grand, Iris had been even more insatiable than usual.

Far be it from him to deny a desperate woman. Too thin for his taste, Iris was at least eager and inventive. She sucked him like her life depended on it, and liked to try to ride him, bucking on him like he was a prize horse at a rodeo. But Cicero didn't let women take control. It was an easy thing to reach up and grab Iris's wrists with one hand, and laugh as she struggled to free herself, while he plunged harder and harder into her. It never failed to turn her on. When he took control of her, so simply and ruthlessly, her half-faked moans of ecstasy turned into surprised, real ones, her pussy slicked up wet and tight around him, grabbing helplessly on to him, and he sensed the contractions just starting to shudder up in her flat belly.

Michael didn't like feminists. He agreed with the fat radio 'shock jock' who labelled them Feminazis. As far as Michael was concerned, the history of the world was the history of men. They talked about equality of opportunity, but for every Ruth Bader Ginsburg or Margaret Thatcher there were ten Irises, ten Diana Foxtons. Beauties who would eschew work for weddings. Still the quickest, easiest route to riches.

'It's not a joke. I got nothing, and I don't cook, so I hope you know a lot of recipes, babe.'

She ranted and raved for ten minutes, and then, as he'd known she would, Iris packed up her stuff and got the hell out.

'And if you think about calling, don't,' she said.

'I'll try to remember that,' Michael said, wryly. To her fury, he patted her on the ass as she swept out the door.

Gold-diggers. Women were gold-diggers, 99 per cent of them. What had the sexual revolution done for them? Not too much, as far as he could work out. Any girl who had the chance would give up her job in ten seconds if she could wind up a kept woman.

He thought of that joke Seth had told him, about the Hollywood studio head who got fired and called his trophy wife from a pay phone. 'But you still love me, right?' he asks her. 'Honey, of course I still love you,' she says sweetly, 'and I'll miss you, too.'

Iris couldn't get out fast enough once she realised that he wouldn't be her cushy ticket to the big time. Michael was glad. It saved him the inevitable scene when he had to dump her. He liked things to be crisp and clean.

He took a week to gather his thoughts, and it wasn't a pleasant one. His dwindling bank account would only make the rent here for two more months, maximum. Susan Katz called, crying and asking when she was coming back to work, and Michael had nothing to tell her. His contacts, built up over the last year, were useless. He couldn't take a job in publishing. He couldn't even set up another company. Foxton had him hamstrung.

Barnes & Noble called. Waldenbooks rang up too. Two of the most prestigious independents in New York City, offering him a buying post. But Michael couldn't reconcile himself to that. He'd be working with books, sure – but not creating, not influencing. He'd be a numbers guy.

He turned the offers down, politely, and rented a tiny space on East Eleventh, where he set up shop as a consultant. Except that Motta told him he couldn't consult to publishers, which made the whole thing academic.

Michael couldn't afford an assistant to answer the phone, but that was OK, because it barely rang. A friend at Amazon gave him two thousand dollars to write a paper for them on finding independent book companies and getting them involved in the online revolution. It was the only commission he'd ever had, and it was a drop in the ocean of expenses that comprised living in New York.

He sat on a rickety chair, in his cramped office, mopping up his sweat and trying to concentrate on the words blinking up from his laptop. It felt like a sauna in here, and the hot, heavy scents of the Dunkin Donuts next door filled the room and threatened to choke him. His jacket had long been surrendered and hung on a peg on the door. He'd downed two large jugs of iced tea and he was going to need to go out for a third one any minute now, because he was thirsty enough in this heat to start licking the condensation off the cracked glass fronting.

Nothing was neat about this place except for the brass plate outside the door. Cicero Consultants, it said, in small, businesslike letters. Michael had it hand made. It cost him seventy bucks he could barely afford, but it was worth it. It felt like the last touch of class he had.

The tiny, hand-affixed bell jangled. Michael sat bolt upright, annoyed to be caught without his jacket on. Finally, a customer. He thanked God. He needed one right now. Maybe a rep from one of the major stores would be looking for a complete overhaul of their stocking policy. Better yet, maybe an agency would ask for his help. He'd managed to make stars of five complete unknowns before he got canned. Who knew who it might be?

The door swung open.

'Hi, Michael,' said Diana Foxton.

He stared at her. She wore a simple cotton dress in an Indian print, flat sandals, and was carrying a tote bag. Her long hair was tied back in a ponytail that made her look even younger, and a breath of perfume wafted in with her.

She wore no make-up, and seemed amazingly beautiful.

'Come to gloat?' Michael demanded. 'If so, please, enjoy yourself, Mrs Foxton, and then get out. I'm a busy man.'

'I can see that,' Diana said, looking around the empty office. It was devoid of furniture apart from a fax machine and a phone.

'Charming as ever.' Michael gritted his teeth. 'Now you have your report to take back to your husband, please leave me to get on with my work.'

She stood in the centre of his room, hesitantly. The thought crossed his mind that it was the first time he'd ever seen Diana Foxton nervous.

'Can I sit down?'

'If you must.' Cicero was puzzled, but maybe the heat was making her faint, or something. He didn't want the chick crashing to the ground on his property. He indicated the hard chair positioned in front of his desk. 'Go ahead.'

'I need to ask you a favour,' she said, quietly.

Michael's brow lifted. 'Yeah? Amusing. What favour would that be? To provide your husband with more amusing anecdotes of how his little spy kept him updated?'

Her eyes flashed. 'I told you, I didn't spy on you. And he's not my husband.'

Cicero shrugged. 'If you're not Diana Foxton, you're a dead ringer for her.'

'I am Diana Foxton. For the moment. I'm also separated, in the process of being divorced.' She tossed a folded copy of the *News* across the desk to him. 'That's me, and that's my ex-husband. I found out about Green Eggs the same day you did. Ernie had served me with divorce papers the night before. I think it was his idea of a joke.'

He was sceptical. Diana sat across from him, blushing with the embarrassment of being forced to wash her dirty linen in front of him. He was so butch. Ridiculously masculine. A big gorilla, she told herself, with all that silky black hair.

'Yeah? And you're telling me you really worked at that job?'

'My work got done, didn't it?' she asked coldly. 'I don't think you need to ask questions about my motivations. I did what you asked me to. And now I need a reference.'

Cicero grinned suddenly. 'You came here to ask me for a reference?'

'Yes.' She shifted in front of him; her slim body, with all those curves, moved deliciously. 'I – I—' she blushed, and fell silent.

'Go on,' he prompted, mercilessly.

'I can't find a job.' Diana's cheeks flamed. 'I had no reference from you, and working for my husband's company didn't seem to count.'

'But you're a rich girl. Why don't you just go back to England?'

'I don't give up that easily,' she said, magnificently cold.

Cicero couldn't help it, he quite admired her. What it must have cost her to come in here and ask him for help. So, the spoilt little brat was getting her first reality check. He looked down at the pictures in front of him. One showed the weary Diana, the other the glittering Felicity, and all he could think was what a moron Ernest Foxton was to pick the second girl.

'I'm not going to ask your reasons,' he said, 'because I don't care about them. But I guess I misjudged you. I suppose I owe you a favour. First, a reference from me would be worthless, because Blakely's discredited me. Second, you need one to get hired. It's Catch-twenty-two. You gotta have a job to get a job.'

Diana lowered her blue eyes. 'That's just great. How the hell can I swing that? I only worked eight months in my whole life, and that was a year ago on another continent.'

'You can come and work for me,' Michael said.

Surprise made her rude. 'Work for you? I don't think so.'

'It's the best offer you'll get.' Cicero shrugged. 'Look, lady, I don't like you either, but this is an office. You don't need to like me, you just need to do what I tell you and turn up on time. I can only hire you for maybe a month. It's real short term, too, but at the end of it you get a reference. I can pay you eight hundred dollars, no benefits.'

Diana looked across at him.

'I'll take it,' she said.

Chapter 25

The days crept by, and the temperature crept up.

Diana learned things she'd never thought herself capable of learning, and it stung her. She learned how to get up twenty minutes earlier to avoid the worst of the subway crush. She comparison shopped at the delis and supermarkets for the cheapest washing-up liquid, and bought last-day discounted meat and fish. To keep the bugs out of her apartment, she learned to clean twice a day. She bought a small portable fan she couldn't afford, and learned how to sleep in her bra and panties lying uncovered on top of the bed. The heat in Manhattan seeped up from the sidewalk, cooked a little more between the close-set concrete valleys, and thickened through the dirty windows of her apartment. It was a full-time job to keep her skin cool and her make-up on her face.

Meanwhile, there was Michael Cicero.

She disliked him, but she had to respect him. Each day he was out there, hustling. Sometimes he left at nine and pounded the pavement until four forty-five. Diana sat in his cramped office, watching a phone that never rang. She did what she could. She tidied the place and swept it, made minor repairs, and even repainted one cracked wall. She fetched coffee and magazines, and pretended she was interested. She talked to a bargain-basement accountant about maximising Michael's tax write-off.

Diana knew she'd have quit long before if she were

Michael. There was stubbornness, and there was stupidity. Cicero had a degree and an employment history; he could get work elsewhere. An English teacher, something like that.

But Michael wasn't interested in some other job. He came in each day, wrote up whatever tiny project he was working on – if there was any work – went to knock on all the doors that stayed closed to him, and then left.

And she sat at her desk in the stifling heat and read magazines.

Time was running out for them both.

The doorbell jangled, and Michael came in, his white shirt crisp, his pants pressed. He didn't look like someone about to go under.

'How did it go?'

He shrugged. 'Same as usual, I guess. How about you?'

'I reorganised the office,' Diana lied. She got the office straight two weeks ago, but she figured it would make him feel better.

'I bet.' He gave her a slow, knowing grin, and she blushed. Cicero had a disturbing habit of making Diana feel undressed when he looked at her. Nobody could be more formal, more reserved, but still, it was as though her dress was being peeled from her shoulders, her bra cups tugged down from her breasts. Annoyed with herself, she felt her nipples harden.

Desire was a trick. It never got satisfied.

He came across to where she was sitting and loomed over her, and Diana shrank from him, like she always did.

'What are you reading?' he asked.

Diana handed over the magazine. 'There was an article on the Internet about how computing is making kids dumber. Concerned Parents of America, that sort of thing.'

'Yeah.' Michael flipped through it. 'I can see why, too.'

'Can I ask you something?' she said.

Cicero was surprised. He looked down, which was a mistake. Diana was leaning forwards eagerly, and her large, lightly freckled breasts were pushed together right under his nose. He caught a glimpse of the caramel lace of her bra. Damn. What a body she had.

'Sure,' Michael said, trying to keep his mind out of the gutter. He hadn't had a girl since Iris had left. An automatic hard-on was already starting in his groin. Shit. He moved out of the line of sight of her cleavage.

'The day Ernie had us fired. What were you going to ask me to do?'

His lips curled upwards. 'You got pretty mad. Actually, I was somewhat impressed with your ability to judge book covers. I was thinking about giving you a shot at working with our illustrators, picking out frames and other in-book graphics.'

Diana's mouth opened slightly. Cicero envisaged shutting it with his. Her lips were plump and red, vulnerably soft. His teeth would tear at them, biting them gently, forcing them apart with his tongue while she pressed those glorious tits up into his hands . . .

'You really thought I could do that?'

Stop. Stop. 'Yes, you had real talent, visually.'

'I liked what I saw,' Diana said thoughtfully. 'I never could draw, but I could pick stuff out. Look at that, for example.' She pointed to a large colour spot detailing the graphics on CD-ROM Encyclopedia. 'Boring, banal. Why would a child be interested in that? I know I wouldn't.'

Cicero looked closer at the magazine in his hand. She was right. There was nothing there to interest a kid . . .

He clapped the page shut and grasped Diana's hand.

'What? What did I say?' she asked, alarmed.

'Nothing. Everything.' Michael stood up straight, all

thoughts of sex vanished from his mind. 'You little beauty. You found it. You did it. We're back!'

He made her put up a closed sign and switch on the answer machine.

'We take the afternoon off?' Diana said.

'Don't be inane. I never take afternoons off. We're going to take a meeting.'

Michael led her westwards, back into the Village at Sixth and Twelfth, and ducked into French Roast. In the chic coffee house, among the louche beat poets and lazy students sipping their frappés, he sensed the old adrenaline bubble up in him like a Louisiana swamp on overdrive. He picked a table, and the lithe young waitresses swarmed round to serve him. Diana had been here alone, and it had taken her thirty minutes to get a menu. She watched the girls play for his attention. Really. They could barely be more obvious if they had just unbuttoned their tops, right there.

'You know I'm banned from publishing,' he said when her vanilla hazelnut arrived with his espresso.

'I had picked that up, yes.'

Michael made an impatient gesture. 'The point is, my expertise has been going to waste.'

'True. I've been in livelier cemeteries than our office.'

'The whole Green Eggs thing was about a new look on old stories. To give children something visual, something worth reading.'

Diana sipped her coffee. 'I understand; they were good books.'

'Today what do kids do? Play computer games.' He rifled through her magazine. 'And the article says most computer games are mind-sapping rubbish.'

'Of course they are.'

'But they needn't be. I proved I can sell high-quality, smart books. American parents are crying out for something valuable to teach their kids. What if we just went into computing?'

An unfamiliar sensation started to churn in Diana's flat stomach. A second later she recognised it. Butterflies. She had butterflies of excitement.

'That's . . . a pretty good idea,' she said, slowly.

'No kidding it's a good idea.' He looked at her, but she had the impression he didn't see her. His mind was picturing a vast empire, she thought: limos, stock offerings, the cover of *Forbes*. Modesty had never been Michael's strong point. 'I still have contacts in publishing who ring me up every day, and most of them have CD-ROM divisions.'

'But that's still publishing, isn't it?'

His face darkened. 'Yeah. Fuck.'

'Language,' Diana said, absently.

'Whatever. OK, so I have to go to a computer games manufacturer, and get them to start educational software.'

'But they don't know you.'

'Nothing good is ever easy, babe. I'll need help. Your job will change. You'll be scouting out hackers and code-writers, and guys who can draw pictures. You'll write my letters and come with me to the banks.'

'What use would I be at the banks?'

'You look classy,' he said, as though pointing out the obvious.

'But . . . but Michael . . .'

'I'm not interested in buts. You were going to say the month was almost done, and how will I pay your salary?'

She blushed. 'Something like that, I'm afraid.'

'Don't worry about it. You let me take care of it,' Michael said intently. 'If your cheque isn't there, you have my permission to walk.'

'Thanks,' she said dryly.

'It's going to be hard and thankless at first. No more

nine to five. No more reading magazines and filing your nails all day. Are you in?'

She glanced at her nails regretfully and wondered if she'd ever get a decent manicure again. 'I'm in,' she said.

He wasn't kidding. Diana started setting her alarm for 6 a.m., and coming home at eight, not that she missed the extra time in her cramped box of an apartment. She started taking a flood of calls, typing up proposals and brochures, registering the new company, dealing with everything from lawyers to labels. Michael had no time to help her with anything. Getting the first slice of funding was like climbing the Eiger without oxygen – dizzyingly difficult. Diana went to so many loan officers that one bank blurred into another. She laid out sample graphics and bound up Michael's papers. She got blisters and learned how to walk on them anyway. At night she came home too exhausted for anything more than a pot of pasta, a shower and the sleep of the dead.

At weekends she cleaned to placate Rita, shopped for food and went over draft pitch letters with a highlighter.

Once or twice Diana even called her lawyer for another helping of bad news; Ernie had everything tied up with pre-trial motions. It might take months to get money out of him.

When Michael finally came home with the funding, they had all but given up. Citibank was prepared to take the risk. The business plan paid off, and they had twenty thousand dollars for staff and one project.

Cicero found their first code-writer. His name was Opie Z., and he was eighteen years old, scruffy, and brilliant. He was a tip-off from Seth Green, miserable in a gilded cage over at Blakely's.

He sat in the offices with the brand-new portable air-conditioner and studied his shoes.

'Dude. I ain't much for nine to five. And I got a record.

Couldn't do that Microsoft thing.' Ruminatively, he spat chewing gum into a wastebasket in the corner. 'Nor the Slick Willy Silicone Valley shit, neither. "The Imagine Arts family".' He made a face. 'I don't got a family, and if I did, they wouldn't ask for my résumé and shit.'

'Quite,' Michael said. The boy was smart; his defiant street gear and low-slung swagger couldn't hide that for a second. What the fuck. 'If you come and work here it's basic wages. You get to write your own stuff. When I get more money, you get more money.'

Opie thought about it. 'But I ain't about nine to five, either.'

'Sure you are,' Cicero said, instantly. 'You turn up at five past nine, just keep walking right past the door, because you won't be wanted. This is for real.'

How can he be cool like that? Diana wondered, hovering in the background with iced water for their guest. We need this guy so badly it's not even funny. Without him, this thing is dead in the water. Opie was scowling at him, daring him to back down, but he was calmly crossing his arms and leaning back, like the little punk had nothing that could scare him.

The kid dropped his eyes first. 'OK. You better not mess with my code, dude,' he said.

'Dude,' Cicero replied, 'I have no intention of doing that.'

He extended one massive paw and took the boy's hand in his own.

'Welcome to Imperial,' he said.

The first attempt at a game was a mess. Clumsy, slow-moving and crawling with enough bugs for a Hollywood horror movie. Diana struggled along on slave wages until Opie got it right.

But when he did, it was glorious.

Michael burst into the office.

'What is it?' Diana sprang to her feet, almost alarmed at the look on his face. He ran over to her and lifted her up in a bear hug, making her gasp and squeal with shock. Michael never behaved like that. He was the biggest tight-ass on the planet.

'It's this. This.' He high-fived the bewildered Opie. 'We got a development cheque from Nexus Games. They loved the ReadWrite code. They want to press ahead. Take a look at this.'

'Wow.' Opie peered at the cheque. 'I ain't seen that many zeros outside of a Backstreet Boys gig.' He chuckled at his own joke.

Michael glanced over at Diana. 'You get a pay rise, too,' he said. 'Call a temp service. Get some extra help. We're in business.'

The funny thing was, she thought a month later, that it was almost enjoyable. There were six people now in the cramped offices, working on the first complete game. She had a secretary of her own, Mona. Mona was a hefty girl and very smart. She didn't bother flirting with Michael. Somehow, this endeared her completely to Diana. It was just annoying to have to deal with all the stupid female hormones.

Her new job was overseeing graphics. She worked under Michael, finding packaging ideas, rewriting the language of the game, trying to make it understandable for children. He sent her out of the office looking for illustrators.

'What will they know about computers?' she asked, perplexed.

He gave her another of his are-you-stupid looks.

'Nothing. We can just scan the work.'

She felt foolish, and it made her snappy. 'Fine. I'll come up with something.'

He was a bastard, a slave driver, and he expected Diana to figure everything out for herself. When she wanted a bag, she went to Hermes. Where did you go to shop for cheap talent? Eventually, after her leads went nowhere, Diana moved to the source. In the blistering heat of the August sun, anyone rich fled the city. The only people left were poor and hungry. When she turned up at Forbidden Planet, Blue Cape, and the other underground comic-book stores, they were happy to give her some names. She met five or six artists, picked two, and brought them back to her boss.

'I can't believe you found these guys,' Michael said.

'I know you couldn't believe it,' Diana retorted. 'But I did.'

Chapter 26

The first game was a bust.

The second, a minor hit. Enough for a bank loan.

By the time summer eased into fall, Cicero had moved offices. He set up in West Fourth Street, in an elegant brownstone house. Five programmers and six illustrators, all scouted by Diana, worked twelve-hour days, but nobody minded. Michael cut them in on royalties and bonuses, and his success was their success.

Diana found she was working too hard to enjoy her newfound status. She wasn't rich, and she wasn't back where she wanted to be, but at least she was kissing the bounds of respectable again. And in September, Herb Brillstein called.

'He has a proposition for you,' Herb said.

Diana clutched the phone in her bedroom in Rita's tiny place and prayed silently. It was neat, but too cramped to take any longer. She wondered if her room-mate was listening in to this call on her extension. The little bit of money she made with Imperial was enough to afford decent clothes, food and health insurance, but that didn't leave much over for rent. Oh, to be rich again. Her ex-husband had millions. What had Herb managed to pull out of the fire for her?

'He doesn't want to go to trial. Plus he's thinking about getting married again.'

Felicity. Diana's hand curled into a tight ball of anger. I was such a moron to trust her, she thought. And I'm going to get my revenge.

'He understands that you can contest the divorce in the UK, and though you weakened your case when you moved out, he wants done with it. But they're pretty hard over in the UK. His lawyers said they would be prepared to wait us out, as you were married less than a year, you took employment and when you moved out you didn't contact your husband—'

'Yes. I know what I did, Mr Brillstein,' Diana said impatiently. 'What's the offer?'

'Seven hundred and fifty.'

She ran the numbers in her head. Seven fifty. With the lawyers' fees . . . That was three twenty-five. Barely enough to buy a one-bedroom flat somewhere decent, and it wouldn't cover the maintenance charges. Ernie was worth about ten million, she thought. If she refused this settlement, though, she'd be stuck here.

Diana glanced out of her window at the pigeons flapping round the white plastic hanger her panties were drying on. Her dry-cleaning had overflowed out of her tiny closet and was hanging on the back of the door, off the end of the shelves, over the back of her chair. She wanted to get out so much it hurt.

'Go back to him and tell him one million. Tell him if he refuses we will put an injunction on all the property we acquired together. I might not have got the apartment in our joint names, but I designed that place.' She took a deep breath. 'The table, the chairs, the antique sofas, the portraits, the carpets . . . I signed for it all. Visa will have a record of that. Tell him that unless he wants to take his mistress home to an empty apartment, he can give me the money. And if he refuses, file for the injunction today.'

There was a pause at the end of the line.

'If I may say so, Mrs Foxton, you should have been a lawyer.'

She smiled to herself. 'In life you have to be tough. Ernie always knew that. And now I'm learning.'

She had to wait a day to discover that she had got the cash. Half a million for Brillstein and his fancy offices, and half a million for her. She signed the papers in the office, and her marriage was over.

Diana pulled the two rings off the third finger of her left hand and FedExed them to Ernie at Blakely's. As the metal and diamonds slipped from her flesh, she suddenly felt as though a chain had been unlocked.

She was on her own again, and it felt good.

To Rita's anger, she moved out.

'Do yourself a favour, *amiga*,' Diana said, thrusting the cleaning brushes back into Rita's hands. 'Learn how to make a bed.'

'What's my job?' she asked Michael one Saturday night, eating Chinese food out of a carton as she laid out plates for the box artwork.

He looked over briefly, his face lit by the glowing numerals on his computer terminal.

'Whatever you make it,' he said.

Typical Michael. He had given her raises and bonuses and professional praise, but nothing more.

Diana shrugged. So Michael didn't like her. The feeling was definitely mutual. As long as she got hers, what the hell did she care?

Besides, she had a friend now. Claire Bryant had cheered her up every step of the way, and had even come apartment hunting with her. Diana was careful not to talk about Michael too much. It was a dead give-away, and why let Claire know he registered with her so much?

She found a new place on Hudson, a smart enough one-bedroom with the luxury of a tiny den that she turned into an office. She decorated the place on a budget, which was a new experience, having no cash and no time. Classic modernism: bare wood floors stained a dark brown, a sleek cream rug, an antique bust, and a campaign daybed. Her only other furniture was a low-slung sofa, a TV and a writing desk. It made the place look less tiny. You might even be able to swing two cats in it.

She invited Michael to her housewarming, but he turned her down.

'I can't make it. Got the new launch in a month. Need to review the distribution contracts,' he said.

'Sure.' Diana ran a hand through her glossy blond hair. It was infuriating, the way he just brushed her off. Not that she cared about his opinion. But the rest of the office would be there. It was like he was snubbing her, and who was Michael Cicero to snub her?

'But there's something I wanted to say about your home.'

She turned to him, hopefully.

'You can get a tax break for the home office, if you declare it.'

'Thanks,' Diana said, pointedly turning her back.

She started shopping again. She had survived on the clothes she had managed to get Ernie to send over, parcelling out her make-up and perfume, dressing simply. She'd been reduced to quietly selling off half her wardrobe in one of the discreet second-hand designer clothes stores that proliferated in the East Village. Now, at last, she could afford to visit Bloomingdales again.

Diana bought a pink silk Miu Miu shirtdress and wore it to the office with a pair of sassy lavender leather slingbacks.

Michael didn't so much as notice her.

She flung herself into her work, annoyed.

'Come and check this out,' Opie said, beckoning Michael with one bony finger.

Cicero sighed, but got up to see what he wanted. Opie

was forever mouthing off about the tight code he'd just busted, or the smooth-jag of his graphic lines. Michael didn't understand it; he left tech stuff to his band of geeks. The point was to encourage the troops. He thought Opie and Jenny Faroe were his two best producers as far as games code went. Part of the success of Imperial Games was the enthusiasm and passion of its staff. Michael insisted everyone show up on time, but that was as far as his discipline went.

His creative staff wore shorts and T-shirts with everything from Metallica to wrestling heroes emblazoned over them, while the business side guys wore suits – mostly. He'd thought about banning the girls from wearing skirts above the knee, but this wasn't publishing. It was an office full of kids, and they didn't thrive when they were being stifled.

Diana Foxton had taken her job as office manager pretty seriously, he had to admit. She'd hit on exactly the right atmosphere for them. They worked out of half a townhouse, and Diana kept it stocked so it felt like a home. She'd found the best hi-tech equipment at prices he found hard to believe, but more vitally, she made sure that each day there were fresh flowers, takeout teas and coffees, baskets of fruit, Coke and cookies for the junk-food programmers. She put hairspray, perfume and cologne in the bathrooms, and had takeouts and beer delivered when the boys were working late.

Michael's staff reported to him that they actually enjoyed coming to work.

He enjoyed it, too. It was a dream in the making. With each little success he felt the blood in his veins pump faster, demanding more, yesterday! He stayed in his tiny walkup simply because he had no time to move. Michael's only luxuries were two or three more suits, which he needed, because he was taking so many meetings.

He turned into the little room that overlooked the

street, where the computer banks were set up under a soothing watercolour of Martha's Vineyard.

'Look at this.' Opie grinned.

He looked. It was from the new interactive classics series. *Henry V*, by Shakespeare. The graphics were fluid and exciting. It might not compete with *Tomb Raider* but he thought parents would have no trouble getting their children to learn with it.

'Pretty good,' he said. 'No, better, fantastic. You keep it up—'

'And maybe I'll get a weekend off?'

'Let's not get crazy,' Michael teased. 'Where's Diana?'

'She's in the front office. She's been locked in there for an hour with some guy.'

'I see.' Cicero turned away so Opie wouldn't see the dark shadow that crossed his face. He'd tried to get used to Diana. Every single day, the woman turned up wearing something guaranteed to make his blood pressure rise. Either it was a body-hugging, light as thistledown, sky-blue suit, or a halter-neck dress that made a mockery of its modest neckline with the way it draped like liquid over the tight, high curves of her butt, the soft swell of her breasts. Even her shoes he found disturbing; tiny little strappy things, even when they were flats, that made him think of garter belts or the lace of her bra. Her make-up was always subtle, but not so subtle it failed to outline the lush fullness of her mouth, the cutting blades of her cheekbones, or her dark, groomed eyebrows, just shaped a touch instead of plucked to oblivion. Her hair was never the same way twice. He wondered, from time to time, what her next look would be. A sleek chignon, a young, fresh ponytail, complex French braids, or a bouncing curl under the ends that reminded him of a shampoo commercial.

Every single day he thought of telling her not to dress so provocatively.

Every single day he realised he had no case.

Diana was wily, Michael thought. She knew just how to keep to the letter of his executive dress code while breaking the spirit. How could he complain about a floor-length white dress with cap sleeves? But how could he ignore the scalloped whisper of lace at the valley of her breasts, the loving grip of the cotton on her butt and her perfectly flat belly, and the way the bias-cut skirt emphasised each tiny, sexy swing of her hips?

She had no meeting today. Cicero prided himself on knowing everything about her calendar. Diana Foxton was a major asset when it came to the formal side of growing his company. Banks and business affairs lawyers just loved her. He enjoyed watching her work them. And work them she did, those long, strong calves tapering off to her discreet shoes that always seemed to match her skirt, her tumbling cascade of hair, that classy, unreachable, ice-queen English voice of hers giving them the summary of what Imperial was about.

He watched the way the men listened, utterly captivated. Was it his growth or her accent, his products or her eyes? The women executives were spellbound too. They took time out from flirting with him to stare at her; always fresh, always pulled together.

But he'd known this time would come. Diana was no shrinking violet, Michael thought angrily, far from it. She knew the kind of pull she exerted over men. She smiled, she brushed back that shiny hair, she dressed to emphasise her sensational body. Sooner or later she was gonna bring a boyfriend to the office, and Cicero was prepared to hate him. He was bound to be a two-faced weasel like Ernie Foxton. Diana had the worst taste in men and he, Michael, was not going to stand for them in his office.

He moved through the front room, ignoring the various requests to review this and sign that. The door to the office where they took meetings with investors and analysts was shut.

He rapped on it.

'Diana?'

There was a pause. He could hear her talking in low, urgent tones to some guy or other.

'Yes, Michael. I'm in a meeting.'

The cool accent infuriated him. Almost without thinking, he turned the handle and barged his way in.

Diana was standing there, with her hand in the grasp of an older man. A rich-looking guy, Cicero noted, with a white handkerchief sticking out of his upper pocket. He even wore a vest, despite the early fall heat. Michael disliked him instantly.

'Can I help you with something?' Michael said, softly.

The man turned round and looked at him like he was something he'd scraped off the sole of his shoe. 'No, I don't think so. I had private business with Mrs Foxton.'

Michael ignored Diana's reddening face. 'Her business is my business. I'm Michael Cicero.'

'Yes, I know who you are, sir.' He made sir come off like an insult. 'But I'm only interested in talking to Diana Foxton.'

Michael folded his arms, and saw, to his great pleasure, the skinny little guy cast a wary look at his biceps under the plain shirt.

'I think I'm done here,' he said hastily.

'I guess you are. Let me show you out,' Michael said, evenly. Diana was pissed off, he saw, but tough. She couldn't flirt with her latest sugar daddy on his time.

'I know the way . . .'

The guy gathered up papers and fled, brushing past Michael with a muttered 'Good day.'

Michael turned to her. Diana was in a pink smock-like thing, with a half-sleeved, jaggedly cut pink jacket. It picked up the warm summer highlights of corn in her hair, and she had teamed it with a light single-note perfume of roses.

She'd dressed up for that guy? He would never understand women. The way money mattered so much to them. Wasn't she earning enough?

Her former apartment flickered through his mind. Well, compared to a penthouse on Central Park, her current place probably didn't cut it. She'd worn a few of the same clothes – in different combinations – twice or three times. Maybe that wasn't good enough for her. She still carried herself like a society dame, and that was what she probably wanted.

Just like Iris.

Then he told himself that that wasn't his business. Business was his business.

'What was that man doing in here?' Michael snapped. 'This is my office. Not a place for you to do your private entertaining.'

'Who do you think you are?' Diana said. She was white-faced and her blue eyes glittered. She marched up to him. 'I believe I told you I was in a private meeting. You think you can just barge in on me?'

'I think I can do whatever I like. I'm the boss.'

She laughed. 'Like I haven't earned the right for fifteen minutes alone? I work night and day for *your* company, *boss*.'

'You think you've sacrificed things for Imperial? You don't have any idea what that even means,' Cicero said, contemptuously.

Diana reached up and slapped him hard around the face. For a moment, Cicero was so shocked he didn't even react. If he had seen it coming, he would have blocked her. He didn't permit girls to hit him. If a guy tried that, he'd be knocked into the middle of next week. From a woman, like Diana, it was nothing but a sting. But the balls of her took his breath away.

He fantasised briefly about tugging her over his knee and lifting that sexy, taunting smock and spanking her. That was what she could really use.

'Would you mind,' he said evenly, 'telling me what you think you're doing?'

'I'm doing what *I* feel like,' she snapped. 'You don't think I've sacrificed anything for this place? Let me tell you something. That man was a lawyer.'

Cicero blinked. 'Explain yourself.'

'Explain myself?' she said, throwing back her hair. She looked wild to him, provocative, a challenge. He thought about shrugging the jacket from her creamy shoulders and ripping her thin dress straight down the middle. Of course it didn't mean anything, I'm just fantasising about her like I would any other pretty chick. 'You want an explanation. How about, you've been so goddamn busy running your damn office you didn't even notice me! I had a life before I came here, Michael. I've been busy trying to get back just a fraction of it. With no support from you. I thought we could be friends; I guess I was wrong.'

Diana picked up the papers and tossed them at him. 'These are my settlement papers. My lawyers just took half a million dollars from me for making a few phone calls.'

Michael didn't bother to pick them up. 'I'm sorry. But it's your own fault.'

Diana gasped. 'Excuse me?'

'Certainly.' God, he could be so infuriating, staring at her with those heavy-lashed eyes, like he knew it all, and she was some bimbo. 'I will excuse your temper, this once. But don't blame me for your inadequacies. You were arrogant. You didn't go to a lawyer at the outset. You could have gotten a better deal, but you had to wait till the last minute. Why is that my fault?'

Diana was thrown. Sometimes she hated him. He was

so cocky. She felt her temper surge again. She wanted to lash out, and without thinking, she drew back her arm and made to hit him again.

But Michael was far too quick for her. His hand lashed out and caught her at the wrist, holding it secure. She struggled, but she couldn't move. In an instant he tugged her to him, and then his hands were cupping her face, forcing her mouth up to meet his, and his lips were on hers, kissing her savagely.

Chapter 27

Dawn broke over Rome, golden and warm, with the promise of another blistering day to come. Felicity Metson sighed. It was so dreary here; traipsing round the world after darling Ernie was more taxing than it seemed. She hoped that he would drop his plan to buy one of the multi-million-dollar apartments set into the two-thousand-year-old Theatre of Marcellus. She really couldn't care less about the endless monuments of ancient Rome, a playground now for wild poppies and quick little black lizards that darted around like the tongue of Ernie's new maid. As for the Renaissance churches with their Da Vinci sculptures and paintings by Raphael and what have you, Felicity felt uncomfortable in them. Such silly moralising. Why keep such art treasures out for the plebs to gawk at? Something in her revolted against the idea of *Moses* by Michelangelo, say, in Santa Maria Maggiore, being kept there so that fat Italian mammas and working men with their sunburned hands and cheap suits could gawk at him after mass. How could they possibly appreciate such refinement? Better it go to a museum, or, preferably, be sold off. Perhaps to her.

Felicity indulged in a small day-dream where *Moses* was delivered to her new townhouse which Ernie would buy her after the wedding, in a hail of media interest and TV cameras. Of course, he didn't have that kind of cash just yet. Hopefully the new deal brewing with Signor Bertaloni of Media Cinque, the Italian conglomerate, would put all that to rest. Why think small? Hadn't Michael Eisner proved that you could get real wealth simply by running a company?

She rang for room service. The Hotel Consul Marcus was Rome's newest and most luxurious haven, a few blocks from the Colosseum and providing all amenities to the more discerning traveller. Felicity had told Ernie that she simply must have a separate suite . . . partly so that her beauty treatments could be applied without him witnessing any of them, and partly so that Jung-Li, the latest of the oriental 'maids' she had hired for her fiancé, could have unfettered access to him in the mornings. Her success in this relationship was all about keeping Ernie happy, Felicity reflected. And it suited both him and her to pretend that the other had no idea what was going on.

The fact that Jung-Li and all her predecessors had been hired by Felicity from a vastly expensive and seriously discreet madam on the West Coast was something Ernie need never know. Or anybody else for that matter. Felicity paid cash and used a false name. She also used pay phones and the good old US postal service, sending her packages from different stations around the city – once, even, from one of the better parts of Brooklyn.

Yes, it was, objectively speaking, a bit humiliating, Felicity thought. But Ernie didn't know she knew and nor did anybody else. The Diana affair had tipped her off as to what it would take to keep Ernie satisfied, and Felicity wasn't into domination. Nor was she into social exile, and Ernie had proved her way out. Felicity could sit on the small part of her heart that still longed for true love, for a soulmate. Love was a fairy tale; at best a matter of luck. You needed to meet the right man in the right place at the right time. The odds had beaten Felicity, and she had never considered giving it a serious shot with her Marine escort. It was hard to live without money. She looked out over Rome, and congratulated herself for her *honesty*. Yes, her therapist had helped her understand that you needed to be true to yourself.

There was no denying she liked her creature comforts. If other girls wanted to be poor and romantic, that was up to them. Felicity was a realist.

Room service materialised; a handsome waiter with a charming accent. Felicity made sure to flash him a lot of thigh, tanned and toned and peeking from her peach satin negligee as she directed him to the sun-drenched balcony. He smiled and bowed, producing Irish crystal glasses, porcelain and silver-plated cutlery. Breakfast was a small grapefruit, some dry Melba toast, a glass of freshly squeezed orange juice and a half-bottle of champagne; Perrier-Jouet rosé. There was nothing like champagne in the mornings, or any time of the day, really. She liked a drop first thing, just to soften the edges.

The waiter brushed against her breasts as she handed him a ten-thousand-lire tip. Felicity arched, very slightly, at the deliberate pressure of his rough fingers. It had been so long since she'd had an orgasm with a man. Ernie would never be able to satisfy her – or any other girl, for that matter. But she pulled back, and contented herself with a frosty smile, dismissing the help.

Felicity knew what they said about Italian men and the bedroom. But no half-hour thrill could possibly be equivalent to her new diamond engagement ring, or her fantastic wardrobe, or the summer cottage in Martha's Vineyard that was Ernie's latest little present to her. Felicity had been highly successful in shepherding her charge through the divorce; a few well-placed charity donations here, a pleasantly coordinated dinner party there, and Mira Chen was forgotten.

Ernie laughed about the fevered imaginations of the tabloid rags and nobody snickered – at least not to his face.

Felicity poured herself a glass of pink champagne and toasted herself. By constantly deferring to the married ladies of New York society, and making no attempt to outshine them, she'd done better than Diana. After all, the girl was English, and didn't understand that if you show up members of the club, you're liable to be kicked out.

Diana had proved herself to be unworthy of the notice of the Jodie Goodfriends of this world, Felicity thought, picking at her sharp grapefruit and gazing out at the scooters that roared through the cobbled Roman streets below. The girl riders in faded denim bitsy shorts, their bronzed, slim legs clutching the metal, wearing no helmets. Here everybody smoked and drank and didn't start the day without an espresso strong enough to stand a spoon up in. Everybody ate *gelati* all day long and weighed two ounces, until they had babies and suddenly morphed into black-shawled, pudgy mammas. It was as though the sun made you immortal. Perhaps Diana Foxton had thought herself immortal, disappearing from the scene without a trace. Nobody knew where she had dived off to. One lousy million, and she was never heard from again.

Felicity sipped and let the icy champagne flow down into her stomach to warm her up. Diana was not her problem; she was nobody's problem any more. The most pressing thing she needed to concern herself with was making a positive impression at Ernie's little party for the Italians. Soon she must buzz her PA to bring her the Rolodex. Signor Emarti liked Cuban cigars; Signorina Vitello was a baseball freak, and Felicity had obtained a signed Mark McGwire ball just for her. She had no doubt that Ernie and she would make the most incredible splash.

The sunlight crept up the ancient walls, bathing the ochre houses in vanilla light. In about an hour, she thought, Jung-Li would have finished off Ernie's 'personal treatments' with a 'massage'. After that she would call him as he went to work; a housekeeping call, to let her dear fiancé know how treasured he was.

'So that wraps it up then.'

Ernie stood, glancing around the small, dark-panelled room with satisfaction. The offices of Media Cinque were cramped in comparison with his glass and chrome palace, but the money behind them was serious cash. He could wing it in any setting. Madison Avenue, Wall Street or even this burgundy and mahogany old gentleman's room, with the quiet air-conditioning failing to remove the smell of cigar smoke and the faint whisper of aniseed from the Sambuca bottle old man Bertaloni liked to leave on the table when he served the coffee. It had been aggravating, sure, the way the fuckers had snickered when he asked for decaff. Nobody in the whole of the wretched country ate low fat, or drank diet sodas or decaff. So fuck 'em, let 'em laugh. He'd have the last one, when Blakely's debuted with a toy division and a slice of European TV action. He, Ernest Foxton, had already taken the publishing house out of the dark ages, and now it was time to spread his wings. He felt invincible.

'*Si, si.*' Bertaloni was giving him that tight little wop smile, but Ernie made sure never to let his warm expression flicker for a second. The businessmen here were just like the mafia in all those movies; big on respect. Bertaloni had carved out a multi-million-dollar empire in this country with its crazy politics and lousy lire, and the old geezer insisted on making out like a *uomo rispettato*. Ernie could handle that, though. He was an expert ass-kisser when it paid for him to be one. 'Tonight we drink, we celebrate, I will meet your wife.'

Ernie thought of Felicity and hoped she had her shit together, all the little gifts and stuff. She must do, right? He had no doubts of her.

'Actually, she's not my wife. She's my fiancée. I'm

divorced,' he said, instantly regretting it. A dark shadow flickered over the old man's craggy face.

'Divorce? Is not good. *Famiglia* is *molto importanta*.'

'Yeah, I agree. My wife left me, though.' Ernie tried to look heartbroken. He grinned inwardly. 'The divorce came through just recently, and me and my fiancée hope to be married very soon.'

'Ah.' Bertaloni nodded. 'Wife leave, that is very sad, Signor Foxton. But marry is good.'

'You'll meet Felicity tonight,' Ernie promised him smoothly, 'and I'm sure you'll just love her.'

His people nodded and chatted to the Italians on their way out of the door, and Ernie was proud of them. He had the ability to select the right men for the job, that much was sure. Once he got back to the States – he gave himself a mental slap on the back – he'd announce the new deals, poach some people for the toys division and become an even bigger star in the entertainment business than he already was. Ernie imagined how all the little bastards who ran scared of him now would just scatter into their corners. He'd be the new Donald Trump, with Felicity at his side, going all the right places with all the right people. And meanwhile his enemies would be crushed. Just like Diana, that stupid bint; she'd had the chance to enjoy all this with him and she'd blown it, big time. And just like Michael Cicero. How sweet it had been to pull the candy out of that baby's mouth! He thought he was such a big man, making Ernie grovel, trying to bully him like some nightclub bouncer.

I crushed him like a bug, Ernie thought. Maybe when I get back to New York I can find out what he's doing now, and crush him some more. It was important to let people see just what happened to boys who crossed him.

Diana didn't think about what she was doing, because Michael didn't give her time. His mouth on hers was ruthless. A second later, his arms wrapped around her, half-crushing her to him. He was so strong, so incredibly – big. She had never felt a man with muscles like this. His arm was almost as big as her thigh. She felt herself overpowered, overwhelmed, her soft breasts pressed up against his pecs. There was a wash of heat in her lower belly, worse than any frustrated wanting she'd felt before. In her head, Diana knew sex was never good. But in her warm belly, she wanted him. The downy hairs on her arms and skin lifted, she felt her nipples, betraying her, hardening into nubby cherries, filling with blood. Her pussy tightened, she felt herself getting wet. She tried to draw back, but he wasn't allowing it. Cicero's breath was hot on her face, her neck. He was hard against her dress. He was huge. He was so different to Ernie's thin, disgusting cock. He seemed a little longer than usual, although she wasn't used to many men, but it was the thickness of him. She half wondered if he would hurt her, taking her. His hands were all over her bottom, stroking and kneading it, rubbing the tender place at the small of her back. Diana's breath quickened. She felt maddened with wanting him.

Michael pulled back an inch, just enough to let him see her face.

'We'll get out of here.'

His voice was low and insistent. It seemed ridiculous even to think of protesting. He just would not permit it. He gave her no room to breathe, no way to see straight.

'Yes,' she muttered.

Michael opened the door and walked straight out. Opie was marching up to them again. Diana felt a sudden panic that he might change his mind, regain his sanity, return to work.

'We have a meeting,' Michael said, snapping at Opie like a turtle. He backed off. When Cicero was in this hungry-gator mode, it was best not to mess with him. He shot Diana a look of pity. Obviously she was in deep shit this time.

Diana kept her head bowed and followed Michael out. She was in an agony of lust and embarrassment. She didn't want any of her colleagues to see her flushed face, her glittering eyes, her lips, moistened and parted. She must look feverish. She fixed her gaze on the strong muscles of Michael's lower back, sliding about under the skin. Maybe *she* was insane. She was. She should back out now—

'Michael,' she said, softly.

A cab screeched to a halt in front of Cicero. He turned to look at her, peeling the clothes from her skin, his gaze stopped right between her legs. It was like a touch of rough fingers trailing over her belly. Unable to stop herself, she gasped.

'Get in,' he said, flatly.

She got in the cab and he piled in beside her. He leant forward to speak to the driver and put his hand on her knee.

'West Broadway and Hudson,' he said.

Diana stepped out of the cab and tried to look relaxed. She'd wanted to pull herself together during the ride, but it had been impossible. Michael had put one hand down the small of her back and had started stroking the curve of her behind, rhythmically, insistently. He was playing with it like it was his toy. Sometimes she had been a little self-conscious about her bottom, but she felt his desire, his excitement, and it turned her on. Cicero was kneading and squeezing while he kept up an easy banter with the driver, discussing the disastrous season the Mets had just had, and all she could think about was trying not to squirm with pleasure and need.

Her panties were a thin chiffon thong. Her behind was bare under her skirt. Diana felt the slim scrap of nothing that covered her start to cling to the moistness of her groin. She bit down hard on her lip and said nothing until the car halted and Michael's hand tugged her out of the back.

He threw a twenty at the guy and punched in the code for the door. There was a maintenance guy in the lobby. Michael greeted him cheerfully, but Diana had to swallow the groan that bubbled in the back of her throat. Surely her condition must be obvious to this man. He didn't seem to be staring at her, but how could he not know? How could anybody miss it? Her whole skin was burning. Michael turned to her.

'It's a bit of a walk. Ten floors up.'

'That's fine,' Diana managed. Her face flushed, hotly. 'I'm used to walkups.'

She deliberately started to mount the stairs. Oh man. Why had he said that? One flight, two, she barely noticed the gradient. Michael was still downstairs, chatting. Great time to pass the time of day. Why not? she thought, angrily. She reached the landing, and heard him racing up the stairs behind her, three, four at a time. He caught up with her. She noticed he hadn't even broken a sweat.

'I can't believe you said that to him.' Her eyes flashed. 'Do you always have to show off your conquests to other men?'

'A conquest.' His dark eyes bored right through her. 'Is that what you are? Maybe you flatter yourself, Diana. I bring illustrators here all the time. Males and females. He's used to it.'

Cicero opened the door and put his hand on her elbow, marching her in.

His place was tiny and immaculate. Diana saw the low-slung, hard-looking bed, made neat as a soldier's, behind him. Suddenly she felt tiny, dwarfed by him.

'Maybe this isn't such a good idea,' she stammered.

He laughed. He reached out and cupped her breasts with his hands, hefting them, as though testing their weight. A fresh rush of electric lust rocked through her hips. She shuddered, and Michael pulled her to him.

Chapter 28

For the first minute, Michael was careful and gentle. His thick fingers fumbled with the buttons of her dress. He managed to pull it from her without ripping it. He laid it carefully across the back of a chair.

Diana moaned softly. Waiting for him to touch her was agonising. Her knees were trembling as though they might not be able to support her. No man had ever touched her with such confidence and command. She forgot that all sex was bad, that it was something women put up with. Her body leapt to his touch, pressing forward, but Michael was holding her back, almost amused.

'Easy, girl.' The whisper of his breath was warm against her bare neck. 'All in good time.'

He reached behind her and unhooked her bra. Her breasts fell out, slipping warm and heavy with blood from the mocha lace, and she heard a quick intake of breath from him at the sight of them.

'Rose-pink. Dark rose,' he muttered.

'What?'

'The colour of your nipples. I was wondering about it.' Cicero reached forwards and rubbed the tip of his thumb over her left breast, not touching the swollen tip, just circling round it.

It was more than Diana could stand. Wantonly, she thrust herself against him. She was nude against the cotton of his shirt. He grinned and reached between her legs, cupping her with the palm of his hand. He could feel the slickness of her through the scrap of her panties.

'I want to look at you,' he told her. 'Turn around. Let me see you.'

Diana turned slowly on her heels as he kicked off his shoes and slid out of his pants. His cock was so hard it hurt. She was stunning; one of the rare women better naked than dressed. Oh, damn, look at that ass. Her stomach was flat enough to balance a champagne glass on, her muscles just slightly defined, and it tapered out to a firm, flaring butt, a perfect peach, rounded and high and tight and so womanly it drove him nuts. Her breasts were soft and full and natural. There was a light dusting of freckles on the tops of them, like powdered sugar. Cicero felt his resolve to tease her wane. He had to have her. Right now. He tore off his shirt and went over to her, his hands ranging all across her warm skin. She was intensely responsive, but awkward. If he didn't know she'd been married, he might have thought her a virgin.

Diana squirmed as she felt his hands grip her, the thickness of his cock press into her back. She was desperate for him, but the size of him made her nervous.

'Will you hurt me?' she muttered, her fingers closing round him.

He pushed her back on the bed, hard.

'No.' His voice was thick with lust. 'I'll go slow. At first.'

His hands reached up and pinned her arms over her head, and his mouth was on her again, kissing her, pinning her under him, and her legs parted, and he entered her gently, half an inch at a time.

'We have to get back to the office,' Diana said, reluctantly.

She kept her head down. She had showered and

dressed again, but she felt self-conscious in Michael's presence. She had had no idea that sex could be like that.

His cock impaled her. There was no way she could think about something else, like she had done with Ernie. His hands were on her, his fingers rubbing the slick nub of her through the silky downy fur even as he took her, turning her over, licking her breasts, directing her body for his pleasure. She had never felt so richly enjoyed. She had come over and over again, little crashing orgasms just teasing her, preparing her, for the way he made her yield to him right before he came, so she was only aware of the sweet block of pressure in her groin and pussy, the way it built up relentlessly driving her forwards, filling her mind totally with his cock, his chest, his strong arms, until it exploded in a white-hot burst across her skin, leaving her drained and panting.

She was astonished to have felt that way. She could hardly look him in the face. Michael had tried to kiss her as she recovered, but she felt shy and drew back from him, going to wash. What must he think of me? she wondered. What a slut he must think I am. Her body's reaction was a shock, and she had stumbled to the bathroom, revelling in the hot water, the precious few seconds left to her to try to gather her thoughts.

My God, she thought, I'll never be able to look the man in the face again.

'What's the problem?' Michael said to her, after he emerged from the shower. Diana had dressed herself, neatly buttoning up her dress as high as it would go, and tying her hair back in a severe French pleat. She glanced down at the coffee she'd fixed from his machine, trying to avoid staring at the thickly muscled chest, the hard, defined biceps. What was he really? Just a jock. I mustn't let myself be fazed by a jock, Diana thought.

Her newfound career was important to her. At Imperial, she'd learned she was more than a pretty face.

It surprised her that she really didn't want to jeopardise that.

And she was scared by how totally her body had surrendered to him. Already she could feel a slight tightness between her legs. Almost – how ridiculous! – as though she wanted more.

'Nothing. We're late for work,' Diana said. 'They'll be expecting us back in the office.'

He turned his back to her and shrugged off the towel, dressing. Diana swallowed hard. The lines from his shoulders to the small of his back were chiselled like some Renaissance statue in marble. His behind was flat and totally hard. He was huge. She looked at the fresh shirt he was pulling on and wondered if he'd had it specially made.

'You're right,' he said, easily. 'We'll get in a cab and get right back.'

She bit her lip, pouting. You're right? Was that all he had to say? I don't want it to get weird, Diana thought, but I *do* think he might have argued just a bit.

It wasn't every day a man got to go to bed with a woman like her. Or was it? He was acting as if nothing special had happened.

Diana tossed her head. Well, two could play at that game.

'Good idea,' she agreed.

When the cab pulled up on West Fourth, Michael got out and held the door open for her. Diana nodded slightly; she could barely thank him. Lower Manhattan had slipped past them in complete silence. Michael seemed totally at his ease.

Diana had gazed out at the warehouses, inwardly seething. How the hell could he be so calm? Maybe things like that did happen to Cicero all the time. That was his reputation.

A horrible thought occurred to her. What if she was

just another notch on the bedpost? Urgh. A lunchtime quickie, just another conquest?

What was I thinking? she asked herself. I didn't play hard to get. I'm worse than a girl who gives it up on the first date. He didn't even ask me on a date. And Michael is arrogant enough as it is.

It was no use pretending it had been nothing special for her. Diana turned aside from Michael, her back rigid with rejection. She blushed hotly, remembering herself leaping in his arms, gasping and crying out, scratching at him, drenched with sweat. But she couldn't help it. The things he had done to her. The urgent, merciless thrusting of his cock, the sweet pressure of his tongue, his wandering hands.

She bit on her inner cheeks. Well, she couldn't help the way she'd behaved then, but she could help how she behaved now.

I'm going to be the ultimate professional, Diana promised herself.

She leant forward.

'Turn off the radio,' she snapped. 'That music is driving me mad.'

The cabbie jumped to attention. Just as well, Diana thought. In this mood, nobody better mess with me.

She stepped out past Michael and marched into her office, closing the door behind her. There were a number of hot graphics designers on her Rolodex to call. She picked up the phone, determined to drive Michael Cicero and his body right out of her head.

'More champagne, sir?' the stewardess asked.

She was flirting shamelessly, but Felicity was lying there with a Gucci traveller's blindfold wrapped around her eyes, and her hands folded neatly in her lap. She was asleep or pretending to be. The stewardesses could bat their eyelids as much as they liked. Ernie was pleased with her. She had thrown a terrific party for the Ities, schmoozing the old geezers like a seasoned pro, not even forgetting the wives. And she knew exactly when to turn a blind eye.

'I thought the bar closed an hour ago,' Ernie said, examining her breasts.

She thrust them forward a bit more. 'Well yes, Mr Foxton, that's true as far as our regular first-class passengers go.' She dropped her voice. 'For our most special guests, we always make exceptions.'

'You can get me another glass of rosé,' Ernie agreed. He didn't really want it, but it tickled him to get what other people couldn't. Really, the world was just his toy shop.

The Bertaloni deal would go through, and Blakely's would have money to spare. Games and toys were big business, and he didn't see why he should be stuck with just books. The more reach you had, the more respect you got. Airlines were just one example. They made their profits on big business, rich travellers like him who would happily pay outrageous prices for a seat that flipped down all the way. Idly, he wondered whether if he took the air hostess upstairs to the private bathroom she'd fuck him right there, or if she'd just slip him her hotel room number instead? Either way, it was too much bother. He could have Jung-Li any time he liked without having to lift a finger.

The girl was leaning over him, pouring out a thin stream of pink champagne that filled up his crystal glass, spitting and bubbling. Ernie reached out and picked up the stem in his thin fingers. Realising she was dismissed, the woman melted away.

He sipped, allowing the chill wine to fizzle on his tongue. Once, a long time ago, champagne had been a treat luxurious beyond imagining. Back when he was a teenager, Asti Spumante was about all he could manage.

Now it was routine, almost boring. Ernie had educated himself on the better houses, even memorising a list of the superlative years. Truth was, it all tasted the same to him. But now he knew to bitch if the stuff was non-vintage, he could say he wouldn't clean his oven with Lanson. Ernie hated being laughed at with a passion.

The plane was banking and turning over Canada, very close to New York. He'd called Jack Fineman with instructions. Firstly, there was the press conference to announce his latest triumph. But after that, Fineman was going to update him. Apparently, there was news on Cicero, and it included a report on his ex-wife. Ernie didn't much care what Diana did; she was out of his hair, and she was never coming back into the social scene. Felicity would see to that. Besides, Diana had no serious cash, and in America, if you didn't have money, you weren't worth a thing. Diana would never embarrass him any more. He didn't think Michael would, either.

But he wasn't going to underestimate the little prick. Once I crush people, Ernie thought, they better stay crushed. Fineman would help him see that they did.

The sun dipped behind the long row of brownstones, flooding rich golden light through the trees outside their windows. Diana tidied up her papers and stacked them neatly on her desk. She had managed to bury herself in her work all day long, calling programmers, supervising the marketing division, writing out copy for the latest batch of games, and running to the water cooler whenever Michael emerged into her area. It hadn't been as hard as she had feared. The company was blowing up, and every day her phone lines and fax machine buzzed off the hook. There was no time to think about what he'd done to her this afternoon, no time to obsess over his flat stomach, his brawny arms, the way his hands pressed and squeezed every inch of her butt. But those thoughts were returning now. As soon as the hubbub of the day died down, Diana felt her body start to betray her.

That's OK, she told herself. I'll get out of here right away. Maybe go down to Bliss and get a massage, or pop up to Bergdorf's for my eyebrows. Anything to get away from him. Hurriedly she packed her papers into her briefcase and turned to leave. Michael was blocking the doorway.

'Can I help you with something?' Diana asked. She was rather proud of herself. She sounded brisk and impersonally friendly. Why let him know he had upset her equilibrium?

'Yes, you can.'

'Of course. Just a second, I'll boot the computer up again.'

'That's not what I meant.' He smiled at her confidently. 'What are you doing tonight?'

'Well, I'm – I'm—'

Diana stammered and cursed herself. Why couldn't she think of something? Her mind had gone blank.

'Would you like to have dinner? I know a great place on Bleeker Street,' he said.

Diana blushed. 'Look, Michael. I think you should know that I don't normally do this kind of thing.' The instant she said it she felt more awkward than ever. I don't normally do this kind of thing. I'm not that kind of girl. How many women had said that after panting in his arms?

His brows lifted. 'You don't normally eat dinner? You should. You've been looking a little skinny lately.'

'You know what I mean. I think we should lay down some ground rules.'

'Yeah, I'm sure you do.' He gave her a wink. A wink! 'We'll do that, OK? At dinner.'

'I can't.' Be firm, Diana told herself. 'I need to go home and have a shower and change. I'm so sticky.'

'Mmm, I know you are,' Michael said, his gaze lingering on her skin. 'So I'll pick you up at eight.'

Diana flushed scarlet. 'I don't know . . . I think . . .'

'You think too much,' he said, and walked out.

Chapter 29

'Michael, I have a suggestion to make,' Diana said.

She brushed her long, dark hair behind her shoulders and regarded him over the edge of her bone-china cup of English tea. Since they'd started dating, Diana had felt confident enough to go back to her natural colour. At first it was a shock, sitting in Oribe's gilt-decorated salon, and watching the bright platinum soften and cool through red right down to a rich chestnut.

'You hate eet, no?' her colourist asked, dismayed.

'No.' Diana could hardly take her eyes from her reflection. 'It's natural, it suits my skin. I look five years younger.'

'Well, eef you are happy.' The woman sniffed. In her opinion everybody should be blonde. But Mrs Foxton had refused to be swayed. Didn't she read the gossip columns? Conchita wasn't discreet, but even she shrank from pointing out that Felicity Metson, the new lady in Ernest Foxton's life, was standard-issue New York: younger, blonder and skinnier than Diana. Maybe she was depressed, now the divorce was finalised, and Felicity was flashing that six-carat rock in front of whatever camera happened to be pointed her way.

But that would not explain why, whenever her client came in for a treatment, she was glowing, her skin shining, her eyes bright. Whatever Diana had in the way of beauty treatments, they must be *very* expensive, Conchita mused, wondering about the size of the settlement.

If Conchita could have seen Diana's beauty secret, sitting across from her in the cramped bistro, she would have been amazed.

Michael Cicero was gulping coffee and drinking in Diana at the same time. Even though she was with him every night and he reached for her in the morning, he couldn't get enough of her. It was like trying to hold a bubble in a cage; he put up the bars of his expectations and she floated past them.

They were having breakfast together outside his apartment. He wore a black suit, tailor-made for him by Gieves & Hawkes in England. Since Imperial's games had started selling, he could afford it. Cicero detested luxury for its own sake, but he liked looking professional. Think Sicilian, dress British. His shirts, shoes and suits were always pristine. A discreet pair of plain gold cuff links glinted in the morning light.

Michael never thought about his appearance, except to require that it be smart. Maybe that was one of the reasons he looked so damn good.

Diana was another matter altogether, though, and it worried him. As Imperial expanded, so had her job. She was his right-hand woman and he paid her commensurately.

Looking at her, he sometimes thought every cent must go on clothes.

Michael was no fashion guru, but he knew about cost. And Diana's things cost plenty. Almost every day, as though to make up for months of relative poverty, she showed up at work in a brand-new outfit. Chanel suits. Prada handbags. Manolo Blahnik shoes. Maybe it was important for all the meetings he sent her to, as Imperial's public face.

But Cicero didn't know. There was still that touch of the pampered princess about Diana. Still, she worked hard, and it was her own money.

Was that why they fought so much? He was doing good, but not that good. Michael regarded Diana. Was she going to turn round and ask him to keep her in the style to which Ernie had gotten her accustomed?

The odd nice suit did not a mogul make. Michael recalled Iris. When his bonus went out the door so did she. He hated gold-diggers with a passion.

But he could not hate Diana. She just wouldn't let him. All his fighting to stay neutral and not hit on her, what had it meant? Just about nothing, when he thought he was faced with a lover of hers.

Michael's groin had refused to be silenced that day.

And it was a good thing. If he hadn't kissed her and taken her home, he might never have known what it felt like to really master a woman; not just an easy lay, the latest of the long string of girls he didn't know, or girls he quite liked, some woman he had selected from all the girls flinging themselves at him because he needed a piece of ass. Diana, he had dreamed of. Thought about. Been distracted by.

She fascinated him. And he admired the way she had adapted to working for a living.

But, Cicero told himself, it was nothing more than that.

How could he fall for an uptown girl like Diana? She sat opposite him, in a delicate pink shift dress worked with tiny yellow daisies embroidered over the hem, a sharp matching jacket that cut under her full breasts and made the whole thing just about work friendly. He had no idea who the designer was. Some logo was emblazoned over the tiny buttons. D&G, Dolce & Gabanna. It was another outfit that looked sensational and must have cost . . . well, best not to guess about that.

He reminded himself she had never asked him for anything. But was that because she thought of him as her boss, rather than her boyfriend?

Their relationship had never been defined. They worked together and fucked like rabbits. Every time he promised himself he would scale it down, his resolve evaporated when he touched her, or saw her, or spoke to her. Maybe she'd be screaming at some delivery company that was late with a package, and Cicero would suddenly look at her mouth and imagine it sliding over his skin. Or maybe she would be bending over her desk, studying cover copy, and that glorious ass would be sticking out in his face, round and firm, flaring out from her tiny waist. The effect was the same. His heart started to race, his groin stirred, he looked at her and had to have her. Sure, he liked Diana and she liked him, but they were too different. They were just friends who had sex.

Michael told himself this daily.

'I'm listening to any suggestions you have,' he said easily. 'I always do. You're pretty bright, for a foreigner.'

Diana raised one neatly plucked brow. 'That's a laugh. In England, you need a satchel and a lunch box to go to school. In America they issue bullet-proof vests at the door.'

'I know you're big on gun control, but that's not the constitution. Anyway, I'm sure you didn't drag me out here to have a political discussion,' he said, dryly.

'No.' She looked down and blushed, and he remembered the flushing of her skin under him this morning, the red patches over her breasts, the long red lines where he had slowly raked his nails across her belly. Diana writhed and gasped more than any other woman he had ever known. They were hot together. Yet when she left his bed, she was more reserved than ever.

She's fascinating. She's infuriating.

'I wanted to suggest that we should be careful. We leave the office together too often. We shouldn't arrive in the same car.'

Michael swallowed a sip of the black, thick espresso and masked his disquiet. Diana didn't want to be seen with him.

'You think people will talk?'

'Yes, I think so,' she said, nodding. Her brown hair – he had told her he wanted her to go natural – suited those sharp cheekbones, those full, pouting lips. Her creamy skin looked warmer, her eyes sparkled. 'It's not business-like. You don't want people thinking you gave me my job just because . . .'

She let the sentence hang in the air.

'Just because we sleep together,' Michael said. 'That's a good idea.'

Diana smiled at him and lifted her glass of freshly squeezed orange juice. She had to draw on all her reserves with Michael to keep from losing her soul. She admired him, and she wanted him and sometimes, when she looked across at him while he was sleeping, she caught herself having deeper feelings. But she ignored them, because he didn't let her get to him.

Diana had been rejected once before. She wasn't going to take any chances now. Michael refused to open up to her. She wanted to end it, but she couldn't. He aroused her like she had never known.

Sex was no longer frustrating and enervating. This time, when she was turned on, she was satisfied. If that was the word for it . . . squirming and whimpering, clutching at Michael as he pounded into her, the thickness of his cock driving all caution away. It was hard to make barriers when she kept remembering the way his thumbs rubbed gently back and forth across her nipples, his palms slipped down to cradle her ass and caress her pussy, softly, until she was twisting in his hands, begging him to fuck her again. And Michael Cicero was not a pretty boy. With the shirt and suit off, the bull-like chest was fully revealed, the thickness of his biceps, the dark, wiry hair that covered his chest and his arms. The face that stared down at her, kissing her hard as his hands pinned her arms over her head, teasing her, keeping her motionless, was a man's face, broken-nosed, dark-eyed, thick black lashes, close-cropped black hair. Ernie's skinny frame seemed even more unattractive and . . . Diana flinched in distaste at the thought of his cock.

Maybe it was true that size didn't matter . . . but she didn't think so.

It wasn't about length, it was about thickness. How long Michael was she really didn't know . . . about average, maybe. What had her biting her lips to stop from crying out was the solid thickness of him, that stubby, wide, sweet plunging, relentless flesh that was so merciless in seeking out her pleasure. Cicero was a master. Outside the bedroom, Diana thought she could handle him, but inside the bedroom, his word was law. Michael wasn't a sensitive lover. He didn't go for poetry and long candlelit, soul-baring dinners. They rarely got to dessert before his hand was rising up her knee and he was shoving her into a cab, touching her breast under her jacket, firing her blood and making her breath come out in ragged gasps. He pinned her down across the bed, a table, his knees. He held her locked in place with his body, one hand holding down both her arms with utter ease as the other roamed across her body, tormenting her. And when he finally agreed to fuck her, Michael knew how to pace it, driving her, forcing her up to the brink, tilting her body so his cock pressed against that soft, melting spot on her inner walls that forced her to yield, the pleasure exploding inside her like a firework, a white-hot, blinding shower of stars.

But he was so stern and disapproving of her.

She tried a million different outfits, and none of them seemed to please him. Sometimes Diana felt they were circling each other like wolves about to strike, not sure whether to mate or fight.

She needed to know how he felt. She had hoped he would tell her she was being dumb, that he wanted to be seen with her.

No such luck. Cicero accepted what she was saying without hesitation. Diana was sure he didn't love her.

'Well, that's settled.' She smiled as brightly as she could. 'I'll go first; I know you like your breakfast.'

'Yeah, see you in the office. And maybe tonight.'

'Maybe,' Diana agreed.

She lowered her glass, stood and walked out. She didn't let the tears prickle in her eyes until she was safely out on the sidewalk.

She is one cold woman, Michael thought, grimly.

He's made of stone, Diana said to herself.

After that, they arrived at the office separately. The irony was that once the office doors had shut behind them, they got on famously, enjoying each other's ambition and dynamism.

Michael drew up business plans and made presentations to software houses.

Diana listened to his vision and increased her hiring. It was amazing to her that he could found a computer-games company when he knew nothing about computers. But Michael's passion was infectious. Book industry insiders who knew him recommended him to colleagues in the tech market. It usually only took one meeting, with Michael's business savvy and Diana's poise, for the fishes to bite.

'I don't know code from crack, but I *do* know kids,' Michael explained. 'If we hire the right people, we can execute the vision. Is David Geffen a musician? Is Donald Trump an architect? Hell no. You don't need to be. You need to hire the right people and come up with the right numbers.'

'But in that case we might as well be selling soap,' Diana protested.

'We might, but I don't want to sell soap. You can work to make money or you can work at your dream. But if you choose to work for the dream, you'll make more money.'

'I guess so.'

'People are interested, aren't they?' Michael demanded.

She couldn't deny it. 'Very.'

'Imperial is going places. Trust me. I know about these things.'

Stung by his arrogance, she couldn't help but needle him. 'You're only thirty-one Michael, and so far you have one aborted book house to your credit.'

'I know about these things,' Michael said simply, shrugging.

Diana didn't press the point. The trouble was, she believed him.

Chapter 30

'Interesting,' Ernie said.

He steepled his fingers, which he thought made him look statesmanlike. Jack Fineman's cool, air-conditioned office looked out over Gramercy Park. Ernie gazed unseeing at the nannies walking their charges and the chess-players hustling the rubes, and considered the information his lawyer had dug up.

'So how much exactly would you say Cicero was worth?'

A nanny in jeans and a soft cashmere sweater strolled by, pushing a double stroller. So many New York wives were on fertility treatments now that you saw twins and triplets everywhere. Ernie disliked kids. He turned back to Fineman, awaiting his answer.

'Imperial's just a small company.'

Fineman shuffled through his papers. Ernie was a seedy operator, no doubt about it. Fineman's firm wasn't used to hiring private eyes to trail people, as though Ernie were some suburban wronged wife with a grudge. But they paid out the big bucks, and clients with egos were always capricious. The lawyer knew that in this matter he had to pander to his client. 'They have an independent distribution deal, plus they write games for some of the bigger houses. But they've also been talking to a lot of banks, even investment banks. I'd say they're gearing up to make an offering on Wall Street. Go public, get serious capitalisation.'

Ernie shifted. 'You didn't answer my question, mate.'

'I'm getting there.' Fineman smiled broadly. 'Right now he might be taking home a hundred, a hundred and fifty a year. He literally takes money from sales and pays off overheads, wages, health plans, etc. But he owns the company one hundred per cent. Any IPO would be based on potential, not the small numbers they're managing right now as a boutique firm. They have a unique product in a small corner of the market, educational software. Kids like learning with their games. Word of mouth is excellent. I think an IPO would be a big success.'

'So if they go public, how much does he get?' Ernie frowned slightly. He wasn't interested in background, just answers.

'The sky's the limit. Conservatively, twenty million dollars. Maybe more.'

Twenty million?

Ernie felt his stomach drop. That would put the little bastard up there with him. He had a lot of toys – the chauffeur on permanent call, the charter planes, the chopper rides – but they were company perks. He was employed, and Michael Cicero owned his product. He glanced out over the park again as though he were totally unconcerned.

'Of course, then he loses control of the company.'

'Not necessarily. He doesn't have to float it all. He could sell off a forty-nine per cent share, or even less than that.'

'I don't like the thought of a rival taking that slice of the market,' Ernie said calmly. 'You know we have an interest in games, too.'

Fineman pushed his spectacles up his nose. 'Then I can only suggest you bring your division to the Street's attention, Mr Foxton. At the moment, his product is unique. And the market loves uniqueness.'

'Right,' Ernie said, thoughtfully. 'I better be going.'

Fineman stood and showed his client out. He wondered how Cicero would take this. They had screwed him over once. It seemed harsh to do it twice, but hey, business was business.

Opie led the applause and then the dive for the beer.

'Great speech, boss.' He grinned up at Michael cheekily. 'Inspiring, huh? Maybe we should get out some brass eagles and send the legions into battle?'

There was warm laughter.

The staff were crammed into the upstairs room at the White Horse Tavern, Greenwich Village's answer to an English pub, which Michael had hired out for the office party. There was a keg of beer and three different wines, and the troops were getting rowdy. Not that he minded.

The Alpha Series of games had recently been launched on the market. After months of code-crunching, rushing the printers and browbeating the independent distribution system, the first Imperial games had finally landed in the stores. Opie had turned to web design and run up a site for direct sales, too, while Diana negotiated shipping contracts with UPS.

The reviewers just loved them. Even the commercial gaming mags had got into the act. Around the room were hung, courtesy of Diana, large blow-up posters of the more notable reviews. *PC World* screamed 'Revolutionary'. *Gamer* said 'Exciting and Addictive'. But the most prominent place was reserved for the tiny inch-long slot they'd got in *Time* magazine that called them, 'The best reason for moms to love a mouse in the house'. Below the brief rave they had printed the website address. And after that, there had been no stopping Imperial. The factory could not keep up with demand. They were limiting the units per store, per region, per customer, which made them must-haves, creating a delicious, sexy little consumer buzz.

'Enjoy yourselves, you deserve it,' Michael told them. He looked round at his troops. 'I'd tell you to give yourselves a week off, but we need the product.'

'Maybe we can have a week off when we die,' Mary Castellano, the new PR girl, suggested.

'Possible, but I doubt it.' Michael grinned. He picked up a glass of champagne somebody shoved at him and motioned to the DJ to start the music.

Michael moved through his staff, pressing hands, kissing cheeks and congratulating everybody. He had the whole office here, right down to the kid who re-stocked the water coolers and photocopier cartridges. It was important for people to feel that they shared in the stellar success of this thing. Next week he would ask more of them and more still the week after that. Everybody needed to be pumped to put in the same kind of hours he did himself. He'd suggested to Diana that she move some beds into the free rooms upstairs so people could shower and sleep there if they wanted to. But she'd vetoed it, firmly. She said people worked better when they had a life.

He wasn't so sure. Work was his life.

He noticed Diana wasn't dancing and looked round for her. There she was, leaning against the back wall in some kind of suit. It was hard to tell the colour under the flashing disco strobes, but it was bound to be something subtle, something tasteful, well cut and extremely expensive. The staff had all been given raises as soon as the cash started flowing in. Diana was his number two, and her raise had been the largest.

She had wasted no time, either, he thought, critically. She had found a new apartment, a beautiful twelfth-floor duplex in a building overlooking the river. She changed her shoes each day and floated into the office in a cloud of some vitally expensive scent. It was almost the same as when Michael first knew her. In fact, now she looked even better.

The excitement of the job gave a charge to her skin, put a glittering gleam in her eye. Her beauty was electric. Maybe he was jealous. The smartly cut suits that spanned her small waist and emphasised the flare of her breasts and her awesome butt, the colours that seemed so right, so elegant, the heels that gave a lift to the sexy curve of her calf ... men noticed her. Even twenty-something puppies and teenagers. From the old weather-worn men on the construction sites outside to the harassed traffic cops, they stopped what they were doing to drool when Diana walked past. Even her soft make-up seemed unnecessary to him. She was so stunning. Her hourglass figure and, supple, sexy sway would make a statue pant. And the way she dressed only made it worse. She was a torture to Michael. Even when she was going out with him, she seemed unattainable. To make love to her was barely to scratch the surface of his desire. She was like a lake which, every time you drank from it, made you thirstier.

Did she really need to put on such a softly brushed, melted-butter, just over the knee Prada suit for a night at the Tavern? Did she have to have her rich brown hair gleaming like that? She looked like a princess, not an executive. But there was nothing he could complain about. Each individual thing she wore was appropriate. It was the overall effect that took his breath away.

He walked up to her and watched as those cool English eyes fixed on him.

'Not dancing?' Michael asked. He breathed in her scent. It was light and fresh today. Sometimes she was rich and musky, or warm and wooded. But today she smelled cleanly of meadow flowers and new-mown grass. It was good, but not as good as the woman smell of her, the personal scent of her soft clean skin. That was how he liked her best; naked, in the shower, with nothing to decorate, nothing to hide, the fantastic body. Her breasts sluicing with water, the tiny rivulets that hung on the peaks of her rose-pink nipples. Her flat belly with the small button he loved to trace with the tip of his tongue, teasing her, circling till she was hot and begging. And for an ass man like himself, the sensational flare of her hips, the rock-hard jutting curve of her butt, which walking all over Manhattan kept firmer than any personal trainer ever could. Desire rose in him. He wanted her more, he felt himself getting hard. Again. He'd thought this morning would have drained him for days, but the sight of her buttoned-up, three-quarter-length jacket was enough to wake him from the dead. She was so ladylike, so correct. But he knew how he could make her leap. He wanted to try again. Each day was a new challenge, to drive her to places she had never been.

Diana smiled slightly. 'I don't like disco.' She nodded at the *Time* review. 'Looks good, huh?'

'It does.' He agreed at once. It was her triumph. Mary Castellano had arranged the interview, but Diana had wowed the journalist, taking him out for a meal that had wiped out a week's petty cash, at Lutece, and dazzling him with her elegance and poise. In a masterstroke of contrast, she'd brought Opie along too. The gawky young programmer and the cold English director fascinated the writer. Diana talked about Imperial's educational philosophy, and Opie blithered on about tight code and graphics scroll and other things the journalist didn't understand. It was alchemy and exciting, and he'd actually sold his commissioning editor on running a tiny plug. As a result, their website was appearing in homes and stores right across the country. 'You did good.'

Diana frowned slightly. She did good, huh? Michael was a sexist, patronising pig. She had made his damn company with that article. He should be on his knees thanking her.

'Glad you think so.'

He noted the tone immediately. 'Don't get snappy with me. I recognise your contribution.'

'Big of you,' Diana said.

They glared at each other, each thinking the other was impossible.

'I'm a little tired, to be honest.' Diana turned her head, and he caught a glimpse of the new diamond studs flashing in her creamy earlobes. 'I think I might go home.'

'Fine,' Michael said, coldly. 'Whatever you like. Are we still on for dinner?'

'Why wouldn't we be?'

'I'll pick you up at eight,' he said.

She stared at herself in the mirror, undecided. What was she today? Was she strappy, sassy, pale-pink Miu Miu shot with lilac and silver, almost a hippyish, short little baby-doll thing? Or was she classic English rose, her rosy cheeks and nut-brown hair set off by a figure-hugging velvet sheath in dark green, with a rabbit-fur trim at the collar and cuffs? The sheath fell to the floor, but it was almost more revealing than the mini-skirted dress. Michael had annoyed her today. Always the stern boss, always the workaholic. She had put in a long day with little sleep last night, and because she didn't feel like chugging down beer in some American pub he was going to give her grief? Michael expected her to be on twenty-four hours a day. She had to make it through a night of energetic love-making – well, nobody forced her, but his body gave her little choice – then get up at six, shower, dress like the businesswoman she was becoming, get into the office, put in a long day, take work home, go out on a date, and do the whole thing again the next day. Michael was professional inside the office, but stern and forbidding. She always felt like she was doing something wrong. Despite her success, maybe he still held her background against her. He seemed so much friendlier around Mary Castellano and Opie and the other staff.

And the way she dressed. It was as though she could never please him. Diana was at her wits' end to discover the outfit that would get a compliment from Michael. Now they were dating, she had thought he might unbend. Her suits got tighter and costlier, finding just the right blouse or pair of hose could take a whole Saturday, and yet he never said anything. It was annoying. Other guys seemed to like how she looked. But if Michael was not kissing her, she would never know he found her attractive.

Diana decided on the pink. Drastic measures were called for. She would shock him out of his goddamn complacency. She put the green sheath back in the walk-in closet and reached for the pink. Classic was failing with Michael, and anyway, the really stylish girl always mixed up her fashion. Guys needed to be challenged. They liked variety; Ernie had shown her that. So the trick was to be as many women as they could handle.

The silky scrappy little dress slithered on over her strapless bra, an amazing feat of engineering considering the over-spilling, creamy flesh it had to contain. It hugged her waist and bottom like a second skin, a luminous fish-scale skin, sparkling in rainbow colours. A fluted hem followed the bias-cut of the skirt which stopped in a froth just above her slim knees and nicely turned calves. With a dress like this there were only Manolos, and she reached for her new yellow leather pair along with the gold, Versace sequined clutch purse. A necklace of pink cut glass looped round the freckled hollow of her throat and she shook her hair loose from its French braid, letting it hang shining and undressed over her shoulders. The effect was sensational. To prevent too many whistles, Diana reached for her latest toy, a three-quarter-length, sixties-style coat in white leather by Stella McCartney. It had big oversized buttons and looked like something Mary Quant might have made. The girl in the mirror was all curves and legs and flashes of pink and gold and white. Diana smiled, flashing her perfect pearly teeth. If this little number didn't knock Michael out, nothing was going to.

It really shouldn't have to be this much of an effort, but she was up to it, Diana thought. Day by day, she was falling more in love with him. He blazed through life like a stallion, thick-bodied, powerful, reckless and single-minded. She loved to see how the guys in the office leaped around him. The women pressed closer and closer each day. She thought they were only deterred from outright pursuit by the thought of being fired and banished from his presence. Everything female just loved to flirt with him. Fifty and matronly, thirteen and menarchal, it didn't matter. Married, single, anything short of an actual nun just loved to bat her eyelids at him. Even old ladies would stare in the street. Despite his roughness and his bluntness he was a natural leader. He was everything her ex-husband hadn't been. And he was a dream to touch. All the fighting stopped when she got him into bed and she could no longer be cool around him. It was hard trying to keep that up, to match his reserve, even when they were fully clothed. Diana thought she would expire of shame if he knew how obsessed with him she had become, while he was still parcelling out the compliments like rations on a battlefield.

The doorbell rang and she hurriedly spritzed herself with Hermes, 24 rue Faubourg. It pitched itself as a sunny day in Paris, and for him, that was what Diana longed to be.

'Coming,' she said.

Chapter 31

Michael just stared.

God, she was something else. Young, vibrant and all body. It didn't matter what your personal tastes were, Diana gave you something to drool over. Like breasts? He'd known guys obsessed with breasts who would have followed Diana around like parched dogs with their tongues on the floor. If only they could see what they looked like when you peeled off the shimmery dress and the lacy brassiere, they'd propose on the spot. Like a small waist? He could almost fit his hands around Diana's. And her butt was the stuff of poetry. In that dress, you just didn't know where to look first. Would his eye trail lovingly up the sexy curved calves and toned thighs that seemed to stretch up like a skyscraper? Or would it burrow into the small hint of warm, freckled cleavage, or try to fix on the smooth curves of her ass under the fluted flickering hem of her dress? She had no make-up on other than a hint of peach lip-gloss, and she looked like a sixties model – except that she didn't resemble a park railing but had curves like Raquel Welch. He wondered how those strappy bits of canary nothing that threw out her ass and aligned her whole body in that sensational way could bear the weight. It was a mystery a man would never understand.

She twirled for him, and the white leather coat and curly hem bobbed in the warm light of the candles. Her place was beautifully decorated in the kind of quiet way that society women were always overpaying their decorators in order to emulate. Usually fruitlessly. Diana had achieved it probably without effort. He was a man, and couldn't be bothered with decor, but the neatness and rightness of her colour scheme took his eye. It was a soft scheme in understated tones of palest yellow and cream; a perfect antidote to the boring all-white or all-beige minimalism you saw everywhere in New York. Her paint job seemed to Michael to be sunny and relaxing. Though she couldn't stock it with the kind of pieces he'd seen at Ernie's joint, she still managed to make you feel like the place had been in her family for a hundred years, instead of being a luxury development put up in the nineties. And still, she'd decided to go out dressed like this.

'What do you think?' she asked.

He thought he'd need his karate tonight. Kicking the crap out of all the lowlifes who would approach her.

'Not bad,' Michael said.

Diana smiled to stop her face from falling. Damn the man. What was he, made of stone?

'I booked a spot at Balthazar's,' he said, after a pause. 'Let's go.' He offered her his arm and she took it. 'Maybe we can avoid shop-talk tonight.'

'But I don't know what you mean by inadequate,' Diana said sharply. They were sitting at one of the nicer tables in the ultra-hip restaurant, eating French cuisine that really wasn't bad for New York, and fighting bitterly. Diana pushed her rocket and goat's cheese salad around on her plate and thought how aggravating Michael was. She'd just finished the office decor and now he was telling her it was inadequate?

'I mean in terms of size. We're going to need to expand.'

'Why don't we wait and see what our sell-through is

like,' Diana said, spearing her salad like she had a personal grudge against it.

Michael regarded her. Great, now she was going to tell him his business. It wasn't enough that he had to deal with all the waiters staring at his date. He swore guys were getting up and going to the bathroom like women just so they could get a shot at trying to look down the front of her dress. Diana was eye candy, and they just couldn't get enough. She irritated him and fascinated him, and he wanted her badly. He wanted to punch out the lights of any man who even looked at her. And he wanted to finish up his meal so he could get her the hell home. Into bed.

'I'm going down to Wall Street tomorrow. I'd like you to come with me.'

'What for?'

'An exploratory meeting at Goldman Sachs. This is confidential, by the way.'

Diana felt her annoyance blossom into anger. Confidential? 'What, you think I'm some ditzy girl who's just going to tell all the other secretaries by the water cooler?'

'I'm just making sure.'

'Making sure of what? That I have a brain in my head even though I have a pair of breasts?'

Cicero stared at her. 'What are you now, some kind of feminist?'

'I love the way you say that like it equals "moron",' Diana shot back. 'Maybe I am a feminist. I'm enough of a feminist to know that you talking down to me is getting tiring.'

Michael crunched into his roast beef with walnuts and took a large swallow of red wine. Maybe it would relax him. It didn't much.

'Could you be a little louder, babe? I think maybe a table on the next block missed you hectoring me. I hate it when women get strident.'

'And I hate it when men get smug.'

'I'm not talking to you as a woman, Diana, OK? I'm talking to you as a director of Imperial. This is business.'

Diana frowned. That was it; she'd had enough. She loved Michael, but if he didn't love her back there was zero point in sitting here and being insulted. She had a good thing going with him business-wise. Why jeopardise both relationships?

The sensible little voice in her head told her it was time to bail out. There was no husband to pay her bills if Michael gave her the boot.

'If it's business,' she said coldly, 'it belongs in the office. Which is where our relationship belongs – in the office. OK?'

'Fine with me,' Michael spat.

Diana snatched up the bill. 'As this isn't a date any more, I'll get it. I can write it off against tax.'

She turned on one of the itsy-bitsy heels and strode out, away from him, and every guy's eyes followed her out.

Michael forced himself to sit there and finish his meal. Deliberately, he took his time with the wine and the coffee. He had just been dumped in public in front of the whole room. He didn't like it. He didn't like it at all.

'Your cash flow's good, but you're going to need some serious numbers to finance an expansion. An IPO could do that for you.'

Diana leaned forward over the mahogany table in the Goldman Sachs conference room. A posse of hip young number-crunchers, most of them men, and a slightly older guy, Richard Demotta, had done a tap-dance for Michael for the last half-hour. The dollar amounts they kept throwing out were so large they seemed like long-distance telephone numbers with a few zeros attached. And yet he still didn't seem to be sold. The stubborn bastard.

Diana had spent yesterday night crying herself to sleep and she was resolved it wasn't going to happen again. This morning, she'd risen and selected the best suit she owned – a Vera Wang champagne-coloured skirt that hovered on the knee, and a jacket with sassy three-quarter-length sleeves, teamed with Charles Jourdan pumps and good pearls. Add a simple cream silk blouse and a little make-up and she seemed to have walked right off the cover of *Forbes*.

Michael's eyes flickered across her body when she got into the office, but he was all efficiency and respect. Somehow it was even worse than his treatment of her last night.

Diana told herself that was OK. He was a good boss. Everything else was a momentary lapse, a spell of adolescent foolishness that would now be behind them.

'But say we do take the company public,' she said, boldly.

The eyes of the M&A specialists flicked across to her. They would ignore a woman here if they could, she knew. Diana wasn't about to give them that chance. She was a director of this company, and she would start out as she meant to go on.

'What are the chances that Mr Cicero would lose control? And how long would our investors wait for a return on their investments? What profits would we need to post, and how soon, before they started dumping us?'

Eyebrows were raised. Then Demotta cleared his throat.

'If I may address your concerns, Mrs Foxton,' he began.

Diana held up one manicured hand. 'Ms Verity. Diana Verity. I go by my maiden name.'

She caught Michael's sharp look of annoyed surprise and grinned to herself. When I was a kept woman, Diana thought, I hated anything feminist. But now I'm doing well for myself it's rather – well – she searched for the word. What was it exactly?

Fun. That was it. Yes, she was actually having fun.

'Certainly, Ms Verity,' Demotta agreed smoothly, and started to outline the risks. This time he included her in what he was saying.

Ernie chewed down on his cigar and blew out a long, thin stream of smoke.

Lunch at the Voyager Club was something he always enjoyed. It was one of Wall Street's oldest clubs and the members were very old money indeed. Bankers, shipping magnates, select judges and landowners all rubbed shoulders and networked here in a subtle fashion. The only women they let through the door wore short black skirts and white aprons as they served the drinks. Members' wives could not accompany their husbands further than the lobby. The Voyager had resisted every attempt to bring it into the twentieth century. Ernie fondly hoped to be made a member some day soon. Every time he got a crony to put up his name he was blackballed. But Ernie had no shame. He wanted in and he was prepared to wait.

His host, Chester Bradfield III, nodded and smiled and thought what an insufferable little man his client was. It was common knowledge around the club that Foxton was banging on the doors to be let in. He'd go fishing for rainbow trout in the Hudson before that happened. Still, he liked to invite Foxton here for drinks, to romance the limey jerk and make him feel comfortable. Foxton's stock was on the rise as Blakely's cut back costs. His venture with the Italians had been well received. Wall Street was always on the look-out for a new Ted Turner or Richard Branson. He didn't think Ernie Foxton was it, but Bradfield hadn't gotten his Park Avenue town house and estate in Dutchess County by burning his bridges.

Foxton and his lawyers were a new client of Bradfield and Smith, the investment banking firm which he had the pleasure of chairing. Ernie seemed eager to acquire new companies, and Bradfield loved nothing better than hostile takeovers. They were great for business, so refreshingly eighties. In exchange for his custom, who wouldn't stand Ernie Foxton roast beef, port and Stilton once in a while, and give him the snippets of information he seemed to lust after so much?

'I spoke with Jack Fineman,' Chester said. Fineman was a good lawyer, too discreet to complain about the client he was saddled with. 'He said you were interested in the progress of Imperial Games?'

Ernie leant forward in his seat. 'Oh, yeah. I am. You got anything to tell me?'

'Nothing important. But they seem to be talking to people about an IPO.'

So it was happening. Ernie felt a rush of adrenaline that made him almost light-headed. 'And what do you think about that?'

'Only that you'd be advised to buy a piece of the stock once they do sell.' Bradfield knew Foxton loathed the man who ran the two-bit little games company, and he enjoyed needling him. 'It's a small outfit, but well fancied. Into e-business. Could do well.'

Ernie forced his body to relax. 'Maybe I will. What exactly makes this firm so special, though? Our new games outfit's doing OK.'

'I agree, very respectably. But you make games. Shoot 'em ups, or whatever they call them. Michael Cicero, that's the name, I think—'

'It is.'

'Smart kid. Going places. Buzz on him. Anyway, he makes educational software, games that teach kids how to learn. The products rate higher than the usual academic CD-ROMs because they're fun to play.' Bradfield shrugged. 'When I was a kid we played with toy soldiers, but whatever floats the tiny demographic's boats.'

He sat back, rather pleased with this. The Englishman looked shrunken, almost drawn-in upon himself.

'Do you know the timetable for the launch?'

Another shrug. 'To get it right – and if it's Goldman they will – a few months, for sure. Maybe four.'

'Interesting.' Ernie stubbed out his cigar, stood and offered Chester Bradfield a weak handshake. 'Thanks for lunch, OK? Talk to you again.'

He raced down the oak-panelled stairs of the narrow, nineteenth-century building and out past the bowing doorman. His driver was waiting for him. Lucky the limo had two banks of phones and an in-car fax. Inspiration had struck Ernie Foxton, and he wasn't going to wait to get back to the office to get to work.

'So what do you think?' Michael asked Diana.

It was the end of the day. The staff had gone home, at least most of them. The phones were stilled, and they were going through the figures with cartons of Chinese food and a pair of biros.

It was hard for Diana to be near him, but she gave no sign of it. Both preserved cold body language. Each waited for the other to make a move. But as neither did, they just got on with the job.

'I think we should do it.'

'We'll need to go to a bank in the interim for a credit line.'

'I know,' Diana agreed. 'But if we can tell them confidentially about the IPO, they'll be happy to give us a credit line.'

'More than happy,' Michael said, cynically. They would love to because then there would be collateral.

And once it was public, the possibility remained that he could lose control. He glanced over at Diana. She was gathering up her papers. She looked so good in that pale-golden suit. But what a goddamn prima donna she was. Diana Verity? Please. Not only had she dumped him, now she thought she was Gloria Steinem.

'Going somewhere?'

'I have plans,' Diana said, sweetly.

'That was fast.'

She arched an eyebrow. 'This may surprise you, Michael, but my world didn't crumble into dust just because we split up. I'll see you tomorrow.'

She gathered her things and was gone in a cloud of perfume.

Bitch, Michael thought. Ball-breaking goddamn frozen English bitch. He would say frigid if he didn't know better.

Well, two could play at that game. There was a 7 p.m. start at Yankee Stadium. He would call his friend Joe and see a little night ball. Beer and a ballgame. Better than a woman any day of the week. Especially that one.

Chapter 32

The ballroom glittered like Aladdin's cave. It was technically only a cocktail party, but you would never know it. Swaths of delicate white tulle covered with minute crystal beads hung from the ceiling like giant spiders' webs covered in dewdrops. Gigantic white pillar candles, scented with iris and lavender, burned at strategic places around the room, casting a warm glow on the golden tables festooned with clouds of creamy lilies and frothing baby's breath, glittering crystal and sparkling Cristal. A twenty-four-piece orchestra, clad all in white, played softly as the beautiful people mingled. And what a sight they were. Instead of the usual command to dress in black or white, the invitation had said simply: 'Wear red'. Guests moved across the expensive white cocoon it had taken Mrs Merriman's decorators a day of flat-out work to create like poppies scattering across a field of snow.

Even the men wore red. Diana thought of the extravagance of it; these were publishers, record executives, television people; corporate Titans and their womenfolk. None of them would own a red suit. They must all have had one especially dyed just for tonight. And the rubies the women were sporting were something else.

'Impressive,' she said to Claire Bryant, her date for the evening. Claire was always inviting her out to society evenings, and now Michael was gone from her life, Diana had decided to accept. It was about time she got back into the flow of things. She had some money again; not enough to dazzle, but enough to be respectable. And she was tired of hiding away.

'Isn't it? Elspeth Merriman throws the most wonderful bashes.' Claire leaned in towards Diana and touched her flute bubbling with a champagne and pressed strawberry juice cocktail. 'This one's to celebrate her fiftieth wedding anniversary. As she gets older, she gets more dramatic.'

'She's got wonderful style,' Diana agreed. Her blue eyes sought out their hostess, a wizened dwarf of a woman who had defied her own rules and come in black. She was wrinkled, like a toe after a long soak in the bath and, from what Diana could see, dressed extremely chicly.

'You can talk,' Claire said, gesturing at Diana's gown. It was a brilliant cherry-red, with a vee that just covered her full breasts then plunged straight down to the breast-bone. The skirt was straight and heavy, and the sleeves long and narrow. She looked like a medieval princess, Eleanor of Aquitaine, ready to command armies and steal the heart of a king.

'It's Ralph Lauren,' Diana said simply. She didn't have the ropes of rubies or the strings of pearl-set garnets that the others were wearing, but she knew she didn't need them. With a truly dramatic dress, less was always more.

'You have a terrific eye.' Claire loved Diana's irreverence; she was wearing a comfortable pair of rope-spun sandals under her couture gown. It was the same eye that had decorated her place so tastefully and, Claire was sure, on a budget. 'Maybe you should come and work for me.'

'Anything would be better than the boss I have now,' Diana said, flashing her friend a rueful smile.

Claire took her arm. 'Come on, let's mingle. If you're sure you can handle Madame Merriman, that is. I do have to warn you, she doesn't pull her punches.'

Diana took a sip of her champagne and smiled slightly.

'Right now,' she said, 'neither do I.'

Elspeth Merriman inspected the young woman being presented to her by the Bryant girl with evident satisfaction. She was exactly the right kind of stranger to meet at a party. Rarely, in a world full of new money where taste and cash were possessed by the Manhattan elite in inverse proportions, had she seen somebody so well put together. The dress, for example, was so exactly right. It fit perfectly, it was daring without being cheap. And the girl had picked just the right tones for her skin. She was thirty or thereabouts, at the peak of her beauty, with an English accent and soft brown hair she had not seen the need to colour. Elspeth approved. There were so many bottle blondes in this town, it was almost like living in Sweden. Dangerous curves on her, too. It was a good job Elspeth's husband had passed the philandering stage long ago. Thank God they had not invented Viagra earlier. It would have caused her such problems.

'Do tell me about yourself, my dear,' she said.

Diana nodded. 'My name is Diana Verity. I work in computer software.'

'Diana is a director of her company,' Claire chimed in. 'She's English. She used to be—'

The claw-like hands clapped almost girlishly. 'Diana Foxton. Ernest Foxton of Blakely's. The Chinese hooker. Am I right?'

'Elspeth!' Claire protested, but Diana waved the protest aside.

'Absolutely right,' she said. 'Luckily I found out quickly enough to get out.'

'But you didn't even take him for every cent,' Elspeth said. She had to hand it to the English girl, she wasn't running off, snivelling, like young women normally did. 'At least that's what I heard.'

'Right again.'

'How independent of you.' Elspeth Merriman beamed,

displaying new false teeth, white and marvellously realistic, that the discreet little man in Switzerland had done such an excellent job on. 'And you used to give the most wonderful parties.'

Diana waved at the scarlet splash of society drifting across the gorgeous cream of the room. 'Not, I'm afraid, as wonderful as yours.'

Claire Bryant smiled into her drink and suppressed a cheer. Diana really could handle the old bat, huh? Elspeth was the absolute queen of New York society at the moment. She chaired every party that really mattered, she knew all the right charity boards, and best of all, she was old enough to enjoy trouble. Elspeth, in her rich, pampered, jet-set way, simply didn't give a fuck. Which was why Claire's grandfather had once romanced her, and why his descendant liked her now. Claire had heard Diana's whole story, and what her friend hadn't spilled, she'd filled in for herself. It was quite easy to join up the dots.

Diana needed a husband. With Elspeth Merriman's help, she could snag a spectacular one.

Claire had never liked Jodie Goodfriend or Natasha Zuckerman. The Wall Street wives liked to think they owned this city. Certainly Diana's fall had entertained the town for a few weeks. But Claire was a New Yorker born and bred. She liked survivors. And clearly the English rose in the silk gown qualified in spades.

Claire glanced to her right and her blond eyebrow arched. Speak of the devil, as the old saying went, and his horns appear. Or even her horns.

'Darling Elspeth.' Brushing Claire aside, Jodie Goodfriend, skeleton-thin with glossy hair the colour of straw, had arrived in a wave of Joy perfume and the standard set of dazzling rubies. She wore a costly cheongsam the shade of spilled blood that showed off her bony hips and non-existent ass. Typical Jodie. She hadn't even looked to see who else Elspeth might be talking to. She just charged in and expected everyone to give way.

Claire noticed Diana was not flinching. She waited for the penny to drop.

'Hello, Jodie,' Elspeth said in her sweetest tone, 'you know Diana Verity, I believe?'

Jodie turned to her left and jumped a little. What was Diana doing here? Wasn't she dead and buried? How many calls from her had Jodie refused to take before the stupid little limey had finally got the message that divorced girls weren't welcome in the club?

'We have met,' Jodie said after a little pause. Her tone was cutting. One party does not a comeback make, sweetie, her pursed lips seemed to say. 'Before Ernie divorced you, Diana, I think?'

'You think right.' Diana found she was slightly amused. 'You came to six of my dinner parties and ate out with me twice a week.'

Jodie waved one hand in the air to indicate how unimportant that was in the scheme of things. 'Oh yes, I recall. So many dinners . . . so many luncheons . . . it's hard to keep them all straight in one's head.'

'It must be, with your busy schedule of shopping,' Diana replied.

Jodie froze. Rather than begging and pleading to be admitted back into the fold – as dear Felicity had done – Diana was actually daring to be rude to her, Jodie Goodfriend, wife of the chairman of Croesus Bank!

People had stopped talking and were looking their way. Enjoying the spat. Well, now was the time to put the little upstart in her place.

'I like to shop. It's important to keep oneself looking nice for one's husband. Part of what it takes to make a marriage work,' she said, cuttingly. 'Perhaps you wouldn't know too much about that. I dare say you have other interests. Shopping for roach-infested apartments in Alphabet City.'

She laughed lightly.

Diana smiled back. The adrenaline was crackling through her blood. So the bitch in front of her had read that article in the tabloid? Of course she had. How can I ever have liked this woman? Diana wondered.

'That *was* difficult,' she acknowledged. 'Of course I moved out of there long ago. I have a little duplex in the Brompton Building now.'

Jodie stiffened. The Brompton Building was the latest fashionable place for rich young things to live. Not in the league of her Bronxville country house, of course, but definitely respectable.

'Seeing a new man? What quick work,' she shot back.

Diana gave her that aggravatingly superior smile. 'Not exactly. I have a business. I am a director of Imperial Games. I find talent, talk to banks, organise personnel and office space, and oversee marketing.'

'Ah. A career girl. I find many women turn to that if they find the social scene a little hard to handle,' Jodie said, after a pause. Director? Of a company? Everybody knew the only thing Diana Foxton could direct was her cook.

'Really,' Diana said, coolly. 'I thought it was the other way around.'

The aggravating, wretched Bryant girl was actually sniggering! Jodie saw the amused faces of that old witch Elspeth's friends smiling as though the most amusing thing had just happened. She racked her brain for a comeback, but there was none to be found. Jodie flushed as red as her tight little dress, and flounced off. She would dig out her mobile and call Natasha and Felicity. Diana would pay for this.

'You made an enemy there,' Claire said once Jodie was out of sight. 'Jodie has influence. You want to be careful.'

'Bullshit,' Diana said. 'If anybody needs to be careful, it's her. You can say one thing for hitting rock bottom. You find out who your friends are. Or in my case, aren't.'

'A wonderful performance, my dear.' Elspeth cackled, squeezing Diana's arm. She hadn't enjoyed herself so much for thirty years. 'I'm having a little party, a dinner really, far more fun than this tiresome zoo. My house on East Seventy-fifth, next Friday. Do come. I have a few people I'd love to introduce you to.'

'I'd like that,' Diana said, 'Elspeth.'

She smiled graciously at her hostess. Next to her, she saw Claire itching to get her home so they could gossip and plan a strategy. How divine if she could get revenge on Felicity, Natasha and Jodie, all the people who snubbed her so viciously on her way out of the safely married circles. The thought occurred to her that Michael would probably call this shallow and stupid, but who cared what he thought?

Diana glanced round the opulent ballroom at the guests who were nodding their appreciation of her verbal spar. These were movers and shakers, the kind she had longed to sit round her own table when she had been married to Ernie. She met everyone's gaze and prepared to do some serious mingling. Claire had taken one of her arms, and Elspeth Merriman the other.

I'm back! Diana thought.

Ernie scanned the figures laid out in front of him and did some quick calculations in his head. If the top-secret sales projections for their software – his marketing whizzes had come up with the name Education Station – were on target, he would bring Blakely's quarterly profits up another 21 per cent by the next report. And with his profit-share agreement, that could mean a bonus of anything up to two million.

Not to mention the delicious fact that he would shaft that little Yank bastard again at the same time.

'Yeah, I like it,' Ernie told Peter Davits.

The Russian grinned back. 'I thought you might, Mr Foxton.'

Their design boys had been up all night for over a week, running off covers, packaging and text that looked and sounded just like Imperial's snazzy product. Better, he could offer the market what Cicero could not – the gaming resources of Signor Bertaloni's company and instant distribution power in Toys 'Я' Us and K-Mart. Just to hammer the final nail in the coffin, he was going for what Michael could never afford – TV spots. Commercials would run coast to coast, from the Cartoon Network to the chat shows that stay-home moms loved to watch. Soon Education Station would be the only name worth having in the house.

Lee Tatton, his marketing vice-president, chimed in. 'Just think, sir. Once our line is known, kids will think everything else is a cheap rip-off. Research shows how brand loyal they are. There are lots of better-made dolls than Barbie, but any kid will tell you what she wants. It has to be right.'

'And if Education Station gets known first, Imperial will look like a cheap imitator,' Davits said.

'Too right.' Ernie smirked.

'But I have to warn you, television is not cheap. The campaign will cost us, of that there is no doubt.'

'I don't give a fuck what it costs.' Imperial was barely weeks away from a launch. 'You get those spots on the air. Find an agency that can pull it together fast. I want to launch and I want to launch now.'

Chapter 33

It barely took two weeks.

Diana smiled when she thought about it. She had blazed back on to the social scene like a comet, her sparks and glow trailing right behind the conflagration of Elspeth Merriman's prestige. During the day, she went over the careful planning of the IPO with Michael, keeping a cool professional distance and never allowing herself to dwell on the way he still made her ache, late at night, when the last kiss had been planted into the air beside her cheek, and the last glass of champagne drained to the bottom. Only in those moments, when she lay tucked up and alone on her Pratesi sheets, looking out through her window, at the night glitter of Manhattan's skyline, did she really let herself feel the hole he created when he left. OK, technically she had left, but he had forced her into it.

Diana shook her head and picked up her new diamond earrings to distract her. She'd said she wasn't going to think about him. It was annoying the way she couldn't control her thoughts sometimes. The business was cracking along, and she basked in Michael's reflected glory. The world was waking up to Imperial. This morning there had been half a paragraph, buried deep inside the *Wall Street Journal*. Goldman Sachs thought that interest in the IPO would be substantial. She had been a part of it. Even though Diana knew nothing about computer programming, she certainly knew about gossip. People gossiped in every circle in life, not just Hollywood and the social-register crowds. Net geeks and comic-book freaks gossiped just as much as anyone else. Her ability to tap that rich stream to find the best, most committed people had made her Michael's best headhunter.

And she couldn't fault him on the business front. He'd given her a chance when nobody else wanted to know her. Now he gave her credit, and not only that but pay and a title to go with it. In his personal relationships Michael was a sexist, domineering bastard – *don't* go there again, Diana – but as far as the company went, he was fair. A slave driver, sure. A stern boss – absolutely. But you prospered at Imperial if you did good work. Black, white, pink with green spots, he didn't give a fuck. He promoted men and women according to just one thing – how good they were.

Last week Michael had hired Jim East, a legendary marketing man who hadn't worked in twenty years. He was excellent at what he did. He was also seventy-eight. The fact that he shared an office with Opie said a lot about Michael's blinkers. He just didn't see anything strange in that.

Outside the office, though, Diana wasn't going to worry about what her boss thought.

Elspeth had been busy. A cocktail party here, a dinner there, mixed doubles at her country club, and suddenly Diana found herself back. It was fun to be worrying again about what dress to wear next, to play with her make-up and be torn between Prada and Lulu Guinness as far as the bags went. She varied what she wore and the tabloids picked up on her style. *Women's Wear Daily* loved her mix of Stella McCartney, Chanel and Richard Tyler when the whole world seemed to be beige and conservative – nothing but Ralph Lauren and Calvin Klein, the Gwyneth Paltrow clones who swarmed everywhere. She met and was sweet to Natasha Zuckerman, and everybody strained to hear what was said. Felicity

Metson was supposedly furious. Diana tried to tell herself she was above petty things like what Felicity thought. But secretly she loved it. It was too much fun.

She selected a pink dress by Ghost, a wisp of nothing that clung to her curves and swept to the floor, and matched it with a rose silk Hermes scarf. The diamond drops in her ears were decoration enough. A quick spritz of the wild rose and lavender scent she had blended for her in Paris, a tug on of her latest Manolos, and Diana was ready to go.

Her phone buzzed. It was the doorman. Her car had arrived.

'I'll be right down,' Diana said.

She picked up her tiny Gucci clutch handbag and made for the elevator. It was a bore that Claire could not be with her tonight, but her fiancé had taken her off for a romantic weekend at his country house upstate. At any rate, with Elspeth behind her, Diana felt confident enough to mingle on her own. New York loves a go-getter, she thought, examining her silken, scented reflection in the glass doors of the elevator as it arrived. There was absolutely no reason why she shouldn't give them what they wanted.

Diana arrived at the Victrix Hotel at quarter to nine. The chauffeur held the door open, and she emerged into a small blast of popping flashlights, the cameras exploding around her. She wasn't famous, but she was becoming a minor celebrity, like Aerin Lauder, or Marie-Chantal of Greece. She smiled and waved and headed inside. They might remark on the fact that she had come alone; they'd probably love it. You had to be pretty secure not to bother scouring the city for an escort.

I'm young, free and single, Diana thought. Why not enjoy it?

Tonight was one of the more vital moments on the

social calendar. A fund-raiser for the new Republican mayoral candidate. Diana wasn't a voter, but that didn't matter; half the people here were registered Democrats. The point was that the place was full of celebrities and power brokers, New York's television and media elite. Donald Trump was flying in from Atlantic City; Si Newhouse, Tina Brown, Barry Diller, the usual suspects were all expected. Hip young movie stars mixed with record moguls and starving artists, who had the thousand-dollars-a-plate tickets courtesy of their patrons in real estate or investment banking. Designers and mafia dons, who these days preferred Wall Street to the fish markets, plastic surgeons and minor princes would all rub shoulders here – and then again at the fund-raiser for the Democrats' candidate two months later.

Diana would be sitting next to Elspeth. Shaking hands, smiling at people she knew – as well as people she didn't, you had to be nice, who knew when it might bite you in the ass? – she made her way through the ballroom to find her table. The Victrix was the most exclusive hotel in the city. It made the Plaza look like a YMCA hostel on a bad day. The parties were usually themed; tonight it was vaguely Republican. Torches that blazed with red, white and blue flames were propped in crystal sconces along the walls, and huge floral pillars fifteen feet high were covered in roses, poppies, hyacinths, arum lilies, any flowers that might contribute to the theme. Diana's eyes widened a little. She was getting rather jaded with American opulence, but – wasn't that an actual, incredibly rare, white Thai elephant in the centre of the room, with a keeper dressed all in gold mounted upon him? She blinked. It was, definitely. You didn't know whether to look at the decor or the guests first. The stars with glasses in their hands were illuminated by chandeliers in the shape of stars and glass bubbles, strategically placed along barely there wires, that made you feel as though you were inside a glass of champagne. A waiter, dressed in a dark-blue suit – his colleagues were in reds and whites, too, of course – bowed and asked if madame preferred Cristal, vintage Krug, or perhaps Veuve Cliquot rosé?

Slightly dazzled, Diana accepted the rosé. She liked Veuve Cliquot and, after all, the bubbly would now coordinate with her dress. She started to repent of having gone for something simple. There were women here in ball gowns. After the austerity of the nineties, it seemed that full-out glamour was making a bit of a comeback. But it was too late now. She took a slow, fortifying sip of the champagne, letting the bubbles sparkle over her tongue. There were table plans written out in beautiful calligraphy all over the room. She found one, and tried to ferret out her own name from the hundreds in front of her by the blood-red glow of one of the lamps. She couldn't see Elspeth's name either, but they were bound to be next to each other—

'Having trouble?'

Diana looked round. The voice, just behind her, was warm and friendly, definitely unusual for a party like this, where the guests would kiss each other all night long then go home and bitch afterwards. It was also male. It belonged to a tall man, with what looked like light-brown hair, though the lamp made it hard to see. He had clean-cut features, sparkling eyes, white teeth and, she noted, a marvellous white-tie suit. Many of the male guests had ignored the invitation and turned up in tuxedos. Not this one.

'Slightly,' she admitted. 'My eyesight isn't bad, but the light—'

'Do allow me.' He offered her a firm handshake. 'My name's Brad Bailey.'

'And mine's Diana Verity,' she said. He was confident, and she liked that. He had an open smile and an easy manner. And he was at least four inches taller than Michael, not that she was going to think about Michael.

'I know.' Brad grinned at her. 'I've seen your picture around. And that accent is beautiful.'

'Thank you.'

'I hope you don't mind that I took the liberty of introducing myself. I just remembered that joke in *Ten Little Indians*, ever seen that movie?'

She shook her head instead of saying no so that her diamond earrings caught the light. It was easy to like this man.

'You should, it's real funny. Anyway, this Irish guy says he'd heard two Englishman were stranded on a desert island for five years and never said a word to each other because they hadn't been introduced.'

Diana laughed.

What a stone-cold fox, Bailey thought, with a body that could make a dead man rise and do the mambo. He loved her dress, her loose, long, brown hair, the delicate scent of flowers that hung about her. And the way she talked. Those English broads just exuded cool. Look at Princess Diana. The woman actually had a nose like Concorde, but she had borne herself with such confidence and classy style that she had been thought the most beautiful woman in the world. This girl was the same way. Brad indulged in a little fantasy of Diana in tennis whites, sipping a lemonade on the court of his country club.

'I'm afraid we can come across as rather stuffy, but on the other hand, we produced the Beatles and the Stones. So you work it out.'

'I'd love to,' he said, smiling down at her. 'But I think I might need some time to do it. Say, dinner?'

'Maybe,' Diana said, surprising herself. 'First I have to find my place at this dinner.'

'Excuse me for just a second,' he said, bowing slightly and moving away.

Diana's eyebrow lifted. He was chatting her up and then excused himself? So be it. After Ernie, she was in no mood to play games. Seething, she bent closer to the table plan and found her name. Table eighty-nine. Now she had to look on the floor plan and see if she could find table eighty-nine, wherever it was. There were enough tables in the ballroom to stock a branch of Ikea, except that these particular tables would not be found there. Solid mahogany and gold accents weren't their style. She scanned the picture, ignoring the flautists and girls in robes with miniature harps who strolled behind her. Eighty-nine . . . but Elspeth wasn't there. She must be ill. Diana frowned lightly. She would have to make conversation on her own, and—

'I'm back.' Brad Bailey tapped her on the arm.

'So you are,' Diana said evenly.

He admired her. Damn, she was cool. An American girl would have harangued him, or batted her eyelids in the face of his money and pretended not to care.

'Please excuse my abandoning you,' he said. 'I had to speak to Fred Layton, he's organising stuff here. I promised him an extra donation if he would alter the seating plan a little.' He leant forward and struck through her name on table eighty-nine. 'You are here now on table three. With me.'

Diana's delicate eyebrow lifted. 'You got the seats rearranged? I'm sure I'm not worth such trouble.'

'It would have been worth a good deal more than that,' Brad told her, thinking of the eight grand he'd had to promise to compensate for the last-minute chaos, the hasty apologies made to the wealthy dowager who was being ejected from her prime seat next to him. He crooked his arm and hoped an English gentleman would have done it in the same fashion. 'Shall we go to dinner?'

Diana's reservations melted. He was funny and charming and solicitous. I *deserve* someone like this, she told herself.

'Thank you. That would be lovely,' she said.

Brad was good at introductions. Even Diana was impressed by the rest of their table. There was Fred Drasner, owner of the *News*, on her left, and the governor's wife on his right. Two film stars and a princess of Monaco were broken up by a Nobel prizewinner and a huge, tall basketball player. She wondered where Felicity Metson was sitting. She would gnaw her heart out if she could see Diana now.

She greeted everyone politely, curtsied to the princess, and settled down to wonder about her escort through the speeches that were bound to follow. Brad Bailey? He knew everybody, he was well liked, rich went without saying. He had a nice body, a gym-lover's body, even if he didn't lift many weights.

'You have the advantage of me,' Diana said. 'You know who I am, but I can't say the same.'

He nodded. 'I'm in real estate. I own Bailey Realtors. You won't have seen the name because we don't advertise much. Mostly we deal in high-end properties in Manhattan, Westchester and Long Island, with a little work upstate.'

'What qualifies as high end?'

'Anything from eight or nine million up, basically.'

Diana studied her menu. Caviar blinis followed by duck with a fresh pea confit, then apple charlotte with vanilla-scented cream.

'How did you get into that?'

'It's a family business. My father built it up.' Brad shrugged apologetically. 'I can't claim to be a self-made man.'

'Let me guess.' She found she was teasing him. She

leant closer, and he breathed in the perfume of roses and tried not to stare at the freckled slopes of her glorious tits. 'A large family house on Brooklyn Heights, and pony lessons at weekends?'

'Almost. A country estate in Westchester, a townhouse in the city, and stables with horses.'

'And a private jet,' Diana suggested.

'Of course,' he said, seriously.

She swallowed. 'It sounds pleasant.'

'It is. I tend to commute in from my place at Scarsdale in Westchester these days, though. I like waking up to greenery.'

'I can understand that,' Diana said faintly.

'It gets me out of the city. I go to things like this because I suppose I have to.'

'Where else would you find people that want to buy and sell places starting at eight million?'

'Exactly,' he said, pleased at her perceptiveness. 'You're a businesswoman too, I know.'

'A headhunter, really. And – it's not quite so high powered,' she said dryly.

'I hope your schedule will spare time for dinner?' he said hopefully.

She gestured to her plate. 'Aren't we having dinner?'

He looked forlorn. 'Ah. You're going to tear a new hole in my heart.'

Diana laughed again. 'Come on, Brad. You must have a million girls chasing you.'

'I do,' he said, factually. 'But I don't like girls who chase. I like girls who are chased.'

'Like me?'

Brad gave her another warm smile. He was golden, she thought, all-American, tanned and healthy.

'Exactly like you. So please put me out of my misery. Say yes.'

Chapter 34

Michael was out running at quarter to six in the morning, the wonderful dawn hour when the city that never sleeps actually sleeps. Apart from the odd cop coming off the night shift and the fresh-produce men driving to the markets to pick up the day's selections, the wide concrete canyons of Manhattan were deserted. He had a membership to several fancy gyms now and kept up the karate, which was good to work off his frustrations over Diana, that ice-cold English bitch. But nothing blew the cobwebs from Michael's mind like running in the empty city. He pounded the concrete and leapt between cross-streets down which no cars were coming. The clean open lines of the New York grid almost pulled his feet along them, challenging him to go faster and harder. Most city joggers preferred the Park, but that was far too bland for Michael. Why circle round and round a fairly ordinary lake when you could be plunging through the shuttered record stores of the East Village, or past the manicured gardens on West Eleventh? Why bother with a hundred other runners on the same beaten track when the Museum Mile, with the stunning apartment buildings of Park Avenue, was so close and could be your exclusive playground? And best of all was midtown, where the giant glass and slate towers jabbed up into the sky like so many accusing fingers. He liked to time his run so that, whatever the route, he finished up with a dash through Times Square, with its massive billboards and scrolling lights dominating the morning sky. Times Square used to be a spot for hookers, but the city crackdowns had tidied them all away. Now it was a place for chic little hotels and cops streaming out of Police Plaza. It was still the neon, beating heart of his city. Cicero thought of New York as modern man's answer to the pyramids. He liked to stop, drenched with sweat, the muscles of his legs worked out, all his tension driven into the ground, and gaze up at the colossal billboards. It was one of the best parts of the day.

But not today.

Today, when he glanced up, he felt anger seethe in the pit of his stomach like molten acid. He found his normal deep breathing was ragged. He frowned, wiped the sweat from his forehead, and frowned again.

EDUCATION STATION, said the caption. The words were emblazoned over a sweet little kid with a pudding-bowl haircut smiling as he glanced at a paper marked 'A'. Underneath that was a blow-up shot of a CD-ROM called *Scientist Sam*. The cute Muppet-like animal that represented Scientist Sam was a total rip-off of Gecko, the character star of his best-selling game.

Michael digested the ad for a few seconds, then turned round. Usually he walked home after his run. Today he was going to wing it. He didn't have time to walk.

The phone purred by Diana's bed, and she reached out a languid hand to pick it up. She was tired; last night Brad had taken her ice-skating at a private rink on the Upper West Side, and then moved her into Le Cirque for dinner, before finishing off with a nightcap at his house on East Seventieth. He'd been funny as usual, urbane and sophisticated, and very solicitous about her wants. He didn't push himself forwards, and after taking her home, had actually asked her permission to plant a kiss on her cheek. His lips were soft and gentle.

He was almost a dream, she thought. So clean-cut and

good-looking he could be a male model if he wasn't a super-successful real-estate broker. Elspeth Merriman had been in fits about the fact that he had asked her out.

'My dear,' she said, placing one wizened hand, glittering with diamonds, over Diana's soft one, 'you must secure him as fast as you can. What a triumph! The Baileys are *quite* the people around town. She is a much sought after hostess and he's retired now, of course, but Bradley has been doing so well. And still single. Every mother in New York has been after him for years, he dated a couple of times, Camilla Vendela, I think, and Tina Fellows . . .'

'I'm not *after* him,' Diana protested. 'Come on, Elspeth. The world isn't like that any more.'

The thought of her first marriage flickered into her mind, but she ignored it.

The old woman snorted. 'Of course it is. Tell Felicity Metson the world is not like that any more.'

Diana smiled and said nothing. That was the wisest tack. But Elspeth did have a point, and Claire reinforced it. How would Felicity take her waltzing off with Brad Bailey, the last single man worth anything on the scene?

'I'm just enjoying his company right now,' she said finally.

Elspeth leaned forward, her crisp Chanel tweed bunching. 'You do that, dear. You enjoy his company. Just make sure he enjoys yours.'

Well, last night had been very enjoyable. She almost didn't want to go to work. But the telephone was ringing, and she had to answer it.

She lifted the receiver. 'Hello, Michael.'

Who else would it be at 6.15 a.m?

After briefing Diana, Michael showered, dressed and prepared to walk round to the office. He had no cell phone and this might be the last minutes of the day he could spend quietly. There would be a frenzy of calls and recrimination later, Goldman Sachs wailing, the marketing people yelling at their contacts, why hadn't anybody gotten wind of this earlier. He could see it now, and he knew how it would end. Ernie Foxton had what they lacked: money. He hadn't needed to float in order to get cash for distribution and marketing. That deal with the Italians, that Michael had read about and dismissed, that was his footing in toys. And he knew the devious twists of that little fucker's mind. Foxton would have spent heavily on this launch. That billboard wouldn't be a one off.

He set out at a fast clip. It cleared the mind to walk. This would ruin the IPO; he realised that straight away. Their product was no longer unique. Without ad-spend or awareness from Joe Public, they looked as though they had come late to their own party.

It was almost as if it was *deliberate*.

He turned the corner onto West Fourth and mulled that over. Deliberate? Ernie Foxton had certainly enjoyed firing his ass and cheating him of his millions. But would he come after him further? Was this an intentional attempt to ruin him?

Michael's thoughts slid to Diana. Ernie had divorced her and had hooked up with some new gold-digging broad, but Michael had given Diana a job. When the company, and she, had started to take off, maybe it had pissed him off.

They did say you hated the people you had harmed worse than the people who harmed you.

He thought about that ad. It wasn't just a kids' educational CD-ROM. It was a total rip-off of Imperial's own ground-breaking product.

Plenty of his best people – Diana's best finds – were staying with his comparatively small salaries because they expected a big pay day. From the start it had looked like Imperial would float. All the staff had small stakes. They would all have become rich to greater or lesser degrees when the IPO went through. But that was over now.

Michael thought it through. They would walk, and he couldn't fault them. This was a business, not a charity. If he was a top-grade code-writer, or a marketing hotshot, he wouldn't take thirty grand a year less than he was worth with no trade-off. A big staff haemorrhage would gut his company. Product would be late and less good. Distributors would fall away. It would be back to square one.

Anger closed a cold fist around his heart. Fuck it. If Ernie Foxton thought this would kill him off, he was mistaken. And if he wanted war, he was welcome.

'So what's the news?' Ernie said. It was a great morning, he thought. Jung-Li had been superbly vicious, the little bitch, this morning. She'd broken in a new pair of steel stilettos on his back. Felicity had kept out of his way, apart from sending up his favourite breakfast, and there was the news from the lawyers.

Goldman Sachs was pulling back from the Imperial offering. The word was out, Fineman said. The ad spots they'd run last night had done well and been noticed. Clearly Imperial was no longer the only player on the scene. The market hated uncertainty and would wait to see how Blakely's did.

'The offering's postponed. Which means they don't have money.'

'They're dead,' Ernie crowed. 'Little cocky bastard.'

'Er . . . quite,' Fineman agreed. 'Certainly I foresee a good many problems for them.'

Ernie hung up whistling. He was a king of the bloody universe. It was great to have cash in New York. He was Ernie Foxton, he could make men and break them.

Michael Cicero once objected to dancing to his tune. Diana the same. But I don't take crap, Ernie told himself, importantly. This would show the world that if Ernest Foxton struck you down you stayed down.

It pissed him off that Diana had apparently taken back her own name. Felicity had come in after the Elspeth Merriman party, whining and carrying on about her. Ernie gave her to understand that he didn't want to hear it. He hated the idea of public fights. Everything round him should be smooth. That was his image. He had to keep up the image.

But Diana Verity? What the fuck was wrong with Foxton? She was lucky she'd ever been his wife. It bugged him that she had the balls to do it.

He pulled himself back to the present. Pleasant reflections on the shitty day Michael Cicero would be having couldn't last for ever. He had the monthly review meeting. Davits, Norman Jackson, his new adult fiction chief, and Emma Datson, who ran marketing, were all lined up around the table with the flunky suits from their departments whose names he didn't bother to remember.

'Lawrence Taylor is going *so* well,' Emma gushed. She was a beautifully put-together forty-something and therefore of no interest to Ernie. Women for him stopped at thirty-five. However, she had survived his purge by being too good to sack. So far. That could change at any second.

'We expect him to go well. He's our biggest author. Gimme the breakdown of the list,' Ernie said.

There was a moment's pause. His executives were looking a bit shifty, Ernie realised suddenly. Staring down at the table, and that.

'Out with it,' Ernie snapped. 'I asked for a fucking breakdown. *Capisce*?'

Mrs Datson swallowed. 'Well . . . there has been a teeny sales problem with some of our new signings.'

Ernie blinked. His new signings were the big-ticket names, the trashy novelists to whom he had cleared out all those literary fuckers and whiny poetry writers. He had spent heavily on ads, mostly using the money he'd saved by firing all the dead wood, the old sales reps who weren't making their quotas, the tweedy fucking American gentlemen editors in the history department, the men who started spouting crap about what the publishing house should be giving back to the community. It was a pretty penny altogether, had done fantastic shit for the bottom line. It was how he got his ruthless reputation. The stock had soared, too.

He was pleased he'd taken out the trash. The star-author drive was part of that. Their blaze of posters, radio ads, in-store dump bins, pro-PR campaigns and talk-show appearances had produced six new bestsellers that had taken turns at the top of the *New York Times* list for the last six months.

'What are you talking about?' He lectured Datson like she was a particularly stupid child. 'Lawrence's book is number fucking one. The rest are doing good too. No?'

'They are,' Emma agreed nervously, 'in terms of chart positions. But since we stopped the advertising, sales have taken a bit of a dip.'

'A dip? What kind of a fucking dip?'

'Twenty-eight per cent on Shoshanna, thirty-nine per cent on Richards, forty-one on Redde—'

He held up a hand. 'I get the picture. Why the hell has that happened? Why did we stop the advertising?'

'We have spent heavily,' Davits said.

'You gotta spend it to make it,' Ernie snapped.

'Yes. But if we spend at the same rate, the profit from the bestsellers cancels out. We must let them try to carry their own weight. And other sales have fallen heavily too.' Davits ploughed on. Nobody else would dare to tell Ernie the way things actually were but if they lost ground at this rate he thought maybe the company would be in trouble, and that would be bad for his career. 'The mid-level writers, the genre romances, the ones the agents brought on board . . . that list is selling very badly. Two of the literary authors we axed, who have advances of no more than a hundred thou, have just had bestsellers for St Martin's Press and Simon and Schuster . . .'

'Who cares what they've done? You're a bunch of incompetents.' Ernie blustered at them furiously. 'If it's not selling, it's your fault. I don't want to hear *can't*. There's no such word as can't. This strategy worked perfect in England and it'll work perfectly here too. Six fucking bestsellers. You make sure they keep selling.'

'But—' Davits started, and Ernie was forced to cut him off.

'But what? Don't talk to me about but. OK? Just get out. Come back when the figures are right.'

They got up and hurried out of the conference room. Ernie glared after the retreating backs, noting with grim satisfaction that none of them was dumb enough to look back his way. Peter Davits was last out. He closed the door quietly behind him.

That showed them, Ernie thought. He wasn't having that bullshit. He was the boss.

Michael sighed, pressed the hold button, and switched to another call. He had an ache in his neck from having had the phone glued to his ear all day. The calls from the lawyers, the distributors, the investment bankers didn't stop coming, but the result was the same. An IPO would be madness right now. They had to watch the Education Station range. Yada, yada, yada . . .

Already he had talked it through with Diana. She was almost as mad as he was. The thought occurred to him that he'd gone almost a whole day without thinking about that Brad Bailey guy she was meant to be seeing. She had rallied the troops. He was going to call a company meeting tomorrow. Michael sighed. Some guys would walk, others he'd have to fire. Right after hiring them, too. Goldman Sachs didn't come cheap, and now he had to find a way to pay them without market capitalisation.

He hated Ernie Foxton.

Tina Armis, their receptionist, walked into the room with a cup of coffee and a muffin. It smelled real good, like it had just come out of the oven. Wordlessly, she set it down before him. Michael talked to his distributors and reached out to touch the muffin. Yeah, it was actually warm.

'Thank you,' he mouthed at her.

Tina gave him a slow smile. 'No problem,' she said.

He finished the call and jumped back to the first, vaguely aware that Tina was hovering in the background still. Michael let his eyes drift back towards her. She was young, maybe twenty-two or three. She had long blond hair and large blue-violet eyes, as well as a small, pert pair of tits and coltish legs that rose up towards a skirt that hovered on the knee. Tina was an all-American beauty. Where was she from? He thought maybe the Bronx, Williamsbridge perhaps. Michael's eye roved to her skirt. It was pencil-line tight on her slender form. He didn't see any panty line. He thought she might be wearing a thong. A cute babe, for sure.

He hung up. 'You want something, Tina? It's been a busy day.'

'Oh, I know.' She twisted her hands nervously. Michael smiled to put her at her ease. 'I'm sorry to bother you, Mr Cicero.'

'No bother. Anything I can help you with.'

'Actually it's kind of more personal.' She blushed, deeply. 'I hope you don't think me too forward but I wanted to ask you out. To dinner tomorrow.'

'What?' Michael said, sputtering. It was so artless. He was used to girls hitting on him, but—

'You're laughing at me.' She looked forlorn. 'I'm sorry. I knew this was a bad idea.'

'No. I'm not.' He said it hastily. She was cute, and why the hell should he sit at home pining after Diana?

'You'll actually consider it?' Tina beamed.

'I'll do more than that.' Michael thought about those long legs wrapped round his waist. 'I'll pick you up at eight.'

Chapter 35

'I'm really sorry, you guys.'

Toby Roberts looked at Michael and Diana and started to shift a little on his feet, like a kid caught smoking pot by the principal.

'I wanted to stay. I really dug it here. We had a blast. But these guys have, like, offered me—'

Diana glanced at Michael. Toby was the latest of their top talent to desert them for Education Station. The IPO had crashed, they had to move the company out of the West Fourth Street house to a far smaller, regular office on Eighth Avenue and Thirtieth, and there was no way they could compete with Foxton's offers. Cars, paid vacations and huge salaries were all being dangled in front of Imperial's best programmers.

Toby was among the last to succumb. Michael looked resigned to it. He'd told Diana this morning he was grateful Toby had stuck it out as long as he had.

'I know what they offered you,' Michael told him. 'You'd be mad not to take it.'

Toby still looked embarrassed. 'Man, my girl wants to get married and shit—'

'That's great. You take the job. I would do exactly the same thing.'

'OK.' Toby offered each of them a solemn, rather grubby hand. 'I hope you guys are going to be all right.'

He looked around at the small, cramped office space, the rented fax machines and dwindling bank of phones, and his tone came out more doubtful than he had intended.

'We'll be fine,' Michael said, in a tone of calm certainty. Toby wondered how the guy could do that. He said it like it was just a fact, like nothing had happened. 'You take care. Stay in touch.'

'Definitely,' Toby promised, blushing again and sidling out.

He felt like a fucking snake. But a hundred thousand a year and a Mercedes? What was he supposed to do? It was clearly the right way to go. Mike said so. But he hated leaving him. He was the kind of boss you'd follow into battle.

Diana Verity was sticking with him, Toby reflected as he waved for a cab. Strange, that. The lady was so high maintenance. Who knew how long Michael Cicero would be able to afford her?

Of course, Michael had some out-of-office consolation. That Tina Armis. Man, she was some piece of ass.

Michael closed the door on Toby and looked at Diana.

'Come on. We'll go to my office and review.'

'Sounds good,' Diana said, determined to remain upbeat. The company was like a sinking ship, complete with rats abandoning it from every porthole, but she had decided – she wasn't even sure when – to stick with it. It felt like her own thing. And if Michael was going down, she was going down with him.

Elspeth had offered to find her another job. 'Interior decor, darling,' she suggested. 'Your old offices were so stylish. I know plenty of wonderful ladies who would love to take you on. You could start with Brad's townhouse. Goodness knows what the fee on that would be.' Elspeth's painted, wrinkled mouth smiled emphatically. 'He has no budget limit, you see.'

But Diana had gently refused. Maybe it was her

encounter with Jodie Goodfriend; she wanted New York to understand that her job, her company, was serious.

There had to be a way back.

Michael led her through the front office, where their sales people were desperately trying to reassure distributors about packaging dates for the new line, to his small private room in the back. Tina Armis had her own little desk just in front of it. She stood up as Diana approached. Diana looked her over. Since she had started dating Michael she had made a big deal of it, Diana thought, annoyed. The girl was barely out of diapers. Glossy long hair, a very unnatural shade of pure platinum, flowed down her back. She wore a business suit, Diana saw, a real short one that let her display long, lean legs in flat shoes – she was so tall she could afford to do that – and probably little else. There were no lines whatever under that suit. Diana imagined her ducking into Michael's office and flashing him, letting him pull up her skirt and force her over the desk, just the way he used to do to her. Tina was welcome to him, Diana thought fiercely. With her brows plucked so thin she needed make-up to restore them, and her lips lined with a darker colour than her lipstick to make them look plumper, not to mention those nails that were far too long . . .

'Good morning, Mr Cicero,' she said.

Good morning, Mr Cicero, Diana mocked in her head. She was just like Marilyn Monroe addressing JFK, all breathy and thrusting forwards those unimpressive tits. Tina was thin, too. Far thinner than Diana would ever be. Diana reminded herself that she liked her body. She wasn't going to get caught up in the skinny blonde thing, which Michael had evidently had the bad taste to do.

'And good morning, Miss Verity,' she added, resentfully.

Diana gave her a brisk smile. The younger woman was eyeing her like she was some kind of threat. Why she thought every woman in the world would be after Michael Cicero was beyond Diana. Don't you read the gossip columns? Diana thought, nodding at Miss Pert Tits. Don't you know I'm dating the last single millionaire in Manhattan?

'Good morning, Tina,' she replied. 'Could you fetch me a coffee? Decaffeinated. You want anything, Michael?'

'Not right now.' Michael opened his office door and went in, oblivious to the undercurrent of hostility outside. Diana noted that Tina flounced off to get her coffee. She was one of those women who loved to dance attendance on men but hated having to fetch anything for another female. Diana knew the type; the air hostess who takes twenty minutes to respond to a woman's buzzer and five seconds to reach the man who calls her.

She also thought Tina was a gossip. Decaf coffee had to be brewed from scratch. If Michael and she were going to talk about the dire state of Imperial, Diana would rather it wasn't all round what programmers they had left in the next five minutes.

'Shut the door,' Michael said.

Diana slid herself into one of the simple, functional chairs they had bought from Staples. Nothing fancy here any more. In fact the fanciest thing in the place was probably his director, Michael thought, trying not to look at her legs. Thankfully he had Tina. He let his mind drift back over their session this morning . . . she loved to wake him up by giving him head, sliding her thin but eager lips over his cock, her fingertips trailing across his balls. Michael loved to fuck in the mornings and Tina could do unbelievable things with those long legs. He liked to put her on her back on the bed and stand in front of her, her slim ankles locked around his neck while he fucked her, letting his cock slide in deep enough just to stroke the G-spot and give her a shuddering orgasm. Tina was undemanding. Not smart, but adoring. She didn't give him any lip, she liked sex, and then to sit around watching TV. Michael was grateful she'd been there. His stress was instantly relieved, in the bedroom. He told himself he hardly ever thought about Diana any more. If he chanced to come across a picture of that rich-ass boy scout in the papers, he simply flipped the page and didn't let it bother him.

'Things aren't good.' He pulled his mind back from the subject of Brad before he got really enraged. 'We've lost Toby, Sarah, Jack and Felix, to that fucker your ex-husband.'

'And your ex-partner,' Diana shot back. 'We were both guilty of a misjudgment.'

He held up his hands. 'Agreed. In my view this is deliberate. Not just that they happened to get into the education software business, but that he has a vendetta. He wants to crush me. Maybe you, as well.'

'With what they're paying our people . . . on our old profit margins, it would eat up most of them,' Diana said slowly.

'Right. It's not profit that's his motive. It's revenge.'

Diana felt a flash of anger. 'He wants to ruin us?'

'Looks that way. Let's consider where we are. We have the new range, the Gecko Math and Science games. All completed before our guys got tempted away. We have some marketing men left. Harry Venture for one. And we also have key talent who refused to walk out. Ernie offered Opie the moon, but he refused to leave.' Michael gave her a rueful grin. 'He's pretty loyal, for an ex-slacker. Our best code-writers are still here. We can build on that.'

'Yeah, but the fact is,' Diana said, 'that our distributors are worried and word on the street is we might close down. That means less racking-out in the stores . . .'

'And that's what we need to counter. The fact is, right now we don't need our programmers. Not right away.'

Michael shot from his chair and started to pace. He looked like a leopard, a jaguar. Feral. Suddenly she almost felt sorry for Ernie. 'We actually have product ready to go. We can package it, sell it, and use the profit to wipe out the bank debt.'

'I can talk to the banks,' Diana agreed.

'Right. That keeps us afloat and buys us time. Meanwhile you look for new code-writers. There must be some out there that are untapped. And we wait for Ernie to fuck up. The fact is, he's going to.'

'How do you know that?' Diana asked.

Michael looked at her, and she had the impression he was looking straight through her, into the future. He was focused like a laser beam.

'Because he doesn't understand children,' Michael said. 'He doesn't care. He just wants money. It's why the new Green Eggs range of books was such a bomb.'

'It was a bomb?' Diana repeated, surprised. 'How do you even know that? We're not in the publishing business any more.'

'I keep tabs on him,' Michael said, and his voice was cold. 'Know your enemy. Now, you go out there and rally the marketing guys and go tap-dance for the banks. I'll handle the distributors. We'll take it slow, and we'll get through this.'

Days turned into weeks and weeks into months. The golden, sunny fall in Manhattan deepened and hardened into winter. Diana bought warm clothes and went dancing with Brad but Imperial occupied all her time. Little by little, under Michael's leadership, they clawed their way back from the brink. The Gecko games were another small success. Suddenly they could pay their bills.

Diana scouted for code-writing talent, but she looked in different places this time. Hackers with criminal records, designers of board games, females who were locked out of the computer boys' club, all came on board. Michael didn't care. He said they were in the second-chance business. 'These guys get one and it means we get one,' he said.

By the time December blasted down across the sky-scrapers, a third line was in production. Imperial was back.

'What are you doing Friday night?'

Diana looked up from her screen to see Michael standing over her with a pair of tickets in his hand. She lifted a brow. 'Asking me out on a date?'

'Since I'm dating Tina, I don't think that would be such a good idea,' he said, easily.

Diana looked across the room at Tina. Since the weather had turned bitter, she no longer skipped around the office in her itsy-bitsy skirts, but she still managed to be fully clothed and look like she was wearing next to nothing. Today she wore a pair of thin, black leather pants that hugged her flat stomach and tiny butt, and a matching silky jersey top with a plunging neckline, about as daring as Michael's dress code would let her go. Diana couldn't stand Tina, which meant she had to make an extra effort to be nice to her. It was annoying.

'Not for Tina, anyway,' she muttered.

Michael said, impassively, 'And you're still seeing Brad?'

'Of course. You know I'm still seeing Brad,' Diana snapped.

'Not really. I'm not that interested in your private life. I guess that means he's flying you somewhere in his personal jet on Friday?'

Diana bristled. 'We have plans. We were going shopping.'

'So he can pick you up a million-dollar trinket at

Tiffany's.' Michael sneered. 'I understand. Forget I mentioned it.'

Diana chewed on her lip. The goddamn guy was as insufferable as ever. 'Wait! Michael. What is it? I can cancel.'

'It's the New York Library Benefit Dinner.' Michael tossed her a ticket. 'Publishing's biggest event this season. I've taken a table. If Ernie Foxton comes after me on my territory, I'm going to come after him on his.'

Diana dressed with more care than usual. She wanted to look good, but not too good. It wouldn't do for that arrogant man to think she was chasing him. This was an important evening for the firm, she told herself. A statement of intent. That was what counted.

'I think that's the one,' she said. She held up the plainest dress in her wardrobe, a silk jersey knit with a square neckline in gunmetal grey. 'What do you think? I could wear my Paul Smith flats . . .'

'Right, and why not add a pair of granny spectacles to complete the look,' Claire said sarcastically. 'You act like you're afraid of something.'

'Of course I'm not. I just don't think I should overdo it,' Diana protested.

Her friend looked at her quizzically. 'This from the girl who wore a golden-mesh chain-mail Versace number to the Fire and Ice Ball last month?'

'So? I was being fiery.'

'The fact that Felicity Metson and Jodie Goodfriend were there had nothing to do with it, right?'

'Sometimes I do like to dress up.'

'You could say that. You know you're driving poor Brad crazy. He feels like he can look at you but not touch.'

Diana nodded. Sex was a sore point in their relationship. Somehow she just did not feel right about taking him to her bed yet. Maybe she was turning into an old-fashioned girl, but she didn't think so. He kept hinting about marriage. Maybe she was subconsciously holding out for a ring. Who the fuck knew? She really didn't herself.

'He knows we'll do it when the time is right.'

Claire made a face. 'Do it? You sound like a teenage boy. How about make love?'

'That too.' Diana smiled. 'You really think this is too plain?'

'You want to put the fear of God into Ernie, right?'

'That's right.'

'Then you need to make a splash.' Claire brushed her aside and delved into the walk-in closet. 'Take the dark green. It sets off your eyes.' She held up a floor-length Chloe gown in rich green velvet with a seed-pearl trim around the waist. It pleated gently over the breasts, to emphasise them, and then hugged her butt and tapered down into a fishtail. It was an exact fit; nothing but a tiny thong would slip under that.

'I can't,' Diana muttered. 'It looks too good.'

'You sound like you're more than afraid of that Michael guy,' Claire said. 'I think you're in love with him. Otherwise why would you care?'

'Nonsense.' She snatched the gown out of her friend's hand. 'I don't care what he thinks one way or the other. Give it to me. I'll wear it.'

Chapter 36

She stepped out of the limo in a rustle of warm, rich velvet and looked up at the hotel. Several press snappers were lined up at the entrance, kept at bay by a red rope and a bunch of liveried security men. A warm murmur and low whistles greeted her arrival, at the sight of the tight plunge of dark green around her warm skin and glorious curves, the pearls which gleamed at her waist and again looped around her neck. Diana had borrowed Claire's family heirloom, the Bryant necklace, a string of pearls the size of small marbles, with a marquise-cut emerald set in the centre. Against the snow, she was a burst of colour, green in the middle of winter. Her dark brows were shaped just a little, her full lips a daring red-plum shade, nothing but a whisper of gloss blush on her sharp cheekbones and a light-brown shadow to bring out the sky blue of her eyes.

The paparazzi were all men and didn't catalogue this. They just saw Diana Verity, the wife in the Foxton rumours, looking good enough to eat, like a Christmas present. Flashbulbs popped like firecrackers as she swept past, ignoring them, into the main hall.

Diana glanced around her at the rich guests. Among the uniform black tie of the men she saw faces she recognised: Rudolph Giuliani, the famous former mayor, Bobby De Niro and his gorgeous black girlfriend, Barry Diller, Ted Turner, apparently flown in from Atlanta . . . but this was publishing's night. Super-agents and the CEOs of the large book houses were all here with their wives, usually thin, blonde girls with bodies like Tina Armis, groomed to perfection and wearing black with diamonds dripping from their lobes.

She was a director, sure. But her company was small, fighting for survival. These were movers and shakers, and at least one of them was out to destroy her.

She gave her name to a receptionist.

'Diana Verity . . . Imperial . . .' The girl scanned her seating chart. 'With Michael Cicero, president . . . ah, yes . . . table twelve. Mr Cicero has already arrived.'

'Yes he has.' Diana stood upright and turned round. Michael was standing behind her in a dark dinner jacket and plain white shirt. It looked as though it had been pressed just minutes ago. The tux picked out his brown eyes and thick, dark lashes and set off his black hair.

'You shouldn't bend over like that. It's too much shape for these old men to handle,' Michael said softly in her ear. 'You could be arrested for giving them heart attacks.'

Diana blushed. 'Come off it, Michael, OK? Look at the women in here. All New York men want is a size-zero teenager in beige Calvin Klein.'

'Don't you believe it. Men like tits and ass. Always have done, always will do.'

'Do you have to be so vulgar?' Diana hissed.

He shrugged unrepentantly. 'You asked babe, I told you.'

'I didn't ask you anything.'

Michael looked down at her. Diana felt his eyes trailing across the plunge of her dress, fixing on her bottom, then running round her small waist and stopping right in the middle of her groin. To her dismay she felt a point of heat burning in between her legs. Her pussy tightened in a way she hadn't felt since . . .

She stopped herself and drew a deep breath. Come on, Diana. You tried it with him and it didn't work out. Anyway, he's seeing that blond, skinny bimbette. You and him are like fire and petrol. Put you together and it's just too much.

'We're not here to fight,' Michael said. 'Let's try to suspend hostilities just for once. We're here to announce ourselves.'

'Agreed. We're on table twelve.' Diana recovered her poise. She wasn't going to allow Michael to disturb her. She couldn't afford that. She was dating Brad and in partnership with Michael, working for him, hadn't she already decided that she needed to keep him at arm's length?

'Then let's go.' Michael offered her his arm, and she laid her fingers gently on his sleeve, as though contact with him might burn her.

The ballroom was packed. Everywhere you looked, moguls swept their wives towards tables round which throngs of waiters were hovering. Of all Manhattan's charity evenings, this was one of the least showy and the most prestigious. There were no big-name rock stars, no themed decor here tonight. Rather there were speeches on literacy from leading educationalists and a short toast by the governor. Tonight was erudite, witty, about books and reading. And the competition for tickets was vast.

Diana moved under a chandelier and accepted a Bellini. She enjoyed fresh peach juice and champagne and she could sip it while trying to get her bearings. Many of the faces here she knew from her dinners as Mrs Foxton. There was Harry Evans, for example, and over there Tina Brown with Harvey Weinstein . . .

'Diana, have you met Richard Freer?' Michael said, introducing her to a tall man with a ramrod-straight back and a shock of white hair. 'I worked with Richard when I was running Green Eggs. He's a buyer for Barnes & Noble.'

'Nice to meet you.' Diana shook hands firmly and smiled up at the man. 'I hope Michael has been telling you about our games. We could supply to your Net operation.'

And they were off. Michael swam through the room like a feeding shark, greeting women and men, introducing Diana, while she gave them the pitch. She noticed the heads put discreetly together after they had passed, the way chatter rose up after Michael had moved through. And the reaction, she was relieved to note, was positive.

'I love selling your games,' the buyer at Amazon told them. 'Parents write us thank-you notes. And that's rare.'

'Michael has such a touch with what kids want,' Greg Bear from Waldenbooks said. 'I'm sure he's taught you a great deal. I have a six-year-old who went up two letter-grades after a month on the Gecko Math game.'

To her surprise, Diana found she was really starting to enjoy herself. Socialising came easily to her, and the executives here were mostly aware of Imperial. Michael was a known quantity and they seemed willing to accept her without question because they knew him.

By the time the announcement for dinner was made, the room was buzzing. A new company was on the scene. Everyone knew that Michael Cicero, still in his thirties, the guy who kept bouncing back like a rubber ball, was a force to be reckoned with. Diana Verity actually looked like more than window dressing. This time last year she was just a trophy wife, they told themselves. But this was New York, where stranger things had happened.

Exhilarated, Michael shepherded Diana over to their table. It gave him the opportunity to rest his hand on the small of her back. He could feel her spine through the soft velvet and rest his thumb just on the curve of her incredible ass. How he missed that firm, curvy butt. The temptation to reach his hands down and just stroke and knead her skin was intense. But he managed not to do it. She was dating Bradley the Billionaire, Michael reminded himself sarcastically. After the divorce Diana has rebounded real fast. Brad would be a big step up for her. Mansions, townhouses, private jets, everybody knew about the Bailey fortune.

I'll never have enough money to satisfy a girl like her, Michael thought. And women who liked men with money were anathema to him. Diana did her job well. That was all he should care about.

If he could just stop thinking about her.

Their table was a good one, just two back from the centre of the room. Michael grinned. All that string pulling had definitely paid off. He could see the floor, see if there was anybody else he should be talking to. And the industry could see him. Thanks to Diana, virtually the only lady present wearing any kind of colour, they stood out as though she was wearing a billboard.

'Michael, look,' Diana said, suddenly stopping him dead.

She pointed.

He saw.

Two of the other six people at their table were Felicity Metson and Ernie Foxton.

Michael squeezed Diana's hand. As far as business went, they had no reservations about each other.

'Ready to show them what we're made of?'

'Absolutely,' Diana said, winking back at him.

Arm in arm, they walked over to the table – well, Michael walked, but the only word for what Diana was doing, he thought, was *sashaying*. Man, he wanted to grab her by that tiny waist and pull up those green folds and slide his hand in between her creamy thighs and start palming that silky little pussy until he melted her ice-core, had her begging him to fuck her like she used to . . . With difficulty, he lifted his eyes from her rear undulating just beside him and fixed them on his enemy. The men automatically stood as another lady approached the table. Michael noticed how Ernie's eyes half bugged out of his head.

They shook hands and slipped into their seats. Michael examined Felicity Metson. Her hair was worn up in an ornate French bun which glittered with some kind of wiring. Her hairdresser had done it tightly enough to stretch the skin on her face. She was bony and the hair made her look angular. He noticed that she was wearing a short black sheath, a plain dress designed to make her look even skinnier. A set of blood-red talons rested on the table and she wore a thin diamond necklace. She was made up with great care: heavy mascara, two thin red lines of blush on her cheeks, and a cat's moue of a mouth in fire-engine scarlet.

Damn, Michael thought. Ernie Foxton had to be insane. He married the girl with the best body in England and then swapped her for a richer version of trailer-park trash.

'I'm Michael Cicero,' he said, offering Felicity his hand. 'I don't think we've met.'

'I don't, either.' Felicity looked him over haughtily. 'I only mix in society circles and publishing, of course.'

He smiled at the rebuke, watching Ernie greet Diana frostily. Whoever had drawn up this seating plan had a sense of humour, that was for sure.

'Then perhaps you'll be seeing a bit more of me. Our games sell to booksellers too.'

Ernie turned on him without preamble. What a thin little weasel the guy is, Michael thought. What a goddamn pity we live in a sue-happy society. I would just love to take him outside and kick his fucking ass.

'I don't think so.' Ernie addressed the other guests at their table, a books editor for *Time* magazine and his wife, who were relaxing in their chairs, preparing to enjoy the fireworks. 'Michael used to be a junior executive working for Blakely's. We didn't see eye to eye so I had to let him go.'

Michael felt Diana tense beside him and gently put one hand on her thigh to stop her from blasting off at Ernie. People knew what the score was with Green Eggs. He silently willed her to understand. Let the idiot dig his own hole.

'Michael runs a small games company. I think it was going to float at one time, huh, Michael?'

Cicero nodded. 'That's true.'

'But then it didn't happen. Funnily enough, Blakely's new software division rolled out its own line,' Ernie said, grinning.

Felicity gazed over at them triumphantly.

'Yes. No hard feelings,' she purred. 'Actually I think it's just *wonderful* to see the *small* businessmen and their staff' – here she shot a look at Diana – 'at industry events.'

'I hope you're not thinking of going back into publishing.' Ernie slipped an arm ostentatiously around Felicity as he said this. He was ruffled by how classy Diana had managed to look. Felicity was starting to annoy him with her endless shopping and jewellery buying. His fucking useless staff weren't coming up with the sales and the board was starting to ask him pointed questions. But what the fuck. He was still a giant compared to this jock sitting in front of him. 'There's a non-compete clause in your contract. Or have you forgotten? I can have my lawyers give you a call, if you like.'

Diana held her breath. Ernie was going to go after them with all guns blazing.

'I assure you I have forgotten nothing,' Michael said, with a precision that made Diana shudder. 'Not the fact that you lied to me and stole my company from me and cheated me out of a million dollars. Nor the fact that you started a games company and poached my people at a cost that cannot possibly have been profitable for you—'

'Hey. Business is business.'

Michael ignored him and continued, quite calmly, 'And certainly not the clause that forbade me from going into publishing for a year. But that's not too much of a problem for Imperial. Because I don't want anything to do with the books any more. Imperial Games is surviving, and we're going to thrive. With the help of Diana Verity, your ex-wife, and our director.'

Diana smiled at Ernie and watched the emotions cross his face; stupefaction, rage, apprehension . . . she watched Felicity freeze in her seat as though somebody had dropped an icecube down her neck.

'I didn't know your company was so small,' Keith Fanning, the *Time* journalist, said curiously.

'Oh, we're not.' Diana turned the full wattage of her smile at him. 'Actually, with the way our second range has been selling, especially our e-business, we're the leading educational games software provider in the city. In fact, we're the largest private company of our kind in the north-east.'

'You can't grow much more, though,' Felicity blurted, unable to contain herself. 'Ernie told me you needed more money for expansion.'

'Oh, he did?' Michael grinned at Ernie as his woman exposed his weakness. 'In fact we are considering a new IPO in a year or so. It seems as though Blakely's games division isn't actually selling that well. I've got no idea why. You guys have good talent over there. It used to be ours.'

Ernie scowled. 'Our division is doing just fine.' He gave a crocodile smile to the powerful journalist. 'I wouldn't believe everything you hear from the competition.'

'Sound advice,' Diana said sweetly. 'I'd say, if you're

interested, you should check with the retailers and Net suppliers. They should be able to give you some accurate numbers.'

Felicity looked with dismay at Ernie.

'But really, enough business.' Michael lifted the wine bottle. 'Would anybody like a little Merlot?'

Michael was amazing, Diana thought.

He led her onto the dance floor after dinner, his arm round her waist and, to her amazement, started to do an expert tango with her. Her skin blazed when he dipped her in his arms, her weight as nothing. My God, she thought, he's so strong. His muscles were like steel knots compared to Brad's. She felt the slow, betraying pulse of blood fill her nipples. Thank heavens the velvet was thick. She tried not to look into his eyes as he spun her round. He had made mincemeat of Ernie, just cut him up into little shreds and left him there quivering. When Michael had extended his hand to Diana and asked her to dance, Ernie and Felicity had been quarrelling publicly.

'You took me out here to talk business?' she whispered.

He shook his head. 'Just to dance. If that's OK by you.'

Diana felt her breath coming a bit raggedly. She was burning up for him. Was there any chance, she wondered, that he still wanted her? That he could actually fall for her?

'Diana,' a voice said.

Michael pulled her upright and close to his chest, close enough to feel those full breasts press against his shirt, then let her go. He felt a wave of anger rock him, but held himself in check. Brad Bailey, in the flesh. He noted the diamond pinkie ring, the very expensive shoes. Bailey was tall, tanned and it looked like he actually bleached his teeth.

'Brad, this is Michael Cicero, my boss,' Diana looked

flushed. Michael wondered why she would react to this vanilla pudding that way, 'my escort tonight. I didn't know you were coming.'

'I wasn't, but you told me you'd be here, so I picked up a table at the last minute,' Brad said. He turned to Michael. 'Cicero, wasn't it? Nice to meet you. I'll be taking Diana home now. Thanks for looking after her.'

'We were in the middle of a dance,' Michael said.

Brad shrugged and he caught a whiff of aftershave. 'Diana doesn't really enjoy dancing. She prefers quiet dinners.'

Diana started to open her mouth and Michael snapped. He really wasn't interested in hearing her back up Mr Moneybags.

'I know what you mean. I got to go myself,' he said. 'My girl needs to get intimate a couple of times a night. Most of them do. I don't want to keep her waiting.'

'I . . . see,' Brad said, discomfited.

Diana flushed. 'Could you take me home, please, Brad?'

She held out her hand and walked away from Michael without another word.

Chapter 37

My girl needs to get intimate a couple of times a night.
Why not just say you're going home to fuck her? I hate
him, I hate him, Diana thought, the way he tricks you
into feeling something for him and then instantly hits you
with that attitude to women. *I hate to keep her waiting.*
Was that the way he'd talked to his buddies about *her*
when they were dating? She prickled with embarrassment. She still wanted Michael a couple of times a night
and a couple of times each day, too. All he'd had to do
was to walk into her office and cup his hands over the
globes of her ass, sometimes less than that, sometimes
just shoot a look at her pussy, for Diana to feel primed
for him, hot, almost panting.

He cheapens everything, she thought, bitterly. I
thought I was special. He acts just that way with Tina
when nobody's looking, I bet.

'Where are we going?' Brad asked.

Diana looked up with a start. She had been thrusting
through the crowd, smiling tightly at the movers and
shakers, seething inside. She had forgotten Brad was with
her.

He was looking down at her. A man that treats me
with ultimate respect, Diana thought. Good-looking.
Good family. Prestigious. And hugely rich.

'Let's go back to your place,' she suggested.

She swooped down on a waiter walking past with a
fresh tray of champagne and grabbed a flute, tilting it
back down her throat in a single gulp. Funny, she felt like

Cinderella at the end of the ball, even though her finery had not turned to rags and she was leaving with the handsome prince.

But this needed doing. It was time. After all, she had been dating him for months.

'Really?' Brad asked, his blue eyes lighting up. 'My driver is waiting outside.'

He looked like a kid who had been told Christmas was coming, as eager and enthusiastic as a puppy dog. Then he checked himself with a visible effort of will. 'Of course I mean . . . we'll have a nightcap.'

'That's right,' Diana said, firmly. The champagne warmed her the way it always did. She felt courageous. 'A nightcap and maybe something more.'

Brad's limo was not a hired ride like the one Michael would be taking back to that little tramp of his. It was a twenty-four-hour, seven-day-a-week convenience whose drivers worked in shifts.

'He'll be ready to take you home whenever you want,' Brad assured her, as the man bowed, holding open the door for Diana.

She smiled gently at him. 'We'll see when that is.'

Brad's home was immensely luxurious. In a cramped city barely five miles long and three miles wide support- ing millions of people, space was at a premium; yet Brad Bailey had a large garden, an entrance hall with an ornamental fountain playing over real Italian marble, and a servant's apartment in the basement. There were five bedrooms and three bathrooms, a library – how Diana had always longed for a house with a real, old-fashioned library – a beautiful roof terrace with a Japanese-inspired Zen-style garden, and modern reception rooms hung with Cubist paintings and a Picasso.

'This place is beautiful,' she told him, as a butler –

wearing modern chinos and a Ghandi-style jacket – took her pale-grey pashmina wrap and hung it up.

'Thank you. I got it for peanuts from a Wall Street arbitrageur who got caught with his fist in the till.' Brad shrugged. 'Benefits of being in real estate.'

Diana wondered what 'peanuts' meant in this context. Probably about the entire worth of her ex-husband.

'Let's go upstairs to the bar. We'll fix our own drinks, Jenkins,' Brad said to the help.

'Very good, Mr Bailey.'

Brad ushered Diana up the black stone staircase, laid with soft red carpet. 'After you.'

The bar was, as Brad put it, his little indulgence. In a house which had been decorated at huge expense to be clean and Euro-modern – sofas from Cerruti, Danish chairs, nothing but dark polished floors and clean simple lines – Brad had kept one room away from the clutches of his exclusive design firm. The bar was an exercise in seventies retro-chic. Fully equipped, it featured huge furry rugs on the floor, fake bear skins, and large chrome bar stools with cherry-red leather. Diana wondered what she could do here if it was her house to go over. It was a stunning property. It definitely needed a woman's touch, though.

'What can I get you? Champagne? We have Cristal, Taittinger rosé, Krug, Veuve Grande Dame . . .'

'Jack Daniels and Coke,' Diana said.

She felt the need to get bombed. Fucking Michael. This would show him, she thought. Let him go back down-town and bang the hell out of Tina Armis. She was up here, being courted, and she was going to have a good time.

Brad raised an eyebrow. 'You're in a party mood.'

'Why shouldn't I be?' Diana demanded, a touch belligerently.

He held up his hands. 'No reason. It's just funny.

337

Before I met you, I used to take out girls, sometimes bring them back here. And they would pick at lettuce leaves all night and then order a Perrier. It drove me nuts.'

He handed her a glass full of golden liquor and poured a splash of black Coke into it. It was almost undrinkable, but she sipped at it anyway.

'Well, they were auditioning,' Diana told him. 'It's a classic good-girl ploy. They were auditioning to be your wife. I bet you they ate before they went out to dinner. It's reverse competition. The girl that eats least at the table wins.'

Brad laughed aloud. God, she was so funny and enchanting. Having her here was like holding the winning ticket in the lottery and having the delicious anticipation of cashing it in.

'Can I be honest with you?'

Diana took a big slug of her JD. 'Hell yes. All the boys are being honest this evening. Why not you?'

'When I first met you I knew who you were and I came after you.'

'Well, I knew that.'

'No, hear me out.' He looked a little shifty. 'I had stayed single for about as long as I could. You know, one day a man wakes up and he knows it's time to get married, to settle down to get himself an heir. And then, if you're a man like me, you want the best. Since I was small, I've been used to the best.'

'I'd never have guessed.' Diana beamed, pleased with her own wit.

'You were famous. You were English, you had a classy reputation. The way you handled the thing with your ex-husband was wonderful. No press interviews, no *National Enquirer* exposés.'

'As if I would.'

'Well, a man in my position needs to know that if the shit comes down, there won't be any scandal. I saw a woman who'd been through the worst that can happen to a society wife and who had kept her mouth shut. Even though you somehow lost out on his money.'

Diana straightened. 'Quite a test,' she said evenly.

'But you passed. And then when I saw you, it turned from being . . . a . . . socially proper decision into being a personal one. You are just so breathtaking. And you kept me at arm's length. You know how long it's been since I had to chase a woman?'

'I don't think you've ever had to chase anything,' Diana said.

'That's pretty much true.' Brad was unapologetic. 'I never have. But the result is I am head over heels, incredibly, amazingly, utterly in love with you, Diana.'

She tossed back the rest of her drink.

'Let's go to bed,' Diana said.

The master bedroom was a fantasy. The flooring was warm chocolate-brown marble, the rugs subtle shades of cream and ivory. The bed in the centre of the room was suspended from a pole made of clear glass, so that it seemed to float above the floor. It was draped with rich satin and silk sheets, down pillows and soft comforters. Diana stared at it. It looked like the most comfortable thing she had ever seen. Sunk deep into a corner of the marble was a whirlpool bath the size of a small swimming pool, with discreet little bottles from Czech & Speake lined up alongside it.

Brad steered her gently towards the bed.

'You're the kind of woman who ought to have things like this,' he whispered. Diana felt his breath hot in her ear, playing against the nape of her neck. The buzz from the liquor was stealing over her, making her languid, making her bones feel like they could just pour flat onto the bed. 'You work, but there's no need for it. You should throw nice dinners, tennis parties at my place in the Vineyard. Decorate. Have babies.'

He punctuated each phrase with a kiss, laid soft as down on her neck and the hollows of her throat.

'It can be like it was before for you,' he murmured. 'Better. Because you'll have the kind of husband a woman like you deserves.'

'Husband?' Diana muttered, dreamily.

Brad scooped her into his arms and laid her on the bed, reddening from her weight. Then his hands were on her back, seeking out her zipper, delicately peeling the clothes from her like a museum director unwrapping a priceless artefact.

'That's what I said,' he whispered, and moved to kiss the slopes of her warm, freckled breasts.

The scent of breakfast woke her. Diana propped herself up, her head throbbing, and tried to deal with the cold winter light streaming through Brad's vast French windows. He was already up and dressed, standing at the doorway taking a breakfast tray from a maid. She smelled fresh roasted vanilla coffee, saw crisp bacon and a fluffy egg-white and fine-herb omelette. There was also a pitcher of squeezed blood oranges, ice-cold spring water and a warm, sun-ripened peach.

Brad walked across the floor and laid the tray across her knees.

'No need to get up,' he said.

'But there is. I'm late for work already,' Diana said, dismayed.

'Sure. Your office,' he said, a little patronisingly. 'I know. I took the liberty of laying out some work things for you on that chair over there. I had one of my contacts at *Women's Wear Daily* guess your size for me, in the hope that one day you'd stay over here.'

'I'm impressed.'

'You should be. I plan ahead. I gotta go, honey.' Brad kissed her on the tip of her nose. 'I have a closing on a luxury block in the Village. Twelve mill. Look, last night was just incredible. You think about what I said, OK? I want us to be married. It's the right thing for both of us.'

He smiled at her and walked out, giving her a little wave.

Diana poured a cup of the coffee, set the rest of the tray aside and staggered towards the bathroom set to the side. Brad's power shower had six jets and a range of shampoos hand-blended in Switzerland. It was inlaid with pale-blue stone studded with small brass stars everywhere. Like showering in heaven, she thought. Anxiously she checked her face. No spots, despite sleeping in her make-up. Diana showered, then grabbed a towel and dried herself, slurping down a little more of the steaming brew and letting the fog in her brain clear.

Last night was . . . what? She had gotten drunk, and obviously had sex with Brad. Except the problem was she didn't remember it. Diana pulled off the towel and glanced down at her body. There were none of the scratches and bruises she'd had after a night with Michael. If they had had sex, it must have been sweet, polite sex. She wondered if she'd actually passed out, from the booze, in the middle of it.

Possibly. Knowing men, though, he would only take that as a compliment.

She walked over to the chair and looked at the clothes he had left. A smart green Prada suit and a crisp white shirt; Woolford hose and sleek Chanel mules. Very nice. Hurriedly she tugged them on and regarded her reflection in the full-length Swedish mirror. A perfect fit, too.

Money buys everything, she thought.

Her life had come full circle. Marrying Ernie for . . . for money. And getting divorced for naivety, for pride.

Now she actually had a job and because she hadn't chased money, money had come chasing her.

Elspeth would be thrilled. Claire would cheer from the rafters.

Natasha, Jodie and Felicity wouldn't know what had hit them.

Diana brushed out her hair with the Mason-Pearson hairbrush laid out by the side of her clothes and rushed downstairs. The butler, who had let her in, was in the hall and bowed slightly when she appeared.

'Jenkins has the car waiting for you, madam.' He handed her a small Louis Vuitton case. 'Mr Bailey took the opportunity of having your things packed up.'

Incredulously, Diana unzipped the rich-smelling leather. There were her pearls, her dress, her lingerie and her shoes, beautifully wrapped between crisp sheets of acid-free tissue paper.

'Thank you,' she said.

'If you'll step this way, madam,' he suggested, opening the elevator to the underground garage.

The journey downtown was fast, but it seemed to take for ever.

The driver was blessedly silent. Relaxing against the comfortable back seat, Diana took advantage of the small silver coffee pot and cup prepared for her and watched the tall buildings of Park Avenue slip past. The noise and bustle of the city was converted to silent images in her sound-proofed luxury, and she could rest her head against the tinted windows with no fear that anybody could look inside at her.

How comfortable, how easy, life as Mrs Brad Bailey would be.

Jenkins let her out right in front of the office. There weren't that many limos in that part of town. The passersby rubbernecked with their Starbucks muffins and deli coffee. Diana thanked the driver and rushed into the office.

'Morning, Miss Verity.' Ellen, her assistant, looked up at her anxiously. 'I left a few messages at your house. I'm sorry. I was a bit worried.'

'That's OK, I should have called in,' Diana said. She wasn't about to explain further. She fought back a blush; what she did in her private time was her business. 'I'm just going to see Mr Cicero. If you could get my call sheet ready?'

'But Miss Verity—'

Diana ignored her plaintive call and marched inside. There was Tina, sitting in front of Michael's office wearing a tight jersey dress which left nothing to the imagination. If you liked string beans, Diana thought viciously.

'Where's Michael?' she asked.

'He told me he was taking a day off,' Tina said, smiling sweetly at Diana. 'He asked me to ask you to look after the business today.'

'Oh.' Diana was floored. She'd had a thousand excuses ready and now he was taking a day off? That was like the Pope taking a day off. It just didn't happen.

'Miss Verity,' Tina said, 'I wonder if I could have a little chat with you?'

Chapter 38

Felicity looked around her dinner table and smiled tightly at her guests. She gave Mort and Natty Zuckerman a little wave, nodded her head so her earrings sparkled, and smoothed down her little black Gucci dress. It was a successful do by anybody's standards. There was Lola Givens, the Met's latest black opera diva, Charles Lenten, the plastic surgeon, Amica, the supermodel, and the usual gaggle of business tycoons and politicians. Monsieur Letrec, Felicity's new cook, had done an excellent job. The duck confit and orange salad was a success, as was the green tea sorbet, the vintage Krug, and the Chateau Lafite 1962.

But the atmosphere was sadly muted.

Annoyed, she looked over at Ernie. His voice was just that bit too loud, braying over the table. They had fought several times this week about his manners. Felicity was tired of smoothing over Ernie's rough edges. Despite her little Rolodex files on every one of his acquaintances, their wives, likes and dislikes, it was getting harder to cover up for his racist jokes and off-colour speeches. Ernie had never been subtle, and since the troubles at Blakely's, things had become worse. She sipped her water – no wine, somebody had to be there to manage things if Ernie got drunk.

'Your ring is wonderful.'

Felicity smiled over at Elise Davenport, the latest young wife of Horace, the paper-mill king. She lifted one slim hand and flashed her diamond. Three full carats and

344

a surrounding band of rubies. Yes, there *was* the compensating factor of Ernie's pocketbook. Despite their little spats, she was getting some wonderful toys out of this. Ernie had to spend to hold on to quality, she reminded herself.

'Thank you. Tiffany's designed it specially.'

Elise nodded. 'It's so wonderful of your fiancé, especially with the way things are.'

Felicity's radar prickled. 'Have you heard something, dear?'

The word was all over the street. Felicity scorned business – vulgar talk of money, she liked to say – but the wives network was a more accurate barometer of current worth than Barron's.

Apparently Ernie was in some kind of trouble. His big-name writers were still selling, but not enough to cover the money spent on promoting them. Then there was the computer games thing. Felicity bit her lower lip. She had so looked forward to rubbing Ernie's new venture into Diana Verity's face, but it wasn't working out that way. The staff, brought in at huge expense from Imperial, chafed under Ernie's strict working conditions. Suits, ties and signing-in didn't suit them. Their work was substandard and the code-checkers had missed the bugs. Games were delayed, faulty and often boring. After the first burst of heavily advertised sales success, the book problem was repeating itself here.

Ernie had told her last night that Blakely's board was worried.

'Please, darling,' Felicity snapped. She had the impulse to reach for a cigarette. 'I'm *so* uninterested in your work problems. Why don't you fix them and leave me to run the house?'

She flounced off before he could bend her ear. All Ernie had to do was keep things going just the way they were. Was that too much to ask?

Felicity was beginning to wonder just how deep the slide would go.

Anxiously she waited for Elise's reply.

'Oh, nothing.' Her guest forked a tiny radichio leaf into her peach-glossed mouth. 'And anyway, I'm sure it'll all soon be fixed.'

Felicity scowled and summoned the waitress over with a snap of her red-taloned fingers. Maybe she would take some champagne after all.

'Of course, Tina,' Diana said. 'We can go into Mr Cicero's office. Did he tell you where he was going, by the way?'

The younger girl pushed herself up and opened the door to Michael's office. A waft of Chanel No. 5 hit Diana. It reeked, as if Tina had taken to emptying an entire bottle over herself.

'No,' she said, shutting the door. 'He didn't have that much time this morning, Diana – do you mind if I call you Diana?'

'No,' Diana said, gritting her teeth.

She did mind, she had worked hard to be made director of this company. But she didn't want Tina to think she was picking on her, because of Michael. Then Tina might get the silly idea that Diana resented her. 'Go ahead,' she said.

I don't like you because you're a vacuous, skinny, itsy-bitsy bimbo, Diana thought. It's got nothing to do with Michael.

'Well – *Diana*,' Tina said sweetly, 'this morning he – excuse me – uh – wanted another round so he left the apartment a little late. He told me just to hold the fort, and ask you to take care of the firm today. He forgot about his appointment. It can happen, when two people are very much in love.'

Suddenly Diana felt a crunching pain in her temples.

She thanked God Brad had magicked up this smart little Prada suit. She thought she could hardly bear it if she had to listen to this crap and not look her best.

Imagine Michael actually missing a business appointment for sex. Tina must be special. Maybe he really was in love with her.

She felt a stab of pain in her heart and nodded briskly to conceal it. OK, I'm not dumb, Diana thought. I have feelings for Michael. I could have loved him. But his attitude made it impossible. So really, I ought to be pleased he's with someone else.

It's just that I don't approve of his choice, that's all. She tried to examine Tina objectively. She was beautiful, slender . . . and young and idiotic. Despite herself the annoyance with Michael bubbled up. So that's what he wanted, right? A woman who would never snap at him, never challenge him, never offer him any kind of rivalry? Michael wanted a low-rent version of the kind of wife . . .

The kind of wife I was to Ernie, a nasty little voice in her head added.

Diana flinched. She looked at Tina's coltish beauty, and the thought of Michael's strong, rough hands on her made her dizzy. Did he bend Tina's slim body forwards and thrust that thick, insistent cock into her the way he had done with Diana? Did he wake up in the mornings and put his hands on the side of her head, pulling her down to him? Did he make Tina come to the office without panties, the way he had commanded Diana to do, so that she would be open and ready for him whenever he chose to take her?

Stop it.

'That's nice to hear that you two are happy,' she said. Diana took command of herself and made her tone as sincere as she could. 'And what was it you wanted to talk to me about?'

'Well, that was it.' The young girl looked a bit awkward.

'I'm sorry, I don't understand. What was it?' Diana asked coolly.

'About Michael and me. I thought – I thought maybe you—'

She looked over at Diana, who sat stony-faced. Damn. Maybe she'd been wrong and Miss Verity didn't have the hots for Michael. Maybe she didn't care. Tina started to blush and stammer.

'Maybe you felt it wasn't right,' she said lamely.

Diana stood up. 'I really don't care what Michael does outside of office hours. He's president and I'm director,' she added, with subtle emphasis. 'We're friends but we don't really see each other socially. Our work lives don't leave any time.'

'Uh, OK.'

Tina stood up again, all gangly legs and bright-blue eye shadow.

'If you could bring me some coffee in my office that would be wonderful,' Diana said.

'Are you seeing anybody?' the American girl blurted out. 'Someone special, I mean?'

'As a matter of fact, I am.' Diana smiled confidently. 'Brad Bailey, of Bailey Realty.'

Tina's mouth rounded in awe. 'Then those rumours in the papers are true? You're actually dating him?'

'I wouldn't know. I don't read the tabloids,' Diana said icily. She levelled Tina with a look.

'I'll bring you that coffee right away,' Tina muttered. *Bitch*, she thought, flouncing out. Always dressing so fancy and acting so calm. Like dating Brad Bailey was no big deal. Well, one day she would definitely get hers. Tina just hoped she was there to see it.

Michael arrived back in the office at five forty. It was

already cold and dark out. A light flurry of snow was falling in Hell's Kitchen, covering the sandwich wrappers and discarded Coke cans before almost instantly turning into grey slush. He felt little of the chill. He had spent the day on Wall Street in warm, air-conditioned offices, juggling figures which made him think he was dreaming.

They were falling over themselves to give him financing. Even with Diana running the publishing side, the bankers adored Imperial. Their reputation and sales increased month by month. And from the start, he had kept the overheads ruthlessly low.

He found he wanted nothing so much as to sit down with Diana and talk it all through.

He marched straight to her office and found Diana handing Tina a sheaf of faxes.

'Hi, Michael,' she said.

'Hi. What are you doing? Can you drop it?'

'Nothing Tina can't handle,' she said. 'Why?'

'I can do the rest of Diana's faxes,' Tina chimed in.

'Good.' He turned to her, absently. 'I won't be able to make the theatre tonight. We have to meet late. Oh, and Tina, it's Ms Verity in the office, please.'

He crooked a finger and Diana meekly followed him out.

'You've been acting very strangely today,' she said, as he held open the cab door for her.

Michael settled on the black leather seat with the standard-issue rip in it. 'East Seventeenth at Irving Plaza. Feel like some sushi?'

'Sounds good.' Diana smiled at him. His mood was infectious. 'Would it be asking to much to want to know where you've been, boss?'

'I'll tell you everything over a bottle of sake. Maybe two.'

*

They pulled up at Yama's, a Gramercy favourite. It was early yet so they managed to skip the queues. Michael found a small table in the corner, ordered a large box with everything and two bottles of warm, clear rice wine. He poured a thimbleful for Diana and gave it to her.

'I've been downtown.'

'Why does that not surprise me?' Diana said, knocking back her drink.

'After you left yesterday I was pretty mad.' He held up one hand. 'No, wait, OK. I know I owe you an apology. I acted like an idiot.' Michael forced himself to add, 'I'm sure Brad Bailey's a great guy. I hope you'll be happy with him.'

'Like you are with Tina,' Diana said softly.

'Right.'

There was a moment's awkward pause.

'Anyway, I was stopped by Art Jankel. You know who he is?'

'JanCorp Entertainment?' Diana asked, leaning forwards on her bench. 'The conglomerate? He runs them. They do toys and games and records.'

'Right.' Michael speared a yellowtail tuna roll with his chopsticks. 'He's a serious player. He asked me if it was true that we wanted financing. Then he took me off for a late-night dinner. We talked about Imperial, the profit margin, the website, the IPO . . . everything. Then he asks me to go have a meeting with Merrill Lynch, his investment bankers. They want to invest in us. Give us office space and funding.'

'That's what you had with Ernie.'

'I told him that. He said that he would pay the bill of any lawyer we cared to appoint. We can check and double-check. I also told him I would give JanCorp no more than a forty per cent stake. He agreed to this.'

'What's our funding?' Diana asked, half holding her breath. Around her, the room seemed to freeze.

350

Michael grinned. 'Funding's not a gift, but he's looking to capitalise us in return for a forty per cent stake at three million dollars.'

They ate a delicious dinner and got quietly drunk. Diana alternated her sake with green tea, but it didn't puncture her high much. At that price they would be able to commission good writers, good illustrators, good marketing men and a competent sales force. There would be no overheads, as a floor at JanCorp was part of the deal.

'He said he'd watched how we grew this place from the ground up, and then rebuilt after the IPO thing,' Michael told her, clicking his porcelain sake thimble against hers. 'He thinks with some real money we can spread our wings. And I agree with him.'

'Me too,' Diana said.

'Look.' Michael stared across at her, his dark eyes warm. 'We've wasted a lot of time in pointless sniping. We make an excellent team. We need to concentrate on that.'

'I agree. You built something pretty amazing, and you gave me a chance to be part of it. I'm grateful for that,' Diana half whispered. Tears were prickling in her eyes; she attributed it to the sake.

'I'd like us to be friends,' Michael said. 'This will be hard work. We'll be in it together.'

'Sure. We should spend some time together. If you have an evening free from Tina.'

'For you, anytime,' he said.

Diana looked at his broad chest, the thickness of his thighs spread over the bench, the hardness of his muscles sliding under the skin.

'This is going to be great,' she said.

And it would be. The question was, why did she want to cry so badly?

They talked for four hours. Diana watched Michael

blazing with excitement, scribbling his plans on the backs of napkins. She was amazed at how badly she wanted this to work. He promised her a rise in salary, even a small slice of the company. But what she wanted was a final opportunity to prove she could do it.

She would go from being a director of a Mom and Pop operation to a hotshot executive.

My God, Diana thought, catching herself. I'm actually thinking like a businesswoman. It was no longer about recovering her former status. Not even about showing up Felicity and Natasha. This time it was about who she had decided to be.

I love him for giving me this chance, Diana thought.

Michael rolled up his sleeves suddenly. His forearm was tanned and covered with wiry black hair, his hand gripped the pen like it was a dagger. Diana gazed at his muscular upper arms, his biceps pushing out at the thick cotton of his shirt. Brad's arms were skinny compared to Michael's. He was much prettier, of course. His features were more even, his teeth straighter, his nose had never been busted up in a fight.

Diana felt her pussy mercilessly tighten and slick up. The wave of desire for him was so intense she wanted to run to the bathroom and stroke herself, just for a little release. But she had decided to try to be friends. Blushing, she pushed herself up.

'Could you run me home?' she murmured.

Chapter 39

Diana flung herself into her work.

It wasn't difficult to do. Expanding Imperial was harder than it looked, even for Michael. She hunted for new talent with a bigger budget; she had to meet headhunters, design salary packages, and reassure all their smaller buyers that the new company would look after them. But her work was as nothing compared to the eighteen-hour days Michael was putting in. Sometimes he slept in their chaotic new offices. It was the company's big chance, and Michael wasn't going to let it slip. He took her for breakfast, took her to lunch, sometimes to dinner, and told her his plans. She knew Brad resented the time she spent with him. But business, for Diana, came first.

'You said you needed time to consider,' Brad complained one night over dinner in Martha's Vineyard. 'When are you going to find the time, exactly? It's Cicero this, Cicero that. I practically have to schedule an appointment with Ellen just to get in to see you.'

'I know.' Diana put her soft, manicured hand over his. She hadn't been back to his bed since that drunken night. She told him she wanted to wait until marriage. She couldn't quite make the jump, couldn't quite commit. Daily she asked herself what was wrong with her. He was the absolute top prize on the New York dating scene since poor, doomed JFK Junior had married Carolyn Bessette. Diana attended operas, jetted off to gamble in Atlantic City, took ski breaks in Aspen; she knew Westchester Airport, where Brad's father kept the family jet, better than Grand Central Station. Claire and Elspeth cooed over each fresh triumph, each new paparazzi snap in the papers. They were hovering like friendly hawks, trying to find something that would motivate Brad to produce a ring. If they only knew he'd proposed months ago, Diana thought, I would never get a second's peace.

'It's not for ever. It's just while the merger gets off the ground.'

Art Jankel had allotted them the ninth floor of the JanCorp colossus on Sixth Avenue. Covered all the way up in polished black marble, the JanCorp building dominated midtown, it had fountains and a tree in the lobby itself. The driven, somewhat anal, JanCorp executives who rushed in and out in their three-thousand-dollar suits, clutching their briefcases and notes, were shocked to pass the Imperial crew slouching into work at ten in Metallica T-shirts and baggy jeans.

'It better not be for ever. Because I don't have that long to wait,' Brad said, giving her his full-wattage white smile. 'There *are* other candidates for your position.'

'Hundreds, I expect.'

'It's just that none of them have your style.' Brad sighed. 'So tell me how next week's looking. Can you squeeze me in between power breakfasts?'

She tried. But mostly she kept breakfasts for Michael.

Building up Imperial was becoming one of the most enjoyable experiences of her life. Funny, Diana thought, looking back, when she'd had such mean little pleasures – always being the best dressed, first on the guest list, the girl with the coolest backstage pass and hottest Prada backpack – she had never known what real satisfaction felt like, what it meant to look down from her sky-high offices in a palette of forest green, cream and chocolate towards downtown and remember how she had cleaned an airless, cramped little apartment just to help grind out the rent. The 'joy' of snagging a rich husband could not be compared to the thrill she got from finding the right marketing guy, or a retired sales king who was so pumped up to get a second chance that at fifty-five he outworked every twenty-four-year-old in the industry.

'You shouldn't be surprised that you're doing well,' Michael told her one afternoon. They were standing outside Yankee Stadium, looking up at the giant bat dominating the forecourt. Michael was determined to get her to understand baseball. He bought her great seats just behind home plate and forced her to eat hot-dogs and down Coors Light; he loved the way she refused to dress down, even for a game. Every other chick in the place wore a sweatshirt and chinos, casual gear for a New York spring. But not Diana. Today she was in a long pink linen skirt with crisp pleats and a tiny shell top in rose cashmere with a matching cardigan. She was completely made up, of course, though she kept it light: clover on her cheeks, a light gloss on her lips, and a touch of bone-white eyeliner under soft beige shadow that made her look bright and alert. Not forgetting the breath of perfume, lily of the valley, he thought; and the string of real pearls around her neck. Her dark hair, sleek and glossy, fell gently just to her shoulders, flipping up at the end. 'You have a great knack of putting things together. Putting the right *people* together is half of what business is.'

'And what's the other half?' Diana asked, watching a young man the teenage girls were calling out to as though he were a rock star of some kind. He was swinging that baseball bat around in the air like it was a cheerleader's baton. She had no idea how they ever hit the ball with those things. It was a bit like rounders, only boys played it.

'Coming up with the right product. Which is where I come in. You need a vision. I don't care if you're manufacturing toilet paper; you better be passionate about toilet paper. And you better come up with a better-sold, better-presented, more comfortable goddamn toilet paper. Because that'll make you a millionaire.'

'Do we have to sit here and talk about lavatory paper?' Diana asked plaintively. 'I'm trying to eat.'

Michael took a gigantic bite of his hot-dog, smothered with chillies and onions and mustard.

'Pretty good, huh?'

'Not really.' She nibbled at a corner of her bun.

'You're lame.' Michael pointed at the young man with the bat. 'That's Derek Jeter. He's one of their best—'

'Batsmen.'

'Hitters. And that's Roger Clemens. Best pitcher in baseball, but he's been having a lousy year.'

'Cricket's much more relaxing.'

'Yeah, eleven guys standing in a field and nothing going on.'

'Nonsense.' She glanced over at him and saw the dark pants and plain white shirt on the barrel chest, the lust for life that he evinced every day. 'Cricket is like war. You and Sam watch your enemy slowly being demolished. He comes back with a new force, you cut the legs out of that one. It can be vicious. Exhilarating.' She shrugged. 'Unless you support England, in which case it's usually embarrassing, but even they can surprise you with a mammoth win.'

'I'll take your word for it.' Michael dragged his eyes away from Diana's chest. 'Tell me how the Count Cloud Nine series is coming along . . .'

She relaxed as they talked through the business of the week. Nobody could hear what they were talking about, no corporate spy could spill their plans to Blakely's. They were not going to let Ernie Foxton win this time.

And he would come after them. If they gave him an inch.

Michael told her not to worry about Ernie. He said he

had it taken care of. And Diana had learned that when Michael said something was getting done, it got done. His word was more than a promise, it was a fact. So she put Ernie out of her mind.

'I'd like to see you tonight,' he said to her when they rose at the seventh-inning stretch. 'I'm hoping to launch an online travel guide. Written by real New Yorkers and aimed at kids. Books can't offer real-time videos of your destination.'

Diana grinned. 'You could make a lot of money with that.'

'That's part of my plan,' Michael admitted. 'So, tonight, OK? My place.'

'Won't Tina mind if I intrude?' Diana made herself ask.

Through Christmas and New Year and Valentine's Day – when three hundred red roses from Brad had been delivered to her desk, making the entire ninth floor smell like a florist's – Michael had still dated Tina. The great advantage to having a bigger office was that Diana hardly ever saw her now. On the rare occasions when she had to go to see Michael, she tried to time her visits so Tina would be having lunch.

Once or twice, though, she hadn't been able to miss her. And the signs were not reassuring. Tina had dropped the itsy-bitsy skirts and tight leather pants for almost demure dresses. Diana noticed she was adapting herself to Michael's taste. He was in favour of ladylike, funnily enough, for a guy who was dating a bimbette. And Tina, while not a smart girl, possessed a certain amount of low animal cunning. I bet she's out in the bookstore right now picking up Italian cookbooks and learning how to serve Sambuca with the espresso, with three coffee beans in the glass, she thought. But she pushed it down. She couldn't let dislike for Tina show. She was getting on so well with Michael.

'Not at all. Actually I told her we'd be spending the evening together. I have plans I want you to see. And the fewer people who know about it, the better.'

'But you can trust Tina, right?' Diana asked.

She didn't know why she asked this. It was like being a kid and having a loose tooth, and being unable to stop teasing it with her tongue.

Michael looked at her with his dark eyes. 'Of course I can. But this is business, not personal. I don't mix the two. You know that.'

It felt like a slap. 'Of course.' She nodded quickly. 'I couldn't agree with you more. Mixing is always a mistake.'

They sat, and she switched her eyes to Tino Martinez, who promptly belted a double down the left-field line.

'Just keep your fucking trap shut, all right?'

Ernie turned on Felicity. Her inane questions about which wedding-cake design and which kind of fancy lightbulb to use in the strings of lights she planned on suspending over the ballroom ceiling were getting on his nerves. He was trying to find some way he could cut costs more, to improve the Blakely's bottom line just a little bit, and she was bugging him yet again. 'I don't give a fuck, darlin'? Understand?'

His thick cockney accent had returned at full force under stress. 'I just want you to fuck off and give me some peace. Just get out so I can do my business, which is what keeps *you* in jewels and fucking Maseratis.'

'I understand perfectly.' Felicity's brow did not crease; she had recently popped down to Dr Wexler for an injection of Botox, the poison that paralysed the muscles in the forehead, making you unable to frown and giving you a permanently surprised look. She had to fix Ernie with a gimlet stare instead. 'You're trying to dig yourself out of the hole the company is in. And you intend using foul language in my presence. So I am going to leave.'

'Oh fucking dear. Boo fucking hoo,' Ernie snarled.

'Just make sure you complete your task properly . . . *darling*. I wouldn't want you to have any difficulties paying for our summer place.'

Privately, Felicity thanked heaven that she had had the estate agent put the deed to that house in her name. Ernie was so busy these days with the wretched little men calling at the apartment, the endless faxes and the calls from Italy in the middle of the night . . . always fighting with somebody and screaming at somebody else . . . he hadn't even noticed the few alterations her private lawyer had put into the deal.

She wondered for a second if Diana Foxton had also had these difficulties. How on earth had Diana reacted when . . . Ernie had never actually fucked Jung-Li in front of her, but with his present frame of mind, that was probably coming. She hated Diana with total passion . . . Diana who once again ruled the scene in New York, this time without even trying. Brad Bailey was actually *pursuing* her. Brad! whom she, Felicity, had set her cap at so firmly three years ago, only to be brutally rebuffed, like most of the Manhattan girls. People had liked to say he was gay, but the trouble was, he was seen with too many women. He had been written off as a hopeless bachelor.

And now wherever he went Diana was there at his side. If Ernie had an excellent box for the opening night at the Met, Diana was in a better one, usually with the mayor or the governor, and on one dreadful night had been seen having drinks with Elspeth Merriman and the First Lady . . . She had the best table at every ball, she lounged on the deck of the largest yacht, she was up there with Mrs Astor, but she was sixty years younger.

And she wasn't trying. Felicity dreaded the day Diana's

dinner parties, twice as glamorous and star-studded as before, started up again – with herself, Jodie and Natasha permanently off the guest list – but it had not come. Diana was past the party-giving stage. She was said 'not to have the time'. And what the hell did that mean? Felicity asked herself, defensively. As though running some wretched company were so much more important than organising the social life of one of New York's premier publishing figures.

Except that Diana's company was no longer so wretched. Felicity had been forced to learn how to pay attention to the business pages of the papers. The JanCorp merger had made Michael Cicero's company a – what was the term? – a player. Diana's books had burst on the publishing scene with promotion, marketing and sales clout behind them. Her ABCs and counting series for infants was a huge success.

Ernie told her bitterly you could spend your way into the charts, but making it last took more skill.

She stood and shook her head sorrowfully in Ernie's direction, but he ignored her. She marched out of the room and slammed the door. She was mad.

Nothing but a couple of emerald studs from Cartier would make her feel better, Felicity decided, rather viciously. And maybe a tennis bracelet, too.

Diana took a cab down to Michael's place. He had moved into a SoHo loft, which was fairly luxurious. She noted the well-equipped gym set up next to the kitchen on the first floor; the neat bedroom, the home office, everything ranged out cleanly and simply. The colours were dark green, burgundy and mahogany. In a city full of teal, cream and variations of beige, Michael Cicero's pad was uncompromisingly dark and masculine.

He had no paintings, just line drawings of the Roman Forum and the Baths of Caracalla. The ornamentation was limited to broken marble heads on display stands. She saw instantly that they were genuine antiques.

'Come in,' Michael said, waving her inside. 'Good to see you.'

'Yeah, it's been at least four hours,' Diana teased. She strolled over to the largest head, that of a masculine, full-figured man with a beard and severe eyes. 'Who's this guy? Could he have more testosterone?'

'That's the Emperor Hadrian.'

'Of Hadrian's Wall?'

'Uh-huh. He was a good commander. Consolidated the Roman gains. A fighter.'

'Very masculine,' Diana said, approvingly.

Michael let his eyes run over her body. She was wearing a simple, elegant light blue number by DKNY, a dress in heavy silk that hugged her ass and her tits, yet maddeningly covered everything up.

'Yes he was. He was also gay.'

Diana laughed. 'Rock Hudson was pretty masculine and he was gay.'

'It doesn't stop you being a man. My first partner was gay. Without Seth, I would never have gotten Green Eggs off the ground.' Michael waved her over to the table in the middle of the office. It was set with illustrations, travel guides, sheets of numbers and a few cartons. 'I got sushi again. Nothing but the best; no California rolls, just octopus, squid—'

'Don't.' Diana tossed back her dark hair, and he felt the first stirring in his groin. 'I can eat the stuff. I just hate knowing what they put in it.'

'Then I'll pour the sake and we can get to it.'

They spent a few hours going over the new games, just enough for Diana to understand what Michael wanted. The important part of a session like this was for her to understand his vision. Once she had clicked, she ran with the ball.

'Dorling Kindersley have the best maps and Insight have the best snaps,' she told him. 'I can poach from both and come up with something even better.'

Diana laid down her papers, aware that Michael was gazing at her. The sun had set outside and his home was lit with softly glowing lamps. She had drunk virtually nothing, but she still felt light-headed.

'I need to ask you something,' he said.

She felt a knot in her stomach. 'Fire away.' If he would only stop staring at her. She had a tendency to imagine his eyes on her breasts, which, inevitably got her hot, made her nipples harden and set her belly on fire as if his fingernails had raked lightly across it. And then who knew what his eyes were doing?

'It's about Ernie. I've been watching him. Building up a position in his stock.'

'A position in his stock,' Diana repeated. 'But Blakely's is huge. You can't own that much.'

'Oh, I don't.' He gave her that trademark Cicero grin. 'I just own two per cent. Which is enough to guarantee me rights to speak for five minutes at the next stockholders meeting. He's in trouble. Real, serious trouble. He has spent so hard on marketing and advances, his sales can never match up. The games division is a joke – the hackers can't work under those conditions, one of them called me last week. In order to make the bottom line look good, Ernie has taken to firing all the high-salary employees and replacing them with cheaper ones.'

'Only the cheaper ones aren't as good.'

'Right. And books and games are leaking money. They have a large market share and a profit margin of next to nothing. Signor Bertaloni thinks his money went to a flake. He's trying to bury the deal.' Michael smiled, cruelly. He had such a handsome, almost callous mouth, she thought. She was trying to listen to him, but her eyes kept fixing themselves on his mouth.

'Most of the business doesn't know how bad it is. I thought I could help them to find out. We'll bury that motherfucker.' He shrugged. 'Excuse my language. But . . . he is your ex-husband.'

Michael stood up and walked behind her chair, and Diana felt the tiny hairs on the back of her neck lift. She could sense his body, his muscles behind the cotton shirt, close to her. She slicked up and shifted on her seat, biting down on her lip.

'I couldn't care less about him,' Diana said. She tried to say it, but it came out as a whimper. Frantically, she cleared her throat. 'You can do whatever you like. I'll be right there with you.'

'OK. Good.' Michael leant forward to clear away her dirty plate. He found himself looking down directly at those magnificent tits. Her skin was warm, silky. Was he imagining it, or was her breathing coming short?

He snapped. Enough control. He pushed closer and kissed her roughly on the lips.

Chapter 40

Diana shuddered. Her reaction was instant, total. There could be no more lies, not even to herself. She moaned lightly in the back of her throat, a soft, small sound, ripped from her by his touch. Her pussy was moist, open and wanting. There was none of the slight recoil, the drawing back she felt in her skin when Brad tried to touch her. Warm blood surged into her nipples, hardening them into tight little pebbles, sensitive and aching so that the soft silk of her bra was almost unbearable on them.

Michael heard her. He instantly tipped back her chair and scooped her up into his arms, letting the chair topple to the floor. He cradled her weight like it was nothing to him. Diana felt his kisses on her mouth, her cheeks, her neck. They were not soft. His teeth half-bit, tore at her. Months and months of frustrated desire were unleashed on her.

'Michael—' she whispered.

'Shut up,' he said, bluntly. 'Just be quiet. You don't make a sound. I don't want to hear it.'

He carried her upstairs and pushed open the door to his bedroom, half shoving Diana inside. She stumbled in front of him, then turned to face him. Michael pulled down the dress from her shoulders, stripping her to the waist, holding her eyes.

'You left me,' he said. His voice was thick with lust. 'You fucking left me. You made me wait for this.'

He tugged the silk bra off her breasts impatiently. They

were warm, swollen slightly. Michael held each one in his hands, as though assessing their weight. Then he brushed his thumb over the aching skin of her nipples. Diana felt an electric shock of pleasure and lust, a silver chain running from her breasts down to her belly, the soft cradle of flesh right above her groin. Her nipples hardened visibly.

Michael said, 'Maybe I wasn't the only one waiting.'

'I—' Diana started.

He shook his head. 'I told you not to speak. If you make another sound I'm going to stop touching you.'

Then he lowered his dark head and flicked out his tongue, circling lightly round the rosy skin, never quite touching it, until she was biting her cheeks to keep herself from begging him. Mutely, Diana lifted herself to him, pressed herself into his hands. But Michael was cruel. He slipped his hands away from her breasts down to her butt, lifting his head to watch her face as he cupped and kneaded it.

'You have such a great ass,' he murmured into her ear. 'Everywhere you go I try to walk behind it just to watch it roll. I want to check it's the same as when I left it. Don't move.'

He tugged her dress down at the waist and kicked it from him, then rolled down her white cotton panties. Diana stood, trembling, her need for him so intense she didn't dare to disobey. She kept her head lifted, staring at the wall. She knew that he was crouching at her groin, staring at her pussy, the neatly trimmed, soft, silky black hairs of it. She was ready for him. She wondered if he could smell it. The thought of his eyes on her made her so hot she started to tremble. She didn't know how long her legs would hold up.

And then he was back at eye level, his hands on her naked ass, stroking it and petting it, condescendingly, letting her know he knew exactly how hot she was, but not letting her move. He would control everything, even her release. Diana's breath was coming from her in great, ragged sobs.

'You want to say something,' Michael murmured, pressing his erection against her. He was so thick, it was incredible. Diana longed to feel him spearing inside her. Her body had never forgotten what it was like to be fucked by Michael. You felt as if you were being plugged. And yet the itch was not scratched, you just wanted more.

Diana whimpered.

'Not yet, girl,' he said. He picked her up again and laid her down roughly on the bed. Her skin, below him, was mottled with lust, reddening across the length of her body. Experimentally, Michael cupped his rough hand over her pussy. She was soaking wet, completely open to him. He groaned deep in the back of his throat and pinned her arms over her head, nudging her tanned thighs apart with his knees. Then he lowered his mouth deliberately onto hers, and entered her, and Diana lifted her body up to him, taking him, loving and lost in him.

The break with Brad proved surprisingly difficult.

He took it well, of course. Brad Bailey would never make a scene. Diana invited him over to her apartment for dinner in order to give him an easy out. But all he did was push the caviar around his plate and raise an eyebrow.

'You're making a mistake,' he said, factually. His handsome face was as open and easy as ever. 'You think you love this man because of your crazy schedule. You two are like . . . brothers in arms, I guess. But what does he have to offer you? A mill, two or three at best? I hear he's a good enough guy, but he's not your kind of person.'

'And what is my kind of person?' Diana asked, sipping

her Chardonnay. 'Michael is a go-getter, Brad. He's a self-made man.'

'But you and I aren't self-made people. We were born into a certain stratum of society. It's why your marriage to Ernie was such a mistake. You had class, and he didn't. I think you're just repeating that mistake now.'

'I may be,' Diana said, neutrally.

'Well.' Brad pushed back his chair and smiled at her as though nothing much had happened. 'I can't promise to wait for you but, assuming I don't find someone else, you should call me when you come to your senses. And take care of yourself in the meantime.'

'You too, Brad. I'm sorry it didn't work out,' Diana said, kissing him on the cheek, then shutting the door behind him.

She sat back down at her table and gazed at the Limoges plates, the crystal cut glass, the abandoned pheasant and herbed potatoes she had had sent in for dinner, bewildered. All the money and extravagant courting had just gone up in smoke for Brad, and he had been so calm.

Diana gazed out over the sparkling lights of the city and it hit her. He didn't buy it. Handsome Brad Bailey could not actually credit that he was being dumped for a nobody, an entrepreneur from the wrong side of town. He assumed she would wake up and smell the Jamaican Blue Mountain, and come back to him humbly asking for a second chance. With Michael, even now, there was the possibility it might not work out. They had been shafted in business before, and it could happen again.

Brad Bailey was offering a future so bright, even the grasping trophy wife Diana had been couldn't have imagined it.

He just did not believe she was turning him down. Claire would be devastated, and Elspeth severely disapproving.

But Diana's body still echoed with the aftershocks of Michael's love-making last night. His tongue, merciless and insistent, dragging over the rich, musky centre of her, had had her thrashing about in his sheets like a landed fish. He had put her on her hands and knees, her belly, her side, he had bent her over and forced her to the ground, his fist in her hair, just to watch her pleasure him. They had spent hours love-making with an almost savage thirst, and then, finally, they had fallen asleep in each other's arms.

And she knew when she woke she would risk everything to stay with him.

Diana and Michael now dated openly, even in the office.

'Look, James Carville and Mary Matalin got married,' Claire told them. 'He was a spin doctor for the Democrats, she for the Republicans. And if they can marry I don't see why you guys can't date.'

Diana smiled over at Michael. Dating. Is that what they were doing? Up at six, working like dogs until seven, coming home, barely through the door before there was a tangle of limbs and skin and hair and mouths? It was amazing to her that they managed to fit in time for eating.

There were problems. Tina Armis had quit, but not quietly. She walked out screaming at Michael, then marched across the hall to Diana's office. Diana could have had her thrown out, but she dismissed Ellen and let Tina rave. No point in adding insult to injury.

The younger woman slammed Diana's door shut and yelled at her. She looked comical, standing there in her string of demure pearls and her long yellow dress, with her blond hair neatly washed and brushed, and her face as red as a drunkard's, her mouth open, bawling at Diana.

'You goddamn lying English witch! Fucking limey

gold-digger,' Tina said, with supreme ignorance of the irony. 'You always had your eye on my man. Home-wrecker! No wonder your first husband fired you. When Michael finds out you're just after his money he'll lose you like a bad habit.'

'Look, Tina, I'm sorry you've been hurt,' Diana said, calmly. 'I love Michael—'

'Love his money,' Tina sneered.

'My ex-boyfriend had a lot more money than Michael does.'

'Right, and now you go around town pretending that you broke up with Brad Bailey when everybody knows he dumped you. Michael deserves better than to be your second choice. And when he realises that he'll be right back with me. Where he belongs.'

'I'll have to take that chance,' Diana said softly.

'That's right.' Tina was practically spitting at her. 'You will. You're older than me and you could stand to lose a few pounds, lady. And you're a goddamn limey who couldn't possibly understand him. Michael and me are two of a kind. We're both from the Bronx.' She snapped her fingers, aggressively.

'Except that Michael is intelligent and motivated, and you're a gum-chewing, skinny little bimbo, who got passed over for a smart girl with tits and ass. If I were you, I'd eat some food,' Diana said, easily.

Tina's mouth dropped wide open. She stared at Diana as though rooted to the spot. She couldn't believe the fucking ice-queen could come out with language like that.

'See you around,' Diana added, opening her door and beckoning to Ellen to show Tina out.

When Tina had gone she grinned to herself. That hadn't exactly been ladylike, but it had certainly been fun.

Maybe she was turning into a New Yorker.

*

Building up Imperial was one of the hardest, most exhausting, stressful, exhilarating and energising times of Diana's life. All day, every day, she met with package designers, ad specialists, code-writers and web experts. She was in and out of planes, limos and cabs, and she took her work with her wherever she went. Diana revamped the Gecko series with her new cash. It was the commercial and critical success which announced to the whole world that Imperial meant business.

But the travel guides, Michael's project, were their greatest hit. Suddenly, student tourists could see and hear the cities they were visiting, in living colour. The guides sold out before the first run even hit the stores. Amazon could not keep enough stock. The only problem they had was rushing out more titles to meet demand.

Art Jankel came to see Diana. He shook her hand and offered her a slim cheroot. He told her he was very pleased, then he left.

The next morning a messenger arrived from Jankel's office on the forty-eighth floor with a slim envelope for Diana.

Inside was a printed card announcing 'an enclosed bonus'. There was also a cheque. Diana opened it carefully.

It was made out to her for a quarter of a million dollars.

'No, I'm not taking any of that money.' Michael shook his head as Diana glanced out at the midtown traffic. New Yorkers were cursing and hooting at each other as usual. 'You earned it. It's about a quarter of what old man Jankel has made on the rise of his stock so far. We're beating the Blakely's games out of sight.'

'Especially now.'

Michael's big paw squeezed her soft hands.

'Right, especially now.'

She fell silent. This was a big day for Michael, and for her. Ernie was about to learn that payback was a bitch.

There was a mass of limos double parked and honking at each other right down Seventh Avenue, forced to line up outside the peepshow stores and Disney musicals that jostled for space a couple of blocks away from the Blakely's building. Michael was glad he'd taken a cab. Jostling for position was aggravating, and worse, it took time.

Ernie and the Blakely's board were nowhere to be seen in the packed conference room, which was as he'd expected. Michael signed up to speak, twelfth on a long list. He did not expect Foxton to realise he was there. The buying had been done quietly and the consolidating even more quietly. He did not have to disclose his stake yet; he'd hovered just below the Securities and Exchange Commission watershed for announcement, set so that targeted companies had some warning of when they were about to be taken over.

He wasn't planning on taking over Blakely's. It was better to have your own business, to build it from the ground up. Michael waited until Diana was seated, then took his place beside her. Around the room were giant blow-up posters of Blakely's latest and greatest best-sellers. Michael recognised them all. Popular novelists, for sure; marquee names. They also had marquee prices. He wondered how Ernie's henchmen were going to spin this. The balance sheet looked good, unless you really knew the book business. If this company was going to survive, the board would need to recognise their mistake.

You didn't throw tradition away to grab at the quick fix, the easy buck. For a quarter or two you were a star. And then the cracks started to show.

Well, Michael thought, settling back in his seat. I'm here now. And I'm their wake-up call.

Chapter 41

'And so, we feel that the improved balance sheet, the cost savings and our gain in market share are positioning Blakely's uniquely well to move forward in this new millennium as the publishing house of the future,' Ernie said, leaning a little into his microphone.

Diana admired his skill. You couldn't help but notice how slickly he dodged the bullets. The overpayment of authors was 'an investment'. The firing of all their best people 'an assault on overhead'. The old-money types who had stock in Blakely's were clearly not too well versed in the nuts and bolts of the book industry. Peter Davits, the tall, Slavonic-looking man, had done a nice little song and dance that made it sound like the Blakely's balance sheet was the leanest in the business.

'Any more questions?'

She settled back into her seat as Michael rose to his feet. A flunky passed him the microphone.

'Mr Chairman, I have a couple of questions, if I may.'

Foxton peered out across the rows of dark-suited men and women in navy and cream. He blinked.

'Mr Chairman,' Ernie said hastily, 'Mr Cicero runs a rival company to ours. I don't think questions from him are appropriate.'

'Actually, you have no choice but to allow me to speak. I am a stockholder of four point five per cent of Blakely's. You will see my name as the twelfth mandated speaker on your list, Mr Foxton.' Michael grinned. 'The Chairman of Romulus Holdings, Inc. That's me.'

'This is obviously an ambush,' Ernie spat.

'As a matter of fact, I tabled my questions two months ago. Besides, as I'm sure you stand behind your running of the company, you won't worry about answering them. Will you?'

Diana watched as half the room turned round to watch Michael, conservatively dressed in one of his black English suits, with dark shoes and a paisley tie. He was polite, but incredibly menacing. The strong body looked like a cobra ready to spring.

Michael's steady gaze and level voice were dominating the room. She could feel the current of electricity, the muted buzz of whispers, that rippled through the investors and Wall Street analysts gathered there.

'Mr Cicero is correct, Ernest.' Flustered, old man Gammon, the chairman of the board, was consulting a lawyer. 'He has the right to speak.'

'I don't mind answering any questions,' Ernie said quickly, 'but I think it's unorthodox procedure.' The set of his mouth was sulky. 'Please say what you have to say. We want to finish up this meeting.'

'Oh, I'll be finished just as soon as I have my answers,' Michael said. 'First, I'd like to ask you about the cost savings. Isn't it true that included in that figure are voided contracts with seventy authors who have gone on to have bestsellers at other publishing houses?'

'It's not as simple as that,' Ernie snapped.

'Perhaps it's as simple as this: isn't it also true that your bestsellers have all cost approximately three times to market and promote as they have made in returns, and that once the spending stopped they disappeared? And isn't it also true that for every bestseller you have produced in the last six months the company has made a loss?'

'Market share is a worthwhile goal,' Ernie replied, a little less confidently.

'Then let's discuss Education Station. Of the moneys invested in new offices, salaries and other overheads, how much have you recouped?'

'Nothing. It's a startup. They are never profitable.'

'Oh, Imperial Games is profitable. But then we haven't had to recall over eighty per cent of our lines because of bugs. I would like an explanation of the fact that money was spent heavily to promote a line of games which was not yet ready, so that the name of the company is now mud among suppliers.'

Ernie sputtered, 'I don't think you are seriously interested in the answer to that question.'

'I am,' said a loud voice behind Michael.

Diana turned her head to see a tall older man with white hair glaring at the dias. She recognised Joshua Oberman, the formidable chairman of Musica Records. 'I have some of my retirement money in this company. I want to know the answers to these questions. Perhaps Mr Foxton will oblige me.'

'And me,' called out a squat woman with thick glasses. She was Katia Hendorf, one of the Street's most respected analysts.

There was uproar. Gammon banged his gavel for quiet. But Michael still had the microphone.

'Ladies and gentlemen, I am extremely concerned about the way this company is being run. Key staffers are fired while an ineffective management retains a private jet for top executives. Market share is being propped up by empty spending. If any investors are as concerned about this as I am, please feel free to stop Ms Diana Verity outside the hall. We have printed our own report on Blakely's.'

Diana stood and gave a little nod to the spellbound room. She lifted up her Gucci briefcase, with its distinctive burgundy leather, so that they could all see it. Inside were the one-page summaries of the disastrous way

Blakely's had been handled. They were easy to read, easy to understand.

They were devastating.

Diana looked across at her ex-husband and winked.

Michael silently handed the microphone back to the conference-hall flunky.

On the dias, Ernie's face was half white, half purple. He shouted over the hubbub. 'This is a disgrace! That cow is my ex-wife, all right? And she's no better than a—'

There was a loud screech of feedback as Paul Gammon reached over and switched off Ernie's mike. For a few seconds, the hall watched in amazement as Gammon and Foxton shouted at each other. Then Ernie Foxton jumped to his feet, knocking his chair backwards and, shoving board members out of the way, stormed out of the hall.

Michael squeezed her hand.

'I think we should be leaving now,' he said.

Ernie Foxton was a survivor. He walked out of the conference room, straight into the lobby, and stepped into the executive elevator that shuttled him from the sixteenth floor to the underground garage where his limo was always waiting.

'Wake up,' he shouted at Richard, his driver. 'Get your fucking lazy little arse up and get me home, all right? Is the fax working?'

The chauffeur jumped out of his skin. He'd been trying to snatch a little rest in between airport shuttling these rich assholes. But Ernie Foxton was the worst of them all.

'Yes, sir, it's all there,' he mumbled. He straightened his cap and hurried to open the door for his boss. Foxton looked like someone had put a rocket up his arse. How great it would be if that were actually true.

'And fucking hurry up about it,' Foxton screeched. He had calls to make. His lawyers in London would be able to get him another job over there. The key thing was that he should lock in the cash before this news broke. His incompetent bloody lieutenants were responsible for all of this crap.

Ernie wasn't deceiving himself. That ball-busting bitch he'd married and that little wop fucker had shafted him. He'd get fired. And run out of New York.

He was going to jump before he was pushed. Paul Gammon's switching off his mike was reason enough. Ernie yanked out the laptop from the back of the limo and hurriedly started to type. If he was fast, he could be back on Concorde by tomorrow. Friday at the latest.

There was a silver lining to the cloud, though. That grasping bitch Felicity would be out of his life. She'd been rubbish when the going got . . . a little bumpy.

As the limo pulled out onto Broadway, it struck Ernie that Diana would have handled it differently. If she'd had the good sense to stay married to him. It was sad the way she had declined since he dumped her. Once, she'd known how to spend money and look good . . . bring a man a touch of class. Real class, the kind that Felicity would never have. But now she was a feminist harridan, *a career girl*, he sneered to himself. Pretending she knew about publishing, about computer games. They had announced her new earnings in the *Wall Street Journal* without comment.

Unbelievable. Could it possibly be that she took herself seriously?

The apartment was empty when he got home. Crispin Morrell, his lawyer in London, was already hunting out prospects. Ernie's resignation was in. He wanted to rifle through his papers and check out the size of his golden parachute. A million or two. Nothing spectacular. He envisaged the immediate loss of the jet, the driver, all the sweet little perks that went with being chairman of

Blakely's. Not even his PR girls were available to issue a refutation of Michael Cicero, because they belonged to Blakely's.

'Felicity?' he shouted. But she wasn't there, of course. She was probably out at Tiffany's.

He quickly called the bank and cancelled her charge card. At least there was one area of his life, Ernie thought viciously, that he still had some control over.

He hated Cicero. Bitter, vengeful, interfering little punk. Ernie wallowed in self-pity. The thought that this guy was fucking Diana caused him nothing but pain. Ernie walked to his bar and poured himself a large Scotch. Diana was frigid, of course. A dreadful lay. But she'd been an excellent wife otherwise.

He knocked back the liquor and thought about her. Her curves weren't to his taste, but she had her admirers: the press loved her, the socialites buzzed about her. And she had dated Brad Bailey. He was serious money. I respect that, Ernie thought, maudlin. He reached for the Scotch. It blurred the edges of his stress, and bathed everything in a calmer, more golden light.

After another glassful he walked deliberately upstairs to Felicity's bedroom. The bitch had a Rolodex with more information on people than the CIA. She was a jealous little madam. She was bound to have something on Diana.

'OK. Yeah. I'm watching it, I'm watching it now. Thanks, Selina.'

Tina slammed the receiver back in its cradle and switched her remote to NY One, the local access channel. Since her break-up from Michael, every girl she knew had been calling up with condolences, which was more sour than sweet of them, she thought. Now Selina Gonzales was giving her a heads-up about Michael and the limey bitch coming out of some meeting. Fascinated and infuriated, Tina curled her long, smooth legs underneath her and stared at the mob of guys in suits pressing round her baby and that slut as they stood together on the sidewalk. Diana was handing something out. Papers. It looked like she was giving away free lottery tickets or something, the way those boys were crushing her. Piqued, Tina couldn't see what Diana was wearing. She always liked to criticise her clothes, with those tits, always dressing so conservative, so boring. Michael was a fuddy-duddy when it came to showing skin. Though after hours he had never objected to seeing all of hers.

She caught a glimpse of sleek black limos parked behind the crowd. Damn. That was the world of money and power Tina had always wanted to enter. By Michael's side she could have done. What the hell was this guy saying?

She flicked up the volume.

'. . . business scandal of the year . . . investors seem to be discounting the personal motivation behind this attack . . . investors in an uproar here'.

'And Mr Foxton fired Mr Cicero a year ago, correct?'

'That's right, Jim, some time ago. While Ms Verity, who heads up Cloud Nine, a new starter that's making waves in the book world, was actually his former wife, and was divorced by Mr Foxton in a messy high-society scandal,' the reporter said, almost licking his lips.

Tina picked up the dog-eared copy of the *National Enquirer* that was lying on her gold faux-satin coverlet and smiled. Maybe there *was* still a way to get back at that bitch. She had an idea.

'We have two choices.'

Michael turned to Diana and put his hands on her waist, tugging the silk shirt loose so he could put his hands directly on her skin. It was amazing, he thought, how he just could not fuck this girl enough. With the

378

others, it had always been the case that his enthusiasm drained before they had finished their first cup of coffee in the morning. Now, he needed to remember to get enough condoms. A couple of three-packs wouldn't cut it any more.

He felt the instant, helpless leap of her skin. He decided he wouldn't let her wear padded bras any more, that way he could actually see her nipples tightening.

'And what are they?' Diana asked, blushing and looking down. Michael always set her off balance. He put himself in her space, he stared right in her eyes. The blazing intensity he had at his work he directed right at her. She wondered if she was a horribly retro creature. She found his muscles, his physical strength, the size of him, his dominance over her, incredibly exciting. Michael didn't beg for sex like other men she had known. He just took. And the paradox was, she wanted him. When he pushed her back on the bed, she was already ready.

'We could go out to dinner and celebrate. Somewhere fancy. Your kind of place. Lutece. Four Seasons.'

'Or . . .'

'Or I could call for takeout and we could go to bed.'

'I vote for the second option,' Diana whispered.

'Somehow I thought you would,' Michael said. He slid her tight, pencil skirt up over her full, firm hips, stroking her butt, and traced his initials over the silken hair of her groin with his finger. Diana shivered and offered him her mouth. Michael pressed his lips on hers, kissing her roughly. His hands came up and palmed her breasts, lightly, over the padded silk cups of her bra.

'Still clothed?' Michael demanded. 'What's the problem? We don't have all day here.'

'I'm sorry—' Diana gasped. She struggled out of the jacket and bra. Didn't he realise who he was talking to? Wasn't he put off by her accent, her class, her elegance? She loved the way Michael just didn't give a fuck. He loved her for her, and ripped the trappings off her the way he liked to tear off her thin lace panties. She had learned to keep an emergency supply in a case here, because Michael had no respect for her wardrobe whatsoever.

'Too late,' he said, softly. He pulled off her skirt and thong panties and picked her up, flinging her over his shoulder. They didn't make it to the bed.

Chapter 42

Tina walked a little more slowly than usual. She was getting used to her brand-new heels, for one thing, four inches of shiny scarlet leather wrapped round a steel spike that thrust up her ankle, jutted out her barely there butt, and made her slim hips swing slightly as she minced along, trying to ignore the pain in her toes. After all, she did look great. No pain, no gain. This way, as she inched down Madison Avenue, she could stop and admire her reflection in every designer boutique window she passed. She had on a fire-red Versace suit, as subtle as a brick, thigh-high, with a military-cut jacket with gaudy gold buttons. Her lips were blood-red too and her eyelashes thick with navy mascara. Her long blond hair tumbled down her back in a shower of gold that caught the light. Men and women stopped to rubberneck. Well, hell, Tina thought, she was glad she'd given them something to gape at. Just last week *Harper's* said red was the new neutral. Which meant she was only blending in.

A cloud of Chanel No. 5 wafted along with her as she turned into the small building on the corner of Fortieth Street. The revolving door and grey slate fronting really didn't do it justice; these were the offices of *Big City* magazine, the gossip sheet that focused specifically on New York. Everybody read it. Marissa Matthews, the *doyenne* of Manhattan's tittle-tattlers, was editor in chief, and she published weekly scuttlebutt about anybody she could think of. If you were a big star, going outside without make-up was sufficient excuse for half a page. If you were a socialite, you needed a really nasty divorce, with fights over child custody and who got the yacht. And if you were a nobody, you needed to be a corrupt cop or a satanist on the board of education to qualify. *Big City* loved dirt. The grime of the New York skyscrapers was mirrored in the delicious celebrity filth that poured forth from its pages.

Tina read it every week. And now she was going to star in it.

She hugged herself. She had always wanted to be famous. Tina minced up to the receptionist, and flicked her flaxen mane.

Maybe some big producer would see it and cast her in a Hollywood movie. Things like that happened all the time. Didn't they?

'I'm Tina Armis,' she announced proudly to the girl.

'Yeah?' came the bored reply.

'I have an appointment at two to see Marissa Matthews. And to have a photo session,' Tina told her. She examined her reflection in the smoky glass panel behind the reception desk. She had never looked lovelier. And of course *Big City* was paying for her clothes.

If only she could see Diana Verity's face when she picked up the mag! That would be the real cherry on the cake.

Diana paced up and down nervously. She wondered if she should do something. Call Michael, maybe. Call the doorman up, at least. How had Ernie discovered her number? And why was he coming round here?

It was early in the morning, but he still sounded drunk. The telephone call had caught her off guard. Rushing back to her own flat to pick up some faxes for the sales presentation this morning, she had grabbed the phone as she stepped out of the shower, still wrapped in her voluminous white Ralph Lauren bathrobe, the soft towelling sticking to her skin. Refreshed and pampered from the L'Occitane lavender and honey bubble bath she'd taken, her body drenched in fragrance and her blood still pumping from the ghost of Michael's kisses this morning, she was relaxed. And not prepared.

'I need to see you,' he said, as soon as she picked up the phone. His voice was slurred slightly, just enough for Diana to notice it. 'Been doing some thinking. You said a lot of true stuff. No hard feelings about today.'

'Yesterday.'

'Yesterday, right. Just business. Anyway, had a fight with Felicity and locked the doors.' Ernie snickered. 'And I'm coming round to talk to my wife. Won't take long, be there in twenty minutes.'

'No! Ernie, don't come round. I – I'm busy. Going to work.'

Diana looked round the apartment for her papers. How quickly could she get dressed and get out of here? What on earth could he want? For a second she wondered if yesterday had unbalanced him, if he'd gone mental.

'I'm calling from the car. On my way into the city to see the lawyers. Going home, darlin'. Got a new job.'

'That was fast,' Diana said, despite herself.

Ernie cackled. 'You know me. I adapt. Gotta adapt, babe. It's why you hooked up with me at first. So, ten more minutes, for old times' sake, all right?'

He hung up and Diana dived for her clothes. Rejecting the pretty dress and tiny mint-coloured cardigan by Gucci she had been planning to wear, she opted for a cream blouse and a severe Dolce & Gabanna navy pantsuit. It fitted her like armour. She wouldn't call Michael, because that would be a display of weakness. Ernie – well – Ernie was an asshole, but yesterday they had cut his world out from under his feet. They were definitely even, and he *had* once been her husband.

She didn't see how she could rightly refuse him.

Very well, ten minutes. She fixed a pot of coffee on the Krups blender and called down to Zachary, the friendly lobby guard who was actually a former Mossad agent. The building housed a lot of UN diplomats, and everybody who was shown upstairs went through a metal detector and a pat-down. If Ernie passed that test, she supposed it was OK that he come up.

Diana let the coffee percolate and settled down to wait.

'So, my dear, tell me how you were forced into this affair,' Marissa Matthews said sweetly to Tina. She was almost beside herself with joy. The girl was young, barely out of college, a twenty-something with a teenager's coltish body. The bright-red lipstick made her look like a tart and the mockery of a business suit, a skirt that was really a T-shirt with pretensions, and the spiked heels, gave the impression of the kind of businesswoman who stars in *Playboy* photo shoots.

What a money-hungry Barbie doll, Marissa thought. And it reflected *so* badly on poor Diana Verity. That she should be dating a man who once dated . . . this! It made you wonder about his taste, about Diana. Her image was far too goody-goody, and that made her ripe pickings for *Big City*. They'd had nothing on her since the 'mistress in the wife's clothes' story had New York choking over its breakfast croissants. 'Extend your leg a little, dear. Slip that jacket off your shoulder. What marvellous skin you have. Do go on.'

The photographer clicked away as Tina gave her story between shots. Marissa had a deadline coming up and was rushing this one onto the cover. They had no time to waste.

'Well, the threat was never said aloud. More like I kinda had to, though. To keep my job,' Tina said.

'You mean it was implicit.'

'Yeah. Implicit, right. Anyway, I fell for him because he was a demon in bed. Hung like a baboon—'

'You don't need to be *quite* so graphic, dear,' Marissa lied, making notes. 'Like a baboon. Right. And he was very successful.'

'Yes, but *I* wasn't interested in his money.' Tina tossed her hair. 'I was a girl from the Bronx, you know, the old neighbourhood. Like Michael. I knew what he needed. But this woman, this little bitch – everybody hates her in our office – she swans in with her limey accent and she marries money, right? That other English guy who dumped her. And she had a heart to heart with me about it. She said—'

Tina smiled for the camera. She'd been using Rembrandt toothpaste for the past four days and she was sure it made her teeth look like ivory pearls. The more she told, Marissa had made it clear, the bigger her piece would be and the bigger her picture. Why, Brad Bailey was looking for a girl, wasn't he?

'She said Michael didn't have enough money for her because she had managed to snag Brad Bailey.'

'To "snag" him?' Marissa repeated, in transports of joy.

'Yeah, something like that.' The thought of lawyers cast a brief shadow over Tina's joy. 'Well, I can't quote exactly.'

'There were no witnesses to this conversation?'

'Just me an' her. She was trying to drive a wedge between me and my man.' Tina sniffed.

Her word against Diana's. They could repeat every word of it, stick in an alleged and they'd be quite safe, Marissa realised.

'She told me though that . . . that men liked a class act. And I wasn't good enough for a rich man like Michael. She was seeing him the whole time she was going out with Brad, you know. Intruding into our private lives. She used to call and hang up.'

Tina was thoroughly enjoying herself now.

'That must have been emotionally devastating,' Marissa purred.

'Sure. Yes, it was.' Tina took her cue and reached for a Kleenex from the box placed before her, holding it delicately to her bone-dry mascara while the snapper moved about her. 'She wrecked the happy home we had together. We were thinking about marriage.'

'Was there any "romance" in the office, dear?' Marissa prompted eagerly. How wonderful if she could break that sensational tidbit.

'That was the rumour. I didn't see any,' Tina said, regretfully. 'But Diana Verity had no skills, nothing, when Michael hired her. That was before I came on board. She was doing my job at first. Which is why she hates me. She feared I would like, unseat her and stuff.'

Marissa did a creditable job of smothering her laugh into a cough. 'Excuse me. Please go on.'

'Anyway, she "worked" in Michael's office when he was at her husband's old place. If you ask me she was the cheating one. He just wanted to get back at her because she was fucking Michael. Why else would he hire her?'

'Why indeed?' Marissa asked thoughtfully. 'Could I get you to put your head in your hands, dear? Just like that. Perfect.'

The bell rang. Diana stood, and walked to the door to let Ernie into her home. The morning sun was streaming through the windows, bathing her apartment in light; it set off the oyster-white decor, the plump cushions imported from France stacked on her chaise-longue, the fresh creamy blossoms of white hydrangeas mixed with brilliant blue irises and soft pink sweet peas which she had delivered each morning. She could be proud of how it looked. It was the luxury of a few hundred thousand rather than the millions she'd had to play with on Central Park West, but Diana thought she liked this apartment better. It was all her; each piece was there for beauty, not ostentation; it was feminine and graceful and simple. The way she had lived her life once Ernie had dumped her.

She stood back as he staggered through the door. There was an unmistakable reek of sour mash whiskey on his breath. Diana glanced down at her watch; it was ten to nine in the morning.

What a way for her fairy-tale wedding to end up, Diana thought. Cinderella's Prince Charming turns out to be a masochistic drunk, and the fairy carriage turns into a rent demand. And yet the irony was that her happiness had begun once Happily Ever After had fallen to pieces.

'H'llo, Di. You look gorgeous. Nice pantsuit. You smell good,' Ernie said. He looked at her rather pathetically with big puppy-dog eyes. 'You always looked good, though. Never better than now.'

Diana smoothed down her hair. She had no idea what to say. Once she had been desperate to make Ernie fall back in love with her, now she just wanted him to get out.

'Thank you.' She moved towards her white marble kitchen countertop, just to get further away from him. 'Let me get you some coffee.'

'Only if you're going to make it Irish,' Ernie said.

'At nine a.m.? Let me get you milk and sugar.' Diana settled into her single armchair so there was no danger he would park himself by her. 'What's all this about, Ernie? I'm glad you have another job. But I have to be at work. I'm late already.'

'Right.' He slipped onto her couch, ignoring the coffee, and gazed across at her. His tone was heavy with sarcasm. 'You're the big working woman now.'

'Yes, I am.' Diana held his gaze unflinchingly. 'And I'm needed at my company.'

''S not yours. 'S Cicero's. Little fucking Yank bastard.'

'I would rather you didn't use language like that,' Diana said. 'Look, Ernie – I need you to tell me what this is all about.'

To her horror he got up from the sofa, lurched towards her, and dropped clumsily to one knee, taking her hand in his.

'We made a lot of mistakes, OK, Di. I was – I cheated on you. But I always loved you.' Mawkish alcohol-fuelled remorse was getting the better of him. His eyes were bloodshot and teary. 'I broke up with Felicity. She was always trying to split us up—'

'You don't say,' Diana interjected, coldly. She had to let him finish, but he repulsed her. Did he expect her to forget everything and take him back so he could cheat on her in England, too?

'She's gone. She was trashy, compared to you. You're a classy lady.' Ernie's breath reeked, and Diana tried not to flinch. 'You need to give up work and come home with me. We can do better there. All your friends. Your clubs. All that.'

'Ernie,' Diana yanked her hand out of his, 'why do all the men in my life seem to think I want to stop working? Maybe I like it. Maybe I'm good at it.'

'Come on, darlin'.' Ernie's eyes narrowed, meanly. 'You got a job because you were my wife, all right?'

His words stung. Diana pushed herself to her feet. 'It's time for you to leave. I'm happy in America and there's nothing between us any more.'

'You don't mean that,' he whined. Then he looked at her face, and saw the expression on it: the hard set of her brows, the look of disdain set over her high cheekbones and full lips.

'I see how it is.' Ernie slouched towards the door.

'You're fucking that guy. And now you're playing Businesswoman of the Year, like you played the good wife with me. Except now you picked some kid from the backwaters of the Bronx.'

'Get out, Ernie,' Diana pushed him from her, revolted, 'before I call security. Michael managed to make it without stepping on people. Maybe that's something you despise. The funny thing is you're finished, and you don't even know it. And by the way – you're hardly from the right side of town yourself.'

'You think you won.' His bony finger jabbed at her. 'You think Cicero can ride off into the sunset with my wife and my fucking life? You got another think coming, girl. I'm not through.'

'But you are, Ernie. That's exactly what you are,' Diana told him.

She shoved him into the hallway and locked the door behind him.

Chapter 43

Michael stepped out of the cab and paused for a second on the sidewalk. The commuters rushing past ignored him. Manhattan was always that way; nobody bothered to look round, nobody had the time. The steam that hissed up from the sidewalks, the clouds of cherry blossom clinging tenaciously to the trees despite the dust and fumes from the honking cabs and backed-up Lincoln town cars, everything got ignored in favour of getting where you were going. Yesterday.

It was early morning. Any second now, Diana would be here and he could get on with the business of making serious money.

Michael gazed up at the black monolith of the JanCorp tower. His office was up there. The phones and faxes would already be starting to buzz with the hymn of success he loved so much. Last week had been fun, sure: sticking it to Ernie, a day he had waited for and planned.

There was that Italian revenge thing. Michael wasn't the type to use a concrete overcoat or a baseball bat, but watching that bastard's career crumble, in his own building, in front of his own board . . . that had been satisfying.

CNN had announced Ernie's resignation on its business news. The shot of him, harassed, rushing out of the conference room in the middle of the meeting had been worth staying up late for. If he had been younger, Michael would have taped that to watch it over and over.

But not now. He was more concerned with the future than the past.

He took a deep breath, sniffing in the scent of coffee and gas fumes and blossoms and doughnuts, everything that made New York what it was. Then he pushed open the door to the lobby.

'Good morning, Mr Cicero.' Sally, the receptionist, greeted him deferentially as usual. She hastily shoved something she was reading out of sight. She blushed. 'Your assistant, Mr Piato—'

'Harry's in already. Good.'

'Yes, sir, he's been in for an hour, supervising the PR response.'

Michael paused and looked down at her. Damn, he was handsome, Sally thought, that square jaw and broken nose, the muscles on him under the well-cut black suit that brought out his eyes. Every woman in the place was half in love with him. And who knew? Maybe after the scandal he'd be a free man again.

She reminded herself to stock up on lip gloss.

'PR response to what? Surely there's not that much more to be said on Blakely's. I thought the phones stopped ringing a day or so ago.'

'No – no,' Sally stammered. She wasn't sure what to say. 'You mean you haven't seen it?'

'Seen what?' Michael demanded.

Furtively Sally kicked away the copy of *Big City* she had let tumble to the floor. Oh man. If he caught her with it . . . Who was going to be the one to break it to him? Not her. They always shot the messenger.

'There's an article in a magazine I think Mr Piato wants you to look at,' Sally whispered, lamely. Cicero was fixing her with that intense, dark stare. 'Please, sir—'

'Don't worry about it.' He smiled confidently, and she was able to stop a tremble before it started. 'Whatever it is, I'm sure you had nothing to do with it.'

'Oh no.' The girl went scarlet and shook her head violently. 'Nothing at all. Really. I never even knew her. Except when she came in in the mornings.'

Michael smiled reassuringly at her. What was the girl's name? Sally?

'I'll sort it out. You have a nice day, honey.'

He stepped into the elevator as Sally looked longingly after him. Most guys here were afraid to wish her good morning in case they got slapped with a sex-harassment rap. But Michael always called her baby, or doll, or honey. How she wished she was his honey.

'You too, sir,' she said wistfully as the chrome doors hissed shut.

The fact was, she suspected, he was about to have the worst day he'd had in a long time.

Michael stepped out on the ninth floor. He instantly noticed something was amiss. The normal early morning office chatter and buzz was muted and subdued. Nobody was even playing Quake on office time. The programmers weren't in yet, of course, but the marketing staff were, and they were nearly as bad; swearing, rock music, empty pizza boxes. This morning they were keeping their heads down. He greeted a couple of his lieutenants. They both just smiled briefly and scuttled away from him.

Michael's radar picked up. Danger, it bleeped at him. He strode to his office, noticing that Harry, the executive assistant who had replaced Tina, had gone inside. He glanced down at Harry's phones and saw all the lights blinking. At least six calls were on hold.

'Emma.' He turned round and gave a brisk order to his office manager. 'Pick up all the calls that are holding, apologise and say we can't speak to them at this time. Take messages. Then divert all my calls to Harry's voicemail until further notice.'

'Yes, sir,' Emma Harris said. She was a pretty, efficient

young woman, usually very exuberant. Today, she was twisting her fingers. 'Can I just say I'm very sorry. I don't believe it, anyway.'

What the bloody hell is going on? Michael thought. He pushed open the door and let himself into his office.

'Fill me in,' he snapped at Harry once the door was shut.

Harry winced and simply handed over a copy of *Big City*.

The picture on the front was unmistakable: Diana, looking regal, as classy as she had ever done, in a long dress of light mint-green silk, with Brad Bailey holding her arm, her hair swept up in a glossy French knot, diamonds dripping from her earlobes and draped over her throat. She screamed class and elegance. Michael had a momentary pang of jealousy; he hated to think Brad had once been her date. Or that any man would touch those curves other than himself.

But that was only for a nanosecond. The blaring headline at the bottom could not be ignored.

IS THIS THE BIGGEST GOLD-DIGGER IN NEW YORK? it yelled. Underneath, in bold red letters, was written, *Home-wrecker . . . Hustler . . . Fortune-hunter . . . The thrilling accusations of the rival she replaced!*

'What the fuck?' Michael said, angry.

'It's your ex-girlfriend. Tina Armis. She spilled her guts.' Harry flicked over to the centrefold article, where Tina was spilling more than her guts. Marissa had coaxed her into a swimsuit and then her lingerie. Her slender legs tumbled out of the staples clad in little more than frou-frou slippers, and a G-string at the top consisting of a tiny vee of dark lace. She was holding a spray of feathers over her naked, tiny little apple breasts. She looked like a young stripper. Michael felt himself flush with rage. Oh, great. Look at the way Harry was biting back a grin. And he couldn't blame him; Tina was a great piece of ass. But it was like having his former sex life splattered all over New York. Michael's thick jaw set in distaste.

'I guess I need to read this,' he said. His stubby fingers flicked through the inky rag, over glossy photos of Tina in a red suit, curled up half nude on a bearskin rug. They had kept it skimming just above *Playboy*, but barely. Next to her were the haughtiest photos of Diana that they had on file. Attending premières and balls, with just that one shot of her in jeans looking for a cheap apartment.

Breathlessly, Marissa Matthews led her readers through Tina's sad tale. She was just a put-upon little girl ... whom, Michael read, blinking, he had apparently forced into bed with veiled threats. Despite this abuse she had come to love him, until Diana Verity had arrived on the scene.

Michael couldn't believe they would try this. He would sue them, destroy them. What proof did they have for any of this?

And then he came to the *pièce de résistance*. Tina claimed she had had a heart to heart with Diana, and Diana had boasted of Brad's colossal wealth. According to Tina, she said she had 'traded up'.

'Ernie Foxton wasn't good enough for her,' Tina was quoted as saying. 'He didn't have enough cash. She was determined to show the world the husband she could snag. But then she found out about Michael's – *my* Michael's – deal with Mr Jankel.'

They stopped for a tiny photo of Art. Michael cursed. Art Jankel was a recluse. He would detest this.

'So suddenly Michael stops being worth a few million and he has serious money, from JanCorp, I mean. And Diana just laughed at me. I wasn't fancy like her. She said she knew moneyed men. She could have Michael any time she wanted.'

Marissa asked Tina why Diana would prefer Michael to Brad. Tina replied ('with tears in her blue eyes,' said the old hag, sympathy overflowing) that Brad could see through her but Michael was hooked. 'He told me once he hated women who married for money. But he's blind and he's forgotten what Diana is.'

His breath coming hard through his nostrils, Michael ripped the magazine into shreds, balled it in his fists, and flung it into the wastepaper basket. He turned to his assistant. 'Diana Verity is head of our publishing division. Our response to any enquiry about this story is no comment. It's not worth commenting on. Got it?'

Harry nodded hastily. 'I got it.'

'Good.' Michael pushed to his feet. 'Where is she?'

Ernie chuckled. He was in the car for the last time, heading out to JFK and his first-class ticket back home. It looked like maybe the new job was going to fall through. Those stupid fuckers, why not take advantage of world-class talent when it presented itself? But whatever, it wasn't his problem. He'd had a couple of lines of blow and nothing could puncture his good mood. He'd find a way through this just like he'd found a way through all the other messes. Meanwhile, there was the fantastic bloody magazine article for the flight over lying next to him on the leather seat.

Ernie glanced at the picture of the thin chick who had sold the story. Nice. Skinny. How he liked them. Probably be happy to try a little experimentation. And wasn't it fantastic to think of Manhattan waking up to this, everybody from the cops grabbing their doughnuts to the socialite wives who pretended not to read trash, but who secretly loved it. Yeah. Everyone he knew in town would be acquainted with it. It made Diana look little better than a hooker, a sort of rich lowlife, just a phony with an accent. He thought of Michael Cicero, the poor boy who carried himself so solemnly. Well, Michael looked like a fool now, didn't he? Once he got back home they'd be calling him to confirm this little story and he, Ernie Foxton, would love to help 'em out.

Diana obviously thought her little appearance at his meeting had been the end of the story – pushing him out of the apartment, that small, ordinary little place she had, nothing to notice in it. Rejecting him. Him, Ernie, who she had set her little money-grabbing cap at, whose money she'd ploughed through. Just like Felicity. All women were the same, of course.

But it wasn't the end of the story. Not by a long shot.

Ernie's only regret was that *he* wasn't the one sticking it to Diana. If he had had a hand in this, it would have been very satisfying.

He flicked through the pages again, staring with hatred at Diana's proud face, while New York slipped past and the limo plunged into the Queens–Midtown Tunnel.

But maybe there was something he *could* do.

He tapped the window in front, making the chauffeur slide it back. The guy had a phone up there.

'Get me Michael Cicero on the phone,' he said. 'Imperial Games. Tell him it's Ernie Foxton calling. And I only want to speak to him, personally.'

Diana couldn't believe it. She'd seen the paper at seven, because Claire Bryant came right round with a copy and a bunch of Kleenex.

'Look at the little tramp,' Claire said. 'Nobody will believe it. And . . . it's a boring story, anyway.'

Her voice quailed on the lie.

'Oh God,' Diana breathed. She sat down. She felt nauseated. Her friend bustled around the apartment, fixing her coffee, chattering, refusing to let her spirits sink.

'Pay it no mind.' Claire brought her a tiny, steaming

cup of espresso. 'You know you married Ernie for love, right? You loved him . . . that's why you married him.'

Diana stared bleakly at her.

'If only that were true,' she said.

Michael scowled at Harry. His day was just getting worse. As soon as Diana had come into the office she had barricaded herself in a three-hour meeting with some Japanese affiliates. He suspected she'd planned that deliberately, but Ellen swore she hadn't, that it had been planned for weeks.

'She told me her day would run as normal, sir.' Ellen quivered. 'Do you want me to fetch her out of the meeting for you?'

'No. That's OK.' Michael turned on his heel and stalked out of Cloud Nine. Now he couldn't even speak to her, to comfort her.

And now Harry wanted him to pick up some damn call. Fuck it. Let the press whistle for it. He wondered if they were waiting outside the building to snap him and Diana as they left the office. More than likely.

'I told you, no goddamn calls, Piato.'

'I think you'll want to take this one,' Harry said quietly. 'It's from Ernest Foxton. And he says he won't speak to anybody but you.'

Michael's brow arched. Very well. He supposed he at least owed the little prick the courtesy of taking this call.

'I'll go into my office. Put him through there,' he said. 'And Harry – tell me the minute Ms Verity gets out of her meeting. I want to see her.'

Michael shut the door softly and sat down. His heart was beating a little fast. Like a predator confronted with a trapped, broken prey, bleeding, with nothing left to lose, he was smart enough to know that he was in danger.

'Michael Cicero,' he said, picking up.

'Hey, Michael. Read the papers? Course you have. It's why I called.'

Ernie's thin little voice was babbling a mile a minute. Coke, Michael thought, with pity.

'You have something to say, Foxton? Or is this a social call?'

'Ah yes, the wunderkind of the *Wall Street Journal*, and all that. So businesslike. So rushed.'

Cicero waited impatiently. Doubtless the jerk would get to it soon.

'I read the papers too. Gotta say, you got nice taste. Girl has an ass like a boy.'

'I always hated that about her.'

'I guess so. Like Diana's big booty, huh? Cold in bed though, ain't she?'

'If you want to swap dirty stories, Foxton, you came to the wrong place.'

'Nah. Not stories, mate, more like a warning. Of course, I fucking hate you, right. Always did. You know that.'

'Yeah. I do,' Michael replied flatly.

'But that's business. Once I get home I'll see what I can do about screwing you over. Return the favour, like. This is more personal. Diana . . . see, I don't know this Tina, but she's bang on about the money. Diana's a gold-digger. She always was, always will be. She married me for money. Never did a stitch of work in her life. She's the same as your ex, but a bit less honest about it.'

Michael felt the blood rise up in his throat. He wanted to reach down the telephone and strangle Ernie with the cord. Lying bastard. Trash-talking asshole.

'That's a lie, and we both know it.'

'Is it?' Ernie gave a sniggering, high-pitched laugh. 'You think she was the poor hard-done-by sweetheart who I betrayed? Wake up and smell the petrol fumes, Cicero. Diana knew you were gonna be rich. She married me for my money. If you don't believe me ask her.'

Chapter 44

Michael hung up the receiver and sat staring into space.

Violence doesn't solve anything, the old saying went. But he thought it might make him feel better. The vision of balling his fist and smashing it into the side of the limey prick's nose was tantalising, but all Michael could do was slam down the phone.

The thought of Manhattan drooling over his woman – women – was annoying. Michael shrank from it. He was a businessman, a private guy. Not some two-bit film star with multiple marriages and a sordid past. He pictured Tina, half nude like a centrefold. Bad judgment on his part. But she really didn't matter; the poor kid was only embarrassing herself. They'd split up. She was no reflection on him.

The trouble was, Michael realised with a jolt, that he loved Diana.

He had been attracted to her from day one. Disliked her, then warmed up to her when her prestige was snatched away. She was a hard worker with a talent for hiring and presentation. All the bonuses and rises he had given her, she had deserved.

But Diana was a high-maintenance beauty. He wondered about the amount of cash it took her to keep it all together. Even when she had nothing, she came into the office in solid designer wear. He wasn't up on women's beauty rituals, but he knew she went to very expensive, very upscale hairdressers, manicurists, beauty parlours.

She wore a lot of diamonds and other jewels. She lived in a fancy apartment. And all this stuff required cash.

Uneasily, he thought about Brad Bailey. An insufferable little jerk living on daddy's money. Well, OK, he admitted to himself, he didn't know if he was a jerk or not, but there was no self-made element to him. He was just an upper-class pretty boy with a ton of cash. Ernie Foxton was self-made, but he was a bastard. What did he have to recommend him besides money?

They said love was blind. Could he have been that blind?

Michael stood and walked to his window and looked out over Sixth. The yellow cabs and crawling cars jostled for position, the sun sparkling off their windscreens, the chaos muted from this height. He had *always* wanted a girl who would love him for himself. There was a sick feeling at the pit of his stomach, a nagging suspicion. Diana had been an excellent manager, but Imperial had always been his thing. The terms of the buyout by JanCorp, if Imperial Games proved a success, had provided for him getting the money.

A lot of money.

Tina claimed that Brad Bailey had dumped Diana. Ernie said Diana married him just for his money. The magazine claimed that Michael was, right now, in love with the biggest gold-digger in New York City.

Michael's reflection stared back at him from the window. He was stocky, muscular, with a square jaw and a broken nose. He looked nothing like thin little Ernie Foxton, nothing like the all-American WASP good looks of Brad. Plus, Diana was an English lady, very refined, very proper. What the hell would she want with someone from the Bronx? But, said that nagging little voice, right now you're someone from the Bronx with 20 million bucks. And Tina says she knew you had that money coming.

Diana had got back together with him barely two months after Tina had spoken to her.

Michael shook his head. It was bullshit, all of it. Of course Diana had married Ernie Foxton for love. She was guilty of nothing more than bad judgment, which he was guilty of too by fucking Tina Armis. He would ask Diana, and that would be the end of the matter.

Meanwhile, he had a company to run.

He buzzed Piato. 'Harry, you can start putting through any calls that are to do with the business, OK? We've wasted half a morning on this bullshit.'

Diana crossed her legs under the mahogany table and listened politely to the interpreter, while not taking her eyes from her guests. It was said that the Japanese liked their women feminine and deferential, but she hadn't worn a dress. She'd chosen a soft Joseph pantsuit in crisp pink cotton, with a matching silky, form-fitting top, and a pair of Jimmy Choo sandals in candy-floss leather, with a low heel. Today it had been more important than ever to get out of the door looking her absolute best. Her lips were touched up with a clover gloss, her make-up minimalist, with light Mac concealer and Shu Uemura blusher hiding her pale, stricken skin and the hollows under her eyes. Drops had removed every last trace of redness. To the reporters – probably from *Big City* – she had managed to look pulled-together and upbeat. There would be time enough to collapse later. She had no idea what Michael thought of it, or how the office was dealing with it. As far as her day went, she had gone straight into her meeting, and then whatever else happened to be on her plate, it could wait.

Thank God for boarding school and the stiff upper lip. It was amazing how often it came in handy. She had met Marissa Matthews before, at balls, charity parties, things like that. She was a bitter, warped little woman who had bad things to say about everybody. Diana vaguely remembered cutting her dead once at a party of Claire's.

Diana didn't like gossip mongers. Now she remembered why.

Of course most of it was lies, she thought, as she nodded and smiled and gave little bows to her guests as they were finally ushered out. But the deadly thing was that part of it was true.

Once the door was closed, she buzzed Michael on the office intercom. He picked up right away. Diana braced herself.

'I'd like to see you,' she said, as calmly as she could.

'I'll be right there.' He hung up.

Diana moved to the small private bathroom at the back of her office. It was her work sanctuary, with fresh flowers by the sink, Tuscan soaps and two vials of her specially blended Parisian scent. The mirror showed her face, beautiful and composed. Her dark hair was fresh and shiny from the wash and set she'd had done in her building's ground-floor salon. Her heart felt like it was in a blender, but at least she looked good.

Michael plunged through the office, waving aside the executives who tried to come up and press their questions on him. Harry could take care of them. Right now, business didn't seem that important.

Diana had left her door open. He told Ellen to hold all calls, then went through and shut the door behind him. She was standing at the window, wearing something in pastels, light pink, form-fitting. It showed off the incredible firm, curvy flair of her butt he loved so much, and the high, full line of her breasts. He had a flashback of her ass on top of him, grinding away, her breasts bouncing above him the last time they had made love, yesterday, at lunch, when they had ducked back to his place because they couldn't keep their hands off each other. How hot she got, how completely she had yielded to him, Michael thought. He remembered Ernie had called her frigid. At least he knew in that way, he was different, at least he knew she liked his touch. She could not help herself, under him. He would not allow it. With some girls, his touch had been light, casual, they meant little to him. But Diana was a woman he had to have, she was in his blood. It was imperative to subdue her, to make her writhe and sob with pleasure and shudder in his arms . . . his fists clenched. There was nothing like it in the world.

His heart lifted just from looking at her. She belonged to him.

The question was why.

'I guess you read it,' he said, lamely.

'Me and the rest of Manhattan.' She shrugged, an elegant, delicate movement that made the sheen on her little sweater sparkle in the light. 'It's fish and chip wrapping. It doesn't bother me.'

She was the old Diana Foxton now, the ice-queen. Daring him to say any differently.

'I have a couple of questions.'

'Fire away.' Diana's blue eyes sought out Michael's. He looked angry with her, disappointed. Oh God. She delved deep inside her for every spare ounce of strength. She couldn't crumple and cry the way she wanted to.

'First, did you speak to Tina?'

'Yes, I did.' Diana saw Michael's eyes flash darkly and she prickled defensively. 'I spoke to her, but it was nothing like she said, OK?'

'It was nothing like that? You didn't discuss relationships? You didn't discuss me and Brad Bailey?'

'Well, yes, but—'

Michael held up one hand, furious. 'That's great, Diana. Talking about me in the office. I guess that wipes out any plans to sue. Tell me, did you also discuss the fact that you were dating a rich guy?'

Diana blushed scarlet. 'Yes, I did, but, Michael, it really wasn't like that.'

'I'm sure.' His dark, thick brows frowned at her. He was so angry, she thought. He was controlling it, but the scornful look on his face just made her want to burst into tears. 'You know, I took a call from your ex-husband today. He's a jerk. He said nothing unusual, except for one thing, he said that Tina was right, that you never loved him, that you married him for his money. I told him that was bullshit. He told me to ask you.'

Michael looked steadily over at her. His heart felt like it was being crushed by some unseen iron fist. Please Lord, let her deny it. I'll never ask you for anything again.

'So tell me. What's the story, Diana? You did marry him because you loved him, right?'

There was a pause.

Michael breathed in, raggedly. He knew what her answer was before she said it. Diana walked over to her window again, and rested her hands on the window, her head bowed.

'Wrong,' she said, finally. Her voice was leaden, 'I married Ernie for his money. I thought we'd be good together. He married me to get a hostess. I thought it was an even transaction.'

'Yeah. Very even. Very romantic,' Michael said. He felt sick. 'And Brad? I guess he dumped you, huh? Did you know about the deal with JanCorp?'

Diana couldn't believe it. She felt the blood drain from her face. She walked back to her desk and picked up her pink leather Prada tote. She had known it was bad, but she had never expected it to be as bad as this. Not from Michael. Not from the guy she loved.

'Of course I knew about it.' She spoke very softly; it seemed to her her voice was coming from far away, like somebody else's. 'I'm a director of this company. Or at least I was. I resign.'

'What?' Michael said. He seemed completely shocked. 'Why? You can't leave. We need you. This is our personal business, nothing else.'

'Yeah, well.' Diana was weary. 'Maybe I can't separate business and personal the way you do. To me, everything's personal. Maybe it's just part of being a woman. Whatever, I'm not staying here with you.'

'All I did was to ask you questions,' Michael said, stubbornly.

'And I answered them. I did certain things, yes. But I'm not that person any more. I've changed.' Diana felt a tear seep out, betraying her, and trickle down her chin. 'I don't need to justify myself to you. Because if you can't trust what we have, it'll never be any good. I thought you loved me. I guess I was wrong.'

He just stood there. He wasn't even looking at her. With a wrenching stab of sorrow in her gut, Diana shoved her way past him. She didn't even say goodbye to Ellen. She marched straight into the lobby and stepped into the elevator, riding down to the parking lot, where she could commandeer one of the company town cars.

It felt weird, so weird, to be going home in the middle of the day. She managed to keep the tears in during the ride home. There would be enough time to collapse when nobody was about. Diana watched Manhattan slip by, and tried to be upbeat. She wasn't destitute this time, she had options. One of them was going home. She had a quarter-of-a-million-dollar bonus, after all. She could take that money and start another business, maybe her own thing. Claire had offered to take her on in the interior design store. She had a talent for that. So it wasn't high-profile headhunting, so what? Diana thought. She could make something of it.

But her internal efforts to bolster herself were a dismal

failure. She didn't want to make it on her own. She wanted Michael. She was in love with Michael. And now, she had lost him.

The car stilled, grinding to a halt in the sweltering traffic. Diana couldn't hold it any more. She started to cry, as quietly as she could. Why hadn't she kept a packet of Kleenex in her pretty, impractical bloody bag?

She finally tumbled out at the lobby of her building almost thirty minutes later. She had shoved a fifty-buck note at the driver, far too large a tip, but she just wanted to get him away from her as quickly as possible without well-meaning questions about how she was feeling. Diana marched straight into the elevator, making sure the lobby guard didn't stop to shoot the breeze either. Today, she just wasn't up to it. All she wanted was a hot bath, her white towelling robe, and Claire's shoulder to cry on. Maybe it would be best to unhook the phone, too. The media were bound to get hold of her resignation. They would take it as confirmation that the *Big City* story was gospel. But the thought of more public humiliation, the tittering of Felicity and Natasha – maybe even Brad's thoughts of a lucky escape – meant nothing to her, compared to the pain of losing Michael. He had been so angry. In all the time she'd known him, Diana didn't think she'd ever seen his face like that. So passionate with rage. She had wanted to reach out to him, to ask for forgiveness, but his eyes had forbidden it. God, Diana thought, I thought marrying a millionaire was such a coup. But all it actually did was keep me away from the man I love.

Her control gave up completely. She put her head in her hand and sobbed, loud, deep sobs that tore out of her breast. Her make-up was running, splashing with her tears. Red-eyed and pale, her reflection stared desolately back at her from the elevator's polished mirror.

Then the doors hissed open at her floor.

She found herself face to face with Michael.

Diana stepped out and turned her head aside automatically. There was no hiding how bad she looked.

'How the hell did you get here?' she whispered. 'What are you doing? Trying to torment me? You can't talk me out of resigning. Please don't waste your breath. Just leave, Michael.'

'I will. Let me say my piece and then you'll never see me again.' Michael fished a handkerchief out of his suit pocket and handed it to her. 'Let me inside for just a second, so we don't have to do this on the landing.'

Diana sighed; it was only 11 a.m., but she felt so weary. 'OK. For a second.'

She let him in and shut the door.

Michael stood there in his work suit. He looked like he didn't know where to begin. Then he faced her, and took a deep breath.

'I'm sorry,' he said. 'I was mad. I was jealous. No other woman has ever made me feel the way you do, and I couldn't bear the thought that you wanted me for money. What that little fuck said made me want to kill him. And then you confirmed it. But after you left, I realised you were just honest with me. You changed, I know you did. You worked too hard to be in it for the money. And you would have been with me all along if I hadn't been so damn arrogant with you at first. I hated you for dating Brad Bailey, but it was only once you walked out of the door that I understood why. It was simple jealousy. Because I love you, and I want you to marry me.'

'What?' Diana said. She trembled.

Michael came towards her, caught up her hand, and pressed it to his lips.

'I look awful,' Diana muttered. It was the only thing she could think of to say.

'You look beautiful.' He pulled her into his arms and

started to kiss her mouth, her tear-stained cheeks, the hollow of her neck. 'You've always looked beautiful. To me you're the most beautiful woman in the world.'

'Michael . . .'

'Just say yes.' His dark eyes locked on to hers. 'Just say yes. It's the only thing I want to hear from you.'

'Yes,' Diana whispered. She kissed him back, fervently. 'Yes. Yes. Yes.'

'That's my girl,' Michael said.

He scooped her up in his arms and started to walk towards the bedroom.